THE REPUBLIC OF NOTHING

Other books by Lesley Choyce

NOVELS
Ecstasy Conspiracy (1992)
Magnificent Obsessions (1991)
The Second Season of Jonas MacPherson (1989)
Downwind (1984)

STORIES
Margin of Error (1992)
Coming Up for Air (1988)
The Dream Auditor (1986)
Conventional Emotions (1985)
Billy Botzweiler's Last Dance (1984)
Eastern Sure (1981)

POETRY
The Man Who Borrowed the Bay of Fundy (1988)
The Top of the Heart (1986)
The End of Ice (1985)
Fast Living (1982)
Re-inventing the Wheel (1980)

NON-FICTION
Transcendental Anarchy (1993)
December Six: The Halifax Solution (1988)
An Avalanche of Ocean (1987)
Edible Wild Plants of the Maritimes (1977)

LESLEY CHOYCE

The Republic of Nothing

GOOSE LANE

Published by Goose Lane Editions with the assistance of the Canada Council, 1994.

Cover photograph by Lesley Choyce, 1994. Reproduced with permission.
Edited by Elizabeth Ann Belyea.
Book design by Brenda Berry.
Printed and bound in Canada by The Tribune Press.

10 9 8 7 6 5 4 3 2

Canadian Cataloguing in Publication Data

Choyce, Lesley, 1951-
   The republic of nothing
   ISBN 0-86492-153-5

I. Title.

PS8555.H668R46 1994   C813'.54   C94-950193-X
PR9199.3.C497R46 1994

Goose Lane Editions
469 King Street
Fredericton, New Brunswick
CANADA E3B 1E5

Nothing has a stronger influence . . .
on children than the unlived lives of the parents.
Carl Jung

Whether you are really right or not doesn't matter;
it's the belief that counts.
Robertson Davies

Destiny is what you are supposed to do in life.
Fate is what kicks you in the ass to make you do it.
Henry Miller

1 My father declared the independence of Whalebone Island on March 21, 1951, the day I was born. It was a heady political time even on the Eastern Shore of Nova Scotia. New, pint-size nations were emerging all over forgotten corners of the globe and my old man decided that the flowering of independence should not pass us by.

He had also discovered that our island, large by local standards, was only somewhat smaller in land mass compared to Bermuda. Whalebone was eighteen square miles while Bermuda was twenty-one. In his mind it was clear that we were large enough to be an independent country. And traditionally, the provincial government had not been kind to the Whalebone Island men and women. Roads were a travesty. Electricity had not made it over the causeway and education was a mere rumour. Men had rebelled for lesser reasons.

My father, Everett McQuade, typed out the Declaration of Independence on the old Smith-Corona that had washed up on the beach in a shattered wooden box. The machine had required many hours of painstaking reconditioning, salt water being exceedingly unkind to abandoned typewriters. In the end, however, the machine worked. The typewriter ribbon, hung up to dry, was still salvageable. The keys snapped cleverly toward the platen with each hammer of his index finger. But the machine was missing a G. The tiny die-cast letter had liberated itself at sea and never washed ashore with the mother machine. Everett had told Hants Buckler to keep an eye out for the G, but it never turned up. Instead, my father tried to fashion a G out of an old fish hook. But no luck.

Carbon paper had been mail-ordered from the Eaton's catalogue and on March 21, 1951, Everett scrolled into his Smith-Corona four sheets of paper and three crisp coal-black sheets of Midnight brand carbon paper, all ready to go. One copy would be sent to the premier of the province, another to the prime minister of Canada and yet another would go to the newly formed United Nations. The new sovereign country that was to exist on Whalebone Island was to be called the Republic of Nothing. My father was an anarchist in the purist sense who despised the petty loyalties of political parties and the inherent evils of patriotism. In truth, he was opposed to having a name for the country at all. But if he had to put a name down for his newly minted nation, a name that suggested total disaffiliation with any existing doctrine or country, it would be the Republic of Nothing.

The document stated simply but unequivocally:

> To whom it may concern —
>
> We the citizens of Whalebone Island do hereby declare ourselves a free and soverei n republic. Our rievances a ainst our former oppressors, reat Britain and more recently, the Dominion of Canada are well known and, in defence of our well-bein and free spirits, we find that independence is our only recourse. We herewith ask for formal reco nition from you and look forward to a lon and healthy career of diplomatic relations (if any) with your overnin body.
>
> Sincerely,
> Everett McQuade
> Actin Head of State

The original copy was kept for archival purposes. The second, a legible carbon copy, went to the United Nations. The third copy went to the legislature in Halifax and the fourth copy, posted to the Prime Minister of Canada, was very faint and most probably the message was unreadable. My father saw the importance of Ottawa to be minimal anyway, so he signed the document and mailed it forthwith as a matter of courtesy. As the weeks passed, there was no reply from the provincial capital or from the United Nations. A reply, however, did come belatedly from the office of the prime minister. It read:

Dear Mr. McQuade,
   It was so kind of you to think of me and take the time to write expressing your views. As you might assume, it is not always possible for me to deal personally with every item of correspondence that crosses my desk. I do, however, wish you hearty good cheer and trust that you will be successful in your endeavours. My regards as well to your family at this festive time of year.

Yours sincerely,
Louis St. Laurent

The letter arrived in July but had a curious Christmas-card tone about it. My father did not question that perhaps the faint carbon quadruplicate had arrived unintelligible. Instead, he celebrated by blowing up the bridge.

Whalebone Island was lashed to the mainland by a tenuous thread of steel and creosote wood that converged on either end with a snaking, gullied, potholed dirt road spiked with jagged granite upthrusts hungry for Chevy oil pans and Ford mufflers. With the bombing of the bridge, independence would be complete, my father reasoned. He had been saving a single stick of dynamite for several years now. It had fallen off a railroad car on the old CN tracks that wobbled from Middle

Musquodoboit to Dartmouth. My mother had tried to remove the explosive from the house many times. She alternated between throwing it in one of the saltwater ponds and burying it in the back yard but somehow Everett always sniffed it out and returned it to its sacred home under the bed. So, when my father carried it away to blow up the bridge, my mother was quite pleased to see it gone.

Not twenty minutes after the prime minister's greetings had arrived that exhilarating July day, my father was down under the bridge with his stick of dynamite. The bridge spanned a narrow tidal inlet that rose and fell in accordance with the whims of the moon. Mr. Kirk was just then driving back to Whalebone from a shopping trip to town. He slowed to see what Everett was tying onto the bridge.

"We're now officially free," he told Mr. Kirk. "Whalebone Island is now the Republic of Nothing."

Mr. Kirk was a man who believed he had heard it all before. There was nothing in life that could surprise him, and he accepted everything with a degree of friendly cynicism. His father had worked around harpoon guns as a whaler so he was familiar with explosives and was probably not overly shocked to see one of his neighbours fooling with a stick of dynamite.

"I'm blowing up the bridge," added my father, feeling that some further explanation was in order.

Mr. Kirk was not perturbed. "Well, it's good to see somebody doing *something* around here for a change," he said simply as he drove on.

After Mr. Kirk's car moved on to fret with the gullies and potholes, my father lit the stick of dynamite and walked slowly islandward. The stick let off a loud CARONG of a blast but failed to drop the entire structure into the water below. Instead, it only blew off the guard rail and the "Go Slow" sign. But my father had never turned around to actually see the damage or lack of it inflicted by his only stick of dynamite. He felt his point had been made.

Lesley Choyce

Almost no one on Whalebone Island seemed to mind that my father had declared them all independent. The only person who showed any serious interest was my father's great ally, Hants Buckler, who would act as a sort of one-man cabinet in my father's non-structured and virtually non-existent government. Hants had sworn to uphold the principles of anarchy that the republic was founded upon and as far as I knew, he never did anything at all that could be considered constructive or organized, which suited my father's plan very well indeed. My mother was, for the most part, disinterested with the secession of the island. She was generally more preoccupied with what she called "things of the invisible world," so she didn't have much to say about any sort of manoeuvering in the political dimension. Her daily life changed very little and apparently the "invisible world" was not ready to offer any insight into the future of my father's political ambitions. Instead, my mother still joined my father once a week in the car to journey outside of the republic to Sheet Harbour where they would buy the necessary things of living, things needed to get by on what my mother referred to as "the physical plane." The fact that the bridge was still standing did not bother my father. Now he claimed that it was handy for "foreign trade." Everything was unfolding as it should.

My father had found my mother adrift at sea in a boat when she was about fifteen years old. My father was only seventeen at the time but already well on his way to becoming an acting head of state. He was a walking, living, torch of a man. His hair was a fiery red, and a soft fur of red hair sprouted from nearly every part of his body. He stood a mere five foot five but he had the presence of a Goliath.

Early in the morning my father would row out to sea in the darkness and wait for the sunrise. It was a windless morning in May when my mother saw the silhouette of a boat headed toward her.

"I already thought I had died," she told me later. "There I was in a little row boat on a pitch black sea. I didn't know how long I had been there drifting. I didn't even know who I was or where I came from. I was cold, I knew that. And then I saw a dim glow. The sun was coming up in the east. It came up like a great overpowering explosion of light and then suddenly I saw something else. A man standing up in a dory looking straight at me. Not a man, exactly, but a boy. And he was all on fire. I felt paralysed by the wonder of it. All around me the sea was alive with light. I grabbed onto the gunwales of the boat to steady myself as I waited for God to scoop me up off the surface of the ocean."

My father was never surprised by anything he found at sea. When he rowed up close to my mother, I guess he didn't know what to say so he didn't say anything at all. After the sun rose in the sky and the flames subsided, he towed her boat to shore. Then he escorted her to live with Mrs. Bernie Todd. Bernie was married to a man from Halifax named Jack Todd, but my father knew very little about her husband who seemed to keep to himself and read a lot of books. But Everett knew that Bernie was the most reliable and competent woman whom he had ever met, and he liked her immensely. He had watched her build almost single-handedly a magnificent stone castle of a house near the shore and believed she was capable of almost anything. He figured if he was going to choose the girl a mother, he was going to choose a damn good one. And Mrs. Bernie Todd was it.

My father himself was without parents — I don't know the full story but they had argued away their marriage into oblivion and then gone off in separate directions. The house was lost to taxes and Everett ultimately lived all alone in a cabin made from boards nailed to cornerposts of living spruce trees.

My mother didn't have a name that she could remember, so Mrs. Bernie Todd named her Dorothy because she had been to Halifax to see *The Wizard of Oz*. When Dorothy was found at sea, her hair had been cut nearly down to her scalp. The theory was that it had been cut off to help rid her of head lice.

Later, when her hair grew in, it was long and rich obsidian in colour, tied in braids and hanging nearly to her waist. She spoke English and spoke it quite properly but could never quite remember where she was from or why she had been adrift at sea. Her accent was a curious mix of dialects that set many theories in motion. In the end, the islanders would agree that it was a good thing she had found her way to Whalebone and that was enough.

My father went back to hand-lining for cod at sun-up and expected to find more girls floating about in boats — as if that was the natural order of things. My mother had a happy life with Mrs. Todd and waited patiently to hear something from the boy on fire. It came in the form of a letter a month after her arrival. My father had apparently decided that there were no other young women in boats to be found at sea, and that Dorothy was, in fact, a worthy catch. He asked her to marry him when she felt she was ready. She said she would unless her memory returned and she discovered that she was already married to someone else. So Everett, still only seventeen, asked old Mr. Kirk for five acres along Back Bay. Mr. Kirk was a cranky old geezer but nonetheless highly respected as the major landowner of Whalebone. My father had no money so he wasn't offering to pay. He just asked for the land outright. Kirk looked at the boy as if someone had just asked him to lop off his own leg. Everett was unflinching.

"I'm asking politely now, Mr. Kirk," Everett continued.

"But why in Hank's name should I give you anything?"

"Because I want to marry this girl. And because I want to build a house. Then I hope to start a new country."

Kirk was taken back by the brazenness of it all. "Why do you want to start a new country?" he asked.

"I need something to do with my life."

Kirk thought about it for a minute. He worked his tongue over his teeth, counting them by twos. Then his jaw fixed and he looked squarely at Everett. "I can see what you mean," he said.

"I guess it just never occurred to me to start a new country, but that would be *something* a fella could do with his life, anyway."

"Yes, sir," my father replied.

"What kind of a country do you expect it will be?" Kirk asked, curious as to what would become of his land.

"I'm not sure, sir. I just think I'll have to study on it and come up with something different."

"I like the sound of that," Kirk said. And the deal was done.

2 The elephant arrived four years after my father declared the independence of the Republic of Nothing. It washed ashore in the night, dead, of course, but otherwise intact. My father was walking the perimeter of the island, one of his many circumspections. He had never seen a dead elephant on the east side of the island before, and recognizing it as a significant moment, he jogged home to get me. He wanted his four-year-old son to share in the find, even if it was a dead one.

Unlike my father, I had a habit of sleeping past sunrise. In fact, sleeping was one of my favourite pastimes. But my father knew that I should not miss out on the discovery of the elephant.

"Wake up, Slim. You'll want to see this." My father called me Slim in those days because I was a skinny little wisp of a kid owing to the fact that I wouldn't eat blue potatoes.

"What is it?" I asked, slipping into yesterday's clothes. I knew better than to ignore my father. When my father discovered something, he had to share it or he would explode. And he discovered something unusual or profound every day of his life. So today it was a washed-up elephant.

"Don't wake your mother. It's just an elephant. Fell off a ship, I guess. Like those crates of oranges we found last year."

Everything that was anything washed up on Whalebone Island. We were targeted, I think, by the Gulf Stream so that ships losing freight somewhere near Bermuda could probably find their goods near Channel Cove, a stone's throw from my house.

In later years, my father would recount the story so I have to admit that what follows comes more from his telling than from my memory.

"I think there's something political about this elephant," my father claims to have said. "It has something to do with the republic. One of the American political parties has an elephant for a symbol but that can't be it. Where do elephants come from, anyway?"

I shrugged a sleepy *don't know*. Since I hadn't gone to school, I was pretty vague on geography. My mother taught me something of ancient Judea from an old Bible but, aside from the ancient Holy Land boundaries, I was unclear about continents and things.

"Could be Africa or could be India," my father reckoned, trying to answer his own question. "It will all add up to something sooner or later. We'll just have to see."

My father led me to the dead elephant. We half-ran, half-walked. "I had a dream about an elephant once," I told my father, slipping on the sun-drenched, sea-drenched stones along the shore. "I dreamed I was riding on the back of an elephant with mountains all around. I was headed somewhere really fast and if I didn't get there in time something terrible was gonna happen."

"You were probably remembering something that happened to you in a previous life," my father said. "You were probably a young prince in India or Africa. What colour was the sky?"

"Blue. Very blue."

My father nodded. "Yep, that would have been one of your former selves, before you came to your mother and me. Ask your mother about it when you get home. She'll know." This is the way conversations went in my family. It wasn't until I was nearly fifteen that I learned that other kids' parents didn't believe wholeheartedly in reincarnation.

"Look at that sun," my father said. He was right. It was something to look at. "When you die, your soul leaves your body and dives straight into the sunrise."

"Dad, did you ever dive straight into the sunrise?"

"Sure, many times. It's like falling off a log."

"Oh."

The elephant was right there where he said it would be on the east side of the island. "The current skirts around to here," my father explained.

"Wow," I said. Before me was a mountain of strange, sad animal. I wanted very badly for it to be alive. "Too bad it's dead." I walked around to look at the elephant's face but it was expressionless, revealing no secrets of its journey.

"Don't worry, Slim. His soul is already as light as a feather."

My father sat down on a beached log and studied the elephant. "A thing like this only happens once or twice in a person's life," he said. "Hants said that a crocodile washed in here once a long time ago. Two days later Canada was in the Second World War. Hants stuffed the croc' and has it up on his wall at his shack. You've seen it. Maybe we better tell him about this. Stay here with her while I go get him. Don't let any gulls or crows peck at it. I always hate to see things tore up by birds."

So I sat and waited. The dead elephant became boring very quickly. I was mad at it for not being alive. I felt cheated out of having an elephant for a pet. Then I started throwing stones at it. They made a dull thud as they hit the leathery carcass. A light breeze came up off the sea and I kept looking for living elephants on the horizon. Maybe there was another one out there who would make it ashore. But none came.

Hants Buckler looked like something made out of erector

set parts. His clothes were tied onto his angular figure with old pieces of fish net and he wore a baseball cap that said SAFE!

"Jesus, would you look at them tusks."

"Ivory," my father said.

"Think we're due for another war?" Hants asked, remembering the crocodile.

"If so, I plan on the republic staying neutral. We're too highly evolved here to go to war."

"Damn straight," said Hants. "It's good having a man like you at the helm."

My father beamed. He always appreciated compliments like that, no matter how tongue-in-cheek. "What should we do with it?" my father asked Hants, the expert on flotsam and jetsam of all sorts.

"The flesh is of no use," answered Hants, "but the tusks and the bones should be salvaged. I have an idea."

Just then the waves began to lap against my shoes. And when I looked out at the sea, I saw that the water looked like it was sprinkled with green and silver jewellery. A war had broken out somewhere on the planet, but it wouldn't reach us here. Pieces of the world's crisis would wash ashore and remind us all of the turmoil elsewhere, but we would live long and free in the Republic of Nothing and when we died and our souls became light as feathers, we would dive straight into the sunrise and ride the backs of living elephants.

3   In reporting all of what follows, I confess that my memory is not as perfect as it appears. The vivid visual impressions persist but so much of the rest, the sense of this thing, was pieced together from later conversations with

Hants, with my father, with secondary versions from my mother and all those loose fragments of my own childhood memory. On top of that, I might have exaggerated my own role in this but I promise to be as faithful to the truth as is humanly possible. I was not quite five and as you must recall from your own memory, life is full of surprises and shocks at that age as you have not carved up the world into sensible categories. The only physical truth that remains of this event is the curious artifact that I still wear around my neck, dangling from a thin gold chain. It resembles little of what it once was.

Aside from the crocodile, there was no precedent on the island for the disposal of exotic animals. Hants wanted the tusks and the bones, all right, but he didn't think he was up to the job of major taxidermy on our sad friend and victim whose soul may have been light on the wind but whose flesh was beginning to stink.

"He shouldn't go back into the sea," my father said. "This is a land animal. Land animals want to rest beneath the earth."

"All I want is the bones and tusks. You boys bury the rest, if you'd be so kind." Hants said it like he was asking us if we would mind helping out with the dishes after dinner. The whole job didn't look that easy to me.

"The main thing is the heart. We need to bury the heart," my father said, revising his previous assessment. "As long as we bury the *heart* in the earth, I don't think it matters much what we do with the rest." But Hants had already gone into his shack and come out with a long machete and a sharpening stone.

I guess you'd have to know Hants the way we did to realize that he wasn't a perverse, unfeeling monster. He saw a task before him and was ready for it — the job of liberating the skeletal structure from the giant beast and then reassembling the parts with wire and concrete outside of his home. In another age and place, Hants might have assembled cathedrals or skyscrapers, but here he had to work with the materials available. He was a born museum man, somebody who wanted to reconstruct, preserve, show off and pester with what he had discovered of the natural world.

As he made his first incision, skilled as a surgeon, straight up the belly of the poor bloated beast, my father made me turn away and follow him to the side of Hants' work shed. From inside the window, the stuffed croc' peered ominously out, its oversize cat's-eye glass marbles looking strangely alien and maligned.

Hants began to sing in a warbly voice an old sad song. With a pick axe and shovel over one shoulder, my father took my hand and led me off in search of some place with soil deep enough for an elephant burial. "The important thing is to bury the heart," he reminded me. "I don't know where we're gonna find a decent grave site around here, though. Nothing but ribs of rock. Can't chip away at bedrock. But we owe it to the creature to get the heart as deep as we can. Maybe the brain. Hearts and brains. The rest can go as carrion meat if it has to."

"How did it find its way here?" I asked, inquisitive as ever. But what I was really wondering was how would Hants know what an elephant heart looked like and how would he go about hollowing out the skull and removing the brain.

My dad looked at me. "A ship sunk somewhere, I suppose. You know how things wash up here. Maybe it was headed to a circus or a zoo. But the real place it came from was where everything comes from."

He stopped and took a stab with the pick axe at a spot that he thought was big enough to bury an elephant heart. It turned out to be a thick clump of goose tongue and sand laying over a face of granite. As the pick connected, it sent a cold chill right through me as I could feel the shudder transmit through every bone in my father's body even though I wasn't even touching him. An aura of defeat swept over both of us as I watched him survey the land around us.

"What about over there?" I offered, pointing.

My father scratched his chin. There were philosophical implications. "The thing about a bog is that you get the feeling it has no bottom. It just goes down and down. It's dark and soft and centuries of peat are all built up." He tapped the tip of his wedge on the granite again. "Bogs are not always trustworthy."

Ignoring my old man, I picked up the fallen shovel and walked way out into the peat bog. I liked nothing more than the feel of the spongy softness, the almost walking-on-air sensation. Beneath my feet, a million living and decaying plants interlaced and interwove. Sundew flytraps sparkled with sticky clear goo that attracted their lunch. Burnt-red pitcher plants, scores of them, were everywhere. I planted a foot on the shovel and dug in. It cut through the surface and sank in.

"I guess you have a point," my old man said, gingerly following me out into the marsh. "A soft damp grave is better than a granite grave," he admitted. "People sometimes say that a bog swallows up things, that it's hungry. Others say that a bog is just the beginning of a thing, the start of solid land before it decides whether it's water or solid land. I don't know about things that are half one thing and half another."

But I had lost track of following my father's concern. I had stuck the shovel in a second time, then a third and a fourth but I wasn't really making much headway. Already I was sinking where I stood. If you just pass through a bog, you hardly sink more than a few inches but if you stand in one place for more than a few seconds, you begin to submerge. If you stay there long enough, maybe you keep sinking and never come back.

I shifted to a new place to stand, pushed down on the shovel again and this time, hit something that sounded like a water-logged tree trunk. I tried scraping away some of the peat but it just kept falling back in, so I leaned over and reached beneath

Lesley Choyce

the muddy water to see if I could pull whatever was down there out of the way. My father watched warily as I got my hand around the better part of the object and began to lift.

One end gave way, although the other seemed attached. "Let me help you with that," my old man said and grabbed hold. It was brown and muddy like an old buried spruce limb but when it was raised to a right angle from the ground, still not wanting to break free, we both recognized it for what it was. A human foot, attached to a human leg, shrivelled to hard leather over hard bone but preserved somehow by the tannic waters of the bog.

My father's wariness had given way to awe as he cleared the mud and debris and counted one, two, three, four, five toes, all intact. "I guess you weren't the first to figure this was a good place for a burial," he said. "What should we do? Let him lie or dig him up?"

There was no doubt at all in my mind. I was overwhelmed by curiosity. There was no way I was going to go home, having found a foot and not having had a look at the full man. I began to pull away at the moss and peat with my hands. My father took the shovel and chipped away at the turf from the other side. "Ever so gently," he said.

The sun was full overhead now and the smell of the bog was sweet perfume — bayberry and juniper mixed with the scent of sweet rotting things. We had carved away a perimeter as if someone had set down a large cookie cutter and stamped the shape of a man on the ground. Then, gently, my father took the shovel and began to roll back the sod of peat and sundew. The first foot was joined by a second, two knees, thighs, torso, arms and a head. The body was all covered with mud and weed at first but my father shovelled some clean water onto him from a nearby depression.

The first thing that shocked us was not the gaunt, hollow, sunken and final face but the metal chest. One arm was bent across the chest, the hand clutching something. My father leaned over and thumped hard with a knuckle on the metal plating. Then he bent over the face. It was like he was waiting for the man to breathe.

As the mud was washed off, the form became cleaner, more lifelike. I still expected to see this once-human thing suck in a breath, yawn and stand up. The eyes were gone, of course, and the dark brown skin was pulled tight against the cheeks like a Hallowe'en ghoul. But it didn't frighten me. I was wondering who he was, how he died.

"Did you know him?" I asked my father, assuming that he had lived on Whalebone Island forever, before the republic, before the rest of us. He would know.

"No, I never met him before," my father admitted.

I rubbed my hand across the metal on the man's chest. What was I thinking? I waited for him to sit upright and come back to life, I'm sure of it. I began to wonder if this was how we came back into this world. The lighter than a feather soul went rooting around in a grave or a bog until it found an old body and then waited for islanders like us to stumble upon it, unearth it and give it a chance again in this world.

"A bog is a funny place," was all my father could say, smoothing more mud off of the metal plate. I tried to pick up the one arm that lay flat against the ground but as I touched the hand, two curled fingers came loose and pulled away. I carefully studied the dried leather over bone.

"I'm sorry," I said to the dead man and set the fingers back in place.

"How long has he been dead?" I asked my father.

"Maybe a thousand years. He's a Viking, I think. He was just here looking for something, I guess. Something happened and he died here. The bog preserved him."

"Is he all right now?" I asked.

"Yeah," my father said, "he's all right. We all are." My father studied the two fingers that I had laid carefully back in place.

"What was he looking for?" I asked.

My father studied the other hand on the chest, the fist curled up around something. A clue.

Delicately, ever so gingerly, he lifted the hand, saw that it was clutching three stones. He timidly removed one, then the other two, returned the hand that seemed to want to snap back into place of its own accord, as if some spring were attached. Then he leaned over, washed the three stones in the puddle around his boots, and held them up to the sun. "White quartz," he said.

I shrugged.

"Look harder." He rinsed one again and handed it to me. I held it up into the blue sky and saw the fragments of gold imbedded in the quartz.

"Is that what he came here for?" I asked.

"I don't know," my father answered, retrieving the stones from me and putting all three back into the grip of the ancient Viking. He shook his head. Later I would understand that the finding of gold on Whalebone never surprised him. I think others had known too, but no one had ever mentioned it. "Gold and dead men sleep together well," he told me. "We should not disturb them. Try not to tell anyone about all this. The world will change for us all soon enough. Let's not hurry it. The island can share a few secrets with us. It can trust us." And he began to shovel the peat carpet back over the dead Viking.

I didn't understand really and I was sad to see that we could not bring the Viking back to life or keep the quartz with the gold in it. As we were covering him, though, I saw that one of the dislodged fingers, the smallest one, had been displaced again and was lying on the ground. When my father wasn't looking, I picked it up and put it in my pocket. It would be a secret shared only by me and the island.

"What about the elephant?" I asked.

"You can tell everyone about the elephant," my father told me. "Hants would want you to."

"But aren't we going to bury the elephant?"

"You're right," he said. And my father proceeded to dig a small square grave to the right of the dead Viking. "We'll bury the heart here. The rest we'll tow to sea for the sharks."

Blood was splattered all over the outside of Hants' house and shed when we got back there. He was covered in a slimy mess of unspeakable proportions, but he seemed cheerful and unrepentant.

"How's it going, Hants?" my father asked, now not even bothering to try to shield me from the gruesome spectacle of a disembowelled elephant.

"Well, I wasn't right sure of which one was the heart, the liver or the kidney," Hants replied, wiping the bloody machete on a handkerchief, "so I got all three there for you in that salt sack. I scooped out the brain with a soup ladle and that's in there too if you want a peek."

"No thanks," my father said. "We'll go bury these and then I'll tow the rest of the carcass out to sea," he said, as matter-of-fact as if it was all in a casual day's work. As my father went to bury the necessary parts, I stayed behind and watched Hants proceed to remove flesh from bone.

"It's all in the wrist," he told me. "Just like filleting fish."

Later, as we towed to sea the remaining carcass of the giant beast enmeshed inside an old fishing net, my father reminded me not to mention anything about the gold or the Viking. "Silence is one of the great skills," he said. "If people talked less and listened more, we'd have a happy planet."

About two miles south of Bull Rock, he cut the load and let it go. We looked back toward Whalebone Island. The republic was a green hump on the horizon. I wondered if I should confess that I still carried the finger in my pocket but as we lay there, dead in the water, the engine silent as we drifted on a faint breeze, I saw the sea come alive with a frenzy of

Lesley Choyce

sharks — violent tails thrashing and fins snapping like knife blades out of the water.

There would be no more elephant flesh. And in a month or so, Hants would have erected the skeleton of the creature with immaculate precision along the shoreline for any stranger to see and consider just how strange and singular was the Republic of Nothing.

And if the bog had still maintained its powers of preservation over the centuries, then maybe some curious archaeologist — or better yet, a curious little kid — would dig again into the bog and find a metal-breasted Viking minus a finger embalmed beside the desiccated heart, kidney, liver and ladle-scooped brain of a giant creature who once roamed freely on the plains of Africa or the deltas of India. I couldn't help but imagine the thrill and confusion of such an odd and wonderful discovery.

4 I was forever thankful that my father had picked Mrs. Bernie Todd to finish raising my mother. There were other options. Bella St. John, a nice old woman from the mainland would have been another candidate. Bella was full of such sweetness and all-embracing acceptance of everything under the sun that I sometimes, as a child, daydreamed that she would have been the perfect grandmother for Casey and me. We could have made so much racket at her house, done so much damage, and she never would have said an unkind word to us.

But perhaps my old man considered that competence was more important than tolerance that fateful morning he towed my mother ashore and surveyed her top to bottom as she stood on her land legs for the first time in who knows how long. She had not said a word so he had little idea of what her personality was like. But my guess was that he already understood that before him was a girl of character and depth and, above all, mystery. And what she needed more than anything in the world was a chance to finish growing up in a good home.

Mrs. Bernie Todd was married to Mr. Jack Todd and neither had been island-born. Jack's telling of the story about how they ended up on our rock would usually go like this. Jack had worked at something in an office in Halifax for too many years, employed by the Cunard Steamship Line. He hated the job where he sat inside a windowless office staring down columns of monetary figures. Jack had schemed to avoid work and go live on the Eastern Shore where he believed life was "more intimate, like in older times." He finally succeeded in getting himself fired by over-billing the Duke of Windsor several thousand dollars. Since the money had already been paid to Cunard, the company was too embarrassed to admit the mistake and return it to the Duke. He saw that he had struck gold, so he threatened to tell the world about the Cunard Line's cheating royalty unless they retired him with a hefty pension. Jack was shocked and pleased to discover how well blackmail worked and lived almost happily ever after as a result.

The first thing he did, however, before settling down on the Eastern Shore was drive down to Portsmouth, New Hampshire and get in a brawl at a tavern near the navy dockyards. He took on single-handedly a large portion of the available U.S. Navy and lost, ending up in a hospital where he fell in love with Bernie Lapham, the granddaughter of a millionaire paint manufacturer. Bernie was the most straightforward woman he had ever met in his life. "Canadian women were all so demure, pretty and polite," he once told me. "Your grandmother had . . . candour. I had told her my story about cheating the Duke and my hefty pension. She called me a selfish, conniving son of a bitch." Right then, at this point in the telling of the story, the colour in Jack's face would be like fire and his eyes would light up like maybe he had just swallowed a big belt of Governor General's Rum. "She said that what I had done was a terrible thing, that it was such an *American* thing for a Canadian man to do that I should go get a job at her grandfather's paint factory as a vice-president or that maybe I should go into politics."

At that, Jack Todd, still propped up in his hospital bed, burst into tears before the nurse. He pleaded with her by saying that it wasn't greed, that all he really wanted was, "TO GET OUT OF THE TWENTIETH CENTURY!"

I guess that's what they had in common and that's why Bernie saw clean through Jack's mistake right into his semi-transparent, natural-finish heart. Bernie, too, said that she wanted out of the twentieth century. She wanted INTO the twenty-first, she said, a time when women would be equal and, quite probably, hard at work trying to sort out the mess left by men in the twentieth century. Jack owned up to the fact that he wasn't thinking of the future but of the past — the days of great sailing ships and times when men were real men who had to lash rigging and haul in the sails and climb the mast to look for land through a telescope. Truth was, he never knew much about sailing or hard work, but such was his fantasy. Well, of course, Bernie said that what Jack was talking about was just "male ego bullshit." Jack said he knew it was but wondered if they might be able to work together to disappear from this century as much as was possible and just sort of go into an alternate time-line altogether.

Jack was all busted up with casts on significant parts of his anatomy. He lay flat on his back and his face was bruised like a Georgia peach after a really rough trip north. Bernie was quite beautiful, I imagine, back in those days when she still had hair down somewhere below her ear lobes. (She never showed us any pictures of herself when she was young. She had destroyed all her old photographs, arguing that photography merely helped to foster vanity.) That was when Jack told her about Whalebone Island on the Eastern Shore of Nova Scotia. "It's like a whole other world," he told her. "People are very tolerant." (He was probably thinking of his old girlfriend, the one he had met on his visits to Whalebone where he had flirted with Bella St. Stephen before she had become Bella St. John.) "There's something about the place — the piping plovers on the sand, the old fishermen who don't give a shit about what anybody thinks, the emptiness and serene possibility of it all!" He talked on and on, through the pain it caused his healing split lip and the mild haze of the heavy sedative he had been given.

At first, Bernie was not convinced. She had heard male bull-slinging before and this sounded like the grandest kind. She tried to turn professional and began to slide a bedpan under the sheets. "No. Wait!" Jack shouted and pointed with a plaster-of-Paris-casted finger toward his wallet on the night table. Bernie thought he was going to offer her money. She stared at the empty bed pan, wishing there was something in it to toss in his face. "Go ahead. Look in!" Jack said, not realizing what she was thinking. My grandmother cynically flipped open the cowhide wallet and immediately saw it: a faded, beat-up photograph of a tiny bay and a rocky shoreline with nothing but straggly spruce and granite rocks jutting up like broken teeth. She was hooked. "What is it?" she asked.

"Whalebone Island," Jack said. I own that little place. The land is mine. Would you come live there with me?" Ever since he quit Cunard, he had become a daredevil. Just like with the U.S. Navy, he'd go in swinging and take his chances, sort out the injuries afterwards.

I guess Bernie must have been puzzled just then at such a bold initiative for a Canadian. Maybe she was almost about to write off Jack for being too bloody American for her, too much of an arrogant male of the twentieth century. But instead, her eyes (or so I envision) were drawn back to the photo of Back Bay on Whalebone Island. "Forty acres," Jack said. "It can be any century you want it to be."

There was a second or two of electrifying silence, I am sure. Possibilities were being explored, destinies rewritten.

"You're on," Bernie answered, surprised perhaps to hear herself say it. "On approval as they say. We try it out. Starting tomorrow I have a two-week vacation. We drive up to your island and I stay there with you for thirteen days. If it works out, I stay. If not, I come back here."

Jack smiled the smile of success, but as Bernie began to slide the bedpan back under the sheets he was painfully reminded of the shape he was in, regretted his declaration of war on the U.S. Navy. "What about all this?" he asked Bernie with some trepidation.

"I'm a nurse," Bernie answered. "We'll work something out."

"Where will we live?" he queried. He owned the land, yes, but there was no house on it.

"I've got a tent. Or maybe we can build something."

Well, I guess Jack was so tired of adding up numbers for the Cunard Shipping Lines and so desperate to escape as much of this troubled century as he could that he found even this trial offer too good to pass up. He had no idea that he was about to shack up with a pioneer feminist and the most fiercely independent woman on the East Coast of the North American continent.

Bernie was somewhat dissatisfied with the tent that housed them the first week during the blackfly invasion and the mosquito attacks. Jack believed he was near death from simple insect bites as he was still immobile and had discovered that black flies and mosquitoes devised ingenious ways to crawl up under the casts on arms and legs and fingers. However, as Bernie ordered the Portland cement and began gathering granite rocks to build a better shelter, Jack turned to daydreams and absolute hallucinations that he was in fact a pirate from a distant time being held hostage by this beautiful but depraved woman who kept him incapacitated by day while she built a castle and then made ferocious love to him at night in their tent beside the fabled treasure cove.

Jack never did forgive her for cutting off her hair. Initially it was a practical move, she argued, as it got in the way with her masonry work. She discovered she liked patching together boulders more than patching up injured seamen, and she always claimed that her plaster of Paris skills were readily transferable to construction work. Jack recovered his health only to discover that he was still madly in love with Bernie but that life outside the city limits of Halifax was not all it was cracked up to be. As the first stage of the granite home grew from the shore line, he did not delight in the blisters that bulged like tiny rockweed pods on his hands or the callouses that followed. Bernie never once called her beau lazy as he sloughed off work during the heat of the summer day or retreated from drizzle and cold, complaining that it was the mortar, not him, that would not work properly in the weather. Instead, Bernie believed this to be her chance, the natural way things would go in the twenty-first century. She found that she delighted in the heavy work of building a stone house — and realized that women had been deprived of it for far too long.

So when one full room was complete with a temporary roof watertight enough to keep out the drenching rains of a northeast gale, Bernie decided her man was not cut out to be a great stonemason like herself. He needed an occupation or at least a hobby better suited to his new role, and realizing that she had found her century but that he had still not found his, she drove to Halifax to buy a typewriter, a case of typing paper and several hundred paperback novels of adventure and intrigue set in olden times. As the house grew towards some semblance of completion, Jack noted with pleasure how happy Bernie was at work. Taking her cue, he settled down and read thousands of pages about swashbucklers and soldiers and pirates and privateers until one day his fingers found their way to the typewriter and began to loosen the tongue of his imagination. As the years rolled by he produced over seventeen novels, none of which were ever published, but Jack always blamed that on the dearth of good literary agents in Canada. He was only mildly disappointed in the failure of his literary career but so buoyed by the sheer joy of writing that he never regretted having chosen a career that brought in not one red cent.

So, when the time came to find a good mother for the girl he had found, my father instinctively knew that Bernie was a woman of highly individualized mind and of fierce independence. In his own pragmatic way, he was selecting a finishing school. My mother was always a bit vague on how she adjusted to the adventure writer and the castle builder. Since her memory was shot, she assumed that this was the natural order of things. Bernie tutored Dorothy in the skills of rock-chipping, cement-mixing and mortar-laying but quickly realized that these were not skills a young woman took to readily. So, instead, she began to coach my mother as she read a select list of books by the likes of Mary Wollstonecraft, George Eliot, Marie Curie, Robert Burton, Sigmund Freud, and Karl Marx, as well as nursing texts and volumes on the human anatomy. But it wasn't until my grandmother ordered several books on astrology, Rosicrucianism and the occult that Dorothy blossomed intellectually. By then, my father had already asked her to marry him and my mother's sense of destiny had taken charge. She regretted that she didn't know where she had come from, but she knew perfectly where she was going.

As for Bella St. John, the tolerant woman who *might* have been my grandmother, she and her husband both slipped into the sea and drowned the night my mother gave birth to my sister. Apparently Bella's husband developed a fanatical interest in the storm as it grew in intensity. It was as if he had finally awakened from a sluggish stupor that had lasted for years. He got all excited and bundled up his wife to go stand on Great Groenig's Point. They were crazy not to stay inside, but Bella went along with her husband's desire to see the raging sea up close and together they were swept to their deaths by a towering monster of a wave.

5 My sister was born during a full moon in August, at one of the highest tides recorded on Whalebone Island in the very eye of Hurricane Irene. I was five years old and I think it was the first time that I understood my mother and father were in love. At five, you tend to think of love as something you feel toward favoured pets more than human beings. I had a one-winged seagull that ate cod scraps and a geriatric dog that had moved into the crawl space under our house. Like so many other wounded creatures, the one-winged seagull who my father had named Khrushchev and the flea-pestered dog that I named Mike had found their way to Whalebone Island and the Republic of Nothing for solace and refuge from the outside world.

What I am trying to say is I loved both these creatures and I think that what I felt towards them — the pity and the compassion and the downright joy of playing with each — I think this was the way my parents felt about each other.

Hurricanes bring out the best in creatures who love each other. At least that's what I learned during Irene. During a hurricane, however, is not a great time to have a baby. The sea heaves enormous waves pounding with incredible force all over rocky parts of an island like Whalebone. Hurricanes pick up anything that isn't tied down and devise lethal flying weapons. Boats, the fisherman's livelihood, become playthings in a maelstrom bathtub where they worry and smash against the wharves until wood gives up its sanity and becomes splinter. Hurricanes shred, suck, spit, stammer, scream, batter, bruise, beat, beleaguer, bend, moan, mangle and molest an island like Whalebone and its usually happy people until they feel they know something of war.

Maybe it was because the skies of earth were jealous that year (my mother would later say) because of that deadly weapon, that H-bomb equivalent to ten million tons of TNT that disturbed the Pacific sleep of the world over Namu islet in the Bikini islands back in February. "For the world has a single soul," my mother argued, "and such an offense might cause her to react — even on the Atlantic thousands of miles away. What is 15,000 miles to a soul as complete and round as a planet?"

For the most part, hurricanes do not batter Nova Scotia with their might. A hurricane is a southern thing, a warm water creature with a supple spine and catty mind that reminds the American east coast it is merely a whim of cities and scum. A hurricane stirs itself to fury in a spiralling soup of skies and crawls like a hungry galaxy toward land to devour houses and businesses and scrape clean the coast, to put it back to normal as best it can. And when the heat runs out, when the bite of the North Atlantic off New England reminds the hurricane that this is far enough, that above here the land is still pure, the glaciers have just barely left, the people are not quite as confounded and corrupt as southerners, then the hurricane usually veers east towards Iceland into a humble retirement of dissolution and repentance.

But such was not the case with Irene. We had boats on doorsteps by the time the quiet eye found us huddled in the living room. A hurricane like Irene reminded adults that something had been disturbed in the clean order of things. My mother, for all her affinity with the future, later admitted she had been misled by the stars, that she had miscalculated the arrival of the baby, for she had predicted the baby to be a Virgo and a birth now would mean a Leo.

I was sitting in my bedroom with Khrushchev and Mike. The gull was on the windowsill eating cod tongues from a plate and Mike was asleep at the foot of my bed. We had weathered the first blast of the storm and I had almost become used to the sound of raging wind and maniac seas. I can't say I was scared of Irene. It was too much fun since it was the first time I was allowed to have both Khrushchev and Mike in my bedroom with me. My father was preoccupied with other things.

Everett MacQuade was the ultimate disbeliever in weather reports. He saw the weather office as a sort of combined misinformation conspiracy and a make-work project for know-nothings. We had listened on the radio about the approach of the storm, how it had ripped through several island communities in New Jersey ("That'll show 'em," my father said.) and how it had carved a deadly trail right across Long Island and Cape Cod ("People should never have lived there anyway."), but when it was reported that the storm was regrouping its strength and gearing up for a full onslaught of the coast of Nova Scotia, that it was already reducing Sable Island to something less than sand and spit, my old man said that it wouldn't dare touch the Republic of Nothing.

So it wasn't until the winds gusted to sixty miles an hour that my old man started screaming at me to find every god-damn shred of rope I could lay my hands on.

My mother was sitting in a chair reading a book on phrenology when my old man relented and admitted that it was a lucky guess on the part of the weather service, a damn lucky guess for them know-nothings. "Sure, the wind is up a little. I've seen onshore winds much worse than this. It won't amount to much, though," he said, looking out at three inches of water in the front yard and a dory slipping by on the road. "Still and all, you better get your creatures inside."

That's when I knew my father was serious. I ran out into

the pelting rain and found Khrushchev hunkered down on his roost by the shed. I had to wake up Mike who was still asleep in the water rising beneath the house. Khrushchev was under one arm and Mike, the big old mangy beast, was in tow by the collar as I went back in the front door.

My old man was headed toward the cove to lash down the boat more tightly when the door — a big square four foot by four foot contraption of one-by-six spruce all nailed together — flew off the shed. It took off like a flying island and sailed past my old man's head, within inches of knocking his brains out. Everett stopped dead in his tracks. Next, he saw a twelve foot wall of water smash up over the granite rock that acted as a breakwater for our tiny dock. The flying door headed straight into the shooting spray and then fell to earth, smashing on the granite. When my dad came back in, drenched and looking shaken for the first time in his life, he said, "Now I get it. Just when the weather office so thoroughly perfected giving wrong predictions, Nature turns around and throws off their entire system by following up with what was predicted." My father had once again, in his own way, made sense of the world. "There could be a little damage to the republic," he told my mother. "We're in for a real blow."

My mother put down her phrenology book and looked at her husband. I was there in my bedroom doorway, my gull on my shoulder and Mike still in tow by the collar. What I saw between my mother and father had nothing to do with the weather. I saw worry and I saw understanding and I saw a kind of wonder, but most of all, I saw between them love, something almost physically tangible, like a heavy silver thread that was strung out across the room from one to the other.

"I guess it was *supposed* to be a Leo after all," my mother said, suddenly grabbing her belly and sucking in a quick, almost panicky gulp of air. Just then the back door flew open and wet wind and tide sloshed into the living room.

Another contraction hit and my mom let out a howl that

roused Mike to howl in empathy. My father fought his way to the wooden door, shoved it closed and, realizing that the lock was clean busted off by the brutal wind, shoved the chesterfield up against it. I probably shouldn't have been surprised to see that there was a smile on my old man's face. He loved weather of any sort, and the harsher it got, the more my old man admired the natural forces that were ready to put us in our places.

"Jesus, did you see that?" he asked me. "That's no ordinary wind. That's a wind that wants to be everywhere. It's not satisfied to stay just outside. You've got to admire a wind with such audacity."

My mother let out another long, low moan. "Something's wrong," she said.

"Not necessarily," my father said. "It's just Nature's way of re-establishing her set of values, testing us to see if we're strong and ready for the challenge." My mother was lying flat on her back in the bed and I could see her grab onto my father's hand and squeeze hard. Now, he clearly understood. The love and concern for his wife cut right through the fascination with the hurricane's political will. "Hang on," he said. "We'll get Mrs. Bernie Todd."

I know that he meant that *he* was going. As I stood there in my bedroom doorway with my gull on my shoulder and my old dog at my feet, it never occurred to me that I was about to head out into the terrible storm. But as my father tried to pull away from my mother, she pulled him back. "You're not supposed to go. I don't know why and I wish it was that simple, but you can't leave."

It could be that my mother was just so scared that she was hiding behind her visionary powers, using them as an excuse to keep her husband by her side. And had she thought it through, did she really think it sensible to send a five-year-old boy out into a raging hurricane? Didn't she care about me? All I wanted was to crawl under my bed with Mike and listen to

Lesley Choyce

him snore through the hurricane. I was in love with the sound of my dog snoring. It was all I needed out of life just then. Things had been whittled down to that simple bit of familiarity.

Khrushchev was back on my window sill, ducking and bobbing at the flying debris that would have been assaulting him had it not been for the window glass. I crawled under the bed, sneezing several times at the dust and amazed at the lost socks and spare toy parts. I had dragged Mike with me and I started singing "Old McDonald" when I saw may father's gum boots before my eyes. "Ian, I need a word with you, son."

At five you believe that if you just close your eyes and pretend you're asleep, nothing bad will happen. At least that was the lesson that I learned from Mike. Since he slept almost all the time, very rarely did anything bad happen to him.

"Ian, son, your mother needs your help. She says I can't leave right now." His face was level with me now, parallel to the rough slate-grey floorboards. Underneath us in the crawl space, small waves crested and broke. As I lay there, face to the floor, I felt as if I was on an old sailing ship, far to sea.

"I know," I said. "I'm scared."

"You should be. It's not fit out there for the likes of you. But your mother's having some problems with her contractions." My father had become quite a literate man and had read books Bernie had loaned him, books on everything from alchemy to gynaecology. My knowledge on these matters as well as my vocabulary was much more limited so I assumed he said, "trouble with her contraptions," contraption being a favourite word of my father's concerning problems created by governments around the world. With a five-year-old's knowledge of anatomy, I could not begin to imagine what sort of machines were involved, biological or otherwise, in the delivery of a human child. Nonetheless, it revived in me a curiosity that caused me to open my eyes, convincing my father I was fully awake and aware of what he was asking.

"Your mother thinks the baby is coming out the wrong way. Nature'll do that to you. I don't know enough to help her. We can't go anywhere in this weather. Mrs. Bernie Todd will know what to do."

"Right," I said, crawling out from under my bed, still reluctant to let go of my sleeping dog who I skidded out on all fours along with me.

"You've got to leave Mike here. He's too slow." Slow wasn't the word. Immobile and unconscious was more accurate. Reluctantly, my hand let go of the dog's collar and he slumped to the floor, oblivious to the human drama.

As my father dressed me up in boots and rain gear, I could see that his hand was shaking. I could feel his ragged breath on my face and saw the worry in every inch of him. It's funny but the fear in him somehow had the reverse effect in me. I felt suddenly adult, responsible, important — more important than I'd ever felt before. I was either about to help save my mother and her new baby or I was about to be swept up into the sky, never to return. My father rooted in the closet and found an old life jacket that he tied onto me with a piece of rope, tight under both armpits until I could feel the bite of the rope even through my oil skins.

My father began to slide the chesterfield away when my mother let out a piercing note of pain. "Wait. Not yet."

"What the hell do you mean, not yet?" my old man said.

But she just held up the flat of her hand and then motioned me to the bed. I went in to her. She held my head between two uplifted hands as if she was praying with my brains sandwiched between her outstretched fingers. And it was more than that. She was pushing back her own pain to use her special skills to determine for certain if I would make it or not.

I can still feel the way her hot palms felt against my ears and the way it made me hear my own blood pounding within my skull. I don't think I had heard my own heart beat until then and wondered at this incredible magical drum that was beating in my head. Suddenly she relaxed her grip, lay back with a brief smile on her face, her eyes closed.

"Wait five minutes, then go," she said, sounding strangely matter-of-fact and certain. A spasm of pain gripped her and my father grabbed onto her hand. He offered her a wooden spoon with a dish towel wrapped around it to put in her mouth but my mother shook her head from one side to the other.

"Better get going, son," my father said, pointing to the door, unprotected now by the chesterfield and rattling at the hook that held it. It sounded like a madman was outside wanting to get in.

"Wait!" my mother screamed. My old man looked down at his watch.

"You're mother knows what she's saying."

The waiting was hard. I've never been good at waiting and never will. Neither is my old man. If a thing needs to be done, better to do it than to stew over it. Still, my mother had an understanding of things. We had an old grandfather clock in the kitchen that ticked away. Five minutes, five years, it was all the same. I was growing older, more frightened, more certain that we would all die in the storm. Why couldn't I just go outside, get launched into space and be done with it?

"Four minutes," my father said. My mother was having more difficulty with her contraptions. Only four more decades to go before I could leave and do my duty. Just then a gust of wind, stronger than anything we'd felt yet, slammed into the house like a runaway truck. I looked out the window just in time to see the entire roof lift off the shed and catapult out into the road. The very house itself, stationed as it was atop loose stone and held to earth only by the basic contract with gravity, lifted up, I believe, ever so slightly. It was enough to wake Mike and make him howl like the living dead.

"It's a girl. Her name is Casey," my mother said. "It's turning out all right because Mrs. Bernie Todd is here."

For a moment my father was stunned. After their many

years together he was still having a hard time adjusting to my mother speaking of the future in the present tense. No baby had been born. No miracles performed in righting the position of my little sister. *Little sister*? God, now the pain had a sex and a name. But there was a big unsaid *if* in there and that was Mrs. Bernie Todd. And the *if* depended on me, my legs and my ability to fend off a hurricane. My father looked at the clock. My mother seemed unable to talk. She tried the spoon in her mouth but spit it out right away and bit hard into my father's wrist, drawing blood. The time had come for action. "Go," my old man shouted.

I was like a cannon ball fired out of a cannon. I vaulted for the door, threw it open, gave myself a quarter of a second to survey the nightmare that was once my yard. "Run!" my father shouted at me, as he rushed for the door and shoved it closed behind me. I took a big leap to get off to a good running start, fell headlong into a foot of seawater, lost my bearings and came up sucking for air. I cleared the water from my face and rolled over, only to find that the life jacket made my body float and I was being carried across the ocean of our yard to who knows where. My old man was halfway out the door to help when I righted myself, got my feet on the ground beneath the water and leaned hard into the wind. The harder I leaned into the wind, the more it held me up. I was momentarily overcome by the exquisitely terrifying and beautiful vision that if I leaned far enough, my feet would simply leave the earth and I would be in flight. I convinced myself that I was about to be turned into a bird and swept away to some distant world never to be heard from again. I tried to walk and couldn't. I tried again and again. My father was inside, at the window now, shouting something to me through the glass but I could hear none of it.

The roar of the wind and the pounding waves was a sound beyond anything which I had experienced. I found myself stuck, tilting ahead, locked against wind, afraid to lean back,

Lesley Choyce

afraid to fall down and float off. My mind wrestled with this impossibility until the wind slapped me with a smack of cold seaweed and turned my head. There, ten feet away, was a granite outcropping. It was behind me but created a ridge against the sea, a jagged buttress of stone that ran an erratic but inevitable course from our house to that of my grandmother. This path had been left here, devised long ago by the glacier, designated for no other purpose than this, so that a small boy in an evil storm could save his mother and his sister from a tortured death.

I leaned left, began to tack towards the rocks. A gust hit me. I fell, as before, onto my back and floated upside down. I scrambled over onto all fours and crawled through the shallow water. At last I made headway and finally I found my granite shelter. As soon as I tucked in behind the ridge, I felt some semblance of control. I ran, stumbled, slipped and floundered onward, not stopping again to look back.

I had never felt so fully alive, so fully human before that moment in my life. I could barely breathe, the very wind stealing oxygen away from my lungs. I tore up the rain gear, bloodied my knees and elbows and was sure I was blinded more than once by the saltwater and rain. Minutes or hours, who knows? But I made it. I raced across a final open space with the wind at my back, ready to drive me like a spike into the side of the house. I slammed hard into the heavy wooden door of the great stone house, having been lucky enough to aim for the only available wood of an otherwise impregnable wall of stone. Jack Todd heard the encounter and looked out, saw me slumped at the doorstep. Together, he and Bernie shoved open the door against the weight of my body and pulled me in.

I said nothing. Mrs. Bernie Todd asked her husband to find her medical bag. He ran to another room as I sprawled on the floor, dizzy, possibly delirious. I believed that I was still out racing and fighting the wind and I felt as if I was looking down at my body contorted on the floor of this place. Bernie did a strange thing. She uncorked a bottle of rum, measured out two tablespoons into a glass, sat me upright against the wall and forced me to drink. "Your grandmother insists that you swallow it hard." This was the first time that she had ever actually called herself my grandmother. In the other room, rattling through a closet, was my grandfather.

It was my first encounter with the demon rum and I assumed that someone had just lit up a fire on my tongue and sent boiling oil down my throat. Had it been anyone else but Bernie, I would have spit it out, but Mrs. Bernie Todd was not a woman to mess around with. She made quick and absolute decisions on her behalf and for others and did not tolerate complainers. As my mind reeled and my stomach burned, I felt the alcohol eventually light fire to my brain where it burned bright as a summer sun. I stood up, saw before me my grandmother and grandfather. "The baby's coming out the wrong way," I said.

"Breech," my grandmother said.

"If you get there in time, it will be a girl. Her name is Casey," I told her. She immediately understood these to be the words of my mother.

"Good, let's attend to your little sister."

My grandfather shoved open the door. It flapped back hard against the wall. My grandfather, with a far-away look in his eye, held hard onto my hand and we followed my grandmother out into the blast, never turning to try to close the door. As Bernie started for her car, I instead pointed to the ridge, for I knew that the road must be even deeper in flood. And it was a longer drive as well. My route was a shortcut. She immediately knew I was right. Jack held on hard to my hand, his eyes fixed firmly on the back of my grandmother.

Almost the minute we were inside my home, a curious thing happened. The wind abated and a brooding, unnatural quiet began to settle over us. The seas still boomed baritone in the background, of course, but the battle of our house to hold

Lesley Choyce

itself together against the blast had subsided. Bernie was not two feet in the house when she saw my father's desperate face. My mother was screaming and my father was bent over her, between her legs. The sight of a woman in labour from any angle is a startling vision for anyone but especially startling for a five-year-old. My father had his arm up between my mother's legs which were spread wide. His hand was inserted up to his wrist and the pain on his face almost equalled that of my mother.

Bernie went immediately into the room, saw the crisis. At my mother's instructions, and fearing we would be too late, my father had inserted his hand into the uterus to try to turn the baby around. "Let me take over," Bernie said in her confident, clinical manner.

"I can't," my father said.

She nodded. Bernie pulled out the bottle of rum, gave my mother a sip, and one for my father. "Everybody just relax," she said.

By then we were dead centre in the eye of the hurricane. "Stay or leave the room as you see fit," my grandmother said to both my grandfather and me. Jack took my hand and we both sat off to one side, not leaving. Bernie put her hand on my mother's belly and studied the opening that would bring my little sister into the world.

Something new hit our front door. Not wind this time but wave. The door held but water gushed in over the doorstep and, if that wasn't enough, the wave rolling under the house forced water up through the floorboards with such intensity that the room was alive with veritable fountains of seawater.

"That's not important," Bernie said, pulling a scalpel from her bag, shoving it into the flame of the kerosene lamp and cleaning it with rum.

My grandfather saw what was about to happen and tried to distract me with a story. "Sometimes, Ian," he began in a soft, controlled voice, "in the nineteenth century, ships out to sea for months in the Indian Ocean would be so dry that the boards would begin to separate and the corking would not hold. They would begin to leak at every seam at once. Just like this. And sometimes the ship would simply pull itself apart, board by board until all her sailors would have to swim for it. Of course, you don't last long in the Indian Ocean with so many sharks. Not unless you can surround yourself with a pod of dolphins or come upon a sperm whale willing to give you transit home."

But the story was not enough. I twisted my head around to see that the scalpel had made a slit and the blood had begun to flow. My mother's face told the story in greater depth. She was tired now, pale, panting hard. Whereas before she was pushing during her contraption, now she looked weak, defeated. "Keep your hand on the baby," Bernie insisted, even though she saw later that she had also cut hard into the flesh of my father's wrist. The blood of my family was everywhere on the bed in pools of red that began to drip down onto the seawater on the floor. Another wave hit the house, this time with amazing force. My grandfather seemed quite calm or maybe he was faking it, for it was his job to keep panic at bay. "They had storms like this all the time in the nineteenth century. Things were much tougher back then. Men had to be able to rig a mast in a hurricane and single-handedly sail a schooner in a typhoon wind."

Bernie was helping my father shift the baby around now. My mother gave one final, feeble push, but then sank back, I'm sure unconscious by now, exhausted. It seemed almost as if they were wrestling little Casey into the world, that she was refusing to come, that nature was against us every step of the way and unwilling to let her waiting soul depart from wherever she was at.

And then I saw her arrive, bottom-first into the world. "Don't pull," Bernie shouted, as my father tried to pick her up, blood still dripping heavily from his cut wrist. "The cord is wrapped around the neck," Bernie said. "Be very still."

The baby was barely out as Bernie began to unwind the umbilical cord that could yet strangle my sister. Bernie then immediately put her fingers inside the mouth of the child and turned her upside down, holding her from the heels and spanked a gentle but firm smack on the bum. My father sucked in his breath, heard the baby cry and he fell backwards into the water on the floor. As Bernie cut the umbilical cord with the scalpel, my grandfather picked up my father, discovered how badly he was bleeding from the wrist and began to wind a bandage tightly. He staggered back to his feet and up to my mother. He kissed her cheek, found it clammy and screamed. "Bernie, I think she's dying!"

Bernie handed me the baby, wrapped only in a single, bloody piece of ripped sheet. She was coated with blood and mucous and, despite that, I held the tiny, bluish face close to my cheek and began to sing, "Old McDonald had a Farm."

When the next rolling wave, more powerful than the last, slammed into our house, I saw my grandfather trying to stop the bleeding of my father while Bernie was pushing air into my mother's lungs with her own mouth. My father, at that minute, looked out the window and, with a vision of pure terror in his eyes, pleaded with some unnamed, unseen force to allow his wife to live.

The eye of a hurricane is an incongruous event in the middle of such turmoil. Even as the next wave, weaker now than the last, made a dull thud into the walls of our house, the sun broke through and sent down a single shaft of light into our yard which was now part of the Atlantic Ocean. The light spilled almost gently into the water of the front yard and little Casey ceased her crying and fell asleep in my arms, perfectly contented, it would seem, to have been born amidst this holocaust.

My mother coughed and vomited and began to breathe, and my father sat down beside her and put his arm around her. Bernie pulled out needle and thread and began to stitch my mother back together. I had to turn away. I could not watch but I held tightly onto the little bundle of flesh and life that was my sister.

And when the hurricane returned and we were all, in varying degrees, alive, I gave my little sister to my father to hold and he could not stop himself from smiling. He began to tell her that she had been more than a little trouble, but that it's probably a good sign of a busy, challenging life to come. Bernie and Jack made some tea, poured some more rum, and kept vigil as I curled up under my bed, even though the floorboards leaked water, because that's where Mike was still sleeping through it all, like it was no big deal. I rested my head on Mike's mangy back and listened to his sad, soft snore and fell asleep through the next blast of wind and wave, wondering if this was the normal way of the world, wondering perhaps if it would be like this every day from here on, if the easy times were behind me.

6   I think the hurricane did more than just clear the island of old sheds, scour the rocks clean, drown the St. Johns and bring my sister into the world. In retrospect I might say that something big was changing somewhere or everywhere and Whalebone, independent as it was, would not be left out. Politics were changing, people were changing. Many were on the move. Some of their own volition, some as refugees.

And refugees had found their way to our island before: my drifting mother, Mr. Kirk's father, Mrs. Bernie Todd and her husband, both wanting to escape this century. Then Casey herself, coming out of the womb the wrong way and strangling, near death, as if some tug of war was taking place and forces on the other side of life did not want her to arrive. She was a quiet, worried-looking baby. Her skin did not settle on a human colour for several days and there was damage to her tiny neck where the umbilical cord, the very conduit of earthly sustenance, had tried to destroy her.

The morning after the storm Hants Buckler arrived on our doorstep to tell us of the wonders that were washing ashore. He said that he'd found wooden boxes of theatrical clothing that appeared floating outside his doorstep — fancy waist-coats and wigs and pointed shoes. Later, Jack would adopt these duds and come closer to realizing his dream of living in the eighteenth or nineteenth century. He now had the garb from each and had a hard time deciding which century he preferred.

Hants had also found live fish left flapping on the boards of his wharf, collected them and already they were salting in the new sun. All except for a two-headed fish that he found in the cutting basin. He said it was a monkfish, a two-headed monkfish at that, and that he would try to keep it alive by building a small aquarium.

"Here's the kicker, though," Hants contended. "Furniture. The shoreline is all lined up with tables and chairs and odds and ends. Some of it's busted, some of it ain't. It kind of looks like a bunch of people set up housekeeping on the beach, got mad at each other and had a fight, knocking over all the tables and chairs. You can come have a look. Plenty to pick from."

"Look what arrived *here* during the eye of hurricane," my father said, holding up my little sister who at that point was sound asleep and looking something akin to a creature from space.

Hants wasn't impressed. "Another one of them," he said. Hants wasn't married and had sworn off women and having kids. Besides, if it didn't wash in from the sea directly, if it had to come from a woman's belly, then it wasn't of any great in-terest in his book. He meant well; he just wasn't much of a family man. He studied the infant, touched her arm with his blunt, squared-off thumb and said, "I guess two is as good a number as one." He meant kids, I suppose. With that, Hants took his knuckles and rubbed them playfully across my flat-top haircut like he was filing down his callouses on a piece of sandpaper.

"The important thing is, though, we can all redecorate!" He meant the furniture on the beach.

"I'll be down a little later," my father said, studying the bandages on his wrists.

"Suit yourself," Hants said, a little disappointed that my old man had reacted so miserly with emotion over the two-headed monkfish, the theatrical wardrobe and the abundance of furniture. But before he left, Hants let go of his secret. In fact, maybe it just dawned on him there on our doorstep.

"You know, there's more chairs and tables down there on the beach scree than any of us will ever need. And I don't ex-pect it was put there for us to use as mere firewood kindling. If so, it would have come in the proper stove lengths and with-out all the fancy lathework. So it can only mean one thing."

"What's that?" my old man wanted to know. Casey had begun to suck on his index finger and my father was smiling at her.

"Immigration," Hants said.

"How so?"

"Well, first the furniture arrives, then the people. The ocean don't do nothing without good reason. You live alongside of it long enough and you grow to realize that."

My father could only nod in agreement, for the sea had given him a wife as well as a livelihood. "You mean the popu-lation of the republic is going to increase."

"Already has," he said, pointing to Casey. "She's just the tip of the iceberg. That little one of yours was just the first to come in with the storm. Wait till the floodgates open."

My father looked confused.

Hants turned to go. "Listen, you get down the beach or

send the boy to pick out what you need. We should get the stuff in out of the sun or 'afore the gulls and gannets have to it. Bird shit'll take the stain right off a fancy set of drawers. I think this stuff is all French or something. Got lots of curlicues and stuff."

Later, I went down alone to pick out furniture for my family. Hants was right, the beach looked like a brawl had taken place and there was stuff knocked around everywhere. I picked out a few things that would have been more suitable for a palace than my old house, but later my mom and dad seemed pleased, sitting at the kitchen in high-back, fancy chairs and eating off of a table that was half the length of our house.

Hants claimed that the two-headed monkfish was an intelligent life form from under the sea and that it could communicate with him which none of us doubted. He stored the rest of the furniture in what was left of his barn and threw big ship tarpaulins over most of it to keep the bird shit off. And he waited for the immigrants that he knew were headed for the Republic of Nothing.

Hants kept a telescope handy and studied the sea for days, waiting for the arrival of immigrants who would need the store of furniture. He studied so long and hard with one eye fixed upon the horizon and the other one squinted shut that he developed a common disorder of chronic telescope users. The overused eye went nearly blind and the unused eye, even when open, began to see things that weren't there. Mrs. Bernie Todd said she had seen just such a thing before with submariners from Portsmouth and she told Hants the only thing he could do was to go soak his head in salt water at regular intervals for as long as he could hold his breath. Hants thought this was a reasonable idea, and seeing a secondary use for his monkfish aquarium, stuck his head in with his favoured sea creature.

I was standing in the doorway to Hants' overly furnished home when I saw him pull his head from the tank for the final time. He let out a maniacal wailing and I could see that he had a two-headed monkfish the size of a medium-sized cod dangling from one ear-lobe like a giant earring.

"Help me, Ian," he shouted, "It's trying to chew its way into my brain!"

In my panic, for I had little experience with intelligent, carnivorous aquatic life, I yanked hard on one head of the monkfish whose teeth still gripped firmly onto Hants' earlobe, tearing the thing off — well fifty percent of it anyway — while the other head of the monkfish looked around, mouth gaping. Hants felt his ear, realized he had lost a minor, insignificant part of his anatomy, shook the water off his head like a dog would and sat down in a faded but immaculate throne that might have suited a king. He blinked the water out of his eyes. "I can see perfectly clearly now," he said. "Tell Mrs. Bernie Todd that the therapy worked."

"What'll I do with the fish?" I asked, for it was writhing in my hand as I held it in front of me with its one head looking up, the other down. It had dropped the earlobe at my feet and I feared that the fish might grab onto either my nose or my pecker and I wanted no more of it.

"Put her in the tank, son," Hants said. "No real harm done. My fault for not feeding her a proper diet." Hants knew when it was wrong to pass on blame and this was one of those times. I heaved the monk fish back in the tank where it fell with a frantic splash.

Hants was probably not expecting to see the first of the immigrants — refugees all — arrive in a brand spanking new two-tone Ford four-door. We were standing in the sunlight in his yard. I was holding up a mirror for him so he could stitch the piece back onto his ear with thirty pound test fishing line. He feared he might bleed to death if he didn't get a set of good double stitches into it. Hants had fortified himself with black tea spiked with thick black Barbados rum intended "to ward off pain and such," he said.

The ear had stopped bleeding by the time that Tennessee Ernie Phillips pulled up to a stop on the crushed clamshell driveway. Unfortunately, Hants had not done so well with the stitching and the lobe fell off again. Distracted by the newcomers, Hants walked away. I picked up the round earlobe which looked kind of like a well-chewed piece of bubble gum and put it in my pocket. A man got out of the newly arrived car to survey the very end of the road. "Where am I?" he asked. He looked far too polished for these surroundings, as did his car.

"You're here," Hants said, trying to get a knot in the final stitch of what was left of his ear.

"The Republic of Nothing," I added, for my father had taught me to say this to strangers, worried perhaps that they would not fully recognize that they were in a foreign country.

"I'll be damned," he said to someone sitting inside the car. The motor was still running.

"Any land for sale?" the man asked.

"Not much," Hants answered. He had not yet recognized that the beginning of his prophecy was coming true.

I saw a woman inside the car who looked like a movie actress. A white miniature poodle was sleeping peacefully in her lap. In the back seat was a girl about my own age who waved at me like we were old friends. As I waved back, I felt a fluttering feeling inside me like I had just swallowed a two-headed monkfish and it was taking the full scenic tour on its way down to my stomach.

Now memory is a funny thing. I was a young man alive on an August day after a hurricane in the republic. I had watched a sister come into the world the wrong way and a two-headed monkfish bite off a grown man's earlobe. I was ready for miracles; I was ready for the earth to open up or for angels to proceed down from heaven. And I guess I was old enough and ready to fall hopelessly in love. I knew that I had never seen anything quite like the little girl in the back seat who sent an electric thrill throughout me not to be equalled again in sheer physical intensity until the time I was thirteen and touched a broken-off branch to the Power Company's fallen electric lines. But history was all around me, as was love. It was all being arranged, I think, like Hants Buckler who retreated from the car to the shoreline where he was organizing the furniture, creating fully furnished kitchens and living rooms and mattressless bedrooms there on the sand.

"I don't know nothing about the land but I'll let you have this here kitchen set," he shouted to the family. "No cost. What's free is free."

Tennessee Ernie eyed Hants with suspicion. It could have been the blood dripping from his ear that made the foreigner think that Hants was a pirate who had just been in a fight where someone had yanked his hoop earring from its socket and torn off the lobe. Perhaps that was what the furniture was all about. Booty. Plunder. Besides, Tennessee was an American and Americans did things for a profit. If anyone was offering anything for free, then that would be proof that he was in a very unusual country.

It was then that a voice from some unseen god spoke up inside me and told me to introduce myself. "Good morning, sir," I said. "My name is Ian McQuade. And I might know of some land available." I was thinking of the fact that my father had gone up to Mr. Kirk years ago and asked for a place to build a house.

"Hop in, son," he said. He opened the back door to the car and I seated myself in heaven.

Unable to speak, all I could do was point and mumble with enough specificity to get us to the home of Mr. Ryan Kirk. As we pulled up to the very doorstep of Kirk's big old house, I saw him out surveying the storm damage to his flowering shrubs. I attempted to introduce Mr. Phillips to Mr. Kirk, but my tongue was still hampered by the tourniquet the girl had put onto it. But Tennessee was a garrulous man, ready to boldly state what he wanted. He wanted land and he had almost no money to pay for it but soon, very soon, he would personally be wielding the greatest power of the universe and then, he would repay with generosity.

Mr. Kirk, pruning sheers in one hand, broken-off sedge stalks in the other, took the request like a man who had just been asked if he would mind laying down on the ground to get beat over the head with a shovel.

"You're not a Canadian, are you?" he asked with some gravity in his voice. Mr. Kirk was the son of a Newfoundlander. His father had never accepted the idea of joining Confederation. Kirk always spoke of that dismal mistake of his countrymen in 1949. When he and his father had left the Rock to seek asylum, they only got as far as Whalebone Island and, refusing to ask what country it was, settled there believing it was an island off Greenland and hence part of Denmark, or maybe even one of the lesser Hebrides. When Kirk's father had learned that they were only in Nova Scotia and hence part of Canada, he shot himself with an old whaling harpoon which launched him straight out to sea. Kirk's final contact with his old man was to cut the line and let him drift or sink, rather than reeling him back in to survey the damage. This explains why Kirk was so pleased with my old man seceding from the Dominion of Canada and setting up the republic. And it helps explain why Kirk took kindly to anyone who was *not* a Canadian. "*Are* you a Canadian, young man?" Kirk repeated, having not received an immediate answer.

"I'm not," answered Tennessee. "I'm from far away."

Kirk needed to hear nothing more. He decided that he liked this man.

"I'll give you four acres over near Back Bay. It's only got an old well on her and a crippled wharf, but it's a place for a man to settle and start a life."

"I'll take it," Tennessee said, offering a handshake which just about wrenched the man's hand off his wrist. "You haven't said the price, though."

Kirk stuck his tongue in a far corner of his mouth. He had put all his mental energy into sedge trimming and had not counted on the prospect of dealing with high finance. "We can work that out later. It's not hard to settle onto a fair price between gentlemen — as long as they aren't Canadian," he explained. And that was that.

"Ian," Mr. Kirk said to me, "do some good with your life, me son, and take this feller over to Back Bay. Show him the old Hennigar place."

"Sure thing," I said. And I threw myself once again into the back seat and back to nirvana.

This is all filtered by the years, remember, but I'm sure that she reached across me to roll down the window and her hand slipped and touched my hand. She smiled, I nearly fainted and she showed me a pad on which she had been doodling. There were hearts and flowers and right in the middle something I didn't understand.

"It's very nice," I said.

"It's the state flag of New Mexico," she said, the first words that ever came out of her mouth.

"Sure is," I said, not wanting to sound stupid. And at that moment, looking at a drawing of the state flag of New Mexico in the back sea of a brand new two-tone Ford, beside a beautiful girl, seemed as exhilarating as anything could ever be.

I pointed down a bumpy lane to the left and Mr. Phillips jammed a hard turn. We hit sand and then a big pothole and scraped bottom. "I'll need a little more advance information, next time, son," he said, leaning back over the seat and addressing me.

I threw up my hands in apology but couldn't get past a loud mumble of consonants which came out like a mouthful of marbles rolling away in my attempt to say "Stop." The tide was still a bit high from the storm and besides he was already half off his new property and parking at a bedevilled angle straight into Back Bay.

"I guess we're there," the woman who looked like a movie star said in a breathy, theatrical manner. The front wheels were in the water and the car was parked at a rakish tilt with the front bumper kissing seawater and seaweed alike. The dog, who I would later learn was named Enrico Fermi, woke up and sniffed the salty, fishy air. From the angle I was at, I saw that the woman had on a tight dress, nylon stockings and high heels. There were what appeared to be diamond rings on several fingers and, as she tried to adjust herself on the hot vinyl seat, the flesh of her thighs gave off a soft sucking noise.

"I love this place," Tennessee said, backing up to level ground and jumping out.

"We call it Back Bay," I said self-importantly as I stepped out of the car.

From out of the trunk, Tennessee took out a squarish metal box with a dial on it. He plugged a set of earphones into it and another cord was attached to something that looked like a microphone. He stood slightly bent over and looked at the ground like a hunter stalking the tracks of animals. He began to walk a zigzag pattern across his new land, holding the device before him. I had no idea what he was up to and not much to compare it to, so I decided it was a sort of religious ceremony. My mother had dabbled in organized religion and taken me to a couple of churches on the mainland where people performed harmless but bizarre ceremonies like this for no clear reason.

"What is he doing?" I asked the girl. Her mother seemed unconcerned and even disinterested as she put on fresh lipstick with the rear view mirror tilted her way.

"It's a Geiger counter," the girl said. "He's counting roentgens."

"That's nice," I replied. Life was a giant jigsaw puzzle missing most of the pieces. Who was I to question any of it? While the dog jumped out to explore the little beach and the mother began to file her nails, the girl began to colour the state flag of New Mexico with a set of perfectly sharpened Crayola crayons. I heard Tennessee cry out that he found, "low levels — nothing to get excited about but the rock formation looks good."

His wife smiled at him and said, "I'm happy for you, dear. I'm happy for all of us." But she seemed somewhat disinterested for she flicked on the car radio, ran the dial up and down a few times, and finding no music save the singing of global and intergalactic static, switched it off. I was afraid to get out and follow Mr. Phillips around. I didn't want to leave my favoured place in the back seat. Attempting to strike up more intimate conversation with the girl, I told her about the two-headed monkfish.

"My father will be happy to hear about it," she answered, genuinely interested. "Could be some sort of mutation from high radiation levels in the water. After the testing, my father's friends found some baby mice with seven legs, and only two toes on each foot."

"Wow," I said. I knew I was out of my depth with these new folks. Just then, I think Mr. Phillips picked up a few more roentgens than expected on the old Geiger counter, for he flicked off the headset and let out a whoop of delight. Mrs. Phillips turned back to her daughter and said, "I'm always so happy when your father's happy."

"Me too," the girl said.

"Me too," I said.

It turned out that Tennessee Ernie Phillips had been a physicist who helped to improve upon the atomic bomb by helping to develop the hydrogen bomb. Tennessee had worked hard on the project and after the initial testings he argued that they should go for an even larger explosion than the Bikini bomb or the tests that followed. If they were capable of making a bigger bomb, they should, until they failed. That would be the only way they would learn their limits. Deep down, though, he believed in unlimited power. But Tennessee Ernie Phillips fell out of favour with some of the big wigs back in Alamagordo.

There was, after all, the honest-to-God possibility that a large enough hydrogen bomb could set off an uncontrollable chain reaction, and that, indeed, the entire sum total of planet matter would go up in a single blast. I guess Tennessee had not been brought up in a household where caution was important. He caused some grief around the planning rooms and, in the end, they drummed him out of the nuclear bomb business, froze all his personal assets and told him to leave New Mexico.

Tennessee wanted desperately to continue with nuclear weapons research but he was too patriotic to go over the wall to the Russians. And the government squelched his attempts to tell the taxpayers that his colleagues were too chicken to make bigger and bigger bombs, that the U.S. could split the world in half if only the scientific community had a chance to live up to its potential.

Phillips was warned: better clam up and keep it all to himself or else. So he packed up the new Ford and his family and drove off into the New Mexico night, his daughter scrawling New Mexico flags in the back seat and his wife punching buttons, shifting from one distant radio station to another. At first, the family drifted from motel to motel. Then, afraid that the Atomic Energy Commission might come after him, Ernie headed north and east as far as the road would take him.

"I've had too much desert," Mrs. Phillips said. "I want to go home."

Always one to leap further than suggested, Tennessee agreed they would go home, but not home to Boston where his wife, Mildred, had been born. Instead, he would drive them home to Nova Scotia where Mildred's family, the Swinimers, had come from in the early part of the century before Bluenosers had gone down the road to the Boston States to get away from poverty and cheap fish prices. Not one to go anywhere empty-handed, Tennessee Ernie Phillips had arrived in Nova Scotia to live out his life, bringing with him a beautiful wife, a daughter, a new Ford and enough knowledge to build an atom bomb (given enough processed uranium) and enough gumption to disperse the planet (given the necessary manpower, cash flow and imagination).

But I knew none of that, there in the back seat of the Ford, listening to the far off static of the radio. For the girl beside me, Gwendolyn, had finished colouring her flag surrounded by flowers and hearts. I watched as she carefully folded it and put it in my hands. I reached into my pocket, wanting desperately to find something to give her, but all I could find was the bit of Hants Buckler's ear lobe. I pulled it out of my pocket and handed it to her. She rolled it around in her fingers and studied it in the light. "I've never seen anything quite like it before," she said. "I'll always cherish this."

7 The year was 1961. I was ten years old and this was the year the foreign government of Nova Scotia caught up with the republic and robbed the children of their freedom. If it had not been for my mother's pacifism and her insistence to my father that bloodshed was not the answer, I might have been spared my fate. I might not have had to go to school.

It was the year Kennedy was sworn into office in the States. Yuri Gagarin had orbited the earth; the U.S. backed the Bay of Pigs invasion (this one really got my old man nervous). More astronauts — Shepherd, Grissom, Titov went blasting into orbit. U.N. Secretary General Dag Hammerskjold was killed in a plane crash. The East Germans built a wall. On August 13, the very same day when the Russians exploded a fifty megaton hydrogen bomb, the largest explosion ever (surely Tennessee Ernie must have been sulking), a small delegation from the mainland arrived on Whalebone to try to eradicate the republic of childhood.

Now, an island is a place where people come and go. Coming and going is always news. Strangers coming and going is bigger news but strangers representing any government outside the republic was even bigger news yet and a major cause for concern. I remember a tall thin woman and a short concrete block of a man. They did all the talking. In tow was a bespectacled, nervous teenage boy who was introduced as "just an observer." Perhaps he was a university student from the Dalhousie School of Education, studying to become a professional educator and touring the outer fringes of civilization for a first-hand view of what he would be teaching.

What can I say? It was August and I was fishing off the little bridge over the Musquash. I can't say I had any ambition about catching anything. In fact, I knew with almost perfect certainty that the big crippled sea trout with the ugly growth on its mouth had already stolen the bait off my hook. I was just kind of lolling around, leaning on the wooden rail, sniffing its perfume of creosote. I was also trying to ignore Burnet McCully, Jr. who was at the mainland side of the bridge, trying to whittle away at the wooden guard rail.

I didn't talk to Burnet very often. He was a mean son of a bitch and two years older than me. Little did Burnet know that we would both be victims that day of an insidious plot to thwart our fun come September. There were only three kids who lived on the island — me, Casey, and Gwendolyn. Burnet lived in an old shack just across the Musquash, but he spent much of his life trying to cause trouble either on the bridge or on the island. For differing reasons, none of our parents had seen fit to send us to the mainland schools. All of us received some manner of education at home. My mother had me reading the entire documented history of Edgar Cayce and so far I was up to the point where Edgar healed a man from Alabama of goitre with information he had received while in a deep trance.

Burnet, on the other hand, had been taught at home by his father the skills of playing card games like Auction Forty-fives, Pinochle, Rummy and Go Fish. He was a quiet, troubled sort of boy who was just waiting for the chance to be around other kids so he could turn into a bully. I tried to avoid Burnet whenever I could. Mostly it was a matter of just getting out of his way.

Poor Burnet, lacking victims, spent much of his time vandalizing the bridge with a pocket knife and throwing rocks. A born killer, he threw rocks at anything living and if he failed in his first attempt to draw blood, he'd go back for seconds and thirds until a bird or gull or frog was mutilated. My father said he was glad that Burnet lived on the other side of the bridge, that cruelty would not be a good trait for any citizen of the Republic of Nothing. "Such folks do little good for an honest anarchy," my father would say. "But he comes by these traits honestly." Burnet McCully, Sr. was a professional lout, the last living specimen of several generations of loutish men who had great swearing skills and could never keep a knife sharp enough to be a good fisherman. Miserable, illiterate Burnet Jr. would be the first among the loutish McCully men to suffer an education.

Gwendolyn, as might be expected, had graduated beyond state flags and, after memorizing the capitals of all the countries on earth, even the newly formed African republics, was hard at work learning the inner mechanics of the atom. Had school not come along and put a roadblock in the way of her education, she probably would have had a fair knowledge of nuclear physics by the time she was thirteen.

But on this fateful day, Gwendolyn was at home drawing three-dimensional models of helium atoms. Burnet was stymied in his vandalism by a duller than usual knife blade, squinting at it in the bright sun. Only I, perhaps, was aware that our lives were about to be radically altered. The tall woman, gaunt to the point of emaciation, walked straight to me and fixed me with an eagle's eye. "Young man," she said, "in September you will begin school on the mainland."

Lesley Choyce

The concrete block of a man was introduced as "Mr. Pig-got," and he smiled the smile of those benignly belligerent souls who hold bureaucratic positions. Leaning against the hood of the car stood the observer, pen and notebook in hand, taking notes. I would never know the name of the woman but later, when learning of a mushroom known as the Angel of Death, would decide that the moniker fit handily. I spooled in my fishing line and everyone focused on the empty hook. "Looks like you're out of luck," Mr. Piggot said.

"Yep," I answered. "I guess I am." Somewhere in the world, probably at that very minute, a fifty megaton bomb went off. I had known that kids were supposed to go to school, but my parents had been very sure that there was nothing worth learning in a mainland school. And I was convinced by my father's insistence that we were indeed an independent country of some sort, that the laws of Canada or Nova Scotia couldn't touch us.

The Angel of Death, Mr. Piggot and their observer went on to visit every house on the island, finally locating Gwendolyn and my little sister, but not before they were harassed by Lambert, Eager and even Hants Buckler who claimed he had never seen any children on the island in his entire lifetime. Mr. Kirk, concerned for the welfare of us island kids, offered The Angel of Death and Mr. Piggot a small parcel of land in exchange for the freedom of Gwendolyn, Casey and me, but they considered him a lunatic. He considered them to be more "ugly Canadians!" Burnet McCully, Sr. made no argument at all and just said that they could do "whatever the hell they wanted" with his son.

My mother would have loved to have held us back from the world longer — especially poor little Casey who had not quite turned six at the time — but she knew it would only bring grief to the island. My mom wondered what her hero, Edgar Cayce, would do under these circumstances and realized that he would let the world interfere if need be, that it would strengthen a soul, not hinder it — if one kept the right perspective and metaphysical attitude about the mundane.

And so, September the fifth rolled around. A school bus was dispatched to us but would go no farther than the mainland side of the bridge to the island. I held Casey's hand as we walked across the bridge and off the island for what seemed then like the last time in our lives. Gwendolyn was stoic as she fell in behind us. Burnet stood alone on the far side of the bridge with that familiar sneer on his face. He was not looking at us, however, but at the bus approaching. As the great, yellow beast neared us, Burnet let fly a jagged piece of granite that made direct contact with a headlight and splashed glass all over the gravel road. Inside the bus, the kids cheered.

What was going on? Burnet must have wondered. After years of being simply despised or at best ignored by islanders, here he had already found a warm reception for his bad disposition with the mainland kids on the bus. He smiled and held his fisted hands up as the bus driver, enraged by the incident, stormed out of the bus towards us. I hauled Casey and Gwendolyn out of his path. We watched as the man lunged for Burnet. The bus driver, a bearded man in a logging shirt, picked up Burnet by the scruff of his thick neck and slammed him down hard on the hood of the sickly orange-yellow bus. "Fish turd!" I heard him call Burnet, then lifting him high off the hood, he gave him a solid kick in the ass and shoved him towards the door. Burnet got in without resistance. However, once inside the strange hallway on wheels he was facing a smiling crowd of mainland kids who applauded him wildly. A legend had been born.

The bus driver turned to Casey, Gwendolyn and me, dipped his hat, smiled what was almost a polite smile and then, through his teeth, said, "Nothin' but island trash. Now get in, the rest of yous, before I kick your butts." We got in.

Maybe I was trying to protect my little sister or maybe I was just too fidgety in the new situation, but I felt my world

Lesley Choyce

crumbling. When I saw Gwendolyn sit down beside Burnet in the seat and then give him a soft, sad look — I suddenly got scared. Exactly what I was afraid of, I didn't know, but I immediately felt a warm hot bead of liquid run down my leg and straight into my shoe and I knew it was going to be a very bad day. Even though it was the last time I peed myself in the twentieth century, I still shudder to think of that moment. And I shake involuntarily, a quaking tremor that issues up out of me much as this poor parent-planet must have shuddered that day in August when fifty megatons of atomic might were detonated inside her ribs somewhere beneath the wilds of Siberia.

8 I think I was fourteen at the time my father began his flamboyant melding of anarchy with the Conservative Party of Nova Scotia. My sister, Casey, had not spoken for three months. My mother believed it was just a phase she was going through. "Silence in children should never be discouraged," she said.

Casey gave up her wordfast, though, the day John G.D. MacIntyre knocked loudly at the back door. My father was in the kitchen trying to sift gold out of the household flour supply. My mother had just walked in the kitchen and was puzzled by my father standing over the table twirling the wheel of the hand sifter, surrounded by a white cloud.

"I had intended to tell you about this, Dorothy, but I got distracted and forgot all about it," he said. He meant the gold flecks he had found in the Musquash stream bed up by the unsuccessfully blown-up bridge. He had been out surveying his kingdom when he looked in the little river and thought he saw gold, a tiny swirling pocket of gold dust nearly camouflaged by three big trout. He had leaned over to ask the fish to move, then he scooped up what was nearly an ounce of gold.

My father was never very interested in wealth. In fact, he worried that if word got out that the island had gold, speculators would want to come and buy up the land to dig pit mines. He thought of simply throwing the gold back in the water but was afraid someone else would see it. Instead, he watched the gold dry in the sunlight in the palm of his hand and grudgingly stuffed it in his coat pocket, realizing that he'd have to keep an eye on the Musquash every day just to make sure there was no more gold showing to attract the wrong eyes. One more responsibility as president of the Republic of Nothing.

So he decided to take the handful of gold home and hide it. He decided the safest place to stash the gold flakes was in the flour bin in the kitchen. He mixed it in thoroughly with the Robin Hood White, satisfied that it would be safe from mining corporations and prospectors. Then, like so many things, he forgot about the gold because it was fishing season and things were busy.

"Dorothy, what the hell happened to my gold!" he was yelling at the very moment the new Tory party leader showed up at his back door.

"I don't know what you're talking about, Everett," my mother said.

"I put a handful of gold in the flour and now it's gone."

"It's gone because I baked at least a dozen loaves of bread with that flour. You never told me there was gold in it."

Everett had sifted to the bottom of the bin. Sure enough, there was no gold left. "Don't you ever sift it first?" he asked.

"Sometimes I do," she answered. "Not always."

So that was it, he figured. We had been eating loaves of gold bread for weeks. He decided that he liked the idea and hoped that gold was good for you. He thought it through. We had eaten the gold. Some of it had been digested and was now part of our brain cells and our teeth. Some of it had been shit out

Lesley Choyce

into the outhouse pit. Archaeologists would arrive here a thousand years in the future, find the remains of his outhouse pit and take core samples. "These people on Whalebone Island were really something," somebody would say. "They shit gold."

But then a dark cloud passed over my father's imagination. Had he poisoned his family? Were any of them different? Yes, poor little Casey had not spoken in three months. What was the old expression — "Silence is golden." Jesus Christ, what had he done?

A cold fear had just swept over my father, for he loved us more than anything on earth. But before he had a chance to burst out of the kitchen, he heard the voice of his daughter. "There's somebody here!" she yelled, her voice loosed finally from silence by the appearance of a political party hack.

"Who is it?" my mother asked.

"It's somebody," she fired back.

My father ran to the front door, lifted his daughter into the air and gave her a hug. "You're sunlight on the cold rocks in the middle of April," he told her.

"I know," she said.

As he hugged her tight, my father found himself looking at the presence of a stranger, a man in a brown business suit with a plump red face and a tie that choked his neck like a dog collar. "Who are you?" my father asked.

"I'm John G.D. MacIntyre," the man said, breathing grain neutral spirits into the living room.

"So?" my father asked. He was mistrustful of strangers with funny smelling breath.

"So I've come to make a proposition to you."

Oh no, not a goddamn gold hunter, my father worried. He stiffened, set Casey down on the rug. "Run along now. I need to talk to this somebody."

The man offered a mickey of grain alcohol to my father.

"You can't have the mineral rights."

"I didn't come to talk mineral rights," John G.D. said, his

voice now noticeably funny like his tongue was thicker than his mouth was willing to hold. "I'm here to talk politics."

That was different. My father hadn't had a chance to talk politics to anyone for a long while. My mother, observing the scene from the white flour cloud of the kitchen, sat down.

"Sit down," my father said to the man.

John G.D. MacIntyre flopped down right beside me on the chesterfield. I was reading a Classics comic version of *Treasure Island* and not getting very far with all the interruptions. He held out the mickey again and this time my father swallowed a hard gulp. His Adam's apple was like a little elevator that went to the top floor and then made a quick express trip to the bottom before returning to an at-rest position in the middle of this throat.

"I'm with the Conservative Party of Nova Scotia," John G.D. said in voice proud but polluted. "Now, we aren't in power in this province right now as you probably know . . . "

My father cut him off. "Just as a point of fact, this isn't the province of Nova Scotia. You are on the soil of the Republic of Nothing and you're looking at the president of said republic."

MacIntyre seemed baffled at first but then his face lit up like a ten-cent light bulb. "Then what they told me in Sheet Harbour was right. You are a politician."

"An anarchist," my father corrected. "The best government is no government."

John G.D. swigged another drop and offered me the bottle just to be polite. I reached for it but my father pulled it away and took a slug. I don't think John G.D. knew what an anarchist was, but he did recognize a man who seemed to be saying he was dissatisfied with the current government, the government of the Liberal Party of Nova Scotia

"Of course, you are right sir. No government would be good government compared to the way the thieving Liberals run things. Look, I'm trying to pull our party back together. We've had our setbacks. But we've got a great leader, Mr.

Colin Michael Campbell. I've been behind him all the way for years and I can tell you he is a giant of a man. And I don't just mean he's tall, neither. Now, he's sent me down here to find the right man for the Tories on this shore. I'm down here today because I need one good man."

"A good man for what?" my old man inquired.

"Look," MacIntyre said. "I won't mess around with you. We have no one to run for the legislature for this part of the shore."

"That's because the last Tory MLA who ruled Sheet Harbour was a corrupt pig who screwed the voters. It was because of people like him that I declared this island a free republic."

"And so you should have. Any upstanding Tory would have done just that." John G.D. was obviously a pro at political wilery. His motto was probably this: always agree with anything anyone says if you want to get them to do your bidding.

The bottle went back and forth. "What do you want, anyway?" my father finally asked.

"I want you to run for us. I want you to represent the shore in the legislature in Halifax."

"Why?"

"Because I been scouring this backwater for days for one honest man who wants to run for us and turn this riding around. And you're that man. Someday this shore will be the haven for free-thinking men like yourself, a place of political idealism and champions of liberty, a home for brave individualism, but most of all a place of integrity and freedom of the heart."

"Freedom of the heart," my father repeated. "I like that."

"They told me up the road that you were our man. Sir, our party is all dried up on this shore unless we bring in new blood. But look who's in power now. The Grits. And what do they stand for? Government ruling the daily lives of the common people. Look at who represents you now — Bud Tillish."

"I don't think I know anything about Bud Tillish. Like I said, we're a separate country from Canada and we are no longer part of Nova Scotia. I don't stay abreast of provincial politics."

"But that's why you're the perfect candidate. You don't have any political enemies. And you have a vision."

"But I'm an anarchist."

"Deep down we all are."

"And I've already declared Whalebone Island a sovereign republic."

"Every town on this shore should do the same damn thing and I'd be behind it one hundred percent."

My father scratched at his jaw and reached for the bottle. "What if I don't like the job?"

"Then you can quit."

"What do I have to do to be elected?"

"Nothing. That's the key to success in this election. Just stay home, stay invisible. If people can't see you, they'll vote for you simply because you won't look bad. All we have to do is wait for Bud Tillish to start giving speeches. Then you're a shoo-in."

"Well, in that case, sure," my old man agreed.

"Great. Can I use your phone?"

"I don't have a phone."

"Oh," John G.D. said. "Well, I better go then and get word to Halifax. But you'll hear from me. Together we'll win this election."

My father hadn't thought that much about an election. As the door closed on John G.D. and his car lurched off over the potholes, my father appeared elated but bewildered. My mother walked in with a tub of clams. "Somebody help me shuck these things."

"Sure, hun," my father said.

Casey jumped up on our father's lap. "That man sure did burp a lot," she told him, possibly her first astute political commentary in her life.

"It's good to have you talking again, Casey," my father said, ruffling her hair. "What was all the silence for?"

Casey shrugged. "I guess I just didn't have anything I wanted to say until the burping man came."

I put down my comic and picked up a kitchen knife. The four of us were sitting in the living room with a tub full of piss clams before us. My father ate three of them raw and sucked back the juice. I never finished reading *Treasure Island*. Things began to change after that. The Republic of Nothing had opened diplomatic ties with the province of Nova Scotia. My father's eyes were like hot red coals and his hair seemed charged with electricity as he shucked clams.

"I had a dream last night," Casey said. "In the dream a horse was swimming in the waves when suddenly it turned into a ship with a bright white sail. I was sailing on the ship all alone and I could make the wind do whatever I wanted it to. Pretty soon it took me to shore and the ship turned back into a horse that gave me a ride home. The horse was golden and very pretty and it gave me back my voice which I had lost at sea. When I woke up, I waited before I had anything to say. And then the man appeared at the door and I knew that it was somebody."

"Who was he, dear?" my mother asked my father.

"An emissary from the next country over. We're negotiating a treaty of sorts," my father said.

---

9   My father, I admit, did have a political mind, but he was so far ahead or behind the times he lived in that my mother was convinced there was no chance he'd be elected to the legislature. So while my father honed his skills for the upcoming election, while he carved in his mind a totally unique

and anarchic platform from which to pronounce policy, my mother ignored his aspirations altogether and busied herself by reading books on memory improvement.

She hoped to eventually recall something from those empty pages of her life, but so far she had only succeeded in memorizing the times table up to 325 times 236. All of us were impressed by her finesse with mathematics and her new system of mnemonics that would eventually allow her to memorize the name of every town in Nova Scotia. She sat in the brassy sunlight of the early morning kitchen all alone eulogizing, "Sheet Harbour, East Jeddore, West Jeddore, Clam Harbour, Lake Charlotte, Clam Bay, Tangier, Ecum Secum, Necum Teuch, Sober Island" on through the morning. The only problem was that there weren't enough towns in Nova Scotia that began with vowels so that she could come up with readily memorizable mnemonic acronyms. Nonetheless, while politics began to ferment in the old man's mind, my mother memorized on toward the east and west.

My mother had not counted on the mighty Conservative forces that were conservatively amassing on my father's behalf. In fact, three weeks after the election had been announced, my father had not even heard one word from John G.D. MacIntyre or any of the flunkies at the Conservative party headquarters in Halifax. But he had not been forgotten. Mac-Intyre had verbally painted a striking picture of Everett McQuade to his cronies and they all agreed that my father was of the correct political cloth if he believed that less government was better government. The fact that he was a fisherman and a dark horse from the boonies was an advantage.

To bolster that advantage, riding workers were sent out daily from Halifax with carloads of rum, enough pint bottles to pickle the gizzards of half the Eastern Shore populace. Mac-Intyre was not a hypocrite when it came to rum bottle politics for he had studied the machinations of government from the bleary side of the pint bottle for many years and he had a dark,

Lesley Choyce

golden crystal vision of a better life for all Nova Scotians, or as his new colleague Everett McQuade would have said, "for all of the great republics that exist or are about to exist." MacIntyre had financial backing in Ontario. He had friends with plenty of money including, of course, manufacturers of rum and rum bottles on his side. How could he lose? He sallied forth headlong into the campaign, blustering and railing and rallying behind him carloads of bottle distributors that issued forth to every nook and cranny of this great province, spreading the golden gospel according to John G.D. MacIntyre.

Cutting government spending was a hot issue in the election. "Why should the little guy have to pay for everything?" MacIntyre taunted the crowds from North Sydney to Church Point. "Why, I ask you, is it always the little guy?" Now Mac-Intyre himself was neither small in girth nor wealth. He was a tall man who also measured in a substantial circumference around his equator. And he had acquired capital by investing in a munitions factory during the war. Fortunately, MacIntyre had pulled out his funds just before it was discovered that the company was selling bomb casings to the Red Chinese army.

In truth, though, it may not have been the loyal and deviously locomotive Conservative machine that was to aid my father the most in the election. I think what my father had most to his advantage was the ever-present public appearances of Bud Tillish, his opponent. Bud was a congenital liar and a cheat which was why he had turned to politics in the first place. He had been appointed to replace an aging Liberal clergyman named Dwight Noseworthy who had died while fast asleep in the legislative assembly during session. The papers said that he died mid-snore, that his sleepy presence would be sorely missed. The premier had appointed Bud as a reward for past services in Ottawa where Bud had been sent to annoy the hell out of the Minister of Finance until the man had quit and was replaced by a minister who felt more kindly towards pumping federal money into Nova Scotia to develop coal, tourism and, of all things, heavy water for nuclear power plants.

Bud had three primary faults: he talked too much in public, he was a bad liar, and the killer — he was a teetotaller. The premier had tried to overlook these worries but urged Bud to closet himself with his thoughts for as much of the election as possible. Instead, Bud stumped the county, promising public swimming pools, paved driveways, unlimited fishing licenses and a heavy water plant for every third town on the Eastern Shore. These lies were simple political whoppers, but then Bud began to get carried away with his own prejudices and on a Friday night dance interlude he gave an impromptu speech at the Masonic Hall in East Chezzetcook. He called for new and higher taxes on cigarettes and booze "for the good of every-body." From then on, Everett McQuade's popularity soared.

My father listened only to shortwave radio, primarily broad-casts from London, Amsterdam and Auckland. He never listened to local media or read any of the local papers. The Halifax papers had already reported verbatim what the Conservative media machine had told them, that Everett was a "reclusive but successful small businessman from Whalebone Island who had studied political science. In his local community he is re-garded as a great family man and a friend to all."

While the campaign proceeded without the active partici-pation of the candidate, Everett was still up at dawn and out to sea in his renovated Cape Islander every day the weather would allow. I'd go along most days to help fish, chop bait, make tea, and puzzle over tangled hand-lines. The day before the fateful election I was in the cabin making a peanut butter sandwich when I felt the boat begin to bob and wobble in a strange way.

"Come out here, son. You should see this," my father yelled.

Outside, I discovered we were surrounded by a mighty

Lesley Choyce

crowd of dolphins. The sea had come alive with roiling waters and ebullient backs reflecting spears of sunlight.

"I've only seen that sight once before," my father said. "Just before you were born. It's a good omen for the republic."

"I don't think I understand," I said, mesmerized by the dolphins but wanting to understand how my father had linked the event with his own politics. And I also wanted to know how working as part of the Nova Scotia government would forward the intentions of the Republic of Nothing.

"It's like this," he said, as the dolphins passed and my father began to bait his lines and feed them back into the waters again. "The Republic of Nothing is based on tolerance of ideas and people. It also holds sacred things like independent thought and the right of any man to shape his destiny as he sees fit as long as he don't tromp on anybody else doing it. It's a basic belief in the littleness of things. Our island is the first fragment of a new world order of little nations. We'll all be too damn small to go to war because we'll be too small to afford it. It's like those hopping dolphins. They are all the many tiny nations of the world who will replace the big bullies. And the leaders of the nations will be non-leaders. Every one of 'em will be a fisherman or a farmer or a car mechanic or a beachcomber."

It had been one of the first times in a long while my father had gone on like this. The election fever had taken full control of him.

"But will we have to move to Halifax if you win?"

Suddenly his face grew dark. "I don't know, son. I haven't discussed that problem with Mr. MacIntyre yet. We'll see."

Everett didn't hear that he had won the election until the night after when John G.D. himself turned up at the door. "Now the fun begins," John said, for his party had crushed the Liberals by distributing enough rum to fill Halifax Harbour twice over. In the Eastern Shore riding, Bud Tillish had received only a handful of votes. Apparently even his family had voted against him. And everyone was curious as hell to find out just who Everett McQuade was. My father was an invisible celebrity. He shuttled John away, said he'd get in touch soon, but right now he wanted to think. After the door had closed on the baffled politician, my father walked into the kitchen and told my mother, "I won. The Republic of Nothing has been admitted into the Nova Scotia Legislature."

"I'm proud of you," my mother said. She looked up from her mnemonics book where she had been memorizing the names of all the stars visible in the night sky.

"I'm going to go for a walk and formulate policy," my father announced, his head swimming in stars.

"I'm coming with you," my mother said.

They walked all the way down to the Channel Cove beneath a canopy of stars that now had names. Alpha Centauri, Aldebaran, Betelgeuse.

"Democracy is a flawed system that beats us all down to mediocrity," my father said to his wife. "The politics of nothingness embraces the sort of negative capability that the poets speak of. It's my job to bring the ambition of the individual and his dreams back into public life, to harness the tyranny of bullheadedness and give the land back to the people and the creatures before the world gets entirely fucked up."

A light was on in Hants Buckler's place. He was up late cataloguing the goods that had drifted in over the last month. He heard my father approach and he snapped on the outside light. Hants had heard the news already. He picked up the walking stick he had carved from the washed-up rib bone of a whale, kissed it once on its pure white shaft and walked outside to give it to my father.

"If you have to go into Halifax, take this with you as a weapon. Them bastards up there might try to give you a hard time. I always knew it would come in handy. You take it. "

"Thanks, Hants." My father accepted the gift but not as a weapon. "I think this could be a useful symbol of something,"

Lesley Choyce

he told his wife who delicately clasped his elbow as they walked. My mother had drifted off into the myriad of stars and whispered their names to herself, "Polaris, Vega, Altair, Deneb, Sirius, Capella, Rigel."

My father looked up at the stars too, and for the first time began to wonder how he could have been elected. As far as he knew, no one on Whalebone Island had even voted and, on the mainland, Everett McQuade was a virtually unknown man except to a couple of fish plant owners. He stirred this thought around for a while until he concluded that he won by a sort of divine intervention. The forces of possibility and nothingness were on his side and had created a perfect vacuum where no one could succeed but him. And when the time would arrive for him to appear on the steps of the provincial legislature, stepping out of a car with a whalebone cane and a head of red hair like a blazing barn, the people of Halifax would know that there was more at work in Nova Scotia politics than a bottle-a-vote strategy.

10 Yes, I'm sad to say that my father's victory truly did go straight to his head. In the living room later that night, he tried to contain himself but he couldn't. "Ian," he said, "in ten years, the entire world will be different. This is just a first, small step. Right now, I bet that individualists like myself are being sworn into governments all over the planet. It's the quietest damn revolution the world has ever known, I'll tell you that." His eyes were like wild lions and electricity seemed to flow out of him at every pore.

Everett grabbed my mother and gave her a big bear hug. She gently pushed herself away and asked Casey and me if we wanted to go for a walk along the shore to give my father time to clear his thoughts. My father turned away from us as if we had already left the room. He began to practice some sort of speech he was putting together in his head, speaking directly to the wall and then to the furniture. My father had gone a little berserk, I guess. My little sister was wide-eyed.

"We're going for a stroll, dear," my mother said to him although he didn't pay any attention. Then she shuttled us out the door in our coats and boots. I don't think my father heard us leave.

"What will it be like?" I asked. "Will everything be different for us?"

My mother was looking out toward the sea from which she had been delivered. It was a cool, clear night. The moon was out and its light had varnished the shoreline rocks to silver. It seemed that every rock was covered in tin foil. The moonlight on the water appeared like a broad, silver highway, alive with tiny ripples. The highway led right to my mother's feet. To the north, we could see stars. My mother gave a sweep of her hand across the entire night sky. "Things will be the same and things will be different. Up there is the planet Uranus which brings about revolution. You can't see it but you can feel it. I can feel it in my heart, tugging. I feel Neptune tugging as well. The stars don't make our destiny, but they are a sort of language from which we can read the plan of things to come."

Casey and I looked up into the grey silvery darkness. We could not see the planets except for Jupiter which was large and stubborn enough to stand out even in the moonlight.

"Yes, Jupiter. Your father has too much of him. Worse yet, Mars." She pointed to a dim reddish glow on the base of the horizon. "Mars is never to be trusted. Ever. I was delivered, however, by Venus, a star alone in the sky the morning your father found me. I came of love by way of the sea. Perhaps someday I'll go back that way."

We were used to our mother speaking this way, but we only had an inkling of what she was talking about. "I'm worried about your father. He has wild dreams. He's safe with us but I don't trust Halifax. Halifax was a city founded by Mars."

"You mean, like Martians, Mum?" Casey asked.

"No, honey. Men of war. It's a city founded by soldiers. A place of killers although you wouldn't know that to see it on a Sunday afternoon, walking through the Public Gardens. I think your father will run into trouble there. Your father is somehow protected here on Whalebone Island. I was sent here from the sea to be with him. I know that for certain. I'll try one more thing to keep him. But I won't argue. That would never work on your father."

"What are you going to do?" I asked.

"Conspire," she said. And with that we walked toward the moon along the shining stones. The tiny lapping waves sang a muted chant with brush strokes of sound. My mother looked long and hard at the moon and then she stooped down to wash her hands in the sea. I was suddenly afraid. All this talk of having been a gift from the sea. I know she believed it but I often wondered if my mother was completely crazy. If she was crazy, she was crazy in such a beautiful, mysterious way that I loved her all the more for it. But I was getting old enough now to wonder if her craziness would be dangerous. It was a time when I should have been allowed the liberty of rebellion and temporary adolescent insanity. But I felt myself becoming an anchor for both my parents. I was all that tethered the anarchist and the mermaid to our home. Casey was young. She drifted through life like a cloud. I watched Casey float around the island on a cushion of air as we walked. Her head was always full of birds and breezes. My mother, on the other hand, was tidal. At times she was there, cooking, cleaning, salting down fish. Other times her mind would slip out to sea or sail her to the stars with her charts.

And Everett, the successful politician, the failed destroyer of bridges, the theorist. He was changed from wild rebellion into something uniquely odd — a Conservative, a Tory. How would he fit into a back bench in the legislature in Halifax? What would become of him?

My mother, in communion with the sea, began to sing a lullaby. She sat down and Casey curled up like a wisp of night smoke in her lap and fell asleep. The power of my mother's soft voice almost sent me to dreams as well, but I was too stirred up. I didn't trust her magic. I sat quietly, skipping small stones into the ribbon of moonlight that had moved further west. "Where is that song from?" I asked.

"I don't know. It's just something that's in me and wants to come out. It's from my life before your father. A piece of it. Some day, I'll know the whole story."

I didn't want my mother to know the whole story. I feared it would break the spell of our own home life. The unknown elements of both my parent's lives were not to be trusted. My mother's singing had unlocked the key to sleep. Hard stones felt like pillows beneath me. The cool, damp air was a warm comforter of down. Leaning on my mother's soft arm, I drifted headlong into darkness.

Then I heard the splashing. The slapping of things wet against the stones. When I looked up I saw that the moon was low on the horizon now. It had melted from silver light to red blood and the world was awash with the setting moonlight, a softer but more sinister glow. The sea was a spectacular circus of jumping things. Fish of all sorts leaped about. Some flipped up into somersaults by the shoreline and landed by our feet.

"What is it?" I asked my mother who seemed to be in a trance.

"It's what I can do to keep your father here. It won't work but it's necessary to try."

"The fish?"

"Yes. For him."

"But he's already talking of the trip to Halifax tomorrow. He doesn't have the boat ready."

"When he wakes, he'll be out there. " Hers was a faraway

smile. I lifted Casey onto my back and we walked home. The fish continued to splash and sprint into the air. My mother and I picked up the ones on the rocks as we walked and slipped them back out into the water.

In the morning when I woke, my father was gone. He had awakened in the dim morning light and, despite the victory, the appointments in Halifax and the politics, he headed to sea. He was back before ten, shouting and hollering for us all to come see. His Cape Islander down at the wharf was a mountain of cod and haddock and hake and halibut. There was barely room for a man to stand and steer and the weight had her pretty well down to the gunwales.

"It was a gift," my father shouted to my mother.

"I know," my mother said softly.

I leaped on to the top of the fish and slipped downward, grabbed at the wrist by my father just a hair of a second before falling overboard.

"What are you going to do with all of this?" I asked him.

"Give it away," he said. "We'll land ashore in Sheet Harbour and give it away to all of my constituents as a way of saying thank you."

It was then I looked up to see my mother's face. The sadness had swept past the softness now but a calm undercurrent of resignation kept her in one piece.

By the end of the day, my father was a small but omnipotent hero along the shore. He had sought out the poorest families to feed first and, beyond that, he set up a spit and cooked fresh fish for all the mainlanders who came to see their newly elected legislator. When the new premier heard of this, he phoned the media and pretty soon camera trucks and newspaper men crawled all around Sheet Harbour asking everyone what he thought of the new MLA. "A saviour," some said. "A real spirit," said others. "A gentleman among savages," quoted one paper.

When the fish was all gone to feed the multitudes, my

father pumped gallons of saltwater all over the deck to clean out the mess. Before the sun had set, he had pulled the boat up the improvised slip back on the island. The boat sat high and dry under a sky of stars and moon that evening, and in my parents' bedroom I heard the bed squeak and shift as my own two parents played their mysterious games late into the night.

11

Changes were sweeping over us all. With nuclear weapons poised east and west, corruption at every level of northern government and bloody revolutions sweeping the forests and deserts of southern nations, my father was about to step off and away from the safety of our island into the colossal catastrophe that was the modern world. For now, at least, we would not go with him. My mother felt a shudder run down her spine over the very idea of Halifax — the busy streets, the busy know-nothing people all caught up in worldly buying and selling.

It was only ninety miles, but it might as well have been light-years. My sister Casey had begun to talk nonstop, although you couldn't exactly call it conversation. She didn't always have anything of her own to say, so she improvised on a half-learned skill of reading out loud. Relentlessly and inaccurately, she would read anything she could find and when she ran out of written words, she made them up.

"It's all a matter of the balance of things," my father explained. "She created a vast silence that was like a blanket around her and now she has to take off the blanket of silence by weaving a quilt of words."

My father, soon to embark upon a career in a small, noisy legislature, was about to learn much about words, how men used them to empty logic and meaning from common everyday actions. Words, he would learn, were tools that could be employed to destroy as well as create, to diminish as well as to augment. He would meet several robust but vacuous men in the legislature afflicted with the same habits my sister had acquired. And often he would wish the blanket of silence wrapped around them.

I must say I enjoyed giving away fish and watching the way people reacted. But I was not sure if I would be proud of my father and his new occupation. I saw it as a traitorous act against the Republic of Nothing. "The republic needs no one to lead," he assured me. "It runs by itself. That's my secret of governing. Leave everyone alone and things will turn out fine. Don't push anybody around." I believe he thought he would take these principles first to the legislature and then to the larger world because there was a strange distant fire in his eyes.

Hants Buckler thought it was good for my father to get off the island and see the world, shake up a few old fogies in Halifax. Hants reminded my father, the ambassador to the outside world, that there was room yet for the right kind of immigrants to our island. He was concerned that the small tide of refugees had stopped. He still had twice as much furniture as he needed and wanted rid of it before the next big hurricane. "If it wasn't my Jesus job to cart and store all this stuff I'd sooner just look after living things. Living things live, they give something back to you and then they die and you can get rid of them. Material things just clutter up your life and your mind."

My grandparents were the only ones who seemed to have any sense of politics and realized that an alliance of basic Whalebone anarchy and Toryism was not a marriage made in heaven. "You're sure you found the right party?" Mrs. Bernie Todd asked.

"The Tories found me, and they wanted me. I sense something pre-ordained," my father answered noncommittally.

"Nothing much pre-ordained about John G.D. MacIntyre," Jack said. "The man's just a loud-mouthed swine."

But my father was above what he called "mere politics" and was off to steer the world into a new tomorrow, although I realized that it was not a formalized plan. Like my mother, he believed the stars were steering him and his past selves were all crowding together in his skull to counsel him through the roughest of hells that a Halifax legislature could set before him.

Only bad news finds its way from Halifax to our doorstep, but occasionally good things leave a place like this and go to Halifax. A city is a city for all that. My father would not accept the offer of a personally chauffeured lift from John G.D. because Everett was "a man of the people" and wouldn't be "seen consorting with politicians." This mightily confused John G.D. who had driven all the way out from town to haul the new MLA back in hopes that a simple-minded man from a place like Whalebone would do nothing but tow the party line. But John G.D. knew that the landslide victory over Bud Tillish had done nothing but good for his party and that whatever my old man was up to was okay with him. "That's good, Everett. You tell the public that. Tell them you don't *consort* with politicians. As a member of the legislative assembly, you will rise above the rest of us consorters and bring a new light to the legislature. A new vision."

"A new vision," my old man repeated there in the kitchen. But my mother had tears in her eyes. Her visions were of a different sort. Behind her my sister was standing on a chair, reading the labels of everything in the kitchen cupboard — "Cow Brand Baking Soda, Uncle Ben's Converted Rice, Paradise Coconut Shreds, Crosbie's Molasses, Lantic Sugar." Suddenly my mother wheeled on her heels and caught her as she leaned too far over to read "Gallinger's Ginger Snaps" and was falling headlong onto the oil stove. As usual, my mother's timing was impeccable.

Dogs barked as we walked my father off the island — the usual assortment of ragged, snarling creatures tethered to posts in the mainland McCully yard. Attempting to join the manic chorus was Gwendolyn's white poodle, Enrico Fermi. Enrico had somehow adapted his cosmopolitan dogself to the island through many happy days of eating raw fish heads down by Hants' place and then heaving them up on the living room floor of the Phillips' household each evening. The dog would not follow us off the island, however. Perhaps it had better sense than at least one member of my family. And as we walked off the bridge onto the mainland, Enrico Fermi stopped barking as if he had already forgotten about us. He turned his attention to the swirling waters of the Musquash below, watching the gaspereau swim by.

So we walked the old man down to Highway Seven, past the ragged line of houses owned by the landlubbers who my father now represented. Further along, one old man with a bent back came out and pumped my father's hand. "Give 'em holy hell," he said. We passed a curious man headed our way along the old road where recent rains had filled the potholes with muddy water. He had on city clothes and a felt hat which he tipped with a soft "Hello" as we passed. He was maybe forty years old and carried himself like he had once lived among polite people who never spat on the ground or chewed beef jerky. He was not from around here and we all recognized that here was another new islander, another immigrant from somewhere. "Hants Buckler can finally find a home for some of his furniture," my mother said.

"A refugee?" I asked.

"Most certainly," she answered.

My little sister, who had not found a thing to read the entire walk, began to make up a story. "Once upon a time there was a man with a black tie and a felt hat walking down the longest, muddiest road in the world and he came across a royal family who he thought were the most beautiful people in the world . . . "

Casey had stopped in mid-sentence because we had

reached the highway and my father grabbed a hold of his thumb and gave it a twist with his other hand as if to loosen it up for the work it was about to do. He was planning on hitchhiking to Halifax, being a man of the people and all and besides, he said, it would give him "a chance to meet a few more constituents and sound out their views." I knew that he was not interested in being persuaded in any way shape or form by someone else's views. He was going to Halifax to see if he couldn't help turn the rest of the province into the sort of political and social utopia that existed on Whalebone Island.

So we left him there, his thumb cantilevered over a paved stretch of Highway Seven. He promised he'd spend no more time in Halifax than he had to and that he'd catch the Sherbrooke bus home every Friday. We turned and headed homeward just as the wind kicked up a gust of cold north air and forced it down our throats and a high grey pile of clouds bullied its way across the sky towards Whalebone.

No one spoke on the way back, not even Casey, until we came to the little bridge when my mother said, "I think that man has just killed Enrico Fermi."

Up ahead, we saw the felt-hat stranger bending over the body of the white poodle. Shock and outrage overcame me and I raced ahead. How could someone have killed Gwendolyn's dog? But as I reached the scene, legs wobbly, heart pounding, I saw that things were different. Both the dog and the man were soaking wet. The man had his face over the dog's and with his hand cupped over its muzzle, he was breathing air into it.

My mother and Casey arrived and we all looked on in amazement. The man stopped, looked up at us and, trying to catch his breath, said, "The dog jumped in the river after a fish. I guess it couldn't swim. It drowned."

"And you went in to save it?" my mother asked him.

He didn't answer. Instead, he went back to his work. None of us had ever seen anyone give mouth to mouth resuscitation to a dog.

Lesley Choyce

"What are you doing?" Casey asked.

"It's okay," the man answered between gasps for air. "I'm a doctor."

But I was absolutely certain there was nothing even a doctor could do to save a drowned poodle. Such a sad wonder for a dog not to be able to swim. What a bitter moment it would be for me to break the news to Gwendolyn for the sight of her dead poodle made me think again how much I loved that beautiful, curious girl who had come into my life. Then I realized how poor I had been, so far, at communicating my true feelings to Gwen. As I turned away, in despair over the fate of Enrico, something happened.

The dog lurched and vomited. Then it sprang free and coughed, vomited some more bluish-white fluid and then some water. Finally it was just standing on all fours shaking itself, sending a spray of water droplets in all directions. It had been a miracle. The doctor, exhausted by his deed, lay on his back now, spread-eagled on the road as the dog walked gingerly to him, wagging its tail, and began to lick his face. My mother leaned over to help the man up. She had never seen a man bring a dead dog back to life before and she wanted to know how it was done.

Casey and I petted Enrico Fermi and let the dog kiss us on the mouth. We were both so glad to see it returned from the gates of heaven — for where else could a drowned poodle go? My mother was helping the doctor to his feet now and I was confused by a new look that had come over her. Her head was tilted slightly upward as she gazed into his eyes and, for a brief second, I had the feeling that she was not here with us on the bridge at all, that she was with this man, this stranger, and they were together and alone in some far-off place, away from us and possibly in another time.

12 Doctor Bentley Ackerman, the man who saved Enrico Fermi's life, had arrived in Halifax four days previously, slept at the Salvation Army and spent a morning studying topographic maps in a book store on Granville Street. He was a man who picked up on things quickly — things like medicine and geography. The owner of the Book Browser, a dour old Scot named Vincent Deacon, had treated Ackerman with great politeness, not knowing that the map browser had spent the night in the Salvation Army or that he had arrived by steamer from New York before that, having paid only fifteen dollars for a bunk on a lower deck among diesel fumes and rats the size of Norwegian house cats.

Deacon probably assumed that Ackerman was a wealthy, eccentric, albeit crumpled American, here to buy land perhaps and ready to tip generously anyone who was willing to help out. Ackerman was served tea at a table by the window. "You're looking on the wrong shore," he told Ackerman, who was studying a map of the coast east of Halifax. "The good land is all on the South Shore. Here. Try this one of Chester or Mahone Bay."

But Ackerman shoved aside the maps of the South Shore and insisted Deacon show him maps of the Eastern Shore. Deacon hitched his bifocals onto his nose and peered with much disdain as Ackerman surveyed the ragged-as-a-dragon's-back coastline of the Eastern Shore until he found something interesting. "Whalebone Island," Deacon said out loud. "Probably lots of heavy drink and inbreeding down that way."

But Ackerman believed otherwise. He had been in search of an island, for a certain place where a man who had seen too much human horror could go to rest and live peacefully. He committed the map to memory, for his brain worked like a great camera, and he drank up the tepid tea. He stood up and thanked Deacon with the words, "You are a man of great courage to be able to live with such a limited intellect and such a rigid view of humanity. A man of great courage, indeed." It was said with such conviction that Deacon didn't know he had been verbally punched between the eyes but instead thought it had been some sort of American compliment, and he was not at all bothered until he realized that the rich American was out the door and had purchased nothing.

Because Ackerman had resurrected Enrico Fermi, he had no trouble making friends on the island. After shaking hands with my mother, saying very little but having a powerful impact with his star-flecked grey-blue eyes, he waved to Casey and me and followed Enrico off to make sure the dog could get home safely. Since he was headed to Gwendolyn's house, I asked my mother if she thought I could go along and I raced to catch up to Ackerman who jogged now alongside the dog like they were old chums.

"Where'd you come from?" I asked.

"From Halifax," he said. A familiar answer.

"No. I mean where?"

"New York before that. I had enough of it. I decided to leave and start a life somewhere else."

"Here?"

"Perhaps."

"What kind of doctor are you? Are you like a veterinarian?"

"No. I help out the sick and wounded of any sort. Back in New York, I worked at a hospital in a place called Bedford Stuyvesant. Very poor people. I saw terrible things. I helped as many as my soul could handle. Then I had to leave."

"Why?"

"Why? Because so much sickness and hurt eventually breeds such a great despair that a man begins to think it wiser to take a life to ease pain rather than to save it to experience more pain. Sometimes he is thinking about himself."

I had stumbled in way over my head with this conversation,

but I knew that this man was the refugee Hants was waiting for. At the home of Tennessee Ernie Phillips, I introduced Dr. Ackerman to the family and explained about the poodle. Mrs. Phillips burst into tears and hugged the dog nearly to death. Gwendolyn looked at me with soft and tender eyes and seemed to say to me that she knew I was somehow responsible for saving the dog and finding the magician who brought him back to life. We sidled away from the adult talk but could not seem to speak. We were friends wanting to be lovers and too young to know anything about love, so what was left was a relationship based on awkward silence, meaningful but abbreviated eye-contact, and an assortment of odd, tangential talk about things we rarely understood.

"Follow me," she finally said, breaking the silence. I followed her to a back room, the place known as her father's shop. A laboratory, I guess one might have called it, but such a word would not have gone over well on an island like ours so it was just a "shop." Even that term was just a tad too inflated in a community where most men worked out on an open boat or inside in a "shed." She showed me a small electronic box hooked up to what appeared to be a comically oversize metal colander with assorted metal strips attached across it. The colander was mounted on a tripod and wired to the black electronic box and a small bank of meters.

"What is it?"

"My father has figured out how to determine how far we are from any given star in the sky. It's so he can pin down precisely where we are located in the universe. And how quickly the universe is expanding."

I looked down to see if my shoe laces were correctly tied. It was the only thing I could think to do. Why would someone want to know these things? I wondered.

"Look," Gwendolyn said, "I'm not really sure what it's all about either but I guess it's like trying to figure out why the sky is blue or something."

Lesley Choyce

Why was the sky blue? I asked myself. Apparently this was a riddle that Gwendolyn had already solved. There were so many unsolved puzzles out there. My head swirled. And then she put one hand on each of my shoulders and kissed me hard on the mouth. She smiled at me and shook her head, then left me alone in her father's shop, my head dancing a fancy jig full of pinpoints of light in the night sky like an unhinged merry-go-round racing uncontrolled through pure, empty, pitch blackness.

My mother missed my father badly and we had no idea as to how things were going for him there in Halifax while he geared up for the first session of the legislature. She read through her deck of Tarot cards a number of times and studied astrology from a book, attempting her first natal charts of Casey and me. Casey had run out of her usual reading material and was beginning to read some of my mother's books. Still incapable of actually reading ninety percent of the words, she would say out loud anything that popped into her head so that a book on palmistry was suddenly transformed into the story of a pink dog who chases a balloon up into the sky, or a book on the occult became the fable of two ducks who live in a small pond and converse with a quarrelsome frog. And so it went.

Because, perhaps, they were all American refugees, Tennessee Ernie invited Doc to stay with them until he could fend for himself on the island. I think Ernie had to overcome a gnawing fear that maybe Ackerman was from the FBI or CIA, but he could not envision a spy from the CIA resuscitating a dog so he opted for hospitality over hostility; life on Whalebone had already improved his spirit and character.

Mr. Kirk had but one spare parcel of land left, and he had been waiting for the past two years for a refugee to arrive so he could give it away. He and Hants had talked about the fact that there was room for one more refugee and that'd be about the quota for our small island which we did not want to see overcrowded like other islands we had heard about — Manhattan, for example. So when a man from New York arrived, a doctor at that, fed up with American distress and wanting a little peace and quiet, it seemed preordained that the final land should go to him, along with the furniture from the Buckler warehouse emporium.

Mr. Kirk was old and tired. "Worn in my ways," as he put it, "and looking for an easy, logical way out. A man doesn't like to die without a sense of purpose and orderliness to it." He was a funny old goat, nasty at times but with a most generous heart. He had no wife or children, but considered all the other islanders as his own family. He felt a deep pride in the success of my father and the creation of his invisible republic not to mention the luck he had at fishing and the crazy good fortune of becoming "the first and last decent politician to ever represent this beloved and godforsaken coastline."

My mother said that no one could have stopped Mr. Kirk from sealing his own fate, but I grieved that I had not done something to stop him from taking his own life. Not long after the deed was signed and two acres of land turned over to Dr. Ackerman, we all heard the final boom of the harpoon gun. We knew what it meant. Mr. Kirk had followed his father back to the sea. I went out with Hants and Mrs. Bernie Todd in search of a body to show the county coroner, but there was nothing to be found. He couldn't have launched himself far from the shore, but the water was deep there and the current stiff and it could have sucked him clear of Bull Rock and out towards the deep in no time if it wanted to. Mr. Kirk would have liked that. Amidst my other baffled thoughts, I think this made at least a fragment of sense, although I couldn't see why he had to live so alone all those years. Why hadn't he found a wife or raised some chickens or had cats in his house? It was the idea of a solitary life that scared me and I felt a little badly that I hadn't spent more time with Kirk.

Lesley Choyce

"Kirk was a good man," Hants told me as we rowed back to shore after a final search off the shoreline. "He had a greater sense of responsibility than a hundred saints."

I guess it was true. In his will he said he was proud of the way he had given the land he owned on the island to good people and that his house should be used by Ackerman until he could build his own and after that, it should serve as a kind of hostel or half-way house to any other pilgrims who came to the island in need of "soul quenching" — the adults at least seemed to have a pretty good idea as to what that meant. He had written that if Ackerman wanted to set up some sort of clinic in his house for lonely people, lame horses, resuscitated dogs, lepers, religious fugitives or what have you, he should go ahead and do it. My father was listed as the ultimate executor of the estate and a codicil to the will recommended that if the legislature ever got too tiresome for him ("what with all the whining and niggling and belittling as well as the pompous preaching, political poaching and philandering") my father should set up the headquarters of the Republic of Nothing in the basement of Kirk's big old stone house because, as he put it, "the basement is a fine, clean and comfortable place with a large wood stove, a bare bedrock floor clean as a polished pitcher and it would undoubtedly serve as a sensible place to sit quietly away from the travesties of this life to contemplate the future of the only true democracy left in the world."

13 Dr. Bentley Ackerman settled into the old Kirk place and went about drawing up plans for a house of his own. Even though Ackerman was an intelligent man with many gifts, I nonetheless saw him as a bit of an idler. When my mother, Casey and I visited him, we discovered he had nothing in the house but what the harpooned Kirk had left him, so we took him food prepared by my mother. I believe she felt that she needed a man to cook for. She took tourtière, baked haddock, buckets of boiled blue potatoes, stuffed cabbage, and pigeon berry pies. And books. Ackerman was lonely for books and Kirk had not been a reader of anything more stimulating than a ten-year-old Eaton's catalogue.

My mother needed talk — man talk. Men were at least rooted in things of a physical nature, things down-to-earth, while her head was flooded with concerns for the well-being of her children several lives henceforward or other conundrums of the psychic/spiritual realm. It's not that she needed to hear talk about changing oil in the boat motor or scraping the hull of a Cape Islander but the other kind of man talk — the search for meaning in the here and now and the pretend power of words that could give shape to the senseless and order to the disorder.

"When I was a doctor at the hospital in New York," Ackerman said, "we'd see a dozen attempted suicide cases a week. People who found life too painful to live. Or simply those who had no longer had purpose. Like Kirk, perhaps, but much different. If I understand you correctly, Mr. Kirk felt that he lived out his destiny and once his job was complete, he was satisfied to die. Like the Blackfoot Indian who might say, 'I have lived a good life and today is a good day to die.' No, the suicide people of New York were different from that. It was like they had been used up by society and no one wanted them. The eyes still haunt me. Some you would see once, twice, three times and then no more. We'd sew up the wrist, pump out the stomach, whatever it took, then send them back to their solitary pain and despair. In the end we had nothing to give them but mechanical repair." Ackerman would look out the window towards the sea that sparkled blue and crystalline. I realized then that Ackerman was doing something to my mother and, although I liked the man immensely, I didn't fully trust him. It was something I couldn't place.

If Ackerman wasn't sketching his house, or describing the many faces of madness in the hospital wards of Bedford Stuyvesant, he could usually be found sitting out on a rock by the sea, looking off as if waiting for something to arrive, waiting to serve some purpose. "Go over there, Ian," my mother told me, "and tell Dr. Ackerman I sent you to help clean up some of Kirk's old things or do any repairs he has. He doesn't look like he knows much about fixing things. Probably spent all his time trying to put sick people straight. Sometimes, I think, if you spend all your time learning to splint bones, defeat disease and mend spirits, you don't have any mind energy left to know how to hammer and saw."

So I went over to do whatever Ackerman wanted of me, a little worried about the strange refugee who seemed much odder to me right then than all the Hants Bucklers in the world. But I missed my father and also needed man talk of some sort even if it was not about the politics of the republic. Perhaps there was a chance that he'd teach me to resurrect animals.

It was a cloudy, turbulent day shot full of a thousand hues of sea grey that only an island dweller would care to delineate. Ever since the hurricane that brought my sister into the world, I had become a lover and connoisseur of bad weather. After all, the hurricane had tried and tested my childish manhood. The wind was gusting today. It was nothing like the great storm itself, but it filled me with a magnificent sense of being alive. I found Ackerman sitting alone on his favoured rock looking off into space. "So far I can't see the purpose of being here," he said to me. He seemed very unhappy about something.

From the shoreline, I picked up a small, water-smoothed bit of slate about the size of a fifty-cent piece. "Watch this," I said. And I skipped it out across the bumpy water until the sea swallowed it. Ackerman tried but failed with three smooth stones. I skipped another six rocks perfectly despite the chop, for I knew how to place a stone lightly upon the water so it would not catch an edge and drown prematurely. My stones skipped like the feet of a ducks landing on water and then took wing again and again before gravity gathered the strength to undo my skill. Ackerman watched intently now as I showed him how it was done. After a few failed attempts, his stone skipped five quick hops before going under. "I guess I came here for a purpose after all," he said.

I smiled.

"Ian, I'm going to tell you something and you are going to have to keep it a secret. Can you do that?"

I said nothing, picked up two smoothed flat stones and held them tight in my hand.

"It doesn't matter. I need confession and you'll have to do because you are, I believe, a lot like me but don't know it yet."

Was I about to hear that he was a murderer or that he was in love with my mother or what exactly was it?

"I'm a liar, Ian. One of the world's great liars. I'm not a doctor."

"But I saw what you did for the dog."

"Oh, that was real enough, yes. In fact, my skills equal that of a doctor and much more. But I didn't leave the hospital on my own. They threw me out and would have had me arrested if I did not promise to leave the country."

"How come?" I asked. These revelations so far did not seem so bad. Some people tell the truth, others stretch it. Each man has his own way.

"I practised medicine but never studied formally. I was born with a skill to learn a thing very quickly and become like others around me. I'm a sort of chameleon of both personality and knowledge with a photographic memory. I wanted to help people. So first I forged some documents and worked as a

Lesley Choyce

social worker. But that was hopeless. I could do very little there to really help people. So I went into medicine. In a month and a half I worked my way up from an orderly to a nurse's assistant to a doctor working in an emergency room. I had to change hospitals each time, though. That's how I ended up in Bed-Sty. They needed a doctor and I was their man — until they checked up on my background."

"What happened? Did you accidentally kill somebody or something?" I asked warily. Perhaps this was why I had felt funny about Ackerman. There *was* something wrong. Something big.

"No. In fact, no one could come up with a single thing I did wrong. I had read medical encyclopedias, anatomy textbooks, studied the functions of the brain and the nervous system and watched other professionals around me. I helped many people — not the suicides I spoke of because no one seemed to be able to help them — but the others, the homeless women beat up on the street, the innocent mugging victim knifed in the trachea for a pocket full of change, the victims of car accidents and train derailments, the children with terrible head injuries. I helped them all."

"Then why did they kick you out?"

"Because I was a liar, I suppose, and that turned out to be a crime that offset all my good deeds."

I studied on this a while, realizing how different we were here on the island. We tended to judge by what a man did, not by what he said he was or where he'd come from. Ackerman, so far, was judged on having saved the life of a dog. That was a good calling card for Whalebone. Aside from appearing to be a bit moody and idle, I could still find nothing really wrong with him, despite his revelation, and I doubted that anyone else on the island did as well. "So the past is the past," I said.

"And the present? "

"Is the present," I said.

"I came here, to this isolated place hoping that I would, as they say, find myself. No more lies. But it's too late for that. Already I've called myself a doctor."

"But you are." All my doubts about Ackerman had vanished. I liked him, liar or no.

"But it's not enough. Now I find I can't give up being the doctor I had become. I need to help people or I'll go crazy and die."

Ackerman was looking at the harpoon gun that blew Kirk to kingdom come. I suddenly realized what a big burden Dr. Bentley Ackerman had placed on my shoulders. He was suddenly the victim and I was the doctor. He needed healing.

14 "One miracle is never enough," my mother said, as I helped her wash dishes that night. "Once a man has tasted victory over death, he can't wait to do it again."

"It wasn't a miracle," I said. "He was a doctor. He was giving Enrico Fermi mouth to mouth resuscitation."

My mother wrung soapy suds from between her fingers and gave me a look. "Not all things are as they appear to be."

This I knew was true. But my mother was correct in assuming that Doc Bentley needed something more than his present existence or he would shrivel up and die. The dog was not enough. And despite the fact that he was a liar of great magnitude and had made me a conspirator in his lies, I knew it was my job as a kind of muddled patron saint of the new refugees to help out.

Weeks passed and nothing presented itself. Not even a wounded gull, a bad case of head lice or a bad back. I thought about asking Ben Ackerman for something to help me with Gwendolyn. Mr. Tongue-tied I was, yet with so much to say. Gwen was patient and sensitive but much smarter than me and

Lesley Choyce

more worldly. I had asked her to teach me what she had learned in the United States schools. There were state capitals and state flowers and state slogans, all with little tests she'd give me at odd and unexpected moments.

"Live Free or Die," she'd say. "Quickly. You only have thirty seconds."

I'd stammer a bit, indecisive between Rhode Island and New Hampshire, eventually picking Rhode Island and getting clunked on the shoulder by Gwen. American presidents, however, for some reason gave me no trouble. Washington, Jefferson, John Q. Adams and so on.

"Tell me something about Canada," she finally said one day as we made our regular circuit around the perimeter of Whalebone Island in our own soon-to-fade republic of childhood.

"It's a very a large country," I told her, "larger than the United States and the only country larger is Russia."

This seemed to hurt her feelings. I would learn later that Americans were like that. To discover that anything is larger or better than something American is an insult of the deepest kind.

"The Russians wanted my father," she confessed to me. "But don't tell a living soul this. We were on our way here, staying at a motel in Concord, New Hampshire."

"Live Free or Die!" I interjected, trying to astound her with my memory retention.

"They came into the motel room in the middle of the night. It was very dark and they had flashlights. A woman and two men. One of the men, who spoke like he wasn't a Russian at all but maybe an announcer at a baseball game, dropped a bag of something on the bed. 'One million dollars,' he said. 'And in Soviet Union, Mr. Tennessee, we will allow you to make any size bomb you want. We don't stifle creativity like they do in America.' I never saw if they had guns or anything. My father, his voice rising up out of the dark, said that he couldn't take their money. 'But why?' the man asked. 'It's good American money earned the American way. In other words, we stole it.'"

"'Your money's no good here,' my dad said. 'I can't let my kid grow up a communist.' There was a moment of silence. Later, my mother would say she expected to be shot dead right there in her bed. She expected to see front page pictures in newspapers of her and my father lying in a pool of blood, her in her delicate pink nightie, as pretty and as dead as Marilyn Monroe had ever been. But they didn't shoot. They picked up their American money, turned off their flashlights and slipped quietly out the door as if they had never been there, as if it had all been a dream. I didn't hear any car so I guess they just ran off somewhere to their hiding camp way up in the beautiful White Mountains of New Hampshire. It was scary but exciting. They never came back."

"I think that it probably gets cold a lot in Russia like it does here," I said, trying to keep up my end of the conversation.

"My father says he still knows too many secrets about the bomb and he wishes he could just give those secrets back to somebody but . . . "

"But you can't give back secrets," I said. "I know."

"After they left and I heard my father kissing my mother — she is the noisiest kisser you ever want to hear — I interrupted them and asked my father what it would be like to live in Russia. 'It would be just awful,' he said. 'The state owns everything.' After that we went to see my grandfather, my mom's dad, in Massachussetts. I had only met my grandfather twice the whole time I was growing up because we were out in the desert and he was back east. My grandmother had died before I was born. Now here we were at his doorstep and he wouldn't let us even in the house. He said my father was a traitor, that the FBI had been to see him and convinced him that his son-in-law had already 'gone over to the other side.' My mother tried to reason with him, but he had already shut us off."

I was wondering why Gwen was telling me all this now, why it had never come out before, and then I realized that it meant a whole new level of trust between us. "Did he ever talk to you again?"

"He's in a nursing home now in New York. Both my father and mother are afraid to go back to the States. They're afraid that my father could be arrested for leaving the country with all his secrets. My mom knows too much, too. They talked about everything. But she misses her father. He never answers her letters any more and when she phones the nursing home, they just tell her he isn't well enough to come to the phone. Once we moved here, she stopped phoning and she was afraid to write and give our new address for fear there would be Russians — or Americans — who would find out."

Bernie and Jack were such healthy, vital, strapping folks that I had no clear image of a faltering, dying grandfather, but I could see that this was a different story. In fact, everything was different about the Tennessee Ernie Phillips family. I could see that Americans carved out problems for themselves of gigantic proportions. While most of us might worry about a little scab on this year's blue potato crop or whether the herring will be good, Americans seemed to be all caught up in problems of such huge proportions that they concerned spies and bombs big enough to split the planet and stubborn grandpops to boot.

"I want to show you my parents' bedroom," Gwen told me at last. "I'm really worried."

Enrico Fermi yapped loudly as we arrived at Gwen's house. Tennessee Ernie Phillips was out tuning up their two-tone Ford. He had a screwdriver between his teeth and his fingers down in the throat of the carburettor. Mrs. Phillips was sitting inside the car, at the wheel, letting it idle as her husband fiddled with the choke. The radio was on a station with Andy Williams singing "Moon River" and every few seconds the music was punctuated by Tennessee's instruction to his wife, to "give her a little more gas," or "ease up on the throttle, I think it's too lean." Mildred Phillips looked decidedly morose. She held a handkerchief to her nose, and I think she had been crying.

"She's been like that for two weeks now," Gwen said with a sigh.

Gwen led me into their house and to her parents' bedroom. Had I been older and more sophisticated I might have thought she was up to something wonderfully romantic, but it was nothing like that. "Look," she said, pointing to one wall that was full of newspaper and magazine clippings of the deaths of famous American movie stars. Marilyn Monroe, dead. Jane Mansfield, dead. Marlene Griffiths, after a private plane crash, dead. The wall was filled with beautiful dead women.

"She's trying to tell us something," Gwen said and suddenly I realized that another secret had been revealed and it scared me to my toes.

Gwen opened the drawer to her mother's bureau and set out an envelope from the Broadview Nursing Home. She slipped out a photograph from it. It was an old, maybe sixty-fiveish guy with rimless glasses and a bald head. He was smiling. "That's the last photograph she ever got from him. She used to look at it all the time and it made her cry. Now she's stopped looking at it, but she still cries."

I was holding onto the smiling grandfather and looking into his eyes when Gwen let out a sigh. She put her hand on my shoulder, leaned on me and began to sob softly. "I miss him too, although I don't think I ever knew him."

I felt her despair claw right down deep through my shoulder blade and find its way into my heart. It was one of those moments when something in me, something smarter, more courageous, more daring, more illogical than anything that could have been me bubbled to the surface. I put my arm around her and felt her forehead against my neck.

Lesley Choyce

"I need to keep this," I said, putting the photo in my shirt pocket.

"I don't understand," Gwen said, looking at the teardrops that had fallen onto my shirt and rubbing the wet spot.

"Trust me," I said.

"I trust you," she said and, looking up, kissed me so softly on the mouth that I wasn't sure our lips had even touched. All I knew was that I had died and gone on to some other place beyond the Republic of Nothing. And I knew precisely what I had to do.

15 "Family is important above all things," my mother said to me as I walked in the door. "I'm going to ask your father to come home from Halifax. It isn't right."

She was feeling lonely again. There was a way she had of tilting her head upward with eyes only half-focused on a far corner of the room. I never knew what to say to her. I wanted to help but didn't know how. Fourteen is not an easy age for a boy to comfort his mother. Not knowing what else to do, I showed her the picture of Gwen's grandfather.

"He has a nice smile," she said. "Who is it?"

"Mrs. Phillips' father. She misses him very much. The woman is lonely and — what's the word? — distressed."

"Depressed. She's very depressed. I was walking by there last week. She didn't even see me, but I could see that she walked as if a someone had put a great weight on her shoulders. She is very depressed. You are a sensitive boy." My mother brought her eyes back down from looking at the moulding in the corner and fixed me solidly with a stare.

"We can't bring your father back from Halifax, right now.

I know that. No one can shift the direction of the wind in your father's sails. He has to do that himself and that will take time. You can't help me, Ian. But you must help those people. They have been driven from their homes and the woman feels loneliness for her father. You must help."

I would probably be exaggerating if I said to you that my mother could read minds. She wasn't like that. She had a different sort of psychic ability more subtle than that. She could not read my actual thoughts but instead tap the deeper undercurrent of intention and emotion and filter my own crazy jumble of ideas in such a way that it would clarify and make perfect sense. Certainly I had already decided to help Gwen. How could I do otherwise? My old infatuation, my friendship, and now a kind of yearning love had just burst into something much more powerful, a force that swept over me like a giant hurricane wave and was driving me onward in the only direction it could.

"I will," I told my mother. "Thanks." I was out the door running because I was a great runner. Why walk if you can run when the world is spinning like a dizzy dancer and all you know is that you are at the centre of things, about to make something happen? That was why you were put in the world, why your mother gave birth to you. You were no longer a little boy, tagging along and trying to make sense of events about you, trying to catch up to life. You were something else now, someone older and filled with a sense of purpose and just given a key by your mother that would unlock the door to . . . what, exactly? I was about to find out.

I didn't knock on the door to Kirk's house. I never had when Kirk lived there — no one knocked on doors on our island. You just walked in. Newcomers, even Americans, had learned to adapt to that. Aside from making a thousand diverse drawings, Dr. Bentley had not even begun to build his own house. He spent far too much time sitting alone by a sooty window that shut out the sea wind; he read books that

Jack had loaned him and got lost in other centuries, other lives. He had grown sluggish and moody of late.

I was about to change all that. I was the hand that would begin to reshape the lives of people important to me. "He's in New York," I said, showing the photo to Dr. Bentley. "You need to find him and bring him here." I pointed to the address of the nursing home on the envelope. "Ever hear of this place?"

"Broadview." Ackerman said the word as if he was pronouncing a death sentence on a loved one. "I know of it and other places like it. Broadview is a place run by men and women of very little intelligence and very narrow minds. It's the end of the line for old people who have been booted from more respectable places."

"Gwen and her mother need you to go to New York and bring him here — for a visit, or maybe to live here. It's Gwen's grandfather." And I explained about her depressed mother and the pictures on the wall.

Ackerman looked back at his book. I was confused. It was like he simply shut me out and was going back to drift into his other century again, as if I had said nothing of importance, as if I hadn't even asked. My blood began to boil and I grabbed the novel with the picture of pirates and large-chested women on the cover. I heaved it across the room straight into the wall. Dr. Ackerman looked up. For a flickering second I believed I saw anger. Maybe he was going to hit me. I didn't flinch. He let out a sigh. "I'd help if I could. But I can't go back there. For one thing, I could still be arrested. Remember, I impersonated a doctor?"

"But you were a doctor. You *are* a doctor!"

He threw up his hands. "Well, yes and no, but it's not really just the worry about being arrested. I can talk my way out of anything — this is one of the great skills of an excellent liar."

"Then what?"

"I can't go back and face all the people I couldn't help. In

New York, Ian, people live on the streets. Hundreds of them. They sleep under cardboard or they curl up inside doorways. Those were *my* people and I failed to help more than a few."

"So, you don't have to see them. You just need to find one old man and bring him back here."

He wasn't listening to me. "That's how I got found out. I let too many of them into the hospital. Each one had an ailment — fluid in the lung, a bad liver, an infected kidney. None of that mattered. When they called me before the hospital board to question my admitting practice, someone did some digging. They found me out and tried to have me arrested. I ran. I went out on the street and lived with them and helped the ones I could, but there was so little I could do without medicine and facilities. So I left them and I came here." Ackerman was studying his hands now in the light of the window. "When I left them it was because I knew that I was a *true* fraud — a fake. I was a failure and when I gave up trying to save any of them, I could barely save myself."

I didn't know what to say. Perhaps I was seeing Dr. Bentley Ackerman for the first time for what he really was — a wimp, a faker and a fraud. I sat down right there on the floor and pounded my fist on the worn floorboards, only to find my hand unclench and go flat, then glide across the wood floor as I studied the straight, strong grain of the old, foot-weary spruce wood. My mother's voice echoed in my head. This was what she meant, what she understood even before this moment had come to pass.

"You're going and I'm going. We're going together," I said, standing up now and grinning like a maniac. I knew that there was something in my voice, a conviction passed on to me just that afternoon by my mother, that could not be denied. Maybe it was the awakened stubbornness passed down to me from my father, only now to surface and move me forward with great deliberation. I knew nothing about cities, about a place like New York. It seemed as far away as the planet

Neptune and as alien, but the words were spoken. There was no turning back.

Just then Ackerman knew that we were going. He had no idea where my sudden confidence had come from, from Kirk's old floorboards perhaps, but he knew that he was being pulled headlong into this thing. "There's nothing more important than family, Doctor Ackerman," I heard myself say. I don't know if Ackerman knew what I was talking about.

"No more *Doctor* anything. Okay, Ian? Just Ben. Call me Ben."

I nodded. "Trust me on this one," I heard myself lie. "I know what I'm doing."

My mother protested. This wasn't what she intended. Ben should go. I was too young. What would my father have to say? New York was filled with muggers and thieves and people fell down dead from knife attacks every minute of the day. Was I crazy? I was only fourteen. I just said that I had to go. There was no other way. My mother was very upset and that got Casey so upset she began to cry and sob until she got the hiccups and couldn't stop hiccupping. "Look what you're doing to your sister. You're not old enough to make these decisions. My God, the whole family has gone crazy and is falling apart!"

"I'm going to visit Dad first on our way through Halifax. We have to go there to get a train." I spoke as if the matter had already been resolved. Why all the protest, you might wonder, if it was my mother who had put the fire in me to begin with? I think I understood even then that my mother wobbled between two poles of being spirit guide and simple mother. The two roles did not always mesh. Now she was coming apart at the seams.

"What did Edgar Cayce do when they asked him to travel to help people? Did he sit still on his butt?" My sister Casey looked at me with new interest now that I had invoked her namesake.

My mother knew what I was getting at. "At first he sat on his butt. He let his mind travel. Besides, you are not Edgar Cayce. Since when can you heal the sick?"

"That's why I'm travelling with a doctor," I answered with perfect logic.

"Why should I trust this man, Ackerman?" she demanded, now holding out a brown paper bag for my sister to breathe into to cure her hiccups.

"Because I trust him."

My mother saw she could not win. She read one possible future before her, several days of arguing before she would finally lose. "You are becoming your father," she said. "I should have known."

My father wanted to save the world. I just wanted to help Gwen see her grandfather again and maybe cheer up her mother. Their pain was my pain. I wanted to ease the sorrow of living for people I cared about. The other future my mother saw for herself was days ahead of living nearly alone with her family diminished to herself and Casey and her fear that maybe I would never come back to the island. Maybe I would get knifed or kidnapped in New York. Maybe my father would go on to become secretary general of the United Nations and she'd never see him again. He had not returned even once since he'd left for Halifax.

Then the spirit guide in her returned from whatever vacation it had taken and I could see the pain in her eyes diminish, the lines of worry smooth out. "You tell your father when you see him that nothing is more important than family. Nothing. And if he gives you a hard time about going, remind him that when he was not much older than you he rowed out to sea all alone one morning just as the sun was coming up and the sea had a gift for him."

"I'll tell him," I said.

16 I told Ben we should ask Tennessee Ernie Phillips for a ride to town, but he insisted, "Not necessary. Besides, something might slip out about our project and we shouldn't get anybody's hopes up just in case we don't succeed."

"We'll succeed," I said. We could do nothing less that re-unite Gwen and her grandfather. Nothing was more important than family.

So my mother walked us to the Number Seven Highway and gave me a final kiss on the cheek. She gave a gentle peck on the cheek to Ben as well and he held her hand in his and told her that he would take good care of her son.

The Shore is a small place where people are concerned and the first car to come by with enough room for two hitchhikers belonged to none other than Bud Tillish who was driving to Halifax to pick up what was left there of his belongings. He would then return home to a life of idle gossip and serious card games.

"Well, get in, the lazy pair of you," he said, a harsh greeting from a man offering a ride.

"We thank you for your courtesy," Ben said as we climbed into the back of his Chrysler. The air was thick with cigarette smoke and the sort of farts that come from eating too much smoked fish.

"Going in to Halifax for a little whoring, I bet," Bud said.

"It wasn't on the agenda," Ben returned, feeling a little embarrassed for me.

"Some skin magazines under the seat there, if you want to have a peek."

"No thanks," Doc said.

"Aren't you Bud Tillish?" I asked.

"Was," Bud answered. "Before some know-nothing from that damn island out there rigged the election and overthrew my ass. Now I'm just nobody at all. Buddy Whatshisname they'll call me, no doubt. After I served this riding fair and square. Done a good job and look what I have left?"

"Nice car," I said. It was nearly as fancy as Tennessee Ernie Phillip's two-tone Ford.

"Won't be mine by the first of the month. I'll be walking like you poor sods."

"Perhaps you'll find work," Ben offered.

"No work on the Shore. Never was and never will be now. It's a place to starve and that's about it. I could've turned it around if the people had given me a bit more time."

Bud had been in government for six years and the best he'd done for the place was to get a little free gravel for some of his friends' driveways.

"The Tories will shove the people of this place back in the dark ages before you know it. We'll all be living in caves and rooting out grub worms to eat. I've seen it happen before."

I think I began to fade about then. I was leaving home for the first time. My head was swimming with the colours that rushed past us outside the window. Suddenly, I wasn't sure I'd ever be able to find my way back home and it scared me. I pulled the photo of Gwen's smiling grandfather out of my pocket and studied it. Was all of this worth it? Why did I think that I had any business in setting right someone else's problems when I barely had a grasp of my own life? But mixed with my fears and self-doubts was the warm anticipation that I was about to see my father again.

Bud let us off at the Dartmouth ferry. He said he needed to do some business with a Dartmouth lawyer before crossing over the harbour. "I'm sorry you lost, Mr. Tillish," I said as we got out. The man seemed like a human skunk but I felt sorry for him.

"There'll be no more gravel for anybody, not even the potholes," he said. "You'll see. A fella can only give away fresh fish once and get elected. That's the way it works."

"We respect you for all your hard work done on behalf of

your people," Doc Bentley said, trying not to let the insincerity of the statement leak out.

Bud was moved by the tone and language. "You're a man who understands," Bud said. "Listen, you and your son stay out of trouble. Halifax is full of sin," he said and sped off.

I wanted to shout out that I was not Ben's son but the son of Everett McQuade, and that there would be plenty more fish to catch and give away if need be. And that the fish came after the election. It was my old man who got himself elected fair and square. But Bud was off to a Portland Street lawyer and never gave me a chance to say it.

Walking towards the ferry and up the wooden ramp, I suddenly felt like Bud had put a strange and terrible curse on me. I didn't feel like my father's son any longer. The man beside me was certainly not my father. We were on a precarious equal footing. Ben needed me and I needed him to show me the world beyond the republic. On the other side of the harbour it was only a few short blocks to the legislature where I hoped to find my father.

I was overwhelmed by the clutter and crazy activity of the people in the Halifax. The legislature was not a particularly imposing building. You could tell it was once a sandy coloured stone edifice, but it was all sooted up like somebody had been burning a lot of trash on the grounds all around the place and the smoke had stuck to the rock. The lobby was beautiful though, with a polished marble floor and a high vaulted ceiling. A commissionaire at the door asked if he could help us.

"We're looking for Everett McQuade," I said.

He raised his eyebrows. "Join the crowd," he said pointing to a noisy little mob of reporters, radio interviewers and a TV camera crew.

Suddenly, two large wooden doors burst open and a crowd of arguing, joking men flooded into the room. The legislative session had ended and reporters took off after one or the other of the well dressed men who approached. I scanned the crowd for the face of my father until I found him, surrounded by five reporters, some of whom dangled microphones in the air above his head. By the way they were all pushing towards him, I thought they were about to hurt him and I moved forward to help. It looked like one of those fights where a bunch of bullies closes in tight around some poor little weakling kid and then allows the cruellest and stupidest of their lot to pound the living daylights out of him just for the sake of bloodlust.

Ben tugged me back and away, though, then led me to the long cascading stairway from where we could get a view and listen to what was going on. A camera man was jockeying for position. A bright light was switched on so that my father's face lit up like a flare. He shielded his face until his eyes adjusted, then quelled the unruly knot of reporters with the raising of his two large, knobby fisherman hands. "One at a time," he told them. I couldn't hear the question, but there would not have been a soul in the room who could not make out the words of the orator who answered. His voice boomed and rolled like a powerful surging wave in the hall.

"While the immediate impression could lead you all to speculate that the act will cause stress to the working environment, I assure you that what we are doing — what my government is doing — is in the best interest of every working man in the province. We are bringing Nova Scotia into the modern international community of commerce and this bill will give us the leverage to turn us forever away from being a have-not province. That's all I wish to say."

He made for the door in long swift strides and the pack trailed him at first like hounds, but seeing that he would not grant another question, they turned as a herd and pounced upon another member of the legislative assembly. Ben and I followed my father to the door and out onto the street. A man, who I later learned to be Premier Colin Michael Campbell, was

Lesley Choyce

getting into a long black Lincoln. He waved to my father and seemed to be congratulating him for something. The premier was inviting my father into his car just as I caught up to him.

"Dad!" I said.

He turned around as if a voice from another world, a sound from the heavens, had stopped him dead in his tracks. "Ian!" my father said.

Turning back to the premier, he introduced me as his son. The premier, a peculiarly robust but pinch-faced man, held out a moist hand and I shook it. His grip was weak and his paw felt like a wad of soft dough. "Pleasure," he said and to my father, "Fine boy." And then he was disappearing into the darkness of the car as reporters began to swarm towards him from the legislature.

"Go on," my father told the premier. "I'll walk." The door closed and the car left.

My father led us away from the legislature, lest the press have another crack at him, across the legislature grounds and we stopped behind a mounted cannon painted pitch black. Suddenly his mood shifted. "Is everything all right?"

"Yes," I said. "Everything is okay."

Doc was my shadow. My father looked at him with suspicion. "Doctor Bentley Ackerman," Ben said, holding out his hand. "You handled them well back there." He meant the reporters.

I then explained to my father how Ackerman had come to the island, about the death of Mr. Kirk and about Gwen's grandfather.

"Someone should have called me about Mr. Kirk. He was a good friend," my father said, his polished, calm demeanour now shattered.

"He was a good man," Ben added. "There was no body, nothing much left. The way he wanted it, I suppose."

"How's your mother and sister?" my dad asked me.

"Fine. We're all fine."

My father suddenly seemed disturbed. Two worlds had just collided for him and he was caught off guard. "Dammit. I should have phoned."

"There are no phone lines, remember?" I said. "You couldn't."

"I'll get phone lines put in to the island," he said. "I can do that now. I can do lots of things."

An awkward silence ensued. My father had always despised telephones. The man who was my father had changed and it scared me. I tried not to show it.

"Let's go get a plate of clams," he said, breaking the impasse.

He led us to a restaurant where he seemed to be well known. I had never been in a restaurant before and it seemed a bizarre sort of place where everyone waited at their tables for a poor overworked young woman with attractive legs to carry food to them. We had a table by the window and I was mesmerized by the people walking by on the street. A world of strangers. I didn't know anyone.

"I can't let you go to New York, Ian," my father said. "You know nothing about that city. A trip to Halifax is enough to get you thinking about plenty. But not New York City. And I don't even know this man," he said, pointing to Ackerman.

Ben nodded. "I can certainly understand the way you feel," he said calmly.

"My mother trusts him," I said.

My father began to fidget with his fork. The waitress came and poured coffee for all of us, even me, without asking. I sipped it immediately before my father could say that I didn't drink the stuff. It was so hot that I burnt my tongue so bad it would hurt for days.

Ben tried to change the subject. "What were the reporters asking you about back there?"

My father waved a hand in the air. "It was nothing much.

Some fool American union trying to set up shop in Cape Breton. If they succeed, the whole steel industry will go down the tubes. Colin says we have to say no, make a law. It's the only way we can save the jobs and keep people from starving. Not the way I'd like to see it, if truth be known." He looked around him as if someone might be listening and catch him in this act of party disloyalty.

I didn't understand the context. But I understood that it was the first time I had ever seen my father give a hog's hair of any concern that someone would overhear what he was saying. He sipped at his coffee. "They say I'm new and I'm green but that I might stand a chance to be party leader. Colin's premier, but he's been around too long. He's made too many enemies and he can't last. If he's lucky, he'll get an appointment to the senate of Canada. There's nobody in line and the party wants a dark horse, somebody who hasn't had time to screw up or get in trouble. I'm being *groomed*." He said the word comically and then laughed at himself.

"Sounds like something you do to a pet," Ben said, but he said it in such a way that it didn't sound like an insult.

My father nodded. "It does, doesn't it?" Then, looking at me, he tried to explain. "I don't know, Ian, but now that I'm here, I have a somewhat better perspective on the world. It's not like on the island. Things are much more complicated. The black and white gets all blurred up. What's good for you and me might well be no good at all for the other ten thousand. I'm trying to adapt my vision to the broader picture. There's no right or wrong. Only compromise."

Three plates of steaming, deep-fried clams arrived. "Chezzetcook clams make the best fried clams in the world," my old man said to the waitress and gave her a wink which sent a shiver up my spine.

There was something about the crusty brown leathery skin of the fried clams that reminded me of something I'd seen before. I reached into my pocket and cupped my hand around my good luck piece. "What would the Viking say?" I asked my father. He seemed startled that I would mention the Viking in front of anyone. "The Viking is dead, and we are alive. He found what he wanted and carried it to his grave. My guess is that a little compromise on his behalf might have carried him back to wherever he came from." And he gave Ackerman a look that said, please don't ask any questions about this, a personal game between father and son.

"Then you'll compromise and allow me to go to New York," I said bluntly. I tried to explain about Gwen's mother, about the circumstances.

"That's a lot to take on as a boy," my father said.

"Which is why I have the doctor along, " I countered. "It's a sort of compromise."

"How you gonna get there?"

"By train to Yarmouth," Ackerman said. "Ferry to Portland and get another train to New York."

"How you gonna pay for it?"

"We were hoping you'd loan us the money," I said.

"What about him? He must have loot."

"I'm retired," Ackerman said. "But I'll figure out a way to repay you."

My father was shovelling clams now swiftly into his mouth, spitting a bit as he talked rapidly. "I don't like the sound of it. A fourteen-year-old boy off to save some senile old man in a nursing home in New York. Maybe we can work something through — I don't know — government channels of some sort. Our people can call their people."

I thought about the complexity of Gwen's father's exodus from the wonderful world of atomic power. Government involvement would lead to disaster. Maybe they would even come after Gwen's family. "My mother wanted me to tell you a story," I began, "about a boy who rowed out to sea all alone at dawn and found the thing he wanted more than anything."

My father stopped chewing. "I almost forgot about that

boy," he said. Then he seemed to be studying the fork that he held in his hand. He set it down and rubbed his hands together, his brow furrowed like waves on the sea. Finally he took a deep breath and bobbed his head. He pulled a roll of money out of his pocket. It was more money than I'd ever seen in my life. He slapped down a collection of twenties and tens on the table in front of me.

"Dr. Ackerman, will you take proper care of this boy?" he asked.

Ackerman folded his napkin. "I think it is likely the other way around. Ian is gifted with great strengths. I think it is he who will be taking care of me. We should be back within the week."

My father called to the waitress and asked her if she had a train schedule. Despite the fact that many other customers were waiting for her to take their orders, she said she'd check and in a minute came back with a dog-eared copy. "The cook had one," she said.

My father studied it intently. "Two-fifteen. If we hurry, you'll make it and be in Yarmouth by tonight."

17 We arrived at Grand Central Station in New York City and stepped off the train into what appeared to be a war. People were shoving and running. Everyone seemed to be trying to get away from something. We had been on an overnight train and it was 8:15 in the morning. I had endured a fitful sleep, upright in my seat, waking periodically and believing that I was dreaming. The train ride seemed unbelievable, surreal, unlike anything related to the life I'd known of island things — seas and tides, sand and rock.

As we walked cautiously through the mobs of crazed New

Yorkers, Ben assured me that all was normal, that I should relax and take in the scenery. We made our way towards the stairway that would lead us up to the street when we came across a crowd of ragamuffin men and women huddled by the doorways, all pushed up together in a corner, as if someone had swept the floor and simply aimed the broom at the farthest, darkest corner. Not one of them was moving.

"Are they all dead?" I asked.

Suddenly Ben stopped walking. "Today, tomorrow or the next day," he said, his voice grown heavy with the weight of his past. "Right now, they're sleeping. Nowhere to go. Those are my people."

Things began to fall into place. I was with the old Dr. Ackerman now, the one fired from his job for trying to help the street people. "Why don't they just leave the city? Go live in the woods or find an island?" I asked.

"Maybe they should. But I don't think they can. This is what they know. Sometimes you can't break free of who you are and go off to an island. Besides, there's too many of them. Some of them have only themselves to blame, others just had bad luck."

"What can we do?" I asked. It was the question that only an outsider would ask. But as they began to stir and waken, I could see that there were so many of them, a small army. And off in a farther corner on the other side of the great railway terminal, I saw another pile of sleepers. A uniformed policeman was going along tapping each gently with a night stick. "You see why I had to leave?"

Maybe I saw and maybe I didn't. "There must be something we can do," I insisted. If I saw a gull with a broken wing, I'd catch the bird and try to set the wing. If I found a starfish left high and dry at the tide's retreat, I'd bend down, pick it up and put it in a pool that wouldn't dry up, wouldn't I?

Ben reached in my pocket and pulled out the folded money. In Portland we had exchanged Canadian for American. He peeled off a ten dollar bill and handed it to me, then pointed to an old woman waking up by door. I walked over to her, bent down and put the ten in her hand. Her eyes had a hard time focusing at first. First there was fear. She thought I was going to hurt her. But I pressed the money into her hand and curled her fingers around it. She looked down at the bill in disbelief. She wasn't any older than Mrs. Bernie Todd but she had lived a different life, one of disappointment and defeat. She started to speak but I moved quickly away. Ben led me out the door.

Charity suddenly didn't feel good. It felt like a stab to my heart. A tide of numbness, of hopelessness swept over me as I was led through a noisy, horrible canyon of concrete buildings, glass, cars like wild beasts threatening each other, and wave after wave of humans in a hurry, running, avoiding something, going somewhere. "It's a long way, but I think we should walk," Ben said. "I want you to see everything. Don't try to understand. Just watch, then take it home with you, live with it but don't let it destroy you."

War, I kept thinking. This is what a war must be like. After hours of walking we arrived at a place that truly looked like the aftermath of a war. Buildings were gutted. Slogans were painted on the remains of brick walls of buildings half torn down. Abandoned cars, some that had been lit on fire and burned from the inside out, littered the streets. What stores that were open had iron bars in front of the windows. Blacks and Spanish speaking kids approached and asked for a spare quarter, but Ackerman waved them away. In the middle of the wreckage, Ben stopped and pointed to a tall, sombre brick building. "And that's where they go to die. If they're lucky."

It was his hospital. And the burden began to descend again on this man who was my friend. He slowed his pace and suggested we sit down on a bench and rest before going on.

"No," I insisted. "I'm not tired. How far is the nursing home?"

"Five, maybe six blocks. Over near the river."

I had this awful feeling that if I let Ackerman sit down there in the dirty little park with newspapers flying around like demented gulls, maybe he'd never get up. I realized then that this foray into this bizarre entanglement of human crisis was to be a commando operation. Hit and run. I wanted us to be out of there before night.

The nursing home appeared to be much like the hospital with institutional dirty brick walls, barred windows, featureless and forlorn except for the fact that it was skirted on one side by a river, a brown, foul-smelling river like none I had ever seen. The river's only saving grace was the fact that its waters were deep and swift and still driven by a primal planetary need to rush itself back to sea, for I could feel the tug myself. Despite the madness and the jumble of buildings, I could feel that we were not far off from the ocean, the Atlantic, and this knowledge reassured me that perhaps I was still on this planet. Ben, almost in a daze now, led us to the front steps. "It won't work," he said. "Look at us. And we aren't even family. They won't let him out."

I realized that we both smelled rather bad. Our clothes had not been changed and Ackerman had not shaved. "There," he said, pointing to a run-down hotel across the street.

We checked in. He seemed to be regaining strength now. We showered, Ben shaved and we changed into our only extra set of clothes. "Let me rest for ten minutes," he said after that, and he lay down on his back on one of the beds and seemed to fall into a deep trance. As I sat in a chair and studied the dingy surroundings, I felt as if I was watching over the corpse of a dead man. What would it be like to be alone in this city without Ben? I half-expected he would not wake up, but he did. Precisely ten minutes had passed. I saw a changed man. "Someday I'll teach you to meditate," he told me. Then he handed me a tie to wear. I tried but failed to get it right, and he knotted it for me.

Inside the front doors of Broadview Manor, a security guard wearing a gun asked us our business.

"I'm Dr. Ackerman from Nova Scotia," Ben said, "and we're here to take one of your patients home for a visit to his family."

The security guard, a short, fuzzy-haired man with oily skin said, "Stay here. What's the name of the patient?"

"Delaney O'Neil," Ben answered. "I believe he's been here for several years."

The man walked away, went into an office, then returned. "You can go in to see Mrs. Claymore. She's the director and she'd like to talk to you." Suspicion was written all over his face as if he'd been born that way.

Mrs. Claymore was a white haired lady with a haggard face and a wary look. Were all New Yorkers afraid of something? Did they all expect the worst? Could she tell that Ben was not a doctor? There was no greeting, no hello, no questions to be asked. "I'm sorry to inform you, doctor, that Mr. O'Neil died some months ago. He had Alzheimer's, as you probably know. His memory went very quickly and then his health. I think that sometimes with cases like his, there comes a time when they simply can no longer remember to breathe. And that's it. I'm sorry that you have come all this way for nothing."

"But why had the family not been informed?"

"Well, let me check." She went to a filing cabinet, pulled out a file, set returned envelopes from three addresses on the desk. "We sent notices. We tried everything. Again, I'm sorry." But there was no real compassion in her voice. So many had come and died in this unforgiving place, this old age brick prison. It would be impossible to care for every one and worry over every single death without losing your mind. Instead, you simply gave up your soul to keep your job. A cloud settled in my brain, a dark, ominous thing that grew cold and dense. It was all for nought. There would be no reunion.

"There was the matter of the cremation. Someone will have to pay." Dying was business. It cost money. It was just another cash transaction for services rendered.

"Certainly," Ben said and pulled out a chequebook from inside his jacket. "But first, could I see the certificate of death?" In a city like New York, I suppose nothing was to be trusted, not even news of death.

Mrs. Claymore produced the document from the file. Ben studied it closely. Handing it back to her, he looked down at his chequebook. "How much?" he inquired.

"Three thousand five hundred."

"And there was nothing left in his insurance or his property to cover this?"

"Not a penny," Mrs. Claymore assured us. "He seems to have timed things almost perfectly. All of his savings had gone into his final days of care, but he had not accounted for his disposal." There was a wry look on her face as if something she had said were witty or intelligent.

Ben wrote out the check and handed it to her. "We'd like his ashes and whatever valuables were left."

Mrs. Claymore got on the intercom. "Harold, get me Delaney O'Neil's remains and his particulars."

Ben handed over the cheque. Mrs. Claymore studied it as if it were a fine and rare work of art. "Chase Manhattan," she said. "That's our bank too."

"I used to live in New York," Ben explained. "I still keep an American account going for, well, exigencies like this."

Harold arrived with a cheap metal urn, shockingly small. To think that a human's remains could fit into such a small thing. Ben studied it. "This is what it all boils down to," he said philosophically. "The body is mostly water. Once you take all of that away, all you have is a fairly unpretentious mound of dust."

I accepted a large manila envelope of valuables. Inside was a watch, three gold tooth fillings, a square Oddfellow's Club ring and pair of photographs of Delaney O'Neil. One showed him as a young man, holding his baby daughter, Gwen's mother, up to the camera. The second was apparently a birthday party there at the nursing home.

"That was his last birthday, but I'm afraid he didn't appreciate it," Harold said.

It looked almost nothing like the happy man I had first been introduced to in Gwen's mother's bedroom. Despite a surrounding throng of smiling old people with faces pushed up close to his, Gwen's grandfather had a look on his face that spoke of nothing save sheer horror and pain.

"Is this everything?" I asked.

"We gave his clothes to the needy," Mrs. Claymore answered. "Now if that's everything, I should be getting back to work."

"Thank you for your time," Ben said. We got up to go.

"It was a waste, wasn't it?" I asked Ben, who seemed a bit too much in a hurry as we walked out. "The first really important thing I have to do in life and it's just a big waste."

"Maybe, maybe not." I was clutching Mr. O'Neil's "valuables" while Ben carried the urn. It had turned to a cool, grey blustery day. The water on the river in front of us was choppy and frothy. Ben walked up to the concrete edge and looked out across it towards the dilapidated tenements on the other shore. He rattled loose the lid of the urn.

"What are you doing?" I asked. I was afraid he had lost his mind. The least we could do was return the grandfather's ashes to Gwen's mother. But it was too late. Doctor Bentley Ackerman heaved the contents onto the surface of the river. The ash caught in the wind and dispersed, almost instantly. Some of it took off in the air as other tiny flecks fell on the choppy little waves and were immediately swirled and churned off toward the sea. With a loud cry — I don't know if it was madness, despair or something else — Ackerman heaved the empty urn far out into the river where it sank instantly.

"Why?" I asked. "What do you think you're dong?" Now I was sure he was crazy. My old friend Ben had dipped a paddle into the river of insanity. He was being carried far away into a world where I could not retrieve him, I was sure.

"I'm about to bring Mr. Delaney O'Neil back to life," he said with a perfect air of confidence. "Could I see all three of those photographs?"

I felt protective of what little was left of Delaney, but I could see no point in confronting Ben with his insanity. All was already lost. I should have never convinced him to come down here. It was all my fault. We sat down on a concrete bench and Ben studied the three photographs. "This is the one that matters," he said, holding up the one I had been carrying all these miles, the one of the older, bald smiling Delaney O'Neil. He gave me back the one of O'Neil holding his little daughter, but with a deft, precise snapping motion, he tore the final birthday shot up into fragments and gave them a toss in the wind saying, "This one doesn't look like him at all. It is of no importance whatsoever."

We began the search that afternoon and it lasted four days. At first the task seemed impossible and the whole scheme foolish. There were so many candidates to choose from. It was not just a matter of appearances. Gwen's mother, after all, had not seen her father for nearly ten years. Certainly she would not have recognized the man at the birthday party. All we needed was a man of the right age, right build, right facial structure and someone who had gone around the bend far enough that he could be convinced that he was, in fact, Delaney O'Neil. It was a bold proposition, the re-invention of Granddad O'Neil, but we had a problem that called for bold measures.

On the fourth day we were back in Grand Central Station. It was that time of day when the homeless would be shovelled out onto the streets for cold, lonely hours, to wait without a roof over their heads until the early morning commuter trains would begin again, the doors would open and they would be permitted to find a corner to curl up in.

He was wearing an old aviator's cap, a frayed rain coat, blue tennis sneakers and a smile that wrapped across his face like he had just won the lottery. Ben studied the photo and then studied the man. Close enough.

"Buy you a meal, my friend?" he asked the grandfather-to-be.

"I'm a vegetarian now," the guy said. "Once you're off meat, you never want to go back."

"How's Chinese?" Doc asked. "No pork, no chicken."

"Sounds good."

His name was Duke, but he couldn't remember his last name. "Duke O'Neil, right?" Ben asked, as we all sat down to a steaming pile of white rice, wok-fried vegetables and a jar of soya sauce big enough to drown a cat.

"Could be," Duke answered. "Is it important?"

"Yes. It's important to your granddaughter."

Duke lit up. "I have a granddaughter?"

"Yes."

"What else do I have?"

Ben looked at me and he didn't have to say it. Duke was perfect. But was he just faking it? And what sort of a guy was this? All I could tell for sure was that he was hungry, and the more I looked at him, the more he looked like the smiling grandfather in the photo.

"What do you believe in, Duke?" Doc asked.

"I believe in the sanctity of all living things," he answered. The words had a strange ring to them there in the nearly empty all-night Chinese restaurant. Ben smiled and so did I.

"Who are you and where are you from, if you don't mind my asking?" I tried.

"I don't mind at all. I'm Duke O'Neil and I live in New York City."

"You do?"

"Sure, I got a good spot just inside Grand Central Station."

"And that's it?"

"That's it."

"Would you mind going to Nova Scotia with us?"

"Would I have a place to sleep there? I'd hate to give up what I got here."

"You'll like it there," I told Duke. "Is it okay if we called you Delaney?"

"Not at all. Duke's just a nickname."

---

18 Ackerman argued that we all have close approximations of ourselves somewhere on earth. He was convinced that it would not be all that hard to replace the dead grandfather with a reasonable facsimile. Despite Duke Delaney O'Neil's amnesiac behaviour, he had retained a mild disposition and a great spirit of optimism during his years on the street. He had no idea as to where he had come from, what his occupation had been, whether or not he had family, but he seemed more than willing to trust us.

"Some might call this brainwashing," Ben told me with a twinge of guilt in his voice. "But Duke is a perfect candidate. Through hypnosis, I'll plant a few suggestions — about his daughter, about O'Neil's past, but no more. Your friends back on Whalebone will have to want to believe that this is Gwen's grandfather and accept him as being a little senile. At least he's alive."

At least he's alive. Yes. I could certainly go along with this second resurrection. We were back in the hotel room on our final night before going home. We had just eaten a large vegetarian Greek dinner and Doc had put Duke to sleep, placed the watch from the nursing home on his wrist, and provided a few final hypnotic reference points. Suddenly Ben looked worried. He hung his head. "Do you think it will work, Ian?" he asked. "I feel as if I'm playing God, a very false one."

"I know it will work," I said. I had the photograph in my hand and the more I looked at it, the more the true difference became clear. I conjured O'Neil's final nursing home photograph and held it in my mind against the smiling man and the sleeping one before me. One big difference: time and trouble had taken a heavy toll on the real grandfather. Duke, however, had remained somehow unscathed by poverty and street life and all the woe that New York could throw at him.

"Ian, you know we could be in big trouble if this doesn't work. Kidnapping, maybe."

I looked at the old guy on the bed, sleeping now like a baby. "I think they'd have to prove he didn't want to come with us. That would be pretty tough to do. Besides we could explain our motive."

"You have to promise, no matter what, that you won't reveal to anyone that this isn't Delaney O'Neil."

I shrugged. What's one more hidden lie, or hidden truth to carry around? I could feel the weight of these things in the back of my mind as I reached into my pocket and pulled out the three gold fillings and set them on the battered wooden table by the bed — three gold nuggets and my good luck piece, the shrivelled finger of a long-gone and unlucky Viking. Ben gave me a curious look but asked nothing. I think I felt a little like old Hants Buckler just then, gathering up the remains of disaster and bolstering up my own life, my own identity with the remnants of those who didn't survive.

As we walked through the big revolving door into Grand Central Station to catch the train to Boston and on to Portland, I could think of nothing but my desire to be back on

Whalebone Island, away from New York and all the daily warfare of life in a dangerous, uncaring city. "Home," Duke said as we walked past the corner of the terminal that was once his favoured refuge from the street.

"Nova Scotia," I said, pointing towards the stairway that would lead down to the trains. "Whalebone Island. The Republic of Nothing."

Much later, on the deck of the big ferry ship out of Portland, the new Delaney seemed to be touched in some profound way by the motion of the boat, the flexing of the waves on the sea. Off in the distance towards Yarmouth, across the mouth of the Bay of Fundy, we could see a squall of rain. "The quality of mercy is not strained," Duke told Ben. "It falleth as the gentle rain from Heaven."

"Where did you learn that?" Ben asked, afraid perhaps that suddenly Duke would remember more of his real life and that his old identity would come back.

"I didn't," Delaney said. "I just made it up."

"It's good. I like it very much."

"'Twas brillig and the slithy toves, did gyre and gimble in the wabe."

We didn't stop to see my father in Halifax but caught the Zinck bus service out of town on its long, bumping and grinding haul to Sherbrooke. It took the last of the money my father had given me that day in Halifax. As we passed through Musquodoboit and Sheet Harbour, the new Delaney became more talkative.

"I know where we're going and why I'm here," he said. "Another piece in the great jigsaw puzzle — you, him, me, that driver up there. All pieces trying to make it fit together."

"Exactly," Ben said.

Lesley Choyce

"You're going to visit your daughter whose name is Mildred," I reminded him.

"Her husband, Ernie and her beautiful daughter — my granddaughter — Gwendolyn," he finished. "God, it will be good to see them again," he said, his face full of such happiness and conviction I think Ben and I were both a little bit shaken. Either his brainwashing had perfectly moulded what was left of Duke's brain into the consummate grandfather or we were bringing into their home some perfect madman, capable of convoluting any fiction into truth.

As the road to Whalebone approached, I walked up front and tapped the driver to stop. We walked the last leg down the muddy road and across the causeway and the little bridge that marked the exodus from the mainland of North America and the emigration to the unaffiliated island republic. I became more and more troubled that this crazy scheme could not possibly work. Ackerman too looked a little timid now and even glum. Only Delaney walked at a good clip and with a sparkle in his eye. As we walked over the bridge, he began to whistle the theme song from *The Bridge over the River Kwai*. Shards of a fragmented past — real but comprehensible to none of us, including Duke.

There was nothing to do but go straight to the Tennessee Ernie Phillips's house. Before we even got to the steps, Mildred Phillips opened the door. I held my breath, afraid to inhale, afraid to speak. I had volunteered to make the introductions but I was dumbstruck at the moment. I was even afraid to look directly at Gwen's mother. Gwen hovered behind. She looked into my eyes and held me, enquiring.

I think that I sensed Ben shuffling backwards, away from the scene. *It wasn't working!* Courage, I called out to the four corners of my brain. Courage to lie, courage to say the new truth, a better truth than the old dumb lie of heartache and pain and loss. Before I could speak, Delaney took over. Looking straight at his daughter he said, "Sometimes the sky is thick with dark grey monuments of despair. Then suddenly a shaft of light slices like a knife through all the piled up gloom. Sometimes it strikes deep through the cold commotion and illumines the earth."

Who was speaking just then, I wasn't sure, not Duke, not Delaney, but a stronger, more illustrious self that was buried inside him. Maybe he had been a poet before his fall from grace, or an actor — that would certainly make sense. But was it anything a grandfather of Gwen's could conceivably say? I searched Mrs. Phillips for a trace of recognition. Her face was trembling. Of course. We had brought a madman to her door. Damn it all to hell, I thought. Why did I believe in Ackerman and his scheme of fraud? I decided I would tell the truth, anything to end this terrible suspense, this skirmish of pandemonium that made me feel as if I was about to explode.

"Who . . . ?" Mildred Phillips began. "Who is . . . he reminds me of someone . . . "

But Gwen let out a shriek just then. She had to physically push her mother out of the doorway and I thought she was frightened, afraid of the three of us, all lunatics, clearly escaped from some asylum and wandering about playing maniacal tricks on the population. I thought she was running toward me, that she was about to slap me in the face or something. I didn't know. Then it happened. She wrapped her arms around the new/old Delaney O'Neil and said one word, "Grandpop."

I looked at Delaney for some signal, some cue. As he hugged Gwen, my Gwen, I could see that the mask was dropped. He was no longer the smiling, happy, crazy philosopher of the streets. I believe that at that minute, under the extreme emotional pressure of the event, his entire lost past flooded back into him. He had me fixed in his stare. He wanted to ask me something and I was afraid. Gwen had her arms locked around him. What now? We had taken everyone in too deep. Some monstrous stupid joke was about to unfold. Please God, I prayed, let Delaney O'Neil live, not this other man! Mildred held onto the door frame and clutched it hard.

Lesley Choyce

"My God, it is him," she said and threw herself at Delaney, almost knocking all three of them over as she wrapped her arms around his neck and began to sob.

Tennessee Ernie could be heard from somewhere deep in the house coming this way, asking, "What is it? What the hell is going on?" As he reached the door, however, wearing some sort of earphones with wires dangling unplugged — for undoubtedly he had been hard at work trying to figure out just how far we were from the centre of the universe — he saw his wife, his daughter and the old man. His face broke into a wide smile, broad as the arc of stars that sweep the night sky calling itself the Milky Way. "Delaney, you old goat. I thought you must be dead!"

Duke/Delaney blinked, for I'm sure his mind was full of the knowledge of his past but also stuffed with the massive overdose of this present, beautiful, impossible lie. Two large tears fell from his face anointing the heads of the woman and her daughter. And he responded to the man who had been scanning the stars, searching for answers to questions few had the courage to ask. "I was," he said. "Until now."

Gwen's father threw his earphones down on the grass and joined in the reunion. I think I knew just then our proximity to the centre of the universe. I could see the stars swimming in the great cosmic soup. I nearly fell over backwards onto Tennessee's two-tone Ford, nearly impaled myself on the hood ornament. But Ben was there to catch me. "And now we fade," he said. And fade we did. And later, much later, I would compare notes. Other young men would deliver themselves from childhood by shooting a deer, by fighting an adversary until blood dripped and bones broke, by discovering the crude thrill of sex with a willing woman. But for me it happened when I delivered a grandfather into the world, by learning that lies can be as good as truth in the proper context and that memory is a mutable thing shored up with hope and fear and the unlikely epithet that all things are possible.

19 So Delaney O'Neil was alive again. The great gaps in his memory concerning his life as Duke and his life as Grandfather O'Neil seemed insignificant. If he was crazy, then I suppose he was no more or less so than the rest of us. Once school had started up again, I'd swing past Gwen's house to walk her to the bus and her grandfather would be standing outside their door, his arms out in a welcoming V towards the sunrise. If I asked him what he was doing, he'd only say he was "embracing the star that feeds us light." A poet he was. The words were stored up inside him and the beauty of them leaked out in aphorisms and metaphors, but his true identity was a cocoon inside his heart. When his granddaughter kissed him goodbye, I thought he would take wings and fly into the sun.

"Step only on the light-coloured rocks," he would offer for advice. "This is what I call the Lesson of Nova Scotia. They won't teach you that in school, though." What he meant, of course, was that if you were walking along the coast at the tide's retreat, the light-coloured rocks would be dry. The darker stones were likely wet and covered with a film of sea algae that could dance you to your death if you weren't careful. And, thus far, the dark rocks were all that Duke Delaney O'Neil had found to fear on the island, for he had tumbled twice and tapped his skull on stone as a result. This was when he had learned what he called his Lesson of Nova Scotia.

Despite my part in the heroic retrieval of her grandfather from the dark realm of nothingness, Gwen and I remained only friends, not that other unspoken thing that should have been. Gwen was taller than me and her true shape was finding her. The other boys noticed and I could not shelter her from the attentions of the older ones, the landlubber no-goods with hearts like fists who talked of hunting and killing for fun, the ones who lived near the highway and bragged of television in their homes, of frequent family shopping sprees to Dartmouth, the boys with metal-toed boots who carried knives and, on weekends, ran chainsaws to cut cordwood for sheer machismo pleasure.

Gwen could probably have leaped three grades ahead of me if anyone had ever tested us but she held back, for me perhaps, and never showed off her great intelligence and hidden wealth of wonderful but seemingly irrelevant knowledge. Only after a gruelling, boring day of school, after the tedium of memorizing math, after the competitions of seeing who could accumulate the most spitballs stuck to the Victorian, high ceiling, after the stares of monster boys at Gwen's beautiful features, after the afternoon lectures on improbable inland provinces like Saskatchewan and Manitoba, after the final spelling quiz with words like "diaper" and "envelope," then and only then, released from the regimented torture of the classroom, would Gwen walk with and only with me to the bus, point up to the nimbus-covered remnant of the same sun her grandfather had embraced that morning and remind me: "Ninety-three million miles." I knew precisely what she meant and exactly why she and I had been positioned in a perfect synchronization that far from a medium strength sun wobbling around somewhere in the suburbs of the Milky Way.

My father had written two letters, both short, both disturbingly skeletal. The first:

> Dear Dorothy, Ian and Casey,
>
> Sorry for the silence. Very busy times as I find my footing here. Powerful men all around me who need taming. I haven't yet found the tools I need here for the job. Coming home soon with a surprise.
>
> Love, Dad

"He's bringing home a dragon," Casey said. Lately she had been having a lot of dreams about friendly, fire-breathing dragons and lonely dinosaurs. She missed her father desperately — the gruff voice, the flaming red hair, the brush of his coarse unshaven cheek against hers like a store-bought rasp file, rough enough to leave her scratched but bubbling with love.

"There might be dragons in Halifax," my mother would answer. "If there are any there, I'm sure your father could find one and I'm sure he would bring it home to you."

The second letter was much like the first. It arrived two weeks after I returned from New York.

> Dorothy and Kids,
>   I trust Ian made it home from New York. He never stopped to see me on his way back. I was looking forward to it. No harm done. The boy's changing. Growing. How's Casey? Any leaks in the roof? Be home by the end of September. Let me know if you need anything. You'll all like the surprise.
>
> Love, Dad.

My father arrived home at 9 a.m. on the thirtieth day of September. He was driving a dragon, or something close to it, a burgundy red '57 Buick with a bumper and grill that could only have been fashioned in a dream by Casey herself. She recognized the car immediately; much to her delight, the dragon was accompanied by smoke. The second he arrived, my father had to pop open the hood and a black cloud of smoke issued forth.

"Just a fanbelt, nothing serious," he said as we breathed in the acrid, exotic smell of burnt rubber. I think I'll always remember that smell coupled with the sight of my father, the new man. Most things new and unexpected seemed to fit in easily on our island — the washed-up clothes and furniture, the refugees, the resurrection of a dog or the arrival of a replacement

Lesley Choyce

grandfather. But this was different. My father was wearing a suit and a tie. My mother, standing behind us in the doorway, had turned to stone. Casey stopped in her tracks as she ran towards the man who must certainly be her father. Even when I had met him coming out of the sooty Halifax Legislature building, he had not been wearing a suit. Now this. *What had they done to him?*

Reaching his arm down into the smoky engine pit of the car, he lifted out a black snake that had once been the fanbelt. But it wasn't the car or the snake that had stolen our ability to speak. It was the change in the way my father looked that shocked us. I decided that it was up to me to break the spell. "Need a new one of them, I reckon," I said, taking charge of the afternoon panic, wanting to grab the source of the crisis by the tail and whip reality back into place. Reading my message, my father looked at the fanbelt, then down at his clothes. He loosened his tie and flipped it up over his head like a sloppy noose, like a man trying to decline the offer of a hanging. Then he tossed me the fanbelt which landed, still hot and smoking, in my hand. "Here, Ian," he said. "A souvenir. We'll make another one out of rope and lash it on to get me to the Irving station in Musquodoboit."

I smiled. My old man took off his coat and vest, threw them back into the car. He tossed me his tie. "Didn't mean to scare you. Just a little costume I bought for the job." He was looking at Casey now. "Y'know? Like Hallowe'en."

"Yeah. Like Hallowe'en," Casey answered and now ran to her father who raised her to him and hugged her breathless. My mother unhinged herself from the doorway and everyone acted as if things were back to normal. Perhaps they were. I held the fanbelt in one hand, my old man's tie in another. The dragon was cooling off. I ran my hand along the sleek, bulging fender. It reminded me more of a sexy woman than a dragon now. But it remained an alien thing, certainly not something of our shore.

My mother did not reveal her loneliness, I don't think, to the man who had pulled her from the seas so many years ago. At supper she spoke of the unusual alignment of Saturn and Neptune and how we had just had a full moon fall within the same month coupled with the highest tides she had ever seen. "It was one of those times when you just wanted to hold your breath and wait for the world to be swallowed by water," she said. "I could see it in my mind as clear as daylight in July."

"You should see what a full moon does to the men in the goddamn legislature," my father said. "I've seen two men actually start barking at each other right in the middle of a debate concerning taxes on a pulp mill in Pictou County. Barking, I tell you."

"A dog is not so much worse than a man," my mother responded without surprise.

"I saw the face of the man in the moon," Casey added, wanting to get in on the dialogue concerning lunar effects. "He talked to me. He told me that he was very sad for everything on earth because he could see us all down here night after night but we were too far away to talk to. He said he was happiest, though, when the sky squeezed him down to a sliver and he could shut one eye and go to sleep."

It's funny that I hadn't been paying much attention to the moon because I was, by nature, a tidal person. I knew almost without looking if it was high tide or low tide. I knew it sitting in school even miles from shore. I had spent so much of my life around the cycles of tides. I knew their patience, their unquenchable thirst for shoreline, their resigned retreats. I knew that a certain moon pushed waves higher, a certain moon of another sort slipped the sea edge far out to lumpy, kelp-laden rocks and left the old shoreline high and dry.

A silence pursued us at dessert. It had been chasing us like a wolf all through the meal but we had been fending it off with small talk. "Do you like the car?" *Uh huh.* "How's the well holding?" *Fine.* "Anything new?" *Not much. The usual.* Finally, my father met the wolf head on, leaning from the table to sneeze from too much pepper. He always shook pepper onto a piece of crab apple pie. His sneeze sounded like a yelp and after he had launched the air out of his lungs he said, "What would all of you think about moving to Halifax?"

It could have been worse. He could have said that we would wake up tomorrow and the sun would never shine again, the moon would never show its sad, expressive face to Casey again or that the sea would dry up for good. I think I had believed that my father's brief infatuation with provincial politics would end as abruptly as it started, that he would shake himself like a dog shaking off seawater on the beach, come to his senses and retrieve himself from Halifax. But I had never expected this.

"No," my mother said. Her voice was barely audible. I don't think my father heard. Or wanted to hear. *No*, I tried to shout but nothing came out. I was thinking of the island, of Gwen, of Hants, of Ben Ackerman. I was thinking of me.

No, he had not heard a thing, not even the wolf silently howling at the door. "I was just thinking," he continued. "Of all the opportunities there for Ian and of course there's better schools. And we'd have more time together — when I'm not in caucus or dealing with constituency problems." He might as well have been speaking Arabic. I don't think any of us knew what a constituency was or what sort of problems it had. Dandruff? Injured limbs? Mental disorders?

"There comes a time in a man's life," he proceeded to orate, "when his perception shifts suddenly and new light comes at him, light he's never seen before . . . and understanding."

"Understanding," my mother repeated now, her voice a bird that had flown about the room flapping frantic silent wings until it had found its way back to the cage of her mouth where it sang a troubled tune. "Understanding is knowing what is true."

Did the words mean anything? Casey stabbed her pie with the fork and began to disembowel it. I shifted uneasily in my seat. *Understanding*. What did I understand about anything now that my father was trying to pull us off the island with him?

"John G.D. took me to have a private lunch with the premier, just the three of us. The premier had some news. He said the party — that he himself was behind it — was grooming me for leadership." Here was that strange word that I had heard before.

"Grooming?" my mother asked.

I thought of horses or girls with long soft hair. I looked at the new man, the groomed MLA. Yes, his hair was more closely cropped and his cheek more finely shaven than before, right down to a red, almost polished neck where all the hairs had been pruned down to the skin. The top button on his shirt was still tight, tight up against the red, ruddy skin where a razor had lopped off what God had grown there.

"The premier is going to take a senate seat soon in Ottawa and they'll need someone new, someone fresh. Someone with a vision."

A grey pall fell over the room. How had the change happened so quickly? It was hard to tell. My father, an anarchist with a fishing boat a few scant months ago, a man who had carved an imaginary country off of Canada and set us adrift in a happy peaceful kingdom, was now turning Haligonian, turning landlubber, turning into a politician, a Tory, a man being "groomed" to be premier.

"Why is it you have to become premier?" I asked. I wanted more information, some key to understanding the change and why my father was willing to uproot us and destroy our happy lives.

"I told John G.D. and the premier about my ideas. The premier said they were good ideas, but that the public wasn't quite ready for them. Perhaps though, he said, there would come a time when I could put them into practice. In the meantime, all I would have to do was keep my loyalty to the party and do the best as I could at my job."

"What *is* your job?" my mother asked, staring hard into the window beside her, at the old, almost liquid pane of nineteenth century glass that had actually distorted itself as a result of gravity. Perhaps she saw the wolf that we all felt to be haunting us at dinner.

"My job is to help people. I can help a whole lot more people if I'm in Halifax. Look, I haven't changed anything I believe in. I'm just learning the ropes so I can be effective. You'll see." He was sounding defensive now.

"I'm not sure I understand," my mother said.

"The ways of the outside world are not the ways of Whalebone Island," he said, trying to explain. But it explained nothing. For the first time in my life, my father's words sounded hollow to me. I watched my mother for a response. She continued to stare at the pane in the glass. If I hadn't followed her glance at that second, I would not have seen it and said it had been there all along, but what happened then was real. The glass cracked, a thin, diagonal line ran southeast to northwest.

"I asked the moon once," Casey said out loud, "why you were in Halifax, daddy?"

"And what did the moon say, Casey?" my father asked, happy to be distracted.

"The moon said that you were tired of being happy and you went there to look for something to make you sad."

My father laughed. "The moon likes to play tricks on you," he said. "I'm happy in Halifax. Would you like to live in Halifax, Casey?"

"No," Casey said. "I don't think the moon would talk to me any more if I lived there."

20 That night we dreamed of dragons breathing black smoke and wolves with long saliva-dripping tongues and a moon who spoke truth to us through a shattered pane of very old liquid glass. In the morning there was no sun, just a ceiling of low grey cloud fringed in dark blue-black lace. I heard barking and howling and finally the shot of a gun which jolted me awake. My father was out the door before me and I was behind him as we ran in the direction of the second gun shot. "It's coming from over by Hants' place," my father said. I could see now that it was my old familiar father who had returned, for he had forgotten altogether about the car which would have made our journey quicker, fanbelt or not.

When we got to Hants Buckler's wharf we saw Hants standing in his long johns in front of what was left of the skeletal elephant. He had blood dripping from one leg in a steady stream and he held a shotgun aimed straight at the sky. "Sonsabitches tore it apart," he said. We could still hear yapping dogs in the distance.

"What did it?" I asked.

"Dogs from the mainland. Big German shepherds with eyes given to them by the devil and teeth stolen from a goddamn barracuda." He looked down at the wounds on his legs. "They went for the elephant bones first and after that, I guess they wanted a taste of fresher marrow."

"How many were there?" my father asked.

"Ten. Ten dogs the size of hammerhead sharks. Mean mothers too. Look at what they did."

The dogs had truly managed to ruin the great work of elephant bones. They must have jumped up and wrenched the ankle bone from the elephant and then gone crazy enough to rattle the thing down, the great monument that had been Hants Buckler's pride and joy. Bones were scattered everywhere. And at Buckler's doorstep were the remains of his pet seagull, Gilbert. The dogs had surprised the poor thing and tore it to bloody pieces before it had a chance to get out of the way. Hants just shook his head. "When I opened the door, they jumped me, the sons of bloody bitches and tore into my legs. They had teeth like ice picks." He showed us his leg and my father stopped to look at it but Hants pulled back. "I wanted to kill them but couldn't," Hants said. "Once you start to kill a thing, even a brute like one of them beasts, you never know what happens to you. It takes restraint at time like this. But I fired the gun to chase them off."

We helped to patch up Hants and get him settled down with a cup of tea mixed half and half with rum. We offered to take him to Mrs. Bernie Todd for a more perfect, professional repair but he'd have none of it. "A body knows how to repair itself, " he said. "Can't blame the dogs," he said. "Can only blame the master."

We all knew who owned the dogs. When we left, we took the inland route back to the house. We skirted the bog and my father pointed to something, a freshly pawed hole out in the middle. We slogged through it to where the Viking had lain asleep so many years. Sure enough, the dogs had dug here too and the leather of the face and a section of the shoulder had been chewed off. It seemed incredible that dogs would sniff out a dead man after so many centuries. The Viking was still to remain our secret and so we shovelled the mud and peat back over him, somehow believing that we were still protecting the lost legacy of the island.

"Burnet's old man raises them for hunting but doesn't hardly feed 'em," I said. "He kicks 'em about and teaches them to be vicious. This was the first time that I know of, though, that they came on the island."

"They'll be back now. We can't let that happen. I'll go talk to Burnet McCully."

But I could have told him there was no talking. The Burnet McCullys were the kind of people that took whatever they could from the world, gave nothing back and then dumped what was left out their back step. I insisted that I be there when my father confronted Burnet's old man. They lived together, father and son, the two of them without a wife or mother.

The next morning my father and I went to confront Burnet Senior. The dogs were in the back yard now all chained to a single post, snarling and biting at each other. Mr. McCully looked like he had maybe slept the night with the pack of dogs in a bed, he looked so dishevelled and disoriented. My father played it cool. The damage was explained with a clinical, unemotional tone, for it was clear that my father had learned a trick or two of emotional control in the legislature. "What do you think we can do to prevent this from happening again and how do you plan on repaying Hants Buckler?" my father asked with the greatest decorum. McCully just stood mute. Burnet Jr. was awake now and pushed out the front door, past his old man, and began to piss on the ground alongside of where I stood. Mr. McCully had one wild eye that just sort of roamed about while the other was fixed like a vulture on my father.

Burnet Jr. was zipping up his fly and snickering like my father had just told some great joke. His own father was coughing and calling up a big wad of phlegm that he spit directly on the ground with a reptile-like hissing sound. "Not my problem," he said. "Just the nature of a dog. I ain't doing a damn thing."

"There are laws that deal with this sort of thing," my father said. Inside him a volcano raged, but on the surface he was the Halifax diplomat. Here was the ultimate anarchist speaking about law and order to a Neanderthal.

Young Burnet picked up an axe from a chopping block and began to split kindling with such malice I expected the wood to cry out in pain. My father studied the vile face of Burnet Sr. a minute and then looked down at me, as if waiting for me to suggest some alternative. I had nothing to offer. I was scared. Something about Burnet and his old man had always scared me — they were brutal, stupid and uncaring. Nothing on the island or in nature rivalled them. At that minute, I hated them both to the bottom of my being.

"Get out of here. And take your skinny kid," McCully snarled.

But my father was not to leave so easily. His face was a study of cool intelligence and reason. "I'm sorry you'll have to see this," he said to me and walked towards the dogs chained behind the house.

Without so much as blinking an eye, my father walked into the midst of the pack of them, picked up the biggest, meanest German shepherd and yanked its leash from the stake. He held the dog's head as he carried it towards Big Man Burnet. He had one arm fixed across its squirming body, the other hand gripping the head tightly with an arm across the neck. I thought I knew what he was about to do. It seemed like a terrible thing, an inhumane thing for any man to do even under the circumstances. My father had always been a power-fully strong man. His days in Halifax had not atrophied his solid muscles; it could not undo years of hauling nets, loading lobster traps and doing the work of the island and the sea.

I wanted to say no. He was about to snap the dog's neck in half right in front of Burnet. Like Hants Buckler, I suddenly felt sorry for the beast. I didn't believe it was the fault of a whipped, maltreated dog that it did what it did. Old man Burnet looked my father straight in the eye, daring him. A faint, sinister grin seemed to appear and as his mouth cracked open, a thin bead of dirty, tobacco-coloured drool slipped out of the side. He was pushing my father to do it. He wanted it to happen and wanted to watch the powder keg of violence set off in uppity old Everett McQuade. "Do you care what happens to this dog?" my father asked. I could hear his voice quivering ever so slightly now. There was anger and hostility pent up in there.

I watched Burnet Jr. pick up the axe now and wield it like a weapon in front of him, ready to pounce, to lop off my head, maybe, or chop my father and me in two.

"I don't give a shit what happens to that dog," Burnet Sr. answered, taunting, trying to push my father over the edge so that he'd have cause to rip into the bloody politician with his own teeth and tear him limb from limb.

"Seems to me, all this dog needs is a little something to eat. He's half-starved," my father said. And with a quick, sudden motion, he wrenched hard on the dog's neck pushing it forward towards Burnet Sr. until the creature's muzzle was square in Burnet's crotch. Then, quick as lightning, my father let go of the dog's head as it chomped down hard on the first thing in its vicinity. McCully fell backwards as his son ran to pull the dog off his old man who lay howling on the step. As we walked away, my father repeated the words of Hants Buckler. "Can't blame the dog," he said. "Can only blame the master."

21 My father seemed particularly rejuvenated as we stood on the little bridge after the incident. "In a true anarchy, Ian, you have this problem about freedom. If everyone is free to do what they want, every once in a while you have some asshole, like Burnet there whose *freedom* causes trouble for someone else. Then somebody has to set things straight or you have an unfair system. Otherwise you have to start creating a bunch of laws and good people start to lose their personal independence."

I guess I didn't realize just then that my father was himself a lawmaker — that was what the legislature was all about. Up until that minute I don't think he had ever seen himself as such. He got elected on a fluke and wanted to change the world. He didn't want to make a bunch of laws.

"Without laws, though, who decides on the punishment?" I discovered that I was unconsciously holding onto my crotch just then, still imagining what it must feel like to have a full-grown, razor-toothed German shepherd lunge at your privates and take a deep bite.

"Me," my father said. "Somebody had to do something or those damn dogs might have gone back one night and killed Hants Buckler." He seemed almost smug now. Even at my age, I could see through his logic. Something was wrong. We both looked down at the clear, cold water flowing toward the sea beneath the bridge. It carried a beautiful mane of long flowing green, gold and reddish seaweed. "Necum Teuch," my father said. "That's how the Micmac would have described this stream. Meant 'hair of the dead'."

As I looked into the water, I could see what the Micmac had seen. Long flowing hair in the channel, long-gone remains of their ancestors, still with them or trying to find their way back to the surface of the earth.

"That doctor friend of yours?"

"Ben. Ben Ackerman," I reminded him.

"Think he knows how to stitch up a man's pecker?" I thought that my father had lost his conscience in Halifax, but something in the little creek reminded him. The dead Indians were speaking, maybe. *It's not fair to let a man die because he doesn't take good care of his dogs.*

"He's a doctor," I said, shrugging.

"I wouldn't want even Burnet to bleed to death."

Ben was meditating in his kitchen when we got there. My father was a little uneasy around him at first, just like before, but I could see that they liked each other. My old man told him what had happened. "I guess I got a bit carried away," he admitted.

"We better get over there quick," Ben said.

Back at the Burnet house, my father and I stood out front while Ackerman knocked on the door, explained who he was and went in. Burnet Jr. let him in and scowled out at me. I knew I was going to pay for this somehow, on the bus or at school. It's one thing for fathers to feud, another what kids have to live with and suffer.

Afterwards, on the walk back, Ben said that Burnet Sr. would be okay. "Gonna hurt like hell to piss for a while though. Couple places the teeth went clean through."

My father hung his head.

"Don't you think your measures were a little strong?" Ben asked.

"It was a political act," my father said. "Besides, those dogs don't even get fed proper."

Ben laughed. They did like each other. I had a funny feeling about it though as I slipped behind and watched the two men walk ahead of me. My mind was conjuring up a comparison of the two and it occurred to me that I knew Ben Ackerman, with all his well-intended lies and half-true past, better than my own father. And it scared me more than staring down Burnet Jr. from thirty paces outside his doorstep.

The dragon was asleep and didn't wake until after lunch when my father had lashed his tie around the pulleys and started up the car. No smoke this time. And then the dragon took my father away. He had said no more of Halifax, of moving. My mother was resolute about that and there would be no persuading her. None of us wanted him to go. We all hoped that it was just a phase of madness, that he would quit, give up his seat in the legislature. I wanted things to be like before. We were island people, ready to welcome the refugees of the world but reluctant to lose a father to the mainland, to the world. The dragon was a promise that he'd return more often, that we'd see more of him, but it was also a reminder that he had joined another society, one that spent time behind the wheel of a gasoline-powered machine, that ate in restaurants and slept in homes rented from strangers.

Later that night when the manic yelping began, I thought I was still dreaming of the day's events. I opened one eye as I lay in bed and saw the full moon through my window. There were howls and barking. The dogs were out there again, prowling the island despite my father's lesson. I thought of my old pup, Mike, who had survived the hurricane with me, that gentle, dumb dog so full of loyalty and happy for a scrap of anything. He'd been dead for several years now, and I wondered how a dog could be so corrupted by its master to become like these creatures of Burnet's.

My father was gone. We were alone: Casey, my mother and I. The barking of dogs came closer. Would they go after Hants again, break down his door and attack him in his sleep? Or had they found their way to my home? At least one had tasted human blood, possibly more. Could dogs with strong savage motivation kill one of us? I was sure that these dogs certainly could. I wanted it all to go away. I wanted to slip back into bed and fall asleep, but as I peered out into the moonlit yard, all at once one of the monster dogs lunged at my window with a horrific yelp. It smashed its face right up against the glass until I could hear its teeth click hard on the pane. It scared the living daylights out of me and I fell backwards off my bed onto the floor. My heart was racing.

There was no gun in the house. My mother refused to allow one. Suddenly, Casey burst through the door and ran over to me, threw her arms around me and hugged me with all her might. She was crying. The dog threw itself at the glass again. It would find a way in. A window wouldn't stop it. I stood up, sat Casey down in a chair and threw on some pants. I surveyed my room for weapons. Not even a baseball bat. A collection of beach stones was the best I had. I picked up one the size of an orange and tried to borrow strength from it as I held it in my hands. Looking out the window I could see someone standing outside. Not a man. A boy. Burnet Jr. This was his doing not his father's. And now I realized that this one was my battle, my test. My father was gone. I felt helpless. I didn't have his politics, his strength or his courage.

My mother was in my doorway now, wearing her long blue gown, her "nightcoat." She saw the rock in my hand and my other arm around Casey. There was no fear in her eyes, only indignation. I stood upright and wanted to say something. I wanted to say, "I'll take care of it," but I wasn't as good a liar as Ben Ackerman and I was scared. Scared of the dogs, scared of Burnet as I realized that my father's ability to settle problems in the Republic of Nothing had diminished to nothing in his absence. It was not a place for part-time presidents and simple violent solutions. But then there was my mother.

My mother in the moonlight is a vision of beauty and power — strange, maybe even dark power. She speaks little to us, but you get the feeling that she is in communion with distant voices, maybe the dead Micmac below the streams, maybe the unnamed voices of her confused past. To some strangers, my mother is so frightening in her ethereal presence that they simply leave without speaking to her. Others, like Ackerman, are drawn to the dark beauty and power that she carries.

The dogs were crashing at the door now. It sounded like the thrashing of monsters. I was reminded of the wind during the night Casey was born. A hurricane of dogs was assaulting our house. Typically the door was not locked and was held in place by a simple hook. It sounded like a battering ram was pummelling the wood. "Fear is always the worst of it," my mother said. "Once you're past the fear, things begin to fall into place."

And with that she left us, closing the door to my room behind. I heard the ranting, growling, thirsting-for-blood madness of the dogs; I heard her footsteps across the kitchen floor, and

Lesley Choyce

I heard her unhooking the latch. The door creaked open and then I heard nothing. The dogs went silent. In a panic I went back to my window. I couldn't see anything but a cold white moon and the silhouette of Burnet. Damn!

I opened my own door, closing it behind me with Casey still sobbing inside. My mother was nowhere in the kitchen. The outside door was wide open. I walked cautiously across a path of blue moonlight on the floor, expecting to feel teeth at my throat at any second, terrified that the dogs had already pulled my mother down. And then I was outside. She was there. Twenty feet away from me. She held her hands out, palms upward. They seemed white, glowing, but it was just the powerful light of the moon on her white skin. And the dogs were all lying down on the ground surrounding her, all ten of them. They might well have been dead for all appearances, but I knew they were simply asleep.

I would not speak and break whatever spell she had put on them. Burnet was now stumbling backwards, his mouth agape. He was watching my mother as she bent down and petted each dog ever so gently. I kept an eye on Burnet, afraid he might do something — throw a stone, a knife, pull out a gun, but he soon disappeared behind some rocks and was gone. He had been let off easier than his father.

I walked over to my mother, but she waved me away. Her eyes were cold blue fire in the moonlight and I felt a severe chill creeping up from my fingertips. My mother saw my dread and gave me a warm, soft smile and waved me back towards the house. I said nothing. As I walked back, I heard a man running, panting in the quiet night air. It was Ben Ackerman. He had heard the dogs barking and come. When he saw my mother petting the sleeping dogs, he stopped in his tracks, didn't say a word.

The door to my house found me and I slipped back inside. I went to my room to tell Casey that everything was okay, but she was gone. In a panic I ran out to the other rooms, the kitchen, the living room. No Casey. Then I threw open the door to my parent's bedroom. Casey was in my mother's bed, asleep, and my mother was fast asleep beside her. I froze and tried to sort out the facts. It was simply impossible. But I would not wake them. Returning to the door and walking outside, I saw the dogs, gently loping away from the yard towards the bridge, towards Burnet's house. And on the dry cold stones of the driveway, I saw Ben standing all alone, peering straight into the moon, like Casey does, as if the man in the moon could offer him some satisfactory explanation.

---

22 The dogs stayed quiet after that. They did not bother to return to Whalebone Island. I never asked Burnet about that night. He never said a word to me about it. It was as if it never happened.

"How did you make the dogs lie down like that?" I asked my mother.

She looked surprised, like I had intruded upon a secret. Then she smiled. "Everything needs to rest sometime and everything is required to change." Obtuse and mysterious — that's the way of my mother. You would have to have been there and seen the love in her face to know that this was enough. I could ask no more questions. There would be no answers. I saw what I saw and it was as it was.

Ben had begun to construct a footing for his house on a barren rocky piece of land behind Mr. Kirk's house. Without mortar he was fitting together loose stones upon a shelf of nearly polished granite. The stones were carefully selected and fit with such geometric precision that it was beautiful. "Notice how one illogical piece of rock can nest perfectly in the shoulders of another and how some renegade dodecahedron of a stone gets rejected from use a hundred times and then suddenly a place opens up for it, cries out for just that stone. A lesson, there. Reject nothing. Save everything. A time will come for use." Was he talking about rocks or about the old Duke, cast off by one society and now fitting so comfortably into the lives of Gwen's family that it would be hard to argue it was not preordained?

And what had Ben seen that night of the full moon and the slobbering dogs of revenge?

"I came because I thought I heard barking. I thought you were in trouble, maybe. I was worried about you, about your mother." He looked away just then. A stone he was trying to place fell off to the side and a section of the kneewall collapsed. A V opened up in the foundation, but Ben looked away from the rocks and across the rugged juniper barren to the sea. I knew that look of longing and hopelessness. I had seen it in my own mirror before as I pondered too much and too intently on Gwendolyn.

Ben Ackerman was in love with my mother.

He pulled himself back from the sea and bent over to pick up the rocks. "Maybe I'm wrong. Maybe there are some stones that never fit." He picked up the rebel rock and set it gently aside, by itself. "Your mother, however, as it was clear, could take care of herself."

"What did you see?" I pushed my point.

"I saw that everything was as it should be," he said.

Bill Lambert and Dave Eager were two old buddies of my father's from years past. They had given up fishing on Whalebone years ago, sold their boats and shacks and moved to Halifax expecting an easier life. They returned with my father the next time he came for his two-day visit. My father's nerves were shattered by their arguing all the way home, but he had agreed to loan them his boat for the lobster season.

"We're both fed up with Halifax," Lambert said.

"Fed up's not the way to describe it," Eager added. "We barely got out with our lives intact."

"Ptomaine poisoning," Lambert said. "From a restaurant. Just an accident."

"No accident. Somebody wanted us out of town. One way or another. If you can't trust the food you eat, what can you trust?"

It was a primal question. The republic would not be as quiet as before and I was personally pleased that my father's boat would not sit high and dry to rot like other boats I'd seen left too long on the land. But my mother greeted the news with less enthusiasm for she knew that the loan of the boat meant my father was even more committed to a life away from the island. Each time he returned home, he was one more step further removed from us. More polished, more precise with his language, more engaged in the workings of the province and entangled in the politics of the world.

"There's talk of tin and uranium mining on the South Shore and a big French tire company wants to put a plant in somewhere, possibly on this shore if we can dangle the carrot the right way. People want jobs and the government would like to satisfy that craving. Once we take care of the material well-being of our voters, I think they'll be willing to see beyond the everyday needs of their families to the larger issues."

Casey gave him a blank look, twirled mashed potatoes on her fork. My mother was looking at the candle upon the centre of the table. The flame flickered. "Whatever happened to free fish?" my mother asked.

"Gonna take more than free fish to get re-elected next time."

The words "next time" spelled gloom.

If gloom pervaded my mother's inner solitude, she tried not to show it to us over that next year. She fed us and fixed our clothes and read stories with Casey from a book about fairies

Lesley Choyce

and witches. She washed and cleaned and tried to make contact with the now-dead Edgar Cayce. Along the cliffs on the bay side of the island, I had found a giant amethyst which I cleaned in salt water and gave to my mother. She greeted it like a long-lost friend and, shortly after, she announced that the rock had acted as a focal point for her energies in making contact with a guide. "Spirit guide," she said. "Edgar was not available, already reborn into someone else. But now I have Diaz."

She explained to Casey and me about Diaz, who had found her. "He was a lost and lonely spirit waiting for someone to ask him for help. He was a Portuguese sailor in the fifteenth century but, he pointed out, not to be confused with the famous explorer. My Diaz was just a sailor who furled in the sails, tightened the sheets, and one day off the coast of Portugal died in the mouths of some hungry sharks while trying to save a companion who had fallen into the sea and could not swim."

Casey thought the rock was magic but my mother assured her there was no magic, that everything was as normal as could be. Besides, it was not the rock who spoke, but Diaz. So now there were four men in my mother's life: my father, myself, Diaz and Ben Ackerman.

Ben had begun to arrive for dinner once a week. He would stay around until nine o'clock and have a strange three-way conversation with my mother and Diaz. The talk was very esoteric and very deep. Sometimes as I sat nearby in the over-stuffed armchair that the sea had delivered to Hants Buckler and passed on to us, I would look up at Ben and think it was my father sitting there. Or he would look over at me while my mother was communing through the amethyst and we would give each other a friendly but worried look. The chameleon doctor, the quick learner, the ultimate Samaritan and paramount fake was changing again, becoming something else in his quick study.

At those moments, I feared that planets were colliding in

space, stars were shifting off route, suns collapsing. Something was being jarred and rattled in the pillars of the world and I worried that we would all tumble off into emptiness. Was it all only a dream, a thin, false veneer of appearances? The night of the yelping dogs still haunted me. What had I been looking at? Where was I really at that moment? How was my mother there in the yard and in her bed asleep at the same time? My eyes were closed and someone was asking me something. My mother touched my shoulder. "Diaz says there is something you want to ask?" she said to me.

I looked at Ben, saw the worry in his eyes. Was he afraid I was about to spill his secrets? *Did* I have a question I wanted to ask of the fifteenth-century sailor who had died at the teeth of seven ravenous sharks? Another loose stone foundation had just proved fragile and a section of wall tumbled down, scattering meaningless, unregimented stones everywhere. I looked at Casey, asleep on the chesterfield, her arm dangling down towards the floor. I could not look at Ben again or at my mother.

"I want to know the truth," I said. "Ask Diaz if he can tell me the truth about all of us."

The words came out with anger, frustration. So much I didn't understand, including all this Diaz madness. Was my mother a seer or a lunatic? Was there a difference between them? Were we all insane and living on an isolated island of crazy people? Why was I forever on the edge of understanding but never certain? Was I going to lose my father forever, lose him to politics and power? Was my mother falling in love with the wonderfully altruistic and fanatically false Doctor Ackerman?

"The truth," my mother said after a brief silence, her eyes closed now as she cupped her hands around the purple crystal. "Diaz says that there is no final and permanent truth. There's nothing for any of us to do but pick and choose as best we can what is true to each of us. He says that he learned that only after he had jumped in the water to save his drowning friend, that it was the last thing he learned in that life, but it had made it all worthwhile. His friend drowned anyway, they both made fine meals for the seven sharks. He said that he had made a big mistake by jumping in. He should have known he could do nothing under the circumstances. He goofed, but it was the best he could do. He's glad you asked so he can pass the news along to you."

23 How or why Burnet Jr. and I became friends remains a real mystery to me. I had always believed him to be a ruthless bully, and perhaps at his worst, a killer. I'd seen him mutilate snakes and frogs just for the pleasure of it. We had plenty of reasons to hate each other's guts. My mother, however, assured me that it did no good to have enemies. "You have no enemies. It's just an illusion that boys have when they are growing up."

"Sure, Mom," I said.

It was a cold March morning when I went to catch the bus. Casey was staying home with the flu. Gwen was not going to school that day. Her father had made some sort of breakthrough in his attempt to receive radio-wave transmissions from a dark star in a distant galaxy. "It's possible that he's about to unlock one of the secrets of the universe," she explained on the previous day to our homeroom teacher, Mr. Dower. He had granted her permission to stay home for the big event.

So I was all alone by the bridge to the republic, just standing there with the big brown paper bag that held my lunch when I heard Burnet Sr. scream above the perennial barking of his backyard dogs. I looked over to their house and saw Burnet

Jr. come running, his pants half undone and his shirt flapping free in the air. It was their car. Old Burnet had been changing a tire and the jack had slipped. The wheel had not been off, but it had fallen down on his hand that had been gripping the bottom of the tire.

I ran over to help. Old Burnet let out a string of ungodly curses. His son was in a panic, flapping his arms as he tried to figure out what to do. His father was not much help trying to explain about the jack. The last time I'd seen old Burnet up close was when my own father had aimed the dog straight at the man's crotch. His was a body that took a lot of abuse, that was sure. Now he had a hand pinned under the wheel. His son was fooling with the jack. I knelt down to help. But we both could see that something had been bent when the car had rolled forward and the jack could no longer work properly.

Old Burnet tried to pull his hand out, but it only made the pain more intense. Then he lashed out with his good arm and grabbed a hold of his helpless son by the shank of his long hair. "Get this goddamn car off my hand you little son of a bitch!" he screamed. He pulled hard on his son's hair until the kid fell over backwards on the ground. Burnet Jr. got up slowly and scowled at his old man. I had the feeling he was about to walk away. Fifteen years of being bashed around by his father was maybe enough. He was trying to help and what does his old man do but pull him down on the ground. I fiddled with the jack again, knowing it would not work. McCully growled now, cursed the sky for giving him such a stupid son. He looked at me with as much hostility. He was a hard man to like.

Then young Burnet slowly and deliberately took the jack out of my hands and held it up in the air. I think he was ready to bash his father on the skull with it. It seemed somehow logical, but instead he threw it over his back and it clattered onto a boulder that sat like a stone Buddha in their front yard. He motioned to me to grab onto the bumper. I bent over along-

Lesley Choyce

side Burnet, our arms touching, our hands gripped onto the rusted bumper of the old Pontiac. I was certain we would not have the strength. Burnet heaved and grunted and I threw my muscle into it as best I could. We could lift the chassis but not high enough to lift the wheel. Burnet let out his oxygen as the car settled back down. His father was taking deeps gulps of air and gritting his teeth at the sky. In a new-found desperation of pain, he'd found the stopper for the hate. Now he looked at his son differently, then at me. "Please, boys. Please?"

Burnet looked at me. "Let's try again," he said. "We can do it."

As we put our muscles to it, this time we were in perfect sync. I could feel the blood rush to my face as I strained beyond what I knew was my limit, and Burnet seemed about ready to break every blood vessel in his body. It was a slow, steady lift. The wheel barely lifted off the ground but gravity relented ever so minutely, allowing old Burnet to pull his crushed hand out and fall over backwards on the ground. We both let go at once and the car settled back to earth. Burnet Sr. was working his hand now in the air. It was not crushed. It had imbedded in the soft muck of the driveway and miraculously he had been spared the broken bones.

Our bus had arrived and the driver, unaware of the crisis, was blowing his horn. I think I expected a heartfelt thank you from old Burnet but obviously I had not grown up in his skin, did not have his way of repaying those who tried to help out. The old coot never even looked at me. Instead, he walked over to his son, and with his good hand curled into a fist let go a punch that caught Burnet Jr. square in the side of the head, knocking him to the ground. "You sure took your time about it, you little bastard." The dogs were watching from behind their fence and began to bark more loudly. They'd seen it all before.

The bus driver lay on his horn again. I sure didn't want to hang around any longer. I helped Burnet up off the ground and we walked ever so slowly towards the waiting bus. At the bridge I grabbed my lunch bag, sitting there like a sleeping brown hawk on the railing. Burnet shoved in alongside of me on the back seat of the bus. I didn't know what to say so I didn't say anything. When Hank, the bus driver, had the big yellow machine turned around and headed properly back on the mainland and the rest of the kids had turned around and stopped staring at us, Burnet yanked my arm up hard against my back and snarled directly into my ear, "You go telling anybody about that and I'll break your face off." I could feel his spit inside my ear, could feel his stupid hot breath on my neck. "You don't ever say *anything* to anyone about my father," he added. My arm was about to break off at the shoulder. Burnet would have been strong enough and mean enough to do it, too.

I didn't have any intention of talking to the other kids about what just happened. That wasn't my style. I was quiet, shy. Language was a tangled fishnet of impossible knots and confusion. I was no storyteller, no gloater.

Burnet let go of my arm and I heaved a sigh of relief. I'd been squeezing back the tears. I worked my fingers in the air, trying to get the feeling back, trying to entice the blood, to suggest it was safe for it to start flowing back into my arm. I didn't say yes, no, or maybe to the guy's demands. Burnet was expecting me to croak out something, but then again maybe he didn't know what to make of me, the son of Everett and Dorothy McQuade. A strange, unorthodox family that drew on powers beyond his recognition.

What to make of Burnet? A complete jerk, a pig, a bully — all of the above. But something else was so clear to me now. All his life his father had been kicking his butt and all he could do was go out into the world and do the same to someone weaker than him. Trapped by his home life, by his madman of a father, unable to break free.

I picked up my lunch bag beside me on the seat. My mother

made meals of heroic proportions for me these days because she knew that food was one of my best friends. Still skinny as a rail, I could eat. Boy, could I eat. Inside were three thick sandwiches, each wrapped in waxed paper and each labelled with a piece of masking tape and a crayon marker: ham, egg salad, sardine. The bread, the home-made brown molasses bread, was cut a full inch thick. Not everyone had the jaw drop to even get a toothhold on one of my mother's sandwiches. The bag also contained a home-made garlic and dill pickle, large as a fist and wrapped also in waxed paper taped with masking tape, two apples, several home-made oatmeal and chocolate chip cookies the size of hockey pucks, and a wedge of bitter chocolate. We were all addicts of bitter chocolate at my house ever since Hants had found a fifty pound crate of it floating up to his wharf and unmolested by the cravings of the sea.

Lunch was my meditative time of day. While other kids cursed at each other, tried to rattle each other's nerves, figure out some way to lie about their homework or cause grief for Mr. Dower, I was quite happy to sit alone in the noisy cafeteria and commune with my food. It was morning. I'd just had a big breakfast. But the excitement and confusion had made me very hungry. The sound of the opening of the tightly furled top of the brown shopping bag was like a prayer for me, or a chant. I opened it and looked in, my mind already running through the possibilities: ham, gouda cheese and sloppy home-made mayonnaise, egg salad with paprika and onions, sardines in mustard sauce. I put my face over the bag and breathed in the options.

Suddenly, I felt Burnet's breath on my neck. He was watching me, still waiting for some kind of an answer to his threat while I had drifted off into less than idle speculation about the food in my lunch bag. I should have been annoyed, felt threatened or maybe even protective, possibly pissed-off at this asshole who could not let a thing drop and let another man get on with reveries more important than revenge. But I didn't. I dipped into the bag, selecting a weapon of peace. I decided on ham, gouda and sloppy home-made mayonnaise. I raised the sandwich out of the bag, studied for a brief instant my mother's delicate black crayon writing on the masking tape label and then, setting the rest of my lunch aside, listened with rapture to the sound of masking tape peeling off waxed paper as I broke the seal. The metaphysics of lunch had just sprung free from the traps of time, from the restricted limits of the usual noon-hour reprieve. I folded back the waxed paper and saw the immaculate beauty of the brown bread, sliced precisely in half — two thick humps of home-made heaven. I lifted one half of the sandwich out of the paper and handed it to Burnet.

Had I the proper occasion I could, in later years, suggest to diplomats how to work out hostilities. I could have told George Bush and Saddam Hussein how to avert war. The proper food at the proper time. Surprise attack of thick sandwiches in the grip of threats and hatred. Maybe I've glorified the moment. Maybe I was just hungry and couldn't eat without getting Burnet off my case, but I believe it went deeper than that. I think it went way beyond the bounty of the shopping bag that I split equally. I would not say to you that I was willing to love this enemy who sat beside me, but the evidence of the morning was clear. Burnet Jr. was not the master of his own fate. All his life he'd been battered by his old man, and long after he had escaped to his own pitiful freedom he would never really be free. A cycle of history would travel around in his genes for God knows how long before all his grief and hatred for the laws of Burnet Sr. would thin out.

I think the word "victim" popped into my head just then. No matter how inarticulate and uncertain I felt about myself in those days, about my ability to catch up with the worldly mainlanders at school or to keep up with Gwen whose beauty and intellect left me grounded on the mundane, I knew this

thing, this big difference between Burnet and m
ter of my own fate. Ben had convinced me
had travelled to hell and retrieved a lost soul
cent back to the cold and immaculate island
My mother had taught me this all my life
inforced it. And as the master of my own fate, I was
how to alter the lives of others, even someone as brutalized as
the oversize monster child who sat beside me on the backseat
of the bus.

So I shared my lunch right down to the jagged wedge of
bitter chocolate, and we became friends. And if it hadn't
turned out to be such a grand mistake, such a dreadful error, I
might say that I had returned to this life from a previous one
as a saint. But the corollary to all the above is that selflessness
creates a vacuum at its core, a vacuum that victims can find
shelter in, a place to style out a plan for revenge against all the
previous deeds. For in the crazy algebra of living, it seems that
victims must create victims of friend or foe. Pain must make
pain and even then nothing cancels out to zero.

24 The world changed yet again during the second half of
the 1960s. Even on Whalebone Island, even in the Republic of Nothing At All. Everything changed beyond repair,
beyond reason. It is wrong to suggest that things do not
change during other half-decades, but there was something in-
trinsically different during those five years. Had I known
what it would all come to, I would have kidnapped my own
father from the legislature in Halifax, pulled him back to the
island, blown up the bridge myself and fended off all intruders. And, presumably, lived happily ever after.

But it didn't work out that way. In 1965, I was fourteen; in

, I was eighteen. Between those four critical years, I was
rged and hammered into something other than a boy. I
would be hard pressed to show you a single physical scar although I am sure there must be something. And on the surface
of things, that untrustworthy monitor of reality, I probably
did not appear to suffer or seethe with change. I grew — my
bones stretched, my body evolved and that was all as normal
as could be.

Maybe other kids experienced the same despair I felt, but
for me it seemed unique. So often it boiled down to something
within me that doubted my own abilities. I did not know who
I was, where I was going or how I could shape my destiny. In
other words, I'd gone a long way downhill since 1965.

My mother blamed it on television. TV had invaded our
remote island home in the 1960s. The grey and white glass eye
presented a world so distant, so alien to our own that it was a
shock to all of us. Then, on rare occasions, my father would
appear on a local news clip with the commentator saying something about "new directions" for Nova Scotia, something about
economic development or social reform, something about
Nova Scotia's role in Canada and "the world community." And
he spoke so eloquently, so clearly and precisely and convinc-
ingly that I was shocked to my roots to realize that he had
become part of the television world and left us far behind. Inside my growing bones, a hollow ringing echoed through me
at those minutes and I would try not to look at my mother or
at Casey as my mother would try to butter over the crisis by
simply saying something like, "Your father looks good this
week, " or "He looks a little pale. Maybe it's just the lighting."

He came to see us sometimes once a week, and sometimes
to stay for a whole month when duty did not call him to his
Halifax office. Other times he would disappear like a ghost
from our lives for as much as a fortnight, only to reappear on
television, surrounded by reporters asking him about a ru-
moured scandal concerning free government driveway gravel

in a riding far from his own, a scandal he of course knew nothing about. He appeared very skilful at sluffing off the reports and shifting to more good news about foreign nations who were interested in Nova Scotia as a place to invest.

It was inconceivable to me how my father had become some sort of international economic whiz kid who could wheel and deal with foreign nations for setting up trade agreements or luring them to build a factory in Nova Scotia. I guess it had something to do with his grand scheme of world unity although I confess it seemed a distant run from pure anarchy and a republic of nothing. My father's mind had intricate turns and weavings and wonderful, wizard-like machinations of plans and possibilities.

One week he was trying to sell spruce lumber to the Norwegians, another he was trying to sell coal to France. The Dutch, he reported, wanted to root around for oil off our coast, and some American corporation was thinking that Nova Scotia might make a good place to produce the railway cars of the future. Jobs were the answer and creative thinking was the name of the game to get them and give us all more money, more growth and more happiness. Or so the story went.

Lambert and Eager were the first of those on our tiny island to directly cash in on my old man's great ideas about world commerce. One day my father arrived unannounced in the old Buick. We all got a hug and a kiss and a bundle of city gifts, and after the preliminaries he held aloft what he called "his latest discovery." "The Spickerton blue-eye clam," he called it, "although the Japanese have a more exotic name for it." I'd seen one like it before, hauled up by accident in a fish net, but always either an empty shell or something we'd toss back. "I'm going to use Lambert and Eager as a test case," he continued. "This is top secret. I found out from a visiting Japanese fish entrepreneur, a chap named Yasuhira, that these little critters sell for a buck fifty or more a pound in Japan. Supposed to make you live longer. Only problem is the

Japanese don't have too many left. They scraped 'em all off the bottom."

My father scooped the Spickerton blue-eye out of the shell and swallowed it, dribbling Spickerton blue-eye juice down the front of his tie. "Nourishment from the fountain of youth," he said, and smiling like he had truly just discovered the miracle elixir, waltzed over to my mother, wrapped his arms around her and danced her into the house and into the bedroom from which they did not emerge for another hour while Casey and I studied the presents he had brought us from town in the back seat of the car.

The Spickerton blue-eye beds were not hard to find off Whalebone. My old man spent a couple of days helping Lambert and Eager adapt some quahog dragging equipment to wrench the Spickertons from their happy homes. The first shipment of a hundred pounds went out from Halifax airport and off to the other side of the world within days, and word came back that Yasuhira would buy from Lambert and Eager all they could provide. Within months Lambert and Eager were rolling in dough, buying a new boat and bringing in loose women for parties at their old shack and as happy as the proverbial muscle-tongue creature they were harvesting.

Lambert took to relative wealth with a certain degree of grace. He spoke of hiring a fancy Toronto ghost writer to write down the story of his varied and intriguing career at sea. Maybe there would be a film starring Sean Connery. Eager stopped complaining for nearly a month until he discovered that, "Money ain't necessarily the equivalent of happiness. Money has a back yard full of problems just waiting like bear traps to trip you up."

So the two men clammed and crammed the money in the bank or spent it like clam piss on anyone who came along. If they weren't up at the cracklight of dawn dragging the sea for Spickerton blue-eye gold, they were on the phone to their Japanese broker, Yasuhira, who every once in a while would send them some exotic present by mail or by truck — a set of silk kimonos or a giant straw mat or a beautiful ten-yard long banner from a Japanese New Year's parade. "Success," Lambert would say, "was always right there just beyond my finger tips waiting for me to go after it. All it took was for your father to help me get a grip on it."

However, when I went to work with the two old geezers in the summer, they'd pay me minimum wage and expect me to bleed from the knuckles to prove I was working up to their expectations. "You're young," Lambert would say while he was pissing over the side of the boat. "The important thing is for you to build character and have that character in place for when you are old and successful."

But I certainly didn't feel like I was building character. I still didn't know who I was. Everything was so damned confused. If I could only have been able to continue the heart-to-heart talks I had once had with Ben or my grandmother or even Hants. But I'd developed what some might call an inferiority complex. The role model of my father was too grand. Even my previous New York courage had diminished, drained off somewhere into a blind gulley.

Burnet Jr., through a quirky twist of fate, had become a handsome young man sought after by the girls. He had also turned out to be not nearly as stupid as all of us had expected. At least he had developed an ability to get by with the brains that his father had passed down to him, and he had learned to hide his inherent cruelty far better as he grew. I was privy, however, to his secrets. He was, alas, my *friend*. I knew that he broke into the hardware store and stole sixty bucks of cash and a chain saw. I knew that he had a .22 rifle and that he would sit on his back step and shoot squirrels and blue jays. And I knew that he had gone down to Sheet Harbour and had sex with a woman there for money. Maybe these are all forgivable in the light of him being a teenager. What was wrong was the false exterior he had created for himself? He had gone from being a snot-dripping bully with an untucked shirt and a fat gut to a clean-cut, high school jock with a manly physique and a politeness about him that charmed the women, young and old.

Meanwhile, I was still a skinny stripling of a kid, a wind-ravaged, TV-addicted, scrawny, scared boy, incomplete in every way. I guess I should give the guy some credit because, despite all my shortcomings, Burnet remained my friend. Our friendship had begun in a genuine enough fashion, fuelled by the shared sandwiches after saving his old man from the fallen car, but it had degenerated into something else. I was the foil. I made Burnet look good. Over that fateful half-decade, while the world wandered toward the brink of nuclear war, while men vaulted into space, while American cities burned, while Martin Luther King and Bobby Kennedy were shot dead, while the Soviets drove tanks in Czechoslovakia, while bigger and better bombs were bursting in the ribs of the planet beneath me, a terrible trade took place.

In the early years of our friendship, Burnet had studied me, I am sure. He'd seen how I succeeded in school, watched how I had "fit in" in a way that was not his own. He learned how to be a civilized human being, something his father could never have taught him. The more he began to fit in and to succeed, the more I began to find myself falling towards the edges. I had to fight to keep my grades up, working long hours into the night to keep my head above water where once it had all been so easy. I had to cause trouble of some sort if I wanted the attention of my teachers where before I was able to command their respect with the limited but quirky sum of knowledge I had accumulated from my father and Hants Buckler and Mrs. Bernie Todd.

While other girls had dazzled me briefly with a flash of eye or a funny little sensual look, I had remained in love with Gwen. The plight of the silent lover is the deepest and darkest of graves, the most tortuous of traps. My guess is that she did not know how deeply I felt for her. I had attempted to write

Lesley Choyce

these feelings down and tell her the shocking truth of my passions, but like so many young men before me, I was scared, scared to my roots, that she would think I was making a joke.

And worst of all, Gwen and I had become "friends." We shared so much, had so much common ground and common experience that there were no surprises left. Gwen had grown into a beauty — long light brown hair styled like the sexiest of the American TV girls. In fact, Gwen had in some mysterious inner way left the island behind her. She still lived there, but the place no longer had the magic for her, the magic that we had shared when she first arrived and we were young. She, too, had been transformed by TV and what TV had done for her was to turn her back into an American. And although Burnet had clearly been born here, TV had also helped transform him. Concurrently I watched my two "friends," Gwen and Burnet, become less like kids from the Shore and more like the polished, slick, sophisticated worldly kids I saw on TV.

And maybe that was why it was inevitable that Gwen and Burnet became girlfriend and boyfriend. I had seen it coming for months. It was almost as if they were two beautiful jungle animals who had stalked each other, circling warily but enticing each other day after day. I was caught in the middle and hated every moment of it. And, in the end, it was me who had brought them together. A cycle of circumstances made this inevitable and there was not a damn thing I could do about it. If I thought that it was good for Gwen, I believe I could have accepted it. I could have been selfless and wished them happiness. But I knew better than that. I knew the dark depths of Burnet, and I knew he had not changed as much as the world believed.

25 My mother withdrew into herself during those years although she always pretended that everything was the same with us. She could see my pain but could not do a thing about it, for I was never to admit how confused and hurt I was feeling. Casey, on the other hand, was growing into a pretty little girl who had discovered she could sing like the superstars on the radio. We had been so thoroughly washed over by television and radio waves from the outside world that our conversation was peppered with worries about what would be on TV or who was at the top of the charts on Top 40.

Casey had gone Motown. She could sing along with Martha Reeves and the Vandellas or the Supremes or any of the best Black soul groups from Philadelphia to Detroit. The girl who once refused to talk was now the girl who could not help but sing in her bedroom, at the breakfast table, all through every class at school in a low or high pitched angelic contralto. She had not known that most of her singing idols were Black. When she first saw Diana Ross on the TV, she was startled and excited at once. "I want to look just like her," she said, pointing to a thin wisp of a fragile-looking, young Black woman with heavy eye make-up and a pile of hair that looked both puffed up and slicked down all at once.

Casey was determined to be a professional Motown singer after that. She began to sit for long hours in the sun to darken her skin, and she took to wearing heavy make-up and hair goo. She made a shiny tight dress for herself and, I must say, the end product, prancing around our living room singing to the record player jacked up to speaker-shattering volume, was nearly convincing.

"That's right, Casey," my mother would say. "You can be anything you want to be."

My mother's weekly intimate meals with Ben continued, only now they had shifted from our house to his. Sometimes

Casey and I would go; sometimes, if we had a lot of home-work, we would just stay home. These events were no secret to my absent father who now reported in to us almost every other day by means of the telephone with news of his latest political triumph or idea for provincial economic development.

I still liked Ben immensely but was so troubled by the inti-mate relationship developing between my mother and him that I decided I had to have a man-to-man talk with the good doctor. After several years of design, planning, revision and study, Ben had only completed the foundation of his ultimate home and was now just laying the floor joists. Forty two-by-twelves were laid out on edge, perfectly in place from side to side of the foundation. Not one had yet been nailed into place, however. One lone plank had been set flat across these floating, unattached joists and Ben stood in the very centre of the house, precarious, pondering. One false move could topple him and all his un-nailed joists like a stack of playing cards. I remained on the perimeter and broached the subject of my mother with caution.

"I could never do anything to hurt your mother or your family," Ben said, looking a little unsteady all of a sudden on his plank held up mostly by air and planning. "I think it's not unreasonable of you to fear that Dorothy and I are becoming, well, lovers." A shudder went through the entire configura-tion of joists. My own vision blurred as the word struck me. "Don't get me wrong," Ben said. "We are not lovers. That is, we don't do things that lovers do. Nothing physical. We have a different relationship. What was it Shakespeare said in the sonnet . . . 'two minds can love whose hands have never touched'?"

"I don't know what Shakespeare said, Ben. I don't know those kind of things. I only know my mother — and my father — and Casey and me."

Ben took a deep breath and began to walk the poem back to the edge of the firm rock and cement foundation. One step shy of arriving, the board beneath his feet gave a jerk and all of the on-edge joists shifted. Ben hopped to safety as they all fell flat with a loud whack. A couple fell into the basement. Ben walked over to me, sat down on a bulb of granite covered with yellow-gold lichen. He began to pick off the growth and flick it to the earth. "We've done nothing to be ashamed of. We help each other. Let me try to explain." He sounded too much like an adult now. Ben had usually treated me as an equal, but I had lost ground, lost confidence since our foray to New York. "I'm working with your mother on memory loss. She wants very much to know about the first fifteen years of her life. Aside from your family, this missing memory is probably the single most important thing in the world to her."

"You're not a psychiatrist," I countered with real anger coming up in my throat. "You're not even a goddamn doctor."

Ben shook his head. He could see that I had lost the little bit of faith and trust that had once welded us together as fast friends. "I know. She knows. Now."

"How did she find out? Did she guess or did you finally tell her the truth?" There was bitterness in my voice.

"Neither," Ackerman said. "She read my mind."

I knew he wasn't playing games with me because I knew my mother. She had powers of some sort beyond what other mothers had. They were hard to pin down, hard to prove, hard at times to believe, but she had psychic skills. It was as if a trade had taken place; the loss of the memory of the first part of her life for these other abilities almost too fantastic and too frightening for a son to believe in if he hadn't seen the evidence with his own eyes. "What have you found out about her childhood?" I asked.

"Very little," Ben admitted, studying a delicate little petal of the golden lichen. "I have read many books, worked with psychiatrists before. Don't ever underestimate me, Ian. I may have been a fraud, but I always helped people."

"I think I know that," I said. "Photographic memory. Chameleon personality. You told me everything."

He smiled. "I did. I told *you* everything. I could always trust you — something about you. I know where you got it from. You got it from her."

"And I inherited a few traits from my father as well." I just wanted to bring him back into this picture. But what exactly *had* I inherited from my old man? A desire to change the world? Foolish dreams and notions? Unfortunately for me, I could not put any of this to real use. There would be no girl waiting for me in an open boat at sea at sunrise. There would be no John G.D. MacIntyre on my doorstep offering glory. I would have to work it all out for myself, and all too often I felt like I just didn't have the courage to do that.

"Your father is a wonderful man," Ben asserted.

"You don't even know him."

"Do you? Any more, I mean?"

It was cruel thing to say and I scratched my fingertips across the granite bolder Ackerman sat upon, wishing right then to do him harm, to hit him. The fucking world was falling apart. I scratched across the lichen and stone until I had cut the tips of my fingers and they bled. Ben grabbed my hand.

"You're much tougher than you think, Ian. You are not as weak as you think. You still have the courage and the wisdom that you had when I first knew you. It's just layered over right now with a shell of confusion. The shell will break. I know what I'm talking about. It will. All you need is time."

I looked at him. There was something about what he had just said, but it wasn't just the words. They were simple enough. It was something else, something like a shaft of sunlight reaching into the gloomy pit of my soul. He was right about the shell and, for what seemed like the first time in years, something had just cracked through the shell. It wasn't that he was just understanding the look on my face and it wasn't just a bunch of words in our conversation. Ben Ackerman had just leaped — he had gone beyond what we had said or what we showed on our faces. He had even gone beneath the surface of what was uppermost in my thoughts right then — my desire to hit him in the face. And it wasn't just a kind thing to say or a good guess.

He had gone right to the core of my problem: I thought I was a weakling — not physically but emotionally. I had lost my ability to assert who I was in a world where everyone else seemed to have it all figured out and were oh-so-confident in who they were. "How did you do that?" I blurted out.

Ben understood immediately what I was talking about. He could tell from the look of astonishment on my face. "I learned it, or at least I'm learning it from your mother. This is our trade. This is our relationship. Call it love if you want because I do think we love each other, but there is nothing physical in it. Ever. I am helping her to recover her past. I think we'll get there eventually, but first I have to help her explore every element of her personality and what memory she has. In return she teaches me to look into other minds."

"And the two of you can actually have like a conversation . . . "

"Without talking," he completed. "It's too perfect. In fact, it's not even a conversation at all. It's more like what I just did with you. I went past what you would have said to what you really were feeling, what you really meant."

"Good God," I said. I was really shaken.

"Your mother has learned to use her psychic skills, if I can use a clinical term, rather well. She's learned to simply blend them into her life in a wonderful way, giving her strength and helping both of her children. And I saw the night with the dogs, remember? We can talk about that sometime if you want. I don't think she'd mind. I think that I've been able to help her to be less afraid of her powers, although I don't think you should see them as being weird or supernatural. She just has certain skills the rest of us have a hard time tapping. She hasn't been able to help you much lately, I think, because

Lesley Choyce

you've been pushing everybody away. Even the ones you love. Your mother, Casey, your father. Even Gwendolyn."

Now I felt like I'd been invaded, violated. "What do you know about Gwen?" I insisted.

"I know you love her and you feel that you've lost her forever. That's how much you've told me without ever even speaking a word. Your mother probably knows a lot more about it. You might want to ask her to help out."

"No," I said. I didn't want my mother involved. And right then I didn't know whether to trust Ben Ackerman, his intentions and his knowledge, not to mention his new-found skill. I felt confused, but in the mass of swirling confusion there was an oasis of clarity. Ben was so perfectly right about my fears and inabilities. Now that he had brought them out in the open, so much about my life began to make sense. I would have to think about all this long and hard. Despite my doubts, however, I felt that I had just seen a way out of a long, winding, dark, horror-infested tunnel. I saw light. I saw possibility. The world, my world, had not disintegrated entirely. I suddenly felt as if I had a chance to pull myself up out of the grave. I was ready to admit it to Ben, to thank him even for this new insight.

But I hadn't opened my mouth. "There's one danger in all this, I think," he said.

I was still thinking of myself. Danger? Hah! I was about to get ready to challenge anything.

But it wasn't a danger for me. "It's Dorothy. I don't know what will happen if she does regain her memory. Something devastating occurred back then. Maybe something extraordinary, maybe something terrifying. I've warned her and she too is wary of unlocking all the doors. It may be very difficult and she may never be quite the same again."

26 It was on one of those nights that my mother went to visit Ben for a dinner and an evening of psychic intermingling that I made my first daring gesture in a long time. I was at home with my little sister who was glued to the TV. From deep within I called on my energy reserves, I dipped into my meagre, dwindled supply of courage, I picked up the phone and dialed. The Duke answered and I asked to speak to Gwen. When she picked up the phone and said a quiet, curious hello, I wobbled on my feet and nearly dropped the phone to the floor.

"Hi," I said. "It's Ian. I'm home alone with Casey and wondered if you would like to come over and do some homework with me."

There was a second of silence and then, "Sure, Ian. I'd like that. I'm kinda bored around here and would love to have a reason to escape. Be right over."

The phone found its own way back into its cradle and I let out a sigh. I was determined to tell her once and for all that I was in love with her. I wanted her to be more than a friend.

When Gwen arrived she wasn't wearing a coat even though it was a cold evening. Frost was growing up from the ground like crystalline flowers, planted there by the damp air. She was wearing an old flannel shirt several sizes too big and a pair of patched and faded blue jeans. The moon was behind her in the doorway and I was rendered speechless. Her cheeks were slightly blushed from the cold and her hair was long, straight and soft as the sound of a whisper erased by the blowing of sand. And something else, something metallic and shiny was dangling from her ears, tangled in her fly-away hair and begging my attention.

Gwen noticed I was staring at them. "Oh these?" She pulled back her hair like it was the curtain of a waterfall. "Do you like them?"

"Wow," I said, vocabulary reduced to a monosyllabic cliché. Two bronze medallions hung from her earlobes. Two peace symbols, that unmistakeable triad inside a circle, these of the slimmest threads of bronze but each large as a sand dollar. As I stared at her earrings, I remembered my first gift to this strange and beautiful girl. Hants Buckler's earlobe. I wanted to say something, to explain the connection, but I desisted. I had clear intentions and I did not want to be unnerved by idle chatter. She had her math and her biology book with her, but I took them and set them down on the kitchen table. "I'd like to just talk for a while," I said, the mute coming back to the world of language, "if it's okay with you."

"Sure." She sat down at the table and tucked a leg beneath her. I sat down across from her.

"How's your father doing with his work?" I asked, deciding that the evening was not ready for me to blurt out deep and passionate and eternal love. I would come at it tangentially after all.

"I think it's great that you've always been interested in my father's work. He misses working with the other men, but I think that in some ways life here has allowed him to be even more creative than before. It's been good for him. He's changed. We all have. He's sick of what's been done with his research — the new bombs, where it's all gone. He admits he was wrong. He says, 'Before, all I had was a brain. Now I have a spine.' It has to do with standing up for what is right, not just doing research. He's figured out how to isolate a single electron in a perfect vacuum and track it. They were never able to do that before. He says he could do it tomorrow if he only had twenty-five million dollars worth of equipment."

"Hard to come by on Whalebone Island," I said.

Gwen laughed and tossed her hair back, revealing again her peace earrings. "He says he's unlocking secrets but he might not ever reveal them to anyone. He's afraid they'll be used for war."

I detected something in the way she said that last word. I wanted desperately to shake myself free of my old self — the one I was at school. I wanted some magic to bring us closer, mind and soul. My mother and Ben came into my mind just then and the idea of that intuitive skill they were learning to share. I jumped. "You've been thinking about the war, haven't you? About Vietnam."

Now she looked at me with her wide open brown eyes. "Yes. How did you know?"

"You've mentioned it. And then . . . your earrings. I've seen that symbol on the demonstrators on TV. The Americans." There, it had not been intuitive at all.

"I'm an American," she said. "I was born there. I think I need to go back some day. Right now, Americans are killing men, women and children in Southeast Asia. I want to go back home to get out on the streets with those others — the hippies, the draft dodgers, the protesters. I want to go back and stop the war. I want to stop all wars."

Coming from Gwen, I knew that this was not a foolish whim. It was the sort of thing one believed, something that made perfect logical sense. All at once I realized that she shared something with my father — my *old* father at least. They both believed they could change the world, that one person could make the difference.

"What would you do if you were an American and you were drafted?" she asked.

I had never thought about it. I'd watched TV like Gwen. I'd seen the American kids protesting, seen the bloody war, but it always seemed like something made up for TV, nothing real. "I wouldn't go," I said, knowing it was what she wanted me to say.

"Even if they threatened to put you in jail?"

"Even then," I insisted.

Gwen smiled, touched me on the back of my neck with her hand. "My father says that if he had the twenty-five million, he could perfect his electron isolation device, that he could create a machine that could project a concentrated beam of highly charged electrons into space, bounce it off a satellite or maybe even the moon and direct it precisely to a target anywhere on earth."

"But then it would be another weapon, right?"

"No. He says it could be so precise as to destroy only other weapons. People could be standing right alongside, say, a missile, and they wouldn't get hurt."

"If he knew the locations, he could destroy all the nuclear arsenal and he could even stop the war in Vietnam by taking out all the weapons."

"Precisely. Only I tell him it will never work because weapons always fall into the wrong hands whoever creates them. Did you know he met Einstein once?"

"No, I didn't."

"Yeah. In Princeton. Einstein was walking down a sidewalk, stooped over to pick up a caterpillar. He was talking to it."

"What did he say?"

"My father doesn't know. It was German. But he did stop to talk to Einstein who told my father that all research that leads to anything useful is probably a mistake because someone will use it the wrong way. The more we perfect our ability to create, the more likely it is we will destroy ourselves, he said, and then let the caterpillar go into the hedge where it could not be walked on by a university student. Einstein told my father that all research should be purely hypothetical."

"Then why does your father continue what he is doing?"

"Because it's what keeps him alive. He's made a promise to us though that he will write nothing down and will tell no one what he learns."

"But now he's told you and you've told me."

"That's because you are you. There's no one like you. You are like some kind of saint. I don't know what the quality is, but there is this kindness inside of you. That's why I'll always need you as a friend."

There, she'd said that stupid word. I heard Casey turn off the TV and go to her room. I stood up and said the only thing I could think of. "Let's watch television." A little baffled, Gwen followed me into the living room. It was the CBC with world news. Planes were dropping bombs on North Vietnam. There was jungle fighting, villages being levelled, women and children running from the flames, some of them with blood dripping from wounds.

"It's called Napalm," she said. "The stuff is sticking to their skin and burning it off. Developed by a researcher at an American chemical plant — Du Pont, I think."

The context was all wrong but I felt I had no choice. Say it or be stuck in sainthood forever. "Gwen, I don't want to be your friend," I told her.

She turned away from the TV screen and looked at me with utter confusion in her face.

"I'm in love with you. It's too hard to be just your friend."

I had to leave the room. I didn't know what she would do. How could this surprise her? Couldn't she read my mind just a little? Couldn't she see the other me inside the outer skin? A bomb had just gone off inside me. I was trying to burn off my outer skin, my shell, and show her who I really was and that I really did love her and needed her more than anything in the world. I would have gone to war for her, or fought against war for her or done anything she wanted if it meant that she would love me.

I walked outside into the cool, clean night air. I walked over thin, delicate shelves of ice that collapsed into sparkling frost as I stepped across the yard. Gwen followed me. "Wait," she said. "Ian, where are you going?"

Now that I had said it, I felt like nothing could ever be the same. Had I ruined everything? Would she reject me outright now? Because I knew she was interested in Burnet, ten times as handsome as I was and slick, worldly, seemingly knowledgeable. Had I ruined my chance to remain a close ally, intimate friend, necessary saint for Gwen? I was walking. Walking towards the bridge, I discovered, walking towards the only route off the island. But I heard her running behind me. When she was right on my heels, I stopped, wheeled around. Gwen was there, panting. It was her move. I wouldn't say another word. And then a miracle happened; she put her arms around me and pulled herself to me. I could feel her warm breasts up against me, I could smell the soft scent of her hair against my face and feel the startling cold metallic nudge of her earring on my neck. "Hold me," she said. "Just hold me."

We stood there embracing in the cold night air. What was she trying to tell me? I leaped to conclusions of eternal love and happiness, retreated to a potential realization that this was only pity; I wandered up and down avenues from ecstasy to despair but never once opened my mouth to ask what it was she felt. I had come this far and, for me, it had taken as much courage as that of some poor fool soldier, brainwashed and walking towards his death at the trip of a land mine or booby trap. And like him, I was not ready to ask what I had gotten myself into.

She let go, took my hand, walked me back to my house and inside. Then she picked up her books and walked off home alone into the night. In the morning, on the bus, she acted as if nothing at all had happened. I got up the courage to pass her a note in English class: "I meant what I said. I love you. I can't live without you." It was ultimate, desperate and absolute. Something other than my own free will had command over me and there was little I could do but follow orders.

A note was returned to me, dropped on my tray at lunch, but she did not look at me as she delivered it. "Love is the most important thing in the world," it said, a cryptic, all too generic message. I decided this was abstract but good news.

We had established a new footing. We were no longer just intellectual buddies. I was no longer just the weird kid who had retrieved her grandfather from the insane asylum in New York. But I would not push it. Over the next two months our relationship was an odd one. Usually we would talk as if nothing had changed, but our conversations grew full of serious issues. We spoke mostly about war and injustice and were even beginning to plot how we could do something useful, however small, to try and alter the course of world events. But when it came to the subject of *us*, she backed off.

And then there was this other Gwen who I viewed, always from a distance, the one who sidled up to Burnet, the one who was able to divert his attention from a dozen other young ladies vying for his favour as they leaned against his locker and flirted with him. No one could flirt with Burnet as Gwen did. But Gwen seemed never to be around when Burnet occasionally flew off the handle. I saw him one day smash a fist so hard into his locker that the metal crumpled. I saw him go home and, as his father yelled some obscene insult at him, kick one of the dogs halfway across the yard.

I would not talk to Gwen about Burnet. I could not bring myself to tell her that Burnet was one of the destroyers. He was stuck with the violence his father had instilled in him. He still got into fights on Friday nights with big punks from Sheet Harbour. He bloodied noses and injured without feeling anything but satisfaction. It was all so illogical, I wanted to say. Gwen, the devout pacifist, should not be attracted to someone like Burnet. Beneath the practised veneer, it was violence and cruelty that made Burnet tick, and you could see it best on those moments when we'd be in the gym locker room and he'd go picking on some easily injured kid like Victor Farthing. Victor, who was wimpish at his most courageous moments, could not take it when the valiant Burnet Jr. stole his towel, picked him up butt naked and asked everyone to "Take a good look at the how tiny Victor's noodle is." That

Lesley Choyce

was the heart and soul of Burnet, and you could tell that humiliating another human meant more to him than all the attention he drew from the girls or the success he had garnered on the sports fields. That was the real Burnet.

But Gwen was never around to see him then. Burnet called her "his little hippie chick" to other guys when she wasn't around. It was a phrase he would not use when he realized I was in earshot because Burnet still considered himself my friend and, despite my feeling towards him, we were locked into some permanent, necessary arrangement although even my sainthood could no longer grant the word friendship to it.

There were few of us who were shocked when Burnet announced one Monday that he would not finish the school year, that he had enlisted in the Canadian Armed Forces and was planning on joining a small group of Canadian soldiers who were volunteering to go to Vietnam and fight side by side with the Americans, under their command. What did I feel there in the cafeteria as he announced it? Was I sickened that he was so ignorant as to go and participate in an unjust war and become himself a perpetrator of some horrific violence to innocents? Was I afraid of losing an old friend at the hands of the Viet Cong, afraid that he'd return in a body bag? Did I try and deter him?

No, I think I was secretly quite pleased. I knew now that Gwendolyn would see him for what he truly was, a creep who thrived on violence and pain and desired to inflict injury. And more than that, I was ecstatic that he would not be there to draw from me the attention of the girl I loved. Me, a fading saint, a dedicated lover who had nothing to show for all his passion but intense loyalty, a greater social awareness and a commitment to world peace. If Burnet was expecting to hear a speech from me against his decision, he might have been shocked when I said, "It takes a lot of guts to make a move like this, Burnet, a lot of guts."

27 After Burnet left, I thought Gwen and I would become closer, but a strange silence crept between us again, this time worse than before. I kept asking her, "What's wrong?" but she wouldn't answer except to say that it wasn't me. It didn't have anything to do with me. I invited her over many times, invited myself over to her house, but it was always no. She was pushing me further and further away and I didn't know why. She had also begun to miss school which was very unusual for her. I figured it had something to do with Burnet, and something to do with the war. Word had come back that Burnet, after training in Canada, would be shipped down to the States for further work with a unit in South Carolina, and then it would be off to Southeast Asia. The crazy bastard was going to have his chance to kill after all. I wanted to explain it all to Gwen, to tell her what Burnet was really like, that maybe it wasn't his fault but that he was a born destroyer. But every time I talked to her, every time I launched into a one-sided conversation with her, I never once mentioned Burnet.

May arrived and the sun reappeared, warming the cold stones, melting the last of the ice. The lifeblood began to flow in the veins and gulleys of the land. I was out walking the perimeter of the island again at night. Ian, alone. A familiar portrait. Seventeen was a no man's land. I felt like I had somehow lost the fun of being a kid but couldn't figure out how to grow up into something that was worth growing into. There were powerful tides in my life and I had no control over anything. Other forces, too omnipotent and too distant, held gravitational sway over my being. I wanted to fucking scream.

Then I saw her. I was on the lee side of the island, near the small crescent beach that my mom used to take us to when we were young. The moon was behind her as she was looking straight out into the water, down that shimmering silver path that my mother called the highway of the moon. The highway danced over the bay. My heart leaped into my throat. It was Gwen. I dropped low and sank to my knees behind a clump of sea oats. She took off a jacket, undid her blouse and stepped out of her skirt. I had only a silhouette to go by, but it was enough to make my lungs forget their evolutionary training. She was light upon the sand, and I watched as she walked into the cold bay water in a straight line centred upon the highway of the moon.

I was, in those days, a dreamer of many dreams; this one seemed closer to imagination than to the fact, so I could not bring myself to waken. Instead, I almost believed I was sleeping the best of sleeps. The water was up to her neck, her throat, up to her lovely nose and eyes but she was not about to swim. How can I describe the way she moved forward, her long brown hair now floating like feathered seaweed behind her, the moon still shining down like cold steel fire?

What happened inside me must certainly have been directed by the moon. Some volcanic thing happened in my blood, something less than the deathburst of a fatal star but larger than the forging of a planet. In a split second, the dream was gone; I was fully alive, no longer a child, forever the next thing to come and sprinting down the sandy beach and into the water.

The water was cold. I sloshed through the shallows and dove forward, tackling Gwen beneath the darkness of the bay. She had no idea what had taken her and she hit me hard in the stomach. I pushed her to the surface and tried to hold onto her hand but she was scratching at my face with her nails. There was nothing to do but hang onto her and pull her shoreward. I felt cruel when at last we were out of the water and I heaved her on the sand, only to watch her fall face down where she sobbed and heaved like some sea thing deprived of its natural environment.

To say it happened like this will seem false, but the truth is

I knew then and there that I would never be the same. What I felt could never be described as anything less than awareness and arrival. Gwen was crying and I had no idea what to say. Too many thoughts were racing, too much was ready to spill from my mouth. I found her jacket and put it around her shoulders, then stepped back and found myself kneeling in the wet sand.

"Ian," she said at last.

She had turned towards me and I could see her face now in the moonlight. For a brief instant the child had returned. We were twelve again. We were kids who played near the shores and picked up sand dollars and put stranded starfish back into the pools. Then it was gone, and she was Gwen, the older one who dazzled in sunlight and walked in grace.

"What were you doing?" I asked.

She didn't say a thing. Her eyes had swallowed me. She dropped the jacket now and slowly stood up, inches from where I knelt. She stood full before me now, the moon at my back, and I could understand that she wanted me to see more than just her beauty. Her breasts were round and full, magnetic above my face, and the skin over her stomach was smooth and taut. It was like the smooth morning sun on the skin of the horizon when the sea has gone perfectly still. I could tell by the way she placed her hands on either side of her stomach that she was trying to tell me something. Still stunned by the intensity of the moment, I leaped to the portent. Remembered the talk at school. I had never heard the words myself from Burnet, only the jokes, the rumours.

My hands seemed to move of their own accord as they reached out and touched those two delicate hands. Leaning forward with what I thought could be my final breath on earth, I rested my head gently against her beautiful belly and then kissed her just above the navel. I could feel her shake with a spasm of sobbing and heard her begin to cry but I didn't move, didn't let go. Kneeling there on the wet sand and getting to know this mysterious, dangerous girl for the second time in my life, I whispered, *It's all right. Everything is going to turn out just fine.*

There was nothing more to be said that night. Things *were* going to be all right. I knew it and I knew that I would somehow take charge of this situation. The old Ian, the rescuer of dead grandfathers, would make something good come out of this. I was filled with a sense of responsibility and necessity and returned to the land of the living.

In the days that followed, Gwen and I walked to the bus together. We talked in soft serious tones in a language that was different from the rattle of nonsense spoken by our peers. And we met at night, out along the same sandy cove, where we walked and we talked.

"It was my idea," she said. "I could have told Burnet no, but I wanted him."

I was probably the stupidest kid my age in the world when it came to matters of sex. Sure, I thought about it. I knew other guys who bragged, including Burnet, but in my company he had never said anything about Gwen. Yet I had believed I understood what sex was all about. I was a kind of romantic pervert, I suppose. I ached for love. I ached to be *in* love and my mind was fixed on Gwen. If I had thought of having sex with her, it was always because that would be the natural thing so closely tied in with that deeper feeling. The other guys spoke about sex so differently — "fuck 'em and forget 'em" was a sort of macho anthem that I heard over and over. The code of the male destroyer. Only this time Burnet the destroyer was also the creator.

"How come you didn't do anything to keep from getting pregnant?" I asked.

"I wanted to but Burnet said that it didn't seem as natural that way."

"What a jerk," I said. "Why did you listen to him? How could you do it with *him*?" I was really mad at her and she looked hurt.

"I wanted to," she said. "I just wanted to, that's all."

I swallowed my anger, my pride. I tried to erase the awful image of the two of them screwing. That's the verb Burnet would have used. It was certainly not lovemaking. "Did you love him?" I asked. I guess I wanted all the pain just then. I wanted her to pick up the hammer, pick up the metal spike and drive it straight through my heart.

"I think so. I'm not sure. I knew it was you I should have been in love with but — I guess it was him. I can't explain it." She came over to me and took my hand, held it up to her cheek, wanted me to look her in the eyes, but I couldn't.

"Do you think he loved you?"

"No," she answered. "I don't know if a guy like Burnet will ever feel real love, not until he stops hurting so bad. That's part of why I fell for him. I knew that beneath his tough exterior he was very vulnerable. I think I believed having sex with him might help him in some way. It sounds crazy, but I thought it might make him more caring, more compassionate."

"Guess that's why he decided to go to Vietnam," I said, the acid of my dark sarcasm carving a new chasm between us. I should have kept my mouth shut.

She pulled her hand away, started to inch backward.

"Sorry," I said. "I shouldn't have said that." I picked up a handful of sand. "What about now?" I asked. There weren't quite tears in my eyes but I felt the sting of their presence. I would hold back. "Do you still love him now?"

She shook her head no, but it wasn't convincing. I wondered if she had any idea of my hurt, my pain. Is that what it would take for her to fall in love with me? I deserved as much pity as Burnet. If pity would make Gwen love me, I would cut off my arm and scream in pain until she was willing to comfort me, to love me, to make love to me.

Fortunately, my good sense prompted me to say nothing. If silence, the inability to express myself, had been my worst fault of late, it was also to be my saving grace. I pulled her back to me — or at least this other Ian did, this Ian with good sense, who had suddenly transcended the boy. He wrapped his arms around Gwen, he kissed her on the neck, he whispered in her ear that he loved her and would do anything to help her and that he didn't care if she loved him or not, that he'd always be there.

---

28 Gwen had not told her parents but she told her grandfather, crazy old Duke who seemed to sparkle with good natured vitality ever since he had arrived on Whalebone and accepted his new identity. He was an easy guy to talk to and I understood why she told him. He was never judgemental and always somewhat askew, never direct with an answer. His answers, like his opinions, were cloaked in mystery and beauty.

"I explained everything and asked for his advice," Gwen said as we walked home from the school bus that had let us off at the bridge. We walked past the barking hounds of Burnet's house. We could hear his old man yelling out the door for them to shut up, heard him fire off a string of foul curses like machine-gun fire. I gulped, wondering what Duke could possibly have to offer.

"He said that there are always waiting souls in the great soul bank. Sometimes they come into the world, sometimes they don't. Usually it's not us here on earth who have anything to do with the decision."

"What's a soul bank?" I asked.

"I asked him the same thing. He just quoted something from William Wordsworth — 'not in entire forgetfulness . . . but trailing clouds of glory do we come.'"

"Trailing clouds of glory," I repeated. It had an eerie, *déjà vu* feel to it. Of course, it was something Duke would say, part of the great mystery of who he was. What exactly had he been before he ended up on the street? A professor? A poet? Himself trailing clouds of ragged glory from his street life outside Grand Central Station? "What do you think he was trying to tell you?"

She looked a little glum. "I'm not sure, really. I think he meant something about the baby." It was the first time she really said the word and a chill ran down my spine. It's incredibly odd how there can be such a big gulf, a huge distance, between the idea of being pregnant and actually having a baby. "I think he was implying that if I have the baby, a soul will come into the world; if I don't have the baby, the soul will still be out there and come into the world another time."

"You're pregnant. You *are* going to have a baby. What else is there to it?"

She hung her head. "Think about it, Ian. Vietnam, nuclear bombs, China, assassinations, dictatorships. A father who gets his kicks by going off to war to kill people. Does it make good sense to bring a baby into the world right now?"

I tried to sluff it off. "You've been watching too much TV. Look around," I said, sweeping my arms around at the blue sky, the yellow lichen-covered rocks, the exotic, wind-sculpted spruce trees and juniper. The air was filled with the tangible smell of clean salt air laced with bayberry and other delicate maritime perfumes. "Look at this. Where's the murder? Where's the bloodshed? No assassinations here. This is a great place to bring a kid into the world." Once again Gwen had ripped me out of my little fantasy cocoon of safety and happy endings. I thought I had it all figured out. I had never said it, but I assumed that I was going to marry her or at least live with her. That she would have the kid and *I* would be the father. Happily ever after. I was refusing to think about the bastard Burnet who I had tried to flush out of my memory. In truth, I secretly wanted him to die in Vietnam. It was part of the package. Part of happily-ever-after. "It's not your decision, " I said to Gwen. "We're going to have the baby together."

The birds flew over — gulls, sparrow hawks, a sweep of plovers. Gwen had grown deaf. "Could we go talk to your friend, the doctor? I'd like to talk to Ben Ackerman."

I looked up at the plovers, now arcing off to the sea. I had to stop myself from saying out loud what was going through my head: *Ben Ackerman is not a real doctor.* "You want to see Ben?" I asked. "Why?"

"I want to know about my options."

"What options?"

"I want to know if I can *not* have the baby."

"I think you should talk to your parents first," I said. I knew her mother and father would be reasonable. I also knew they would try to talk her out of it. "And I think you should tell them I'm the father, not Burnet." This was a very important point to me. Yet another lie I wanted to add to my life. I don't think I even cared any more that Burnet was the father. *I wanted it to be my baby.*

She gave me a look of soft defiance, but behind it I saw the fear. What exactly was she afraid of? What was it that had sent her out into the cold water the other night? A fear, deeper than anything I could understand, a sad, haunting despair. She had told me nothing about her actions. I had wanted to believe it was just a test of herself, something she could not explain to me. Something I could never fully understand.

"Were you really trying to drown yourself?" I blurted out.

"I felt like I had thrown everything away. I wanted to change the world and if I had a kid now, I would be bringing up a child in a world that was ugly and cruel and full of hate.

If I have the baby, I won't be able to make this a better place. Once it's better, then I'll have kids. I'll have ten of them and you can be the father." She sucked in her breath. "No, I don't think I would have been able to kill myself." She looked almost embarrassed now. "The water was too cold." She laughed at the absurd point she was making. "People who are serious about killing themselves slit their wrists indoors in bathtubs full of warm water. It's hard to explain, but I just needed to do that. I needed to push myself a little, to toy with the idea and to feel the pain. You weren't supposed to be there."

Did I believe what she was telling me? I don't know. But she had brought me back to a possibility more frightening than any I'd tried to understand yet. I suddenly forgot about the invisible baby, the sweet martyrdom of my fatherhood. Gwen was mysterious and unpredictable in ways I could never fathom. *I was suddenly aware that somehow in all this mess I could lose Gwen.* She might simply vanish from the island, from my life. And I could not let that happen.

"I think we should go see Ben now." I said.

He was wrestling a section of framed wall into place when we arrived. It would take him forever to build this house. He was too much of a perfectionist and it was slow going. Gwen and I walked across the floorboards and I grabbed onto the wall to steady it as it wobbled in the breeze. Ben smiled at us both, picked up a level and began to readjust the framed section so it was perfectly vertical. He began to hammer it onto the subfloor. When he was certain it was anchored, a great grin of satisfaction came over him. One modest item had been set right in the world, one fraction of perfection achieved. He threw his hammer down with a loud bang on the floor and rubbed his hands together. "How are you two kids doing?"

"Gwendolyn's pregnant, " I answered.

Ben pulled three nails out of his nail apron and studied them as he rolled them between his fingers. "That's a bombshell," he said.

"I'm thinking about having an abortion," Gwen said. "I'd like your advice as a doctor."

Ben gave me a puzzled look. I don't think he had considered himself a doctor any longer. No one had called on him for medical advice in quite a while. I think he was happy to have grown out of the lie and into another role: the world's slowest, most meticulous and grudgingly perfect house builder.

"Abortion laws were beginning to loosen up in New York State when I was leaving the profession." Ben looked at me, silently asking for my compliance with the lie. His voice, however, had assumed a cool, clinical tone like he had used at the nursing home in New York City. "My colleagues had performed some at the hospital. I had been involved in one or two emergency situations. I'm no expert. How far pregnant are you?"

"Fifty-two days," she said. She knew exactly the night. It had only been once.

"If you want an abortion, then it should be soon or it will be much more complicated. Have you thought all of this through? It's an important decision."

"Yes," Gwen said immediately.

"Are you sure it's the right thing?" He was looking more at me than her now. I think he was shocked to think I was the one who had made her pregnant.

"Yes," Gwen answered again.

"Do your parents know?"

"No. It's my decision."

"I think you should discuss it with them."

"Would you be willing to give me an abortion here on the island?" Gwen asked.

"I would be breaking the law. But even without that, the answer is no. Why do you want one?"

"I'm too young. I want to live more of my life more first. I want to help stop the Americans from killing people in Vietnam. I want time to change things, to make people see how bloody cruel they are. I want to fix up the world as best I can and then have kids. Ian understands."

"Yes," I lied. "I do." It was so odd again to see my father in her, to recognize that same flawed, possibly fatal drive to improve upon the human race somehow, to take the whole global problem in hand and fix it. I would never understand this deep-seated motivation. Now, in order to stop the killing in the world, she would have to postpone the arrival of one new soul into it.

Ben shook his head. "I think I understand what you're saying but I can't help you. I'm not licensed in Nova Scotia to practice medicine, certainly not abortion and abortion is not legal here. I think you should go home and discuss this with your parents."

I guess I knew then that Ben had ceased, once and for all, being a doctor. It seemed to cause him pain to be brought back into the difficult moral arena that medical decision-making created. He walked across the floor of his someday home and picked up two two-by-sixes and began to measure them, marking them with the T-square and trying to pretend we weren't there.

"Thanks. Bye," Gwen said as we walked down the plank to the ground.

"Why can't you tell your parents?" I asked her. "They aren't like other kids' parents. They're smart. They don't see the world in black and white. They'll understand how you feel."

"No," she said. "I can't."

"Why?"

"Because my mother wanted to have an abortion once. She was young and pretty and thought she had a career ahead of her as a dancer, maybe an actress. Then she met my father. She got pregnant and decided to have an abortion — it was illegal in those days, of course, but she had found a 'safe' clinic in Las Vegas. She was all ready to go. My father was in Alamagordo making new bombs. He went to see her, found the note she had left for him. He drove to Nevada and stopped her. He forced her to go back to New Mexico. He convinced her to have the baby, and she resigned herself to it. They ended up getting more serious with each other and getting married. "And somehow a little tiny soul waiting in a soul bank somewhere had its way and came into the world."

I tried to think of a world without Gwen. Now I could begin to see the difficulty of her situation.

"But this is different. Very different," she asserted, rubbing her hands across her face. "*I* need to make the decision. Correction. *We* need to make the decision. What do you think we should do now?" The ball was back in my court because I was inextricably involved in the game.

"C'mon," I said. "There's somebody else on the island we can talk to."

29 My grandmother was the most no-nonsense woman who ever walked the face of the earth. A woman who possessed warmth, kindness and compassion, she also possessed that rarest human quality: common sense. We arrived while she and Jack were drinking tea and discussing a book they had both recently read and admired: *The Feminine Mystique* by Betty Friedan.

"We need your advice," I began, looking at Bernie. "It's of a private, medical nature." I lowered my eyes but hoped that Jack would get the drift.

Jack, always humble, always willing to slide out of this century and back into the days of pirates, scraped his chair back and said, "I have some reading I need to do anyway. Good to see you again, Ian."

But Bernie grabbed him by the cuff. "Stay, Jack," and turning to Gwen, "I tell Jack everything, anyway. That's the way we are. No secrets. No weapons. Everything plain as the nose on your face. That's our relationship. So he might as well stay."

Gwen gave me a shrug. She trusted me. I trusted them. Maybe pretty soon the whole island would know. Gwen wasn't really all that troubled about that. She was probably infinitely different from a thousand other North American girls who got pregnant. She wasn't trying to cover anything up. She just had her priorities. Fix the world, then have a pile of kids. She looked down at *The Feminine Mystique* sitting on the table.

"Jack's a feminist, too, I might add," Bernie said. "Read all of Wollstonecraft, Simone de Beauvoir. He understands women better than most women do. We're both tuned into the battle for equal rights."

"I'd beat the faces off the sons of bitches who try to dispossess women of their fair share," Jack said, sitting back down now, a male radical feminist streetbrawler.

Bernie shushed him, apologizing, "We're still trying to work out a few bugs in the male evolutionary system — aggression, tendency towards violence, defence of the indefenceless by punching their lights out, that sort of thing." She sounded very professorial just then. Clearly, we weren't going to shake Jack from the room. No book of nineteenth-century piracy or even twentieth-century feminist rhetoric would lure him away from our nearly public real-world crisis.

"It's nice to see you both again," Gwen said.

Bernie looked her in the eye. "Haven't talked to you for a while, Gwendolyn. You look all grown up. I remember the day you arrived. Another family of Yanks. So how do you like it here on the island, compared to The United States of America, I mean?" She asked the question like Gwen had only been around for maybe a week. Old people had this funny thing about time.

"It's not so bad, really, I guess," Gwen answered, "except for the fact that I'm pregnant and I don't want to be."

There. It was out. Didn't surprise me any. Jack lifted his eyebrows a couple of centimetres above their normal at-ease status. Bernie was taken back for only a second. It would have been a sign of defeat for her to show any real shock or surprise. "I like that," she said to old Jack. "The girl has balls. She comes here with a problem looking for advice. Cuts through all the small talk and gets right to the point. That's something."

Jack nodded.

Bernie reached her hand out to Gwen. "Give me your wrist, honey. Jack, could I have your watch." Gwen held out her hand. Jack set his watch down on the table beside his wife. Bernie grabbed Gwen's wrist, pressed her index finger down on the vein and watched the seconds tick by. After a full minute of silence, she said, "If I had the proper instrument, I'd really like to check the blood pressure, but you have a good count and the pulse is strong. You're in good shape. Probably no reason why you shouldn't have the baby if you wanted it."

"It's all wrong. I just don't think it's the right time," Gwen said defiantly. "After all, it should be my decision, not anybody else's."

Bernie was scratching at a longish hair that was growing out of her neck. Jack was the one to answer. "Damn straight. About time women had the right to control their own procreative processes." You could really tell he'd been reading the female liberationists.

Bernie went over to a bookshelf in the kitchen that held maybe two hundred cookbooks and one other volume not usually kept near the wood stove in the kitchen. "There," she said, handing it to Gwen. It was an oversize volume of something with a slapdash cover that looked more like a catalogue than a book. The title shouted out in big bold letters, *OUR BODIES, OURSELVES* by the Boston Women's Health Book

Collective. Bernie leafed through until she found what she was looking for. "Read this chapter. Then, if you're still sure it's what you want, come back. We'll talk. How far pregnant are you?"

"Not quite eight weeks."

"Then we better talk soon. Read it tonight, honey. Consider all the moral implications. Consider the future. You're gonna have to do what you believe is right and you're gonna have to trust yourself. Come back tomorrow. If you are sure you want it terminated, you can fly to Boston. I'll phone and make the arrangements. I'll pay for the tickets. Ian will take you down and stay with you. I'll come if you want me to."

Gwen seemed now reassured and relaxed for the first time in days. She took the book, promised to read it carefully. "You won't need to come. Ian will be enough. He's the best friend in the world." Gwen took my hand and squeezed tight.

I bet that Bernie and Jack believed her one hundred percent, and I bet they knew immediately that I wasn't the father. They would never hint at it. I think my grandmother was thinking just then about the night Casey was born and how I'd braved the hurricane to come find her. This was a curious reversal. I was older now, and I was helping someone I loved avoid childbirth. For me, it most certainly did not seem right. But Jack had said it. *It was her body, her decision.* Someday, perhaps, we would all be liberators of women, we would all be willing to let people decide for themselves what was right.

I had a harder time seeing things the way Gwen did. If it was up to me, would I *not* have a child because I thought I was bringing him into an evil, incorrigibly violent world? That assumed a belief that some day the world would be better — fixed, as Gwen had called it. I didn't share the vision. The world would get better; the world would get worse. I didn't think it would ever be *fixed.*

"Ian's a good boy," Bernie said.

"The best," Jack added.

30 It was a bright, clear morning as we sat in the Air Canada plane on the runway. Gwendolyn pressed herself tight up against me and held my hand as we watched the stewardess show us how to adjust our seatbelts and what to do if the plane were to ditch in the open water. "The cushion of your seat will act as a floatation device should the plane have to land in the water," the woman said matter-of-factly.

I looked down at the seat cushion I was sitting on and I thought of the open Atlantic Ocean — frigid, uncaring, always willing to absorb the death of one or hundreds. No, I didn't think the piece of foam rubber I was sitting on would do much good out there. It was my first plane ride and the first for Gwen as well. Maybe everyone on their first plane ride has this sensation, but it seemed frightening and unique to me; I felt like I was leaving Nova Scotia forever. We would crash, we would burn or we all would drown; the plane would be hijacked to Cuba and we'd never be allowed to leave. Or when the doors opened at what was supposed to be Boston, we would have arrived in some twilight zone alternate universe and there would be no point in trying to use our return ticket.

Gwen closed her eyes and leaned against me. She was more nervous and worried about this decision than she had let on. But we both knew it was the right thing for us to do. We'd read *OUR BODIES, OURSELVES* and I had been suddenly thrown into the world of women's concerns — anatomy, gynaecology, politics and liberation. Like Jack, reading the book had turned me into a feminist, a liberator of women. First stop on the road to liberation: Boston, for a legal abortion as Gwen asserted her right to have control over the biological processes of her body.

Miraculously, her parents didn't know. They knew we were both flying to Boston alone for a weekend. They knew the trip was being paid for by Bernie. We were to visit museums, universities, take in a Boston Red Sox game and stay, in separate sleeping quarters, at the youth hostel just off Harvard campus. Her mother approved. She trusted me immensely. Her father was a little leery of the trip, paranoid that the CIA or FBI would try to kidnap his daughter in order to bring him and his military secrets back into the country. In the end, it was Duke who persuaded him it was okay, that we were old enough and dependable.

I told my mother the same lies as to why we were going, but I think she saw through the story instantly. Nonetheless, she didn't say a word. Once more, I knew that she was not only seeing past the lie and into the truth but even deeper than the surface facts, into what my motives were. She regretted that I lied to her and so did I, but I could not bring myself to tell her part of the truth without telling all of the truth and what I did not want her to know, if such a thing was possible, that it was Burnet, not me, who had made Gwen pregnant.

My sense of foreboding began to dissipate as the plane took off. I felt a rush of adrenalin as we left the ground, and as Gwen leaned across me to look out the window, we both stared in wonder at the spruce trees that turned to green matchsticks beneath us, at the cars on the highway to Truro that suddenly became toys and the houses so miniature, so perfect, so orderly. To a veteran flyer, these sights would not mean much, but to us it was a thing of much magnificence.

My arm had found its way around Gwen as she leaned across me and it was all very dreamlike — her warmth, her body pressed into me and the vision of Nova Scotia transforming beneath us into a three-dimensional, almost cartoon-like map of forest and rivers. As the plane arced out towards the sea, I saw the ragged caricature of a coastline and the brilliant, flashing blue and silver of the sea. Beneath us, all those lakes, each stretched like a snaking finger north to south, all left there by the scratching retreat of glaciers a million years ago,

Lesley Choyce

the same glaciers that had scraped off the topsoil and left pro-truding bedrock. Then the pilot banked the plane and we were back over the centre of the province, so high up in the sky now that we could see water on both sides: the Atlantic to the south and the Bay of Fundy to the north.

"We're doing the right thing," Gwen said, sitting up now and kissing me lightly on the cheek.

"I know we are," I said.

"Ian, do you know what a quasar is?" Gwen asked, a typi-cal shift for our conversation, away from the immediate and into some abstract realm.

"Is it a kind of television?" I asked. I knew it was; I had seen it advertised on my own TV. But I also knew it wasn't what she was asking.

She sat up and punched me playfully on the shoulder. "No, silly. My father says they are some kind of star or something way out in space that gives off funny electromagnetic signals because they are moving away from us at such high speed."

I wasn't sure what to do with the information. "Why are they moving away from us?"

"I don't know. They just are."

"Maybe we frightened them."

She knew I was teasing. "I think it has more to do with the universe expanding. Everything is moving away from the centre of the universe where it started. The quasars seem to be moving away faster."

"Do you think they know where they are going?"

"Do we know where we are going?" she countered.

"Yes," I said. "We're going to Boston and I love you. I'd love you and stay with you even if you were a quasar and racing away from me. I'm that kind of guy."

"I know you are," she said. She held tightly onto my arm again. "And I think I'm falling in love with you. I think I had forgotten how much I needed you just because you were al-ways around. I guess I thought you were still a little kid and that I was a little kid, too. I think I expected that I would wake up one morning and you'd be outside in the sunshine waiting to take me for a walk around the island — to put the jelly fish and the starfish back in the water."

"Yeah, I keep thinking the same thing. How did we grow up so quick?"

"Like quasars, something was driving us, racing us away from where we started. I want to go back."

For a split second the crazy euphoria was broken; I thought she meant that she wanted to go home, that she had changed her mind about the abortion. "You do?"

"I want to go back to being a little girl. I want to go back to a time when I didn't have to think about war and about stupid mistakes. I don't like feeling so responsible for everything."

I was a little surprised by what she just said because that was how I felt so often. I felt like I had too much responsibility; I was never free to be myself or to just goof off. But right now, I wanted to be the martyr. I wanted to take on all of Gwen's worries. "I want you to stop thinking about anything at all. I'll take care of everything and I'll be with you the whole way."

The immigration agent in Boston airport was a tough young man with a black mustache who leered at Gwen and asked us insulting, stupid questions. I guess we were both a bit sensitive about the abortion. We didn't mention it was why we were there. I told him we were there for the museums and the ball game. "Good. We like tourists here," he said. "We just don't like radicals who come in to stir up trouble. Remember that."

"Right," I said. I had no idea what he was talking about. As we walked through the terminal, I saw quite a few other kids our age, maybe a few years older. They all had long, long hair, both the guys and the girls, and they wore bright flowered shirts and torn blue jeans. One tall character with a knapsack and major beard looked at Gwen, at her peace earrings, and flashed us both a two-fingered V. At the far end of the terminal I could see a group of maybe fifty long-hairs had gathered

Lesley Choyce

and were chanting something, holding up signs as a small knot of American soldiers were lined up at the ticket counter to Delta Airlines.

Gwen's interest was aroused and we walked through the crowd of business people and tourists to where the contingent of hippies were now shouting, "No more War. Stay home and fight the system!" Just as we got there, one of the soldiers broke out of line and smacked into us on his way toward the beard who had flashed us the V. In a second he was on top of the beard, smashing him with his fists until two other soldiers came to pull him off. I led Gwen quickly away from the demonstrators and outside to the bus that would take us downtown.

I guess we didn't look too far off the mark of the local hip community because it seemed everywhere we walked on the city streets, other long-hairs would flash us the peace sign or say, "How's it going, man?" or just smile and nod. Heck, my hair had always been longish and uncontrolled. I had on country clothes — slightly beat-up dungarees and an old flannel shirt. We both had knapsacks.

At the clinic, we were greeted warmly and asked to sit in a waiting room with one very young looking teenybopper and her overwrought mother who chain-smoked as she kept telling her daughter to stop fidgeting. After about twenty minutes we were led into a smaller office where a woman doctor gave a somewhat bland lecture on birth control and asked us how much we could afford for the procedure. Bernie had already given us the full amount, one hundred and twenty dollars, which I tried to give to the woman immediately.

"Just pay at the front desk please," she said, refusing to actually take the money. I don't think she wanted to touch it and, for a minute, the whole affair seemed odd as she suddenly slackened her professional self and looked at us closely. "Are you sure you can afford this? We can perform the abortion for free if you are hard pressed for money."

I guess we looked like a couple of hicks from Nova Scotia. "We can afford it, thanks. What I'd like to know is if I can stay in the room with Gwen for the abortion."

"No. But it will only take about twenty minutes and then you can be with her in the recovery room. You'll be able to leave within two hours after that. Do you have some place to go to where she can rest?"

"Yes," I said. According to my map, we were close to Harvard and the hostel, but I was having second thoughts about going there.

Gwen was led into yet another room and I went back to sit on the vinyl chairs with the mother and her pregnant daughter. I tried reading. It was the longest twenty minutes of my life. Twice, I think, I felt a wave of hot nausea sweep through me and I wanted to jump up and run into the operating room. The mind that leaps to horrible, tragic conclusions is a weapon of great irrational power. But another voice kept reaching up from within me. It was the voice of my mother, an echoing whisper, telling me to be calm, to keep control of myself.

"You can go in now," a nurse said at last.

I found Gwen lying peacefully asleep in the recovery room, the shades pulled down to keep out the daylight. "Everything went just fine," the doctor said to me, then checked her watch and left me with Gwen. She was so full of peace at that moment that I knew she was okay. I knelt down on the floor and put my ear close to her mouth and simply listened to her breathe. I tried not to think about the whole business of abortion but couldn't avoid it. *Nothing is lost*, came the voice from within. *All things are renewed. It's the way things are.* It was my mother again, inside me. And I knew she was right.

31 Gwen woke up a little groggy but feeling cheerful. We were given some pamphlets concerning potential problems and a phone number to call if we had any worries. They were very nice people at the clinic. I asked them to call me a cab because I had no idea if I'd succeed at simply walking out into traffic like the Americans could and waving one down. I led Gwen out to the noisy city street. When the cab stopped and asked where to, I hesitated. We would not go to the youth hostel after all, I decided. We would not sleep in separate rooms. That was all wrong. We would sleep together in the same bed.

"A hotel nearby," I said. "Some place nice but not too expensive."

The guy looked at us in his rear-view mirror. He looked at the name of the clinic on the doorway we had just come out of, smirked and bit down on a toothpick in his mouth. "You got it," he said. He drove us eight, maybe nine blocks; clearly we had passed a dozen or so other hotels on the way, all of which didn't look too fancy, but I kept my mouth shut. The streets were full of university students and pretty freaky looking people — seemed like a lot of police too. Some of them were walking the streets, some sitting in patrol cars, others on horse back.

We were dropped off in front of a sooty brown brick hotel with a sign out front that said, "The Waverley." I paid the driver and said nothing when he shook his head at Gwen and clucked his tongue. The desk clerk inside the dingy lobby was a very unusual looking man of about forty with yellowish, almost translucent skin that seemed like it was pulled too tightly over his skull. You would have thought him sinister if you did not look closely at his eyes. There was something about them — sad and compassionate, friendly even.

"We'd like a room," I said. "A nice room." Gwen stood

beside me. She looked very tired, very weary, almost as if she were pleasantly drunk. The clerk looked at her briefly and smiled — not the leer of the cab driver but something deferential and fatherly.

"Sign here please." I took the pen and signed my name and Gwen's name, then put our address: Whalebone Island, Nova Scotia.

The clerk looked at what I had written. "My father was a worker on a ship once. It was a very bad company and they treated the men badly. When the ship came into port in Halifax, he complained to the authorities and the captain was arrested. A very bad ship, a bad man. In Nova Scotia, my father told me, you will find real people. That's what he called them. *Real people.* He visited ports all over the world and he said there were only a handful of places where he found real people. Are you real people?"

I wasn't expecting the litany to my home province. "Yes," I said. "And those are our real names." I wasn't sure if he was playing a game, accusing us like so many who had probably come here before, checking in without using their real names.

"Are you married?" he asked. I had been ready for this question but there was not a trace of accusation in his voice.

"No," Gwen said. "But we've known each other for a long time. We belong together." She said it as if in a dream. I felt suddenly so proud, so happy. I looked the clerk right in the eye and there was no judgement. His eyes sparkled with a distant fire.

"Of course you do. You are real people. Real people belong together. Here is your key. Top floor."

We took the ancient elevator to the top floor and I led Gwen down the hallway to our room. It was an old, run-down but surprisingly clean hotel. Cheap, but somehow honest. A surprise. And then an even greater surprise. When I opened the door to our room, I saw that it was some sort of large, well lit suite of rooms with a magnificent view of the park below.

Lesley Choyce

Gwen yawned and looked around with a sleepy angelic smile on her face. "It's beautiful," she said. And it really was. Everything was perfectly old. My guess would be 1930s. Things were shabby but neat, authentic but not improved. Gwen zeroed in on the bed and waltzed like a somnambulist to it and collapsed. She was exhausted and her body needed rest.

I closed the door, walked to the bed and lay down beside her. She was in a near fetal position as I tucked up around her, feeling her warmth, meditating on her soft, childlike breathing. I hugged her and she squirmed in a most comfortable way, and despite the strangeness of our day and the less than romantic nature of our circumstances, everything now seemed perfect. We were together, alone. I loved her very much. We were boyfriend and girlfriend, husband and wife; we were two people who needed each other very badly and had found our way to ourselves.

As I closed my eyes on the impossibly neat but tattered 1930s suite, I fell asleep and travelled far into some deep warm mysterious universe where nothing was tangible but light and voices. I recognized at once that this was some place familiar, a place of spirits, a domain that was one my mother must have known well. It was her other world. I was, for some reason, being given a glimpse into it. Voices were speaking; I could not understand the words. It was all indistinct, but I understood the nature of what I was being told; I had found, maybe for the first time in my life, a perfect moment. With Gwen I had found peace and contentment through love. The spirits around me were suggesting it would not last but the echo, the reverberation of that feeling, would linger with me forever. Then a solitary voice was asking me to look down.

I hadn't even realized that I was "up." I looked down and saw my own body pressed against Gwen; we were lying there, cupped together, fully clothed on the bed, and I could read the message on my face: perfect peace. But where was *I*? Was I dreaming? Was I dead? *No, definitely not*, someone answered more distinctly now. The voice was decidedly Nova Scotian in accent but I didn't recognize it. I wasn't even sure if it was a woman or a man. As I looked down on us sleeping, I suddenly grew frightened. I felt as if I might fall from my height, but a hand reached out and steadied me. *Am I about to be punished?* I asked. I remembered the abortion and how we had come to the decision, that in the end it seemed like the right and logical thing to do. But was I wrong? Had we performed some grievous sin and was I now about to be penalized? *No*, came the answer. *Nothing like that. Nothing is ever lost. Everything goes on and on. The way it should. Only actions made without thought, without compassion, do any harm.*

I was still looking down at myself asleep. The fear was gone and I had been returned to a mild euphoria tinged with what I had felt before. I looked up to find the voice again, but as I did, I felt myself falling like a rock and then I hit the bed. I bounced. Not high, but I bounced. Gwen pulled away slightly and tugged at the bed cover, pulling it up over her shoulder. I sat up and looked around. I shook my head, looked for the lights, listened for the voices. Nothing. A dream, I decided. An important dream, perhaps, but a dream. Nothing more. I covered Gwen more fully with a blanket and went into the bathroom to splash some water on my face.

I looked at myself in the mirror. The afternoon light was warm and yellow. In the mirror, I did not look like me. I remembered a boy there once. I remembered the face of a confused, excited, nervous little kid who expected miracles each day and often found them. Now there was this: a young man who needed a shave, the mug of a skinny but tough looking fisherman. It was the face of a stranger, but after a brief study, it became likeable, agreeable. I looked for the fear, because that fear, lurking in the corner of the eye and in the corner of the mouth was what had made me turn away from mirrors so often in recent years. Fear and doubt and an aura of impending doom. It had been the face of some poor kid who

Lesley Choyce

was just about to receive bad news from a stranger. That was the old face. This one was different. Unsophisticated perhaps, the face of an island kid now too big for his old boots, but it had, I decided, character. I sat in an old overstuffed chair by Gwen and watched her sleep as the sun set over the tall buildings. As it grew dark, I saw bright lights turned on below in the park. I saw a gathering of young men and women. There were placards and a guy with a megaphone talking about the war. I heard shouts of anger and outrage and saw people thrusting fists into the air. There was a war on the other side of the world and outside the protestors were performing some sort of anxious ritual in an attempt to stop it. Gwen heard the guy yelling on the megaphone and woke up. She rubbed her hand across her stomach and came to stand by the window with me. I held her as we watched the pageant below. So much anger down there behind all the good intentions.

This was almost like watching TV or a movie. Clearly, it couldn't be real. How could there really be a war on? How could men be killing women and children, burning villages, dying of sniper wounds, falling into human traps or stepping on land mines, burning jungles and pouring living fire of Napalm on families while I stood by a window with Gwen, feeling so peaceful and so full of love? Such things could not be. I can't remember if we said anything just then. There were syllables, there was the syntax of lips kissing, of shared breathing, of the soft rustle of hair, of the slide of her hand across my sandpaper chin. After a while, the outrage outside subsided and the crowds dispersed. I had hoped that the protestors concluded that a war could not possibly be raging on a night like this, a night so full of love for clearly, I had enough love in me right then to overwhelm any living soul within a six-mile radius. Then Gwen and I went to bed and fell asleep. No dreams returned save the vision of a warm dark sea lapping at the shore of Back Bay in the moonlight on the warmest night of the year.

When I woke the next morning, Gwen was already up and dressed. Someone had just slipped a newspaper under our door and she picked it up. I watched with one eye half open as she sat down and began to read. For a second I felt very adult, very old. I had just slept the night with Gwen. We were here together, like man and wife on a honeymoon in the strange old-fashioned honeymoon suite (that was my theory) and it all felt so right. I was lying there trying to think of something really romantic to say to Gwen to start the new day, and our new "life," but my brain was fuzzy. She beat me to the punch and it wasn't what I was expecting.

"Nixon's bombing Hanoi again," she said, holding the newspaper headline up for me to see. "It's one of the heaviest bombings yet. Right on the city. He's escalating the war."

I rubbed my eyes, felt more than a little puzzled. The spell was broken. "How are you feeling?" I asked.

"I'm a little sore. But I'm okay. There's going to be a march today from Harvard to the Federal Courthouse. It starts in about an hour. I'd like to be in it."

Downstairs, checking out, I asked the man about our room.

"Belonged to a big guy in the crime syndicate. Louis Longines was his name. You probably never heard of him. He killed lots of people, but he had a heart of gold. Kept his girlfriend there and treated her like a princess until she died in the flu epidemic. After that he paid the rent on the room for the next hundred years. Said all the owner of the hotel had to do was change nothing, keep it clean and, you know, special and every once in a while let it out to a nice couple that looks like maybe they deserve something extra nice."

"Wow," I said, handing over the money I figured I owed.

The clerk pushed back my hand. "It's okay. Compliments of Louis Longines. How was everything? Okay?"

"It was perfect," Gwen answered. "Just perfect. Thanks."

"What became of Louis Longines?" I asked. "He end up in prison or something?"

"Nah. Somebody shot him."

"Oh," I said. I suddenly felt a bond to this invisible, kind-hearted criminal.

"Killed in World War Two by a German bullet. He was a major at the time. Go figure. It was the war that got him, not the crime. But he was a good guy. Real people. Like you two."

"Yeah. Well, thanks."

After a massive breakfast in a little coffee shop that only charged ninety-nine cents for the whoppingest breakfast I ever had, we walked on to Harvard and saw thousands of people, mostly our own age, rallying around the steps of a building. There was the feeling in the air of something about to explode.

32 Nothing I'd ever known on Whalebone Island in the Republic of Nothing had prepared me for this. "Gwen, are you sure you want to get involved in this? Are you sure you're okay?" She had just been through a heck of a lot and, to tell you the truth, I didn't trust this crowd. All around us people were holding up placards against the war and shouting, "No War!" or "Impeach Nixon!" They were loud and they were angry.

"I'm okay. Ian, I'm really glad we're here for this. I'm tired of watching the protests on TV and we're here now. We can finally do something, let the world know that we want the war stopped.

Somebody was starting up a chant of, "Ho Ho, Ho Chi Minh. If he can't do it, no one can." It was like a cheer from a soccer game back at high school.

Gwen was leading me now towards a table where a couple of long-hair freaks were handing out placards. I held onto

Gwen's hand, afraid I'd lose her in this mob and never see her again. If I could have had my way, I would have told Gwen that we had to leave. It looked like trouble to me. We'd been through enough in Boston. Couldn't we just go to a museum as planned, or even a Boston Red Sox game? I liked those lies we threw around and wanted to go home having done something that I could say was true. We weren't scheduled to be on the plane until 6:30. We could just take a nice easy day, get out to the airport in time and be home, asleep in our beds, ready for school tomorrow. It could be that easy.

"Where you from?" the guy handing out protest signs asked. "Who do you represent?" The guy was maybe a couple of years older than us. With his long hair he looked so much like the paintings of Jesus Christ in my Bible back home that I did a double take.

"We're from Canada," Gwen said. "We want to march with you.

"Right on," Jesus said. He pulled out a massive magic marker and began to produce a masterfully psychedelic scripted message on the posterboard reading, "Canadians Against the War!" He handed it to Gwen. I could hear the guy with the megaphone trying to get people to line up for the march and everyone began to shuffle in that direction. "We don't have an official permit for this march," said the voice, "because the pigs wouldn't give us one. They said they won't recognize our march as legitimate."

Everyone booed.

"That means that they might come and try to bust a few heads. But they can't stop us because we are here to end the war. People all across America are out on the streets today. We might not do it today, we might not do it tomorrow, but we're gonna get this thing stopped and nothing can push us back!"

A cheer went up. We were moving now. I felt like a cell in a blood stream. Thousands of people around us. We were moving in the middle of a mass of Americans out exercising

Lesley Choyce

their right of free speech, only something in the bureaucracy wasn't quite right and we were all part of an illegal march. People began to sing, "We shall overcome," and I suddenly thought I was going to cry. It's funny how just then I was thinking of Burnet. Would he be in Nam yet? Probably still in training. I began to realize that the guy on the horn was telling the truth. How could a war continue if a tide of protest like this was going on across the country, if it was happening week after week? I truly didn't want Burnet to come home in a body bag. I think at that moment, tagging along with Gwen whose face was radiant with the passion of a righteous cause, I still felt a hatred for Burnet for seducing Gwen, for getting her pregnant; and then I hated him because he had gone off to be a soldier, to fight for the Americans. He was the perfect sucker for a government that had to preach and package hate in order to create and prolong a war that nobody would have otherwise wanted. It would always be so easy to sell hate.

But most of all, I can now admit, I wanted the war to end because I didn't want to see Burnet come home a hero. I didn't want to believe that you could go away from home, maim and kill and destroy in the name of a patriotic cause and then come back a winner. The irony of Gwen falling for a guy who craved going to war still haunted me. Sure, I knew that Gwen's motives of protest were pure. How could they be otherwise? But now I knew that mine were different. I wanted the war to end quickly so Burnet would never have a chance to fight, never have a chance to come home and gloat and probably get his way for the rest of his life. I wanted to save his stupid ass so he couldn't be a stupid hero, dead or alive. I took the placard from Gwen and held it high in the air. Then I joined her in singing, "We shall overcome some day." We both had our back packs and I didn't want her to have to carry anything else.

"This is beautiful," Gwen said. "I think we should stay here in Boston and work for the peace movement."

I pretended I didn't hear her over the chanting of the crowd.

She did it again; she just scared me to death. We had to go back to school. We couldn't throw that away. I decided I would say nothing. Once again, Gwen had made a leap I was not ready for. How could I ever hold her back? How could I hold onto her? I couldn't live in Boston. I couldn't give up my family and my island. I knew that I had to be sure she was on that plane with me today, no matter what.

Our island seemed so far away as we walked toward the centre of the city and the buildings grew taller all around. Marchers shouted slogans for peace or against war and, as we passed each side street, I saw groups of policemen. They had on helmets and were carrying wooden clubs. I heard their bull horns telling us this was an illegal march and that we should disperse, but not one person was intimidated. I tried to glimpse forward and back to see how many people were ac-tually marching, but I could tell nothing except the fact that there was a flood of protesters as far forward and as far back as I could see. The immensity of the crowd scared me, but if I looked sideways at a stranger who gave me eye contact I would receive a flash of the two-finger V and a warm smile.

There was a division in the street ahead where a small park interrupted the normal flow of the traffic. We were pretty far back from the lead; I could see that the crowd was divided into two now as it streamed around the little triangular park. At the centre was a monument to war and it was being guarded by a group of maybe twenty cops. I saw the hippie with the megaphone try to walk up onto the steps of the monument. At first the police looked like they were going to let him through, but then one of the troopers decided to stop him. The war memorial was surrounded now on all sides by the marchers, thousands of them.

Our leader, still wielding the megaphone, turned back to the crowd and said, "Remember, whatever happens, we are messengers of peace. No violence. No fighting. Passive resist-ance will stop this war. Peace above all things." With that a night stick came down with a hard crack on his head. He slumped onto the steps of the war memorial. A roar went up from the crowd, and all at once, as if a giant living thing, it began to press in towards the centre. The cops left in the middle protecting the monument looked as if they could be crushed. They held up plexiglass shields and began to wave their clubs blindly at anyone who came near.

Gwen was craning her neck, trying to get a look. "What's happening?" she asked.

I tried to edge us away from the centre of the crowd. Already I was feeling as if we were being compressed, packed tight by the hundreds of people surging forward. It was very scary. Up at the monument I heard a pop and saw two small clouds of smoke. "Tear gas," I said. "I have to get you out of here." Then I heard women screaming and I heard the pounding of horse's hooves on pavement. The police were trying to get in to rescue their fellow cops who were trapped inside the mob. They were charging through the streets, scattering the marchers into smaller groups. I heard another pop and saw another cloud.

Pure white terror went through me as people began to drop their signs and try to run. A new batch of uniforms on horses stationed themselves several yards away from us in a line. They had on helmets with dark plexiglass shields so you couldn't see their faces. They carried long wooden clubs and I could see that the numbers on their badges were taped over. I dropped my sign, held tightly onto Gwen's hand and tried to squeeze us out of the crowd. But there was nowhere to go. One young woman reached up to grab the bridle of one of the horses and she was immediately cracked on the head with a stick. I could see blood on her face as she fell to the ground. Four protesters grabbed the cop and pulled him off the horse onto the street. All around I could hear people screaming and crying. I could hear police shouting orders to disperse. But for us there was no place to go.

Our section of the protest, cut off from the rest, was being surrounded by twenty or so horseback policemen and we were being pushed up against the giant glass wall of a bank tower. If Gwen was scared, she didn't show it. I saw only defiance in her face. Any minute she might do something really stupid. We slipped to the back of the crowd, but there was nowhere left to go. We were right up against the green glass wall and people were crushing in on us as the horses paced slowly forward. A whiff of the gas made my eyes water, my mouth sting. Gwen began to cough. Out on the street, I saw bodies of protesters writhing in pain from injuries or from the gas. Hundreds of other protesters simply lay down right in the street, surrounded by dozens of uniforms. We were being crushed now, surrounded on three sides by men on horses slowly but steadily inching in, purposefully jamming us against glass and concrete. I held on tight to Gwen. She shouted out, "It doesn't matter what you do to us. We'll stop the war." Others shouted too as we found it getting harder and harder to breathe. Someone began to cry hysterically. "Back off!" somebody screamed.

We were trapped. Now we were going to be crushed. Certainly they were doing more than just their duty. It was impossible to see their faces; they were faceless, emotionless machines doing the will of the government.

More people began to scream and hysteria was sweeping the crowd. I felt the glass behind me actually begin to flex like a weak skin of ice on the surface of a newly frozen pond. We were about to be crushed to death or killed in an explosion of broken glass. A woman fell under the hooves of the horse and she shrieked. Except for the cry of the injured, a curious quiet had come over the crowd and as I looked around I saw pure, undiluted terror in the faces around me.

Why I did what I did next cannot be fully explained. Desperate options come from deep within. Maybe it was my mother, although it was so absurd that it seems unlikely it would have been in her psychic bag of tricks. Maybe it was one of those vague, distant spirits I had met in a dream. I knew I had to do something. It was just like someone had thrown a switch. And what I did was begin to sing, "Oh Canada." I sang it like I was a kid in grade two who would belt it out on a good morning as he just arrived at school. I'm sure it must have sounded off-key and warbly as I belted out, "Oh Canada, glorious and free!"

My guess is that most people in the crowd, including the cops whose horses were in breathing distance of my face, had never heard the national anthem of their northern neighbour. Gwen joined in, sounding shaky but celestial. And at that moment the horses stopped, backed off ever so slightly. This mob, taut as a living, single wild creature, suddenly relaxed its communal muscle. One single policemen lifted his face shield and looked straight at me. Horses shuffled backwards and protesters began to leak out of the crushed crowd from the sides. Gwen sang a few more lines, stumbled on the words and then stopped, out of breath. The only cop with a face was looking straight at me and, in his eyes, I recognized pure hate. He had wanted to see us cave the glass wall in. He wanted to see blood and jagged glass driven into the bodies of anyone who would speak out against the American war. He had that ugly passion of a true patriot in his eyes.

I could not look away from his face. I should have sidled out of there like the others, safe now on the side street and making a run for freedom. But there was something in the locked horns of our stare. It was what I felt then and what he told me in his silence that suddenly made me understand war, understand how someone becomes an enemy. I blinked back my hate and tried to move away with Gwen, but he was headed toward us. I could see the eyes even better, see the puffy, half-shaven face. Whatever level of calm had overtaken me to save us all with a national anthem was now gone. I felt animosity, not for anything this man had done but for the fiendish look in his face. Gwen was tugging at my sleeve now. We had a clear exit, we could have got away but I stood my ground. He towered above me now, his foaming horse breathing heavily. I saw the billy club raised. Why would he use it on me if I was posing no physical threat? I believed that this was the line he would not cross over. He would not actually hit me because, I wanted to believe, there was still some common bond of humanity that would prevent him from hitting an unarmed good intentioned kid from Nova Scotia.

I was looking at his face, his eyes. I saw the stick raised in the air, saw it shudder and hesitate, and then without seeing it, I could feel the air slice, feel it descending towards my head. I dodged out of its way and as I did, I saw Gwen dive forward at him. I screamed. She was about to take the goddamn thing on her own skull to save me. I knew I had made a big mistake. We should have run. But another hand, the anonymous hand of a fellow protester, had reached up and grabbed the end of the stick and was trying to pull the cop off his horse. Gwen grabbed the cop's wrist and was biting it hard enough to draw blood. The horse reared up and I nearly fell over backwards but kept my footing enough to pull Gwen off the policeman and away as the horse came back down on all fours and a can of tear gas went off.

We got far enough away from the gas so that we were not blinded with tears or choking, but we were disoriented and shaky enough that two other patrolmen on foot came up and pushed our arms up against our backs. "We saw that," one of them said. "You're both under arrest." They handcuffed us and led us quickly to a nearby van. We were thrown into the back of the paddy wagon onto the floor. The truck was nearly full of other protesters. We lay panting and coughing, and it took some time before I could speak. I pulled Gwen up off the floor as the truck began to speed off. "You all right?" I saw blood on her mouth. "Are you hurt?"

Still unable to speak, she shook her head, smiled at me and

Lesley Choyce

wiped the blood on her sleeve. Finally, holding her throat and gasping, she pointed to the blood on her clothes and said, "It's not mine. It was his. I have very sharp teeth."

Once Gwen got her bearings, she shook off the fear that we had both felt and treated our arrest as an adventure. I took a bit of glory from my comrades as the "Crazy Canuck who sang some wacko Canadian song."

In the cell, along with at least twenty others, we waited for two hours, singing together and swapping stories about what had happened on the street. For the most part, the outrage we had felt was gone and I couldn't help but think that this was the jovial comraderie of soldiers who had just done battle. A strange irony. We were called out in pairs or one by one, and word came back that we would all be released after the posting of bail.

Much to my shock, it was the horse patrolmen who had tried to bash my brains out who came to ask Gwen and me to join him in an office. My first surprise was that his voice sounded strangely familiar. He had a New York accent like Ben and he was about the same age. Inside a small, windowless office with a silent uniformed policewoman present he asked me, "You both Canadian?"

"Nova Scotian," I answered. It was a typical Bluenose reflex.

"Nova Scotian, huh? What are you doing down here?"

"We came to protest the war," Gwen answered defiantly. She looked very weak now and tired. I needed to get her out of here, to get her home, and my mind was filled with a wasp's nest of impossible entanglements.

"It was an illegal protest. You need permits for this sort of thing. You were breaking the law." He was rubbing his bandaged wrist now and it looked like the blood was leaking through the bandage.

"I didn't know that," I lied. "We didn't come down to try to break laws. We only wanted to try to stop the war."

He breathed heavily. "I got a kid over there. He's about

your age. Fighting for his country. Doesn't want communists to fucking take over. You kids know nothing." The cop was looking down at the floor. The hate was all sucked out of him and a profound sadness filled the room. Gwen looked over at the policewoman but she looked away at a small framed picture of a Vermont hillside on the wall.

"Maybe we don't want to see your kid get messed up over there," I said. "Maybe we care, too."

But he wanted no more of war debate. He had let his other self out of his uniform for a brief instant and now he had crawled back into his job. "You want to know what I can have you charged with?"

We said nothing.

"Unlawful assembly, assault and battery of a police officer and crossing international borders for the purpose of creating a disturbance. That's a federal offence, by the way."

"We don't care," Gwen sassed back, but I didn't let her get anything else out.

I decided to forgo any sort of logical argument now. I acted like I was scared. It didn't take too much acting. "We'd like very much to go home if we could — to our families."

The cop shook his head. "Jesus H. Christ," he said. "You come down here and disrupt a city and you want to go crawling back home to mommy and daddy like nothing happened?"

We said nothing. I was looking for a way out. I was thinking about Gwen's father, realizing that if they actually did some sort of check on us they'd figure out who she was. I didn't want it any more complicated than it already was.

"Can I make a phone call or something?" I asked.

"Gonna call the Canadian Communist party to come bail you out?"

I shrugged. The policewoman got up and brought a desk phone with a long extension over to us. "Here," she said. "Call."

I guess I had already sorted it out. It was very simple.

There was only one person who was going to get us out of this and, oh boy, did I want to get us out of here and on that 6:30 plane home for Halifax. I pulled out a phone number from my wallet and told the operator I was calling collect. My father answered the phone. It was the middle of the afternoon, but he sounded like he had been taking a nap. "Where are you?" he asked.

"I'm in jail. In Boston. Gwen is with me."

"In jail? What the hell for? I knew about the trip, but what on earth did you do?"

"We protested the war."

"Oh." There was a bit of silence. It was hard to know what my father was thinking. "What do you need?"

I asked the cop. "What do we need to get out of here?"

"You need a goddamn lawyer and probably about a thousand dollars in bail."

"Dad?"

"Yeah," he said. "I heard."

"I want to get Gwen home," I said, my voice cracking. "Today. She's not feeling too well." It was true. She looked pale and for good reason.

The cop was shaking his head. "No way are you going to get out of here by supper time, kid."

My father heard that too. "Tell me where you are, what you're being charged with and who I can talk to there. We're going to hang up and I'm going to have you out of there within an hour."

I gave him the whole scoop. All the while the cop was nudging me like my time was up.

"Sit tight. I'll have you out. Put the officer on the phone."

"Thanks Dad." I hadn't called him that for a long time. I handed the phone to the cop. "He wants to talk to you."

Reluctantly the man whose son was at war took the phone. Whatever it was my father said, it had some sort of impact on the cop, because by the time he hung up, he had already begun to treat us nicer. Less than an hour later, the cell door opened. We were told to leave. No charges, no nothing. "Need a ride to airport?" the lady cop asked. Gwen was very sleepy now, very tired, and I had to help her to walk.

I gulped. "Yes please," I said as politely as I could.

Two hours later we were on the Air Canada flight headed for home. My head was swimming with love, swimming with war and swimming with history. When my father met us at the airport as we cleared customs, he gave me a big hug and hugged Gwen as well. I thought he was going to gush all over us but he said very little. "Get in, kids. We're going home."

Gwen lay down in the back of the Buick and fell asleep immediately. I sat up front and it was so good just to be with my father again that I felt a warm glow of pride. He had come through for me. "How'd you do it?'

"Politics, son. It's a powerful tool. I talked to Colin as soon as we hung up. He agreed it would look very bad on my career if my kid spent much time in a Boston jail. It might make the party look bad, make the province look bad. He got on the phone to the governor of Massachusetts who got on the phone to the mayor of Boston who immediately told the police chief to have you released. It was all in the politics. Colin didn't want this little blot on any of us."

I was suddenly puzzled. I had guessed he had pulled a few strings, but I was annoyed by the motive. "Is that why you got the premier to make the phone call, because you didn't want it to look bad?" For a minute I felt like I didn't know who this man was. Did he save our asses to protect the goddamn Tory party?

My father shook his head. "No way, Ian. I went that route because I knew it was the quickest way to get you out. If I had to, I would have gone down there with Kirk's harpoon cannon and blasted you two out of jail. Can't allow some foreign government to hold hostage two citizens of the republic."

I sank back in the seat. I knew he was telling me the truth

and knew it had been a long while since he had mentioned the republic. It was still alive, somewhere inside him. And right now we were headed back to the island. Tomorrow I would wake up and I'd go to school. If Gwen was feeling up to it, we'd catch the bus together there in front of Burnet's house, and by mid-morning we'd be taking a vocabulary test in English as if nothing at all in our world had changed.

33 The lights were on at Gwen's house but the car wasn't there. I walked her inside and there was no one at home, no sound except for the static of the interstellar receiver back in her father's shop. It was picking up intermittent static bursts from a quasar perhaps or a failing star somewhere in a distant galaxy, and it gave me an eerie feeling of my own insignificance. Gwen sank one last time into my arms and she said, "It's okay, really, Ian. They probably all went out for a drive." It was, after all, a warm pre-summer evening.

"You're sure?"

"Yes," she said, kissing me on the lips. Planets tilted slightly out of kilter on their axes, stars slowed down on their breakneck race away from the centre of the universe. A burst of hot static shot through the room. My father was waiting in the car. After I left Gwen and sat down in the dark Buick, he said, "Someday you'll tell me about Boston, okay?"

"Right." I knew exactly what he meant. He knew that it was more than the war protest, more than the arrest. He had watched me kissing Gwen through the window and he knew that while he had been gone, his son had grown up; he knew I had changed and it would take more than a few minutes of father/son heart-to-heart to get to know me again.

As we drove back to our old house, the sound of pebbles

and shells crunching beneath our tires on the gravel road, I felt the bond again with my old man. Maybe he had not changed so much after all. Maybe he still was my old man. Soon he would find his way back to his island home and to us. It's one thing for a man to storm out of his home in a rage after years of pent-up frustration and chase across the continent, perhaps to Alberta, for a new job, more money and a new life. But Everett McQuade would never have done that. His had been a silent, almost unadmitted parting, a melting from the old ways. His intentions had been good. Maybe one day he would become a great politician, an international statesman, someone who would bring world unity and global peace. But even that, to me, would not be quite enough. I wanted my father back with us. I wanted him living and working on the island. A weekend replica of my old man was not enough.

"Potholes are in the exact same places they were forty years ago," he said, his face lit up by the red and green lights on the dash.

"Oughta have it paved. Somebody should get the MLA to look into it," I said.

He shook his head. He knew that none of us on the island wanted paved roads. We'd live with potholes. Pavement meant more traffic, more tourists, more change. We wanted the island to stay roughly the same. No one was more adamant about that than the refugees — Ackerman and the Phillips family. My mother, Casey and I agreed. Let the rest of the world be paved black and blue with asphalt, but let us have our island without tarmac.

We pulled to a stop in front of the house. The light was on in the kitchen. My father turned the car off and killed the headlights. I went to open the door, then noticed that his face was frozen, his eyes fixed on the light of the kitchen window. My mother sat at the table, her hands outstretched on the table top in front of her. Directly across from her was Ben Ackerman. His hands lay on top of my mother's. Their eyes were

Lesley Choyce

wide open, locked intently on each other. They weren't speaking.

If it wasn't for the cold glacier that set up camp in the back of my skull just then, if it wasn't for the fact that I had marshalled all of my forces of disbelief into action, and if it wasn't for the fact that my father took a short choking gulp of air into his lungs, I might have believed I was looking at two people in love. But I could not believe that. "Ben calls it psychic transfer," I said. "It's his scientific name for it. Mom has been teaching him how to read her thoughts. He says he's always been interested in telepathy. He and Mom have become close friends." I tried hard to contain the rattle in my voice.

"What are they doing?" he asked me. I don't think he had heard a word I said.

"They're communicating," I said.

"Why is he looking at her like that?"

"Eye contact is important. It puts them on the same wavelength, I think."

My father jerked open the door. I saw the look of anger; I could feel the brooding, smouldering fire. I half-expected to see his clothes in flames. I grabbed his sleeve as he started to get out of the car. "You've been gone a long time," I told him. "The weekends, the vacations, the visits. They're not enough. She needed a friend." I saw, for maybe the first time, a heavy weight on my old man's shoulders, a blanket of defeat trying to smother the wrath. "Let's go in," I said.

The door opened and I stepped through first. Dorothy and Ben had let go of each other's hands and had unlinked their minds. Or so I supposed. I, too, as my mother's son, had become a disciple of these psychic games. But I had always been an observer. Not like Ben who dived into the metaphysical pool headfirst and had barely come up to gulp the air of the real world again.

My mother was on her feet rushing towards us. "What a treat," she said. "Both of you here at once." And I didn't know just then if she meant Dad and me or Ben and her husband. Both of the men she loved. Oh, I doubted very much that the two of them had been physically intimate, beyond the language of hands and "eyebeams," but I knew deep down that they had developed a love for each other and from what we had seen through the window, theirs was a more passionate intermingling of minds than any I had ever seen.

"It's so good to be home," my father said, the weight of defeat still tugging on his frame so that now he seemed a heavier, bulkier man who had shouldered the worries of the world. He and my mother locked in an embrace and I saw one minute tear trickle down my mother's face, spill from her cheek and disappear into the dust on the hardwood floor.

"I should be going," Ben said. Guilt was written all over him, even though, I suppose by civilized standards, he had nothing to be guilty about. Ben was a gentleman and a good friend to both my mother and to me. He had never understood my father, but the two of them had never had the chance to get to know each other. Maybe in some other world with some other set of mores and values, the two of them could have shared this exquisite woman who was my mother. Maybe one could have been intimate with her mind and soul while another loved her heart and body.

My father did not look at him. My mother did, but said nothing. Her eyes simply told him it was okay, that nothing was wrong; it was not his fault.

On his way out the door, Ben turned to me and asked, in a half-whisper, "Did everything go okay in Boston?"

I could not begin to recount the whole tale. "We were treated very well in Boston," I said. "Dad came to pick up Gwen and me at the airport."

Before Ben had a chance to walk out the door, the phone rang. I moved across the room and answered it. It was Gwen.

"My parents just came back," she said. "My grandfather's missing. He took Hants Buckler's dory out fishing late this afternoon but didn't come back. At first my mother wasn't worried. She said he'd always been around boats. She said he could swim like a dolphin if anything went wrong. She was sure he'd be okay. It would be good for him. But it's so late. No sign of the boat. My parents have driven all around the island and can't find him."

Everyone in the room could tell from my face it was an emergency. "We'll be right over," I said. "Stay put." The simple act of cradling the phone back in its place seemed painful. I was thinking about the lie that had brought her grandfather back to life; I was thinking about all the lies.

"Gwen's grandfather went out in Hants' boat and he didn't come back."

My father let go of my mother. "It's not a cold night. If he stayed with the boat, he should be okay. Not much of a sea running. Light onshore breeze, down to nothing at all by now. Wouldn't drive him out to sea." This would have been something my old man would have known instinctively, even in the dark, even though he had not even had a look at the sea since we arrived on the island. Some things "stay with you in the blood," as he was fond of saying. Like wind direction. And wave height. In the old days, my old man could wake up, open one eye and only get a glimpse of the sky through a crack in the window shade and know the weather for the day.

I looked at Ben and we silently admitted our conspiracy to each other again. Could Delaney swim? Did he know anything about boats? What other infinite number of details had we forgotten in our attempts to save a hound of the street and give Gwendolyn her grandfather back from the dead?

"I'll call the Coast Guard," my father said. "They'll be a while getting here, though. We'll pick up Ernie and get on over to Eager's boat. It's big and it's fast."

"What can I do?" Ben asked.

"Better come too," my old man said. "Might need a doctor."

"I've got a pot of tea already hot," my mother said, as if the sweet elixir of bitter tea would be enough to save a man lost at sea. But it was the kind of thing that would mean so much to my old man. She was off to the kitchen and back before the call to the Coast Guard was through. She handed me the giant thermos. "You take care of your father," she said, as she handed it to me.

The tea was a link to our past. It was the old thermos my father and I had used when we went to sea on those early, magical mornings in the days of fishing, in the days when life was simple, when life was good.

My father next called Lambert and Eager who said they were ready to go, any time. We drove over to pick up Gwen's father who was pulling the two headlights out of his old Ford. He had a spool of wire around one arm and jumped into the car with us. I saw Gwen standing in the doorway but I didn't get out to say anything. "We'll wire these up to the battery on the boat," Tennessee Ernie said. "I've never been out to sea before," he said. "What's it like for him if he's out there now?"

"It's dark and it's lonely. And there's two kinds of luck you have out there alone in a boat."

"It doesn't look good, does it?" Ernie asked.

"Just relax," my father said. "It doesn't look one way or the other until you get out there and stare it in the face. We got half a moon and lots of stars. That's a good start."

As we bumped over the road towards Lambert's wharf, I wished for once we did have the roads paved. I wished we could get there faster. I closed my eyes and tried my mother's trick. If anyone could tune in old Duke, it should have been me. We had become good friends. I loved that crazy old saint and felt a sudden pang of loss. I tried to reshape his image in my mind but it wasn't there. I tried to remember how we had conjured him up, so near perfect to the photograph, conjured him up out of the rabble, the pile of old clothes and battered souls who had huddled in Grand Central Station. But he just wasn't there.

The car smelled of man sweat. It wasn't the high school locker room smell. It was the smell of men on a mission, the smell of men with a job to get done, a life to be saved. It was the sweat of fear and necessity. My father pulled up to Lambert's wharf and lay hard on the horn as we all piled out. Lambert and Eager came charging out the front door. They were cursing at each other and pulling themselves together as they came. A zipper up here, a shirt tail tucked in there. A hoist of a suspender over the shoulder.

"We got no lights on the boat," Lambert admitted as we piled onto the boat. "Have to go at it near blind."

Ernie held up his two headlights and wire. "Show me where your battery is. Only take me a few minutes to rig these."

Lambert handed me a flashlight and pointed towards the battery box. I led Gwen's father to it as they fired up the boat and started to untie the lines. Despite the darkness, we were already underway as Ernie hooked up the wires and ran them outside. It was the first time I'd ever been alone with Gwen's father, and as I held the light for him in the cramped corners and he made the sparks fly as he wired in the lights, he spoke first. "I know all about Duke Delaney," he said. "I probably could have stopped him today. I knew he wasn't my father-in-law. Gwen's grandfather was a mean son of a bitch who hated my guts. He was a very cruel man to Gwen's mother and he carried the hate around in his heart. Duke is just the opposite. I don't know how you did it, but you saved Gwen's mother from cracking up. You might have saved our marriage as well."

"But I made a mistake. Look what I got him into."

"You didn't make a mistake. I should have stopped him but Gwen's mother insisted. He had been a great man on the water, she said — boats, fishing. It was all he had lived for at one point."

"Unfortunately, it isn't him out there in the dory," I said.

As he connected the final wire, the car headlights lit up the inside of the boat with stark, intense light. We looked at each other in the blinding white illumination. "When I saw the first bomb go off in the desert," he said, "I thought it was the most beautiful thing I'd ever seen. I thought I had been part of one of the most splendid creations anyone had ever attempted. I had this feeling that the world would now be safe, it would be perfect. There'd be endless energy, unlimited everything for everyone." Ernie taped up the wires and then handed one of the lights through an open window to my father, then another to Eager on the other side. The cabin was now a pale yellow. I had looked at the headlight and I was half blinded. All I could see were white spots. "Then Hiroshima, then Nagasaki. But I still believed. Then I thought that if we could do it bigger, do it so big and horrendous that no one would ever dare challenge us or go to war with any nation for fear we would step in and annihilate them, I thought we'd have a peaceful world."

"But it didn't work out that way," I said.

"And then all the magic was gone. If nothing could save us, then there was no point in further research. I didn't know that for sure until I got here. You did more good in a few days by taking Duke Delaney off the streets of New York and bringing him here than Einstein and Fermi and all those years of research did — along with millions of dollars."

Ernie pulled something out of his pocket. A folded sheet of paper. "Read this," he said.

I unfolded it and aimed the flashlight on it. It was a poem without a title. It read:

I'm near the end but stumble on —
the haunting truth, I'm nowhere near.
The coast goes on like this, too far to match.
Its million miles will call my bluff,
remind me I know nothing yet.

The sun stains the other side
of the inlet now.

Lesley Choyce

I see the other shore.
With a narrow blade of copper light
I see the green, tall crown of trees.

The farther shore reminds me this:
if I were set to circle round
the continent's coast
I'd end back here, a stranger still.
I could not come back to tie the knot
of ending to beginning
since change still rules this ragged edge
and sets my seasons spinning.

I realized that Duke Delaney had been a poet after all. I had tangled him up in a beautiful conspiracy of hope and he could not help but accept the lie. Now this.

"Whatever you do, Ian, don't feel sorry for him. I think Duke believes he had dreamed you and Ben Ackerman into existence."

Up on deck, I surveyed the darkness beyond the skim of the headlights. "Where are we going?" I asked my father, standing by the wheel with Lambert.

"Only two places to look," Lambert answered.

"Shag Rock and The Singing Sisters."

"Right," my old man said. "What's the tide doing?"

It was a rhetorical question. Tide was like wind and wave. He knew it instinctively.

"Low," Eager answered. "She's all the way out. That's good news and that's bad news."

"What does he mean?" Ernie asked me.

"Means that it's likely pulled the boat further out, but it also means that Shag Rock and the shoals at the Singing Sisters will be up out of the water. Anything that washes off Whalebone seems to go to one of those two places. Duke could be on one or the other."

"Gonna be tough getting in close to the Shag," my father said.

Shag Rock was a low stark island of rock that was visited only by gulls and crabs. No trees, no shrubs, only lichen and sea creatures in the sea ponds and little lagoons. All jagged rock everywhere, not a place for a big boat like this to get in close. The Singing Sisters were a series of small island rocks, each one at this tide probably not much bigger than a man stretched out. If Duke was out here and if he had landed, I hoped he had made it to Shag Rock.

"Pull in close to the boot," I told Lambert. "Water's deep there. I'll jump off onto her and you go check out the Sisters, then come back for me." The boot was a little peninsula of Shag Rock that stretched out into the sea. It looked a lot like the boot of Italy without Sicily trailing off at the end.

Ben didn't like my idea. "Sounds dangerous."

My father agreed. "Yeah. I don't like it. It's dark out there, and all those slippery rocks. But you're right. We'll never be able to get a look at everything — can't get in close to all those nooks and crannies. I'll go with you."

"No," Ben said. "Let me go. You need to make sure that somebody can find their way back to us."

My father was shaking his head but he knew there was truth in it. Lambert and Eager were good fishermen, but they were not to be trusted. My old man was probably remembering the fire on their boat from years back.

"Coming up on the Shag," Eager said.

"Cut the Jesus engine 'fore we gouge a hole in us, for Chrissake."

Eager throttled the engine down.

"See if you can find the boot," my father told Lambert. He grabbed my flashlight and checked it. "Don't try anything fancy," he told me.

"Why don't you let me go with the boy?" Ernie asked now.

"Can you swim if you fall in the drink?"

"I could give it a try," Ernie answered.

"Stay put. What about you, Ben?"

"I once won the fifty meter freestyle in college," he boasted.

"Here we go," Lambert said. "Good thing there's no sea runnin'."

"Good thing is right," echoed Eager. "Give us just a few seconds here. We'll drift in close. You jump and then I'll rev her up quick so we don't turn her into loose lumber."

"Ready. Go!" Lambert shouted as we saw the shiny wet ledge of rock creep up close alongside from out of the darkness.

---

34 My previous visit to Shag Rock had been when I was maybe eight years old. It was a hot, clear summer day. No wind. No waves. I'd been up at sunrise with my old man and we'd been fishing all morning. No luck. Not a single bite. It was exquisitely beautiful on the calm sea, but it was also a dead world with not a bird, not a fish anywhere. With nothing to catch, the morning had turned into something other than work.

My father cut the engine and let us drift. We wouldn't go far. Like so many things drifting away from Whalebone Island, we found our way to Shag Rock. Without saying a word, my father dropped anchor, tore off his shirt and pants and dove straight into the deep, immaculately clear, dark blue water. I did the same. It was the first time I'd ever actually gone swimming off a boat at sea. But we were only yards away from Shag Rock and we swam for it. Instead of hoisting ourselves up onto the first ledge, my father led us up a narrow channel cleft between the rocks to a sheltered pool surrounded on all sides. Long fronds of kelp slithered along my body as we swam, a feeling that still haunts me to this day — those long, almost silky, fingers of seaweed stroking me.

All was stillness once we were in the pool. But if the sea had been a lifeless place today, it seemed that all of the watery kingdom was here in this basin of crystalline water, thirty feet across and maybe only ten feet at its centre depth. I dared not put a foot on a single rock for every square inch was covered with spiny sea urchins with long, needle-like probes or grotesquely huge barnacles sharp as razor blades. Blue crabs scuttled everywhere. Magnified by the clear water, everything looked surrealistically large. I cocked back my head and just floated.

Suddenly there was noise. Chaos above us in the sky which was now a jumbled puzzle of black and white laughing gulls who, after a few minutes of studying us, decided we were harmless and settled back to roost on the rocks around this little sea within the sea. I noticed now that the shores were populated with adolescent sea gulls — large, brown mottled, fluff-ball gull chicks, each as big as a hen and looking nothing like a full-fledged herring gull. Some were tucked into clefts, others simply strolled leisurely along the rocks until a parent was found for company.

I don't think I was looking at him at all. Maybe I had forgotten my father was there, forgotten how I got here and what this was all about. Clearly, I had been transported into another world. The sound startled me at first. A loud whoop echoed off the rock walls, followed by an uncontrollable laughter. I turned myself around in the water to see my old man floating on his back effortlessly, as if he was lying on a bed, his arms locked behind his head, his elbows cocked out to the side, floating and laughing.

I'm sure I had heard him laugh before but not like this. I admit, it scared me. Everett McQuade was a man with a sense of humour. Yes, he chuckled, he told a joke, but I had never heard him laugh like this. He let out a whoop, turned over on his stomach, dove to the bottom of the pool and came shooting like a Polaris missile back to the surface, his arms outstretched with a lobster the size of a small motorcycle lofted above him. As he shot up into the air, he let out another laugh, heaved the lobster half-heartedly in my direction and I watched as the giant claws pinched the sun from the sky as it descended, then touched the water and began a slow, comical descent back to the bottom.

"Today, Ian, the world has no purpose and we are obliged to do nothing, kiddo. You and me. We are free." Later, we lay sunning ourselves on a rock shelf, dozens of the half-grown sea gulls sleeping just feet away from us. We went home fishless but happy. And I would never understand why neither of us said a word about that morning to my mother.

But now it was a world of dark, not light. The Shag was a dangerous place to be, even on this rather placid night. Ben and I watched the lights of the boat skirt around the rest of the tiny island and move off to check the Singing Ladies.

"Just for the record, I *can* swim," Ben said.

"I think I believe you. Anyway, I'm glad I'm not here alone."

With flashlights on, we groped our way to a somewhat higher, dry ledge. "Turn off your light," Ben said. "Just sit here for a minute. Let's let our eyes adjust. There's probably enough reflection off the water to allow us better walking if we don't use the lights."

He was right. I could sense the pupils of my eyes dilate until they were willing to allow for vision just by sucking in all of this cold empty moonlight, starlight and sealight. There was even a faint phosphorescent glow of the sea. And again the surreal quality of this place seemed so gripping that I wondered if anything was ever real. Could any of this be connected to the real world of the mainland or even Whalebone

Island? In the distance, I could see the headlights of Lambert's boat and further to the north I could see scattered lights of houses and the odd street light or two strung out like a haphazard carnival in the dark beyond.

"It's ironic, isn't it?" Ben said, not quite ready to stand up, find his island legs and begin the search. "Delaney, I mean. It reminds me of being a doctor. Cure a man of one ill only to set him up for the next one. Fix up a kid with a knife wound only to make sure he's in good health to be gunned down by a neighbour. Rescue someone from the streets of hell and drop him on the beaches of paradise only to ... well, the story's not over yet." But I had a feeling we were not to find a city man like Delaney pulled to sea in a tiny boat, happy and healthy.

"Let's stay together," I said. "Follow me."

I led Ben along the ridge of the loose rock. Gulls awoke and took to the night skies with awful, terrifying banshee shrieks. I took careful steps and advised Ben at every toehold of loose stone or jagged rock. On the lee side of the island I found an oar and carried it with me.

"It looks like one that might have been with the dory, but it's hard to tell."

There was nothing else on the perimeter, nothing save gulls, each one a nightmare of white wing and flapping air as it launched itself into the darkness. Dozens were in the air now, a swirling maelstrom of angry wings and beaks. I trusted a gull, though, not to attack a thing it did not understand and clearly these gulls would not understand our presence nor trust our intentions. They'd know it was best to stay out of harm's way. I used the oar as a walking stick as we stumbled around the moonscape toward the pool at the centre of the island. And then I saw him. The half-moon was high now and allowed enough light to see with great cold clarity. I saw the body of a man face down in the centre of the pool where my father and I had once discovered pure freedom.

As we scuttled down to the water line and the scree shifted

and slid beneath us, I felt again how unsure my footing was in the world of the living. At every turn I felt my good intentions would be swallowed up, digested by some great haphazardous, incomprehensible scheme. It was a vast, impersonal network of events that insisted there was no purpose, no action worth attempting that would not be undone by the permeating, nauseating madness that directed life.

Ben took the oar from me as I stood mute and helpless on the shore line and he jumped out onto a rock outcropping in the pool, then carefully, delicately, pulled the body to the shore. I helped my friend, my accomplice in this unintended murder; I helped him lift the bloated, cold and sea-ravaged remains of what was once a man to the shore. As we rolled him over on his back, some stupid impulse made me shine my flashlight in his face — a horrible, empty portrait of what was once old Duke. His cheeks were bruised and scraped and something had been biting on his neck. And then I stepped back, tripping, nearly falling into the water as I saw the mouth appear to move. I half-expected the dead man to talk which might have been less gruesome than the sight of the small, blue-green crab that emerged from the mouth, still tugging with one claw at the tongue it was trying to steal from the victim.

Ben kicked at the crab and sent it catapulting through the air into the water. I switched off my light and breathed the salt air of this sad, cold night into my lungs, thinking of Gwen, and wishing I had not been born. He rolled Duke back on his stomach and tried to empty him of the enormous weight of the sea he had swallowed. A drowning man, he explained, can swallow almost half his weight. "We'll never be able to carry him like this." It was a slow, difficult job accompanied by ghastly sounds made as the water was released and given back to the sea.

As we saw the boat lights approach, we staggered and lurched, our poor dead brother in tow as we made our way back to the boot. Ben and I never again said anything to each other about how we had inadvertently led old Duke to his death by falsifying his life, turning him into a grandfather and a fisherman, a man who understood boats. I was sure that what we had done was to bring more pain and suffering into the lives of Gwen's family.

The next day I awoke to the sound of someone knocking at my door. I got up and threw on an old pair of pants and walked shirtless through the cold house. It was Gwen. She had her books with her. I could read nothing from her face, though.

"I'm not going to school," I said. "Not today. I'm so sorry about your grandfather." I didn't know what else to say.

Gwen walked in and closed the door behind her. She let out a sigh. Her face looked pale. I knew she had been crying. So much had happened in such a short time. Was it possible that we had been punished somehow for our decision to go to Boston, to end the pregnancy? She sat down at the kitchen table. I saw the bedroom door to my parents room open a crack. My mother looked out but then closed it again, left us alone. I sat down at the table across from Gwen. She leaned across, cupped my face with her two warm, beautiful hands. "Don't look so sad," she said.

Out of her math textbook she pulled a folded square of paper. "Read this," she said. "It's a poem he wrote yesterday. He's been writing poems ever since he got here." And so I read the second work of the man from the streets of New York. The words were printed in a neat, stylized handwriting:

> *The shrunken man, indifferent, nameless, faceless in despair*
> *finds new strength in strangers turned towards heaven.*
> *Yet reaching back to earth with arms*
> *that lift the roof of hell*
> *they find me floating up into the sky of blue,*
> *the sun a net of warm love on my pain*

until I find I have surpassed the one I was
and settle in to sleep the sleep of seas and sons
and sheets as soft as floating air.

"I think I understand this," I said. "I'm sure I do. Your grandfather was quite a guy. He was very deep."

Gwen shook her head. "He wasn't my grandfather."

"Of course he was."

Gwen knew the truth, though. "My mother believed he was my grandfather. I believed it until last night when I found this and his other writings. I guess my father knew for quite a while."

"It's hard for me to explain," I said.

"It's okay. I read all his stuff." She pulled out a notebook from her pile of books. "It's all in here. Some poetry, some other things. It all fits together. I think you gave me a very precious gift. I don't think Duke Delaney would have regretted any of it. He drowned at sea and it wasn't your fault. That part was an accident. Duke had believed that part of him was my grandfather. He was fitting the puzzle together of his unlived life from what my mother told him. He believed he understood boats. Funny how well he had become the best of what my grandfather actually was."

"How's your mother?"

"Not good. But I think she's still better than if he had never come into our lives. My father and I have decided not to tell her the truth. I don't like the feeling of it, but I guess that maybe there is something to the notion of a *good* lie."

I hung my head, thinking about all my attempts at the necessary lies, the good lies.

"How are you feeling?" I asked.

"I'm glad we went to Boston. I feel terrible about the drowning. But I don't want to hang around home today."

"Why?"

"Because I want to be with you."

I looked at the pile of books. "Are we going to go to

school," I asked, thinking of all that had happened, "and pretend that nothing has happened?"

"No," she said. "I think you just changed my mind. Let's forget about school today. I want to spend as much time with you as I can right now. I think I'm still trying to figure out who *you* really are."

~~~~~~

35 My father stayed for a few days until he felt that there was just too much pressing business in Halifax awaiting him. He tried again to convince my mother to bring us to the city with him where, he assured us, we would all be very happy. But I'm sure he knew it was a lost cause. My mother would have none of it. And neither would Casey or I.

I don't think they ever talked about Ben. And as I watched my old man's Buick spit gravel from its tires as he left us once again, I wondered if there could really be anything wrong with my mother's relationship with Ben. What did I understand of adults? Not much. My mother would always be a mystery to me, but so would my father. How could he leave us here like this, anyway? What could possibly be so important that it would take him away from the island, away from this family? Maybe it was right then that my mother had this other "lover." After all, my father was deeply smitten with politics. Maybe there are irreconcilable powers that pull things apart, push others together.

It was like Tennessee Ernie's lecture to me about the forces of the universe, the "news" he received daily on his backyard dish-like antenna. Galaxies colliding, suns blinking out, black holes sucking everything into an intense overwrought gravity pit of nothingness, the entire universe pushing outward, everything driving away from the centre of its creation, then at some point flagging, slowing down and reversing, drawing itself back together.

As my father drove to Halifax, I went to visit Ben again. The first floor of his house was framed in now. There was no sheathing on the walls but the two-by-six studs made for wonderful walls of air. He was sitting in the middle of the subfloor, now solid, now nailed down, and watching a sparrow that had alighted on the lintel where a window would be.

"Someday there will even be a roof," he told me.

"And then what?" I asked.

"Then I'll move in," he said.

"But you'll still be alone," I said. "This is a house big enough for, well, a family."

He ignored my point. "As I build, I'm using my mind to put a kind of personal life force into the walls. Nothing you could see or even detect, but I believe that as a person builds, he puts more into a thing than just the physical elements. Cutting wood, piecing it together, it's only logical that you transfer some of your own energy, some of your own spirit into a thing until it becomes well, sort of, alive."

"I believe that," I said, because I knew what construction was like. I knew that there was always a return above and beyond the mere physical creation of anything.

"A metaphysical dividend," Ben said.

"Something like that. But you, Doc, you need more than just a house. You need to find someone to share this with." My voice had finally formulated what had been in my thoughts. I wanted to see Ben with a woman, a woman other than my mother. Perhaps if he could find himself a lover or a wife, his alliance with my mother would ease off and maybe, just maybe, that would help bring my mother and father back closer together. Maybe it would cause my old man to give up on his Halifax mistress — Tory politics.

Ben looked down at a galvanized ten penny nail in his hand. "There have been women, kid, believe me. Very sophisticated women. New York ladies. With money, with education, with heels this high." He held the nail between his two palms up to the sunlight. "But it never worked out." He pressed the nail between his hands until the tip began to drive into the soft flesh. "They had a bad habit of doing nasty things to me." The tip of the nail now broke the skin. I saw blood. I snatched the nail away from him. "They had a way of using me up, Ian, until I felt like someone had hollowed me out with nothing left inside but pain and hurt." He rubbed at the spot of blood in his palm. "No, I'm happier here. Like this."

I walked around the perimeter of the house and put my hand on the corner posts, ran it along the smooth window sills and the diagonal supports. The wood smelled fresh, new. It was still a bit green, recently cut spruce from Gaetz Mill at the Head of Chezzetcook. Felled, cut, planed in a matter of weeks. It would crack and dry and twist a little as it gave up its moisture, but this would be a strong building. I could feel the energy field in the structure, the metaphysical dividend.

"This is going to be a great house," I said.

"Your mother likes it, too," he said, but then realized the subtext of what he was saying. "She says that this exact spot was once the summer camp ground for migrating Micmacs. She says I will have many uninvited guests in my living room and that I should learn the language if I want to understand them."

"Sounds scary."

"She says the only thing that will keep the dead Indians away is television."

"Are you going to get a television?"

"Only if it gets too crowded," he said. Then he sighed, and got up to go sit on the saw horse. "Tell your father there's nothing to worry about. I'm not that kind of a man. I don't want to cause any trouble. But Dorothy and I are good friends."

As I walked on towards Hants Buckler's, I wasn't sure I was convinced. Love, for me, was still a tumultuous, out-of-control emotion. I wanted to be with Gwen all the time, every minute, and that did not seem possible.

After things settled down, after the death of old Duke, Gwen spent less time with me and more at home in front of her television. She had become addicted to watching TV news reports about the war. When we were together, she told me body counts, details of massacres, tonnage of bombing raids, daily costs of the war in terms of money and casualties.

"I guess we didn't stop it, did we?" I meant Boston.

"No," she said. "But we will. They've been marching in New York, San Francisco, Los Angeles, Philadelphia, at the Pentagon, even in Ottawa. I think we're on the verge of a full scale revolution."

Again I heard the echo of my father from years ago. *Revolution*. How peaceful and wonderfully unproductive life was on Whalebone Island. Why couldn't the world stay away and let us be? Too bad my father hadn't successfully blown up the bridge and figured a way to move us further to sea, away from the coast. Maybe Gwen's old man had a theory about how this could actually happen. Certainly a man with a brain capable of developing a thermonuclear device could figure out a way for us to overcome limits of geography.

"Hants Buckler found a bale of marijuana," I told Gwen, wanting to change the subject from politics to the story of the old guy's latest gift from the sea.

"You're kidding?"

"No. Just washed in yesterday. He knows what it is but doesn't quite know what to do with it. I think he's been feeding it to his chickens."

Suddenly a devilish grin came over Gwen's face. "I think we should go over and give him some suggestions."

The door to Hants' house was open, but he didn't seem to be anywhere around. I heard an axe blade biting into wood from his nearby woodlot and figured he was out there cutting down black spruce for firewood. Chickens were running around chasing each other in crazy patterns in the dirt. A couple were pecking away at the bale of what looked like dried timothy. Gwen shooed the chickens away and we sat down on what was left of the burlap covered bale of marijuana. She picked some off with her fingers and put some in my mouth. "Chew it."

I chewed. I think I was expecting to hallucinate immediately. She sucked on a stem herself and split some seeds with her teeth. I spit out the stalks and kissed Gwen long and hard on the mouth. For once I had driven the devils of the war out of her. She was mine again. I had suddenly turned into a big fan of marijuana. Hants walked towards us out of the stunted forest and found us like that, kissing. He set his axe down by the wall of his shed, wiped his forehead with what looked like the remains of a very old sock. "You found the dope," he said calmly, tugging at what was left of his ear lobe.

"Quite a bit here," I said.

"Chickens like it for the seeds. I'm not at all sure what it'll do to their laying habits. You kids don't know nothing about this sort of thing, do you?"

"Smoked any of it yet?" Gwen asked. "That's what people do with it, you know. They smoke it."

"Like tobacco?" Hants asked.

"Sort of," Gwen answered.

"Makes you go funny in the head?"

"Some people like it."

Hants scratched on his stubbled jaw. "Think I'd get in any trouble if the law found it here?"

"If they thought it was yours, they might send you to jail. They'd think you were a dealer," I told him.

Hants looked unmoved. I don't think he believed that the law of the land, the Mounties, had any jurisdiction whatsoever over him. "Only one of two things to do, then," he said. "Either bury the stuff or use it up."

"Smoke it, you mean?" Gwen asked, looking down at what must have certainly been at least a hundred pounds of densely packed pot leaves.

"I got some rolling papers in the house. Let's see how much of it we can get smoked. I need a break anyway. If we can't get too far into it, I'll just spread it around for the chickens and hope it doesn't stop 'em from laying eggs."

We tried to keep up a conversation about tides and wind conditions and Hants attempted to explain how life was different when he was growing up, how the sea was a different colour, the sky a different hue, how it was a time when something meant something, but mostly we fell to coughing and giggling. The chickens were hysterical to watch and the sea sparkled like blue-white diamonds and, after a bit, Hants went inside and brought out an old warped fiddle and proceeded to play an out-of-tune version of "Farewell to Nova Scotia." He said that the song always reminded him of a woman he met years ago.

"She come up the road there in a car — a little woman with pretty eyes full of spark, and she asked me if I knew any old songs. I said I did but they were mostly dirty songs — the kind the sailors sang at sea. She asked me if I could sing them to her. I said sure and she opened the door to her car and pulled out this big tape recording machine. She set that thing on the hood of her car and plugged it into the car battery.

"I told her I couldn't sing no good without a glass of rum, only I didn't have any, so she went into the trunk of her car and pulled out a demijohn of Governor General's. She never touched it herself. But I had suddenly developed a powerful thirst. I just kept getting better and better with each song. I felt like a kid again. And this little lady, she just kept looking at me and smiling and then looking off to sea as if she knew there was some special surprise out there, just waiting. I tell you, I fell in love with that woman. Mind you I hadn't seen a woman from the mainland in some seven years, but I think this was the prettiest, most alive little beauty who ever set foot on the shores of Canada. Then I had run out of the bawdy songs and all I had in me was one more, a kind of sad one, but it was all I had left and I was afraid if I stopped singing, I'd lose this vision, this goddess with a tape recording machine."

Gwen and I had stopped giggling as Hants picked up his fiddle for the third time and began: "Farewell to Nova Scotia, your sea-bound coast, let your mountains dark and dreary be . . . ".

I wrapped my arm tighter around Gwen as we picked seeds out of the marijuana and spread them around for the clucking chickens at our feet. When the song had finished, there was a tear running down a deep crease in Hants' face. "And then she said she had run out of tape. I helped her pack up the machine in the back seat and waved goodbye as she drove away. She promised to come back, but she never did."

Hants set down the fiddle, spliced two cigarette papers together and rolled a joint as thick as a thumb. When he lit it and passed it to us, he said, "Sometimes, for an outcast like me, you only run into the right woman once. If you're lucky, she stays put. If not, she's gone. That's all there is to it. Call it what you will. I gave that woman my songs, gave her my heart and then she drove off."

"You could have gone after her," I said. "You could have tried to find her. That couldn't have been too hard."

Hants squinched up his face into the smoke, looked far off to sea. "A man has his pride, I guess," was all he said.

While I might have been a little confused the next morning as to what had actually happened at Hants Buckler's that day, years later it would all come back to me as I discovered patch after patch of the plant growing wild, free and haphazardly throughout the island. That was all on a day in the cusp of June, 1969. June of 1969 will never come around again on your calendar or mine. We had, for that one brief day, untethered the island from the mainland and swept ourselves far off to

Lesley Choyce

another place beyond the reach of war and politics and government. We were, in the best sense, free, ebullient and alive. And when you are only young once, you never fully recognize the brief tenure of such happiness or the instability of the dream that anchors you so far from the shores of madness and maturity.

36 It was the last week of June. Gwen and I were about to say goodbye to high school forever. At a school like Memorial High, you didn't have high expectations as to what would come after the big event. Some of us would go to universities, but very few. Most of us took a traditional Eastern Shore wait-and-see approach. Gwen wouldn't tell me what she had planned for herself. We had talked about marriage, but I guess we both knew that we had a lot of growing up to do first. We'd talk about living together here on the island, but each time we started into a discussion it went nowhere. We couldn't really visualize it.

As for me and my career, I was going to have to work my way into owning a boat. Probably a good summer aboard The Lucky Lucy with Eager and Lambert would give me enough for a down-payment. I still had rights to my father's fishing permit.

Gwen kept bugging me about Burnet, as if I would have some secret inside information, like maybe Burnet would sit down at regular intervals and write his old buddy a letter. It still shook me in my socks every time I thought of a blind and stupid young bulldog from the Eastern Shore of Nova Scotia actually getting himself into the *American* military because he wanted to see action. I was sure he would come home one of two ways: as a stiff in a black body bag or as a hero in a neatly pressed uniform, glittering with a chestload of medals.

Mrs. Skinner, my English teacher, had cornered me after school one day near the end and said I was wavering between a B and a B- in her class, that she couldn't make up her mind. Then she changed the subject, asked me about Burnet; she said she was dying to hear any news at all before she left for the summer to study in Greece. She admitted to having had a run-in with Burnet's old man and that she didn't have the courage to go visit him. But if I could do this one little thing, just go and talk to Burnet Sr. and find out if his son was still alive and kicking, well, it would just plain be appreciated.

It was a bribe, I suppose. And I could tell that Mrs. Skinner was not a person used to bribing her students. Prim and proper were words that fit Mrs. Skinner, whose favourite poet was Keats, whose eyes were amazingly blue and whose skin was an olive sort of colour. She must have been part Acadian. I had always liked her and she had always liked me, but she had always liked Burnet better, fooled by Burnet's good looks and brutish charm. Mrs. Skinner would have passed Burnet if he had stayed all year, even if he did little more than blow his nose on the final exam.

"Sure," I told Mrs. Skinner. "I'm not exactly on good terms with his old man though, you understand this?"

"No one is," she said. "I've asked other students. They've refused. But Burnet was your friend." Then she fluttered her eyes, hesitated. Had she intended the past tense?

"I guess he's still my friend," I said. "I just haven't heard from him lately."

There were no dogs at the Burnet homestead. I heard them though in the distance, chasing after some poor wild creature. I knocked on the kitchen door. No answer. I heard a TV on inside. Through the window I could see Burnet's old man sitting at the kitchen table. I knocked again on the window and it rattled in its frame.

When Burnet Sr. looked up, I waved as if I was an old friend. He looked at me like I was someone dropping by to sell him a vacuum cleaner. When I waved a second time and pointed to the door, he reluctantly got up from the table, clicked off *The Price is Right* and opened the door.

"Yeah?" he asked.

"I came by to ask if you've heard from your son," I said.

"Jesus H. Christ," Burnet Sr. spit in my face. "Why would I hear from him? He doesn't live here any more. How the hell should I know what he's doing?" He left me standing there with the door open, walked back and sat down at the bare wooden table. Before him was an open bottle of Keith's and a plateful of what appeared to be baked beans. There was an open loaf of Ben's Holsum White Bread beside it. After a slug of beer, he grabbed a slice of white bread, sopped it in the beans and stuffed it in his face. With his mouth full, he looked back at me. "Come in and close the fucking door."

So I came in and closed the fucking door.

"Sit down somewhere. Anywhere."

But there wasn't much to choose from. A three-legged chair, a green vinyl-covered chesterfield with springs protruding. I opted for a seat on a pile of firewood sitting squarely in the middle of the room. It looked like the most stable thing around.

"Aw fuck," Burnet's father said, like he had just been pushed over some invisible limit inside his head, as if I had been the final straw to a really bad day. He spit the beans and bread back onto the plate in one great tan bolus and he pushed his plate away. "Now my goddamn dinner's cold."

It was my fault of course. "Sorry. I don't mean to keep you from your meal. It's just that some of us at school, we really wanted to know about Burnet."

The man got up and slugged back what was left of the beer, then threw the bottle into the case of empties behind the wood stove. Burnet Sr. studied a black and blue thumb nail like he was reading a newspaper. "Who ever cared a fuck about him? No one. Only me."

"I cared," I offered. "He was my friend." I did the same as Mrs. Skinner. *Was.*

"That's a laugh," he said, belching loudly to punctuate his point. I was remembering the morning Burnet and I had lifted the car off of his old man's hand. All that hate, all that anger. This was not, I admitted to myself, a family that was easy to get close to.

"How is he?" I asked. All I could do was pursue the point.

"He ain't never coming back. That's how he is," Burnet Sr. said as he picked up his plate on the table and scraped the cold beans and bread into the garbage, then threw the plate in the sink where it broke in two. "It's almost like I never even had a son."

"What happened?" I stood up now and went over to him. I dreaded hearing the words, but my worst fears had come true.

"What happened was that he turned chicken shit. He got over there and he just fucking couldn't take it."

"You mean he's still alive?"

"He won't be if he ever comes back here." The man's eyes were kind of glazed over. Rage or sadness or something of both mixed together.

"But he's not dead?" I asked. I already had him buried and gone. Now Burnet was back in the world of the living, somewhere. God knew where. "Is he still in Vietnam?"

"My guess is that he's got a fucking job wiping the ass of Ho Chi Minh by now. He deserted. Went AWOL the first day in the field. That's what he did." Big Burnet's fist came down hard on the table. He glared at me like it was all my fault.

I tried to conjure up a picture of Burnet alone in the jungles of Southeast Asia, on his own, AWOL. He was in deep shit. Where would he go? What would he do? "Maybe he just figured out that killing was the wrong thing to do," I said.

Burnet picked up the chair he was sitting in by the back and brought it down hard on the table until it splintered. "If he ever comes back here, I'll turn him in," he said. "If I don't kill him first. Now get out of here."

I guess I had what I had come for. I stood up and began to back slowly towards the door. "I'm sorry," I said. "You might be wrong about him. It might be something other than just chicken. He might have just figured out he was doing the wrong thing."

"Shut up and get out!"

I gingerly pulled open the door, slipped out and began to walk away. I was halfway across the muddy, littered yard when I heard the door open again. I was almost afraid to turn around, afraid I'd see him standing there with his twelve-gauge aimed at me. I had always known this was going to be a dangerous mission. I should have settled for the B-.

"Wait," Burnet Sr. said. I spun around to see he was out the door. He heaved what was left of the chair into the wild rose bushes and walked towards me. I stood stone still. He didn't have a gun. Just a pair of clenched fists. He walked up so close that he was breathing down on me. I could smell his beer breath and his foul stench. I looked him right in the eyes as he spoke. "If you tell anyone, *anyone*, I'll break your fucking neck."

I shook my head. I could never explain to the raging father what I felt just then. I didn't think less of Burnet for what he did. I was beginning to think that maybe he had finally woken up. Even if he went AWOL because he was scared, that was okay by me. I figured it might have been the best that could happen. If he could keep his butt out of jail and alive and find his way to a safe haven somewhere, he might just get his act together. "I'm not going to tell anyone," I said. But it wasn't the threat. It was because people wouldn't understand. They'd jump to the wrong conclusions. I wanted Burnet back here to tell his own story. But I didn't want his old man to think I was intimidated. So I looked the ugly old fart in the eye and added, "If you hear from him, you tell him he still has friends here. You tell him to get in touch with me." Then I let fly a long, sleek line of spit onto the ground, the sort of act of defiance Burnet's old man would understand. I was, by nature, not a spitter, but Burnet was. His old man would recognize the style of my spit, know that his son had taught me to spit that way; he would recognize that it landed perilously close to his foot. He would wonder what other tricks his son had taught me. I turned to go.

Mrs. Skinner would not hear the news. I would not even tell Gwen, for despite what I had said to his old man, I still worried that Gwen might be attracted to Burnet if he came back, especially now *if* he had turned into a deserter. I guess I really didn't want him to come back, but I hoped he was safe somewhere. I would not tell a living soul what his father had said.

There is nothing to report of graduation because it is a blur. I had bought a car by then, an old 1957 Chevy station wagon that someone had driven here from Alberta so it was not all rusted out. After graduation, Gwen and I were going to drive on down the Shore to a "secret spot." We were going to make love for the first time. We wanted to be alone somewhere away from Whalebone Island, away from our past selves. I had bought a pack of twelve condoms. I had a sleeping bag in the back of the car. There was a bottle of cheap wine rolling around under the back seat.

Somewhere that night on a dark lonely and beautiful stretch of sand, my car parked right on the beach with waves lapping near my tires, we were going to make love over and over and sort out what we were going to do for the rest of our lives. With the graduation ceremony ended, we turned down the various invitations to get drunk with our fellow graduates. We said goodbye to our parents who made feeble protests about being out too late but knew that whatever we were up to, we would not be dissuaded.

It should have been the most natural thing in the world for us. There would be no guilt, no feelings of mistrust. It was a cool night, so instead of lying out on the beach at Excelsior Point, I uncurled the sleeping bag in the back of the station wagon and we both took all our clothes off. At first we lay in each others arms, hardly moving. The night was perfectly quiet and still. I could hear the blood pounding in my own ears, I knew this was a thing to approach slowly, that we had all night, that nothing could ruin it, that it was the beginning of a new phase for us. We'd been through so much together, knew each other so intimately, had shared so much that I felt like Gwen was already part of me. This mere physical thing was the obvious and ultimate commemoration of who we were.

She licked her tongue inside my ear and then I slid down to kiss her mouth, her slender, beautiful neck, and further down to where I put my mouth around her nipple and took a gentle suck on it which made her body twitch. I was prepared to keep descending to kiss her body all over, to test her reactions to anything I could do if it would bring her pleasure. My eyes closed, my tongue exploring the contours of her flesh, I discovered that, right then, I was more interested in giving her pleasure than caring about my own. Was this the way other men felt? Was this the key to love? Not the taking but the giving? It seemed like a wonderful concept and I continued to caress and kiss, to explore with my tongue. I could keep this up all night. As I burrowed further down, licking the light fine hair that followed below her navel, she suddenly stopped me and pulled me back up.

"What?" I asked. I was drunk and stoned and delirious with something, but had not even remembered to open the bottle of wine.

She kissed me hard on the mouth in that funny way we had of kissing until our teeth clicked hard against each other. Then she held my head in her two hands. "There's something I have to tell you first. Otherwise you'll think that I tricked you."

"Tricked me? What are you talking about? Do you think I'm letting you take advantage of me?"

"No. It's not that."

"What is it?" I asked. A light wind had come up out of the northeast. I looked away form her, up and away towards the sea, towards the dark clouds scudding along further up the coast.

"I'm going to Boston tomorrow for the summer," she said abruptly.

"Why? What's going on? You didn't tell me."

She was very cool now, very clinical. "It might be longer than the summer. I have to see."

"See what?" My world was shattered.

"See if I can do any good. I'm going to work for the peace movement. I want to do something to help stop the war. I can't do that from here."

Before I could speak again, before I could question, I suddenly understood Gwen and I knew that our island world was too small to contain her. I knew she wanted to protest, to work in whatever way she could to fix the world. It was selfless, not merely ambitious, and I knew she was capable of doing some real good. But I also realized that she was now willing to sacrifice me, to sacrifice us, for this more noble cause. And that made me very angry.

"You can come with me if you want," she said, kissing me on the forehead like I was a little boy.

"No. I don't want to leave. I want you to stay." But it was hopeless.

"I have to do this," she said then kissed me again, sucking my tongue into her mouth, wanting to make up by drawing me back into the interrupted lovemaking.

At first all desire had fled. My mind whirled. I wanted to turn back the clock by minutes, by hours, to any time before the bomb had been dropped. I wanted to be there on the gravel road again, a boy, watching as the strange American car pulls up and out steps Tennessee Ernie Phillips. I wanted to be there looking at the little girl in the backseat who would hold my love, my adoration for years. I wanted to start all over again.

Lesley Choyce

Gwen became more animated despite my confusion and seeming indifference. Now it was she who began to explore down my body with her tongue. That soft tongue dancing over my bony chest. I was ready to get up, to open the door, and plunge out into the dark night, go running naked and screaming along the beach, crying, wailing in pain to let her know how much all this hurt, how much harm she was doing to me. But I couldn't move.

And then the anger swelled up in me again. I grabbed Gwen's hair, twisting it in my fist, pulled her face back up to mine and assaulted her mouth with a kiss, biting her lip and pushing my hand down to grab one of her breasts. Love had turned to lust and the lust was mingled with the hurt pride of the male ego and pain. I still wanted Gwen, I still wanted her then and there but I knew it was no longer making love. It would be something else.

I pushed myself over on top of her and pulled her arms out to the side. As I entered her, she made movements with her body to let me know it was okay, that she wanted me. I looked down at her as I lifted myself up from the waist, still pinning her with my hips, still possessing her. We were both gasping for air and I could not look for more than a second at her sweet face because I feared she would see the anger in my eyes. Instead, I went about my work, feeling the thrill of sex and the hammerlock of lust on my brain until it was over and I was satisfied and I slipped off her sideways, gasping for breath.

I lay there nearly unconscious, feeling I had done the most awful of things because it had not been love. Gwen had betrayed me, but I had betrayed her and myself. I could not understand why I had done this. I could understand nothing. I was both a victim and a criminal, jailed forever in some crippling emotional prison.

But Gwen was still lying there naked beside me. She ran her fingers through my hair, pulled herself gently to me. I could see that her lip was bleeding. I tasted the blood as she kissed me gently on the mouth. If time had continued to flow, it was indifferent to me. I was locked in some expanding present, a place of grim loss and solitude. And then she was whispering in my ear. "Let's do it again. This time more slowly because I love you so much and I want this night to go on and on."

She knew how much she had injured me and she had not held me to blame for the way I had acted and then, through her gentle encouragement, she led me back to the land of the living and helped me translate lust and guilt into love. Soon we were making love again, the way it should have been. We spoke very little for the hours that followed but made love, then rested, made love, then rested until we were both exhausted. A dim silver sun was coming up over the sea. Outside, the world was grey and dismal. The wind, up out of the northeast, was setting the coast up for a stormy blast of ugly weather. We were two slightly sore, overwrought kids in the back of a '57 Chevy who were still very much in love and who had forgiven themselves but not the world that was about to drive them apart. But we both knew it was what had to be and there wasn't a damn thing anybody could do about it.

37 By three o'clock the next day she was gone and I was alone with my island. My mother sent Casey looking for me. I had already wandered, lonely and lost, to the beach at Back Bay, to the stony barachois where the gaspereau would pass upstream, to the look-off ledges that jutted out over the sea. I made my pilgrimage to all the old sacred Gwendolyn places.

Casey was fourteen now — a funny, awkward girl with long black hair and glasses. Smart in some ways but not school smart. It had been a rough year for her and she had almost failed. She had lost all self-confidence and I had not been much help to her. For me, there had always been problems larger than Casey's, crises more important. She still didn't understand why our father was around so rarely; she couldn't fathom politics or the expansive geography of our family. Casey was a child who had gone through phases so diverse, so striking that I sometimes didn't know who she would be when I woke up. When she first came into the world during the hurricane, she had screamed and wailed but then fell asleep and when she woke, she made very little noise for almost a month. When she opened her mouth again, she had learned to coo a musical sort of melody that sustained her for nearly a year. Then more screaming, more silence, a Niagara of language at one point, silence again. Moodiness followed by alert, perceptive insight.

Casey missed her father and had not even had those few "good years" that I had experienced with him. I think I'd been a poor excuse of a brother for her. Casey and my mother had a bond deeper, stronger and weirder than any I had with my mother. My mother, wanting to pass on to her daughter what protective powers she could, got her started on the occult quite early. It would be years before her intuitive, psychic powers were honed but by the age of eleven, Casey could make salt shakers fall off the table for no reason, cupboard doors open and bags of flour slide to the floor. She claimed that she could make a sparrow go silent at fifty feet or start singing up a frenzy at her mental command and "proved" this to me time after time although I always believed that there were other more natural forces at work.

Now that she was fourteen, I would come home on an evening and find a pair of twisted spoons on the table. "Your sister is developing a sharp mind," Dorothy would say, pointing at the warped silverware. Now that we were both older, my mother preferred that we call her by her first name. I guess I conceded to myself that they could mangle spoons with their minds but it was never actually performed in my presence. Casey even claims that, in a desperate moment while failing a geometry test, she made Mr. Hawkings' belt come loose and his pants fall to the floor as he leaned on the chalk trough, waiting for his pupils to finish. The class dissolved into an uproar. Casey still failed the test, but she had realized another survival weapon in her psychic arsenal. Soon after that, however, Casey decided that she would set aside all interest in the paranormal. She had decided that she wanted very much to be "normal."

Everyone on the island lived somewhere near the perimeter — by the bay, by the sea, or along the several little inlets. The bulk of the island was the unused and relatively uninspiring interior, about a hundred and fifty acres of bog, jutting rocks, tundra-like field and a few briny ponds. For the most part we considered this communal land although no one had ever tried to "do" anything with it. In the winter it would freeze up, the snow would glaze over and it would be a good place to trek around as if lost in the frozen arctic wastes — or so I used to pretend. But now, early summer, it was generally a damp, dismal place where you might sink up to your elbows in the bog or trip over the tangled juniper roots that snaked over the lichen-covered rocks. But it was a place that Gwen and I had not visited often and it was, on that unhappy, lonely day, where I wanted to be.

I was hiding, I guess you could say, behind a high granite boulder that perched like an egg on a flat shelf of rock. It had always looked off-balance, like it would topple over any second. As a kid I'd tried to budge it and found it strange that it could not be moved. There was a small pond below. I assumed it would one day roll off the ledge and plug the pond and that would be the end of its journey, its final destination after being left here high and dry from the retreating glacier. I often thought about that old dead-and-gone glacier that had scraped this island clean and left the odd deposit of boulders to sort out their fate through geological time. I was sitting alone there on the pond side of the rock, ready to accept my fate if forty-five tonnes of granite should decide that today was the day to slip free of the whims of stasis and let gravity have its way.

"I knew I'd find you here," Casey said as she arrived, scaring me half to death. She was lying of course. I'm sure she had searched the island's shores first and had finally turned inland in a final attempt to locate her morose brother. She parked herself beside me. "What are you doing?"

"Nothing," I said. "I'm doing nothing. It's what I was cut out to do."

"That's good," she said. "People do too much of everything and it takes patience and practice to do nothing." Casey picked at the dry bayberries on the ground, crushed them to make them give off that fragrant scent of summer — last summer trapped in its fruit. "Weren't you and Gwen in love with each other? Why did she leave?"

My little sister was in her blunt phase. She'd ask anybody anything directly. But her question annoyed me because of the illogical answer that was necessary. "Question number one: yes. Question number two: she had to."

"It was only a quiz, not a final exam."

"No more questions, okay?"

"Okay." Casey tried to sit quietly by me as I brooded. A low bush nearby was filled with starlings eating dried berries. We sat in silence again until Casey grew bored and pulled out her pocket transistor radio. "Want to listen?"

I shook my head no. She plugged in the tiny earphone and started to move side to side to the music. I couldn't bring myself to show it, but I was glad she was here. I started to get my mind off Gwen. I began to think about the upcoming election. The Tories would have to choose a new leader. Colin was in some sort of hot water — some hints of scandal, kickbacks, minor corruption just as the political clock was ticking down to election time. I tried to follow the papers nowadays, wanting to keep up with my dad and his party. It was always so strange to read his name in the *Mail Star*. They made him sound so very important.

But the Tories had been slipping in popularity since my father was first elected. It was possible the Grits would return to power. It was possible my father would not be re-elected. For selfish reasons, I was praying for his defeat. Bud Tillish had already announced he would try to regain his seat. Bud had cleaned up his image and brought himself some local favour by luring a couple of small manufacturers of fishing gear to our part of the Shore. But I just couldn't see how Bud's recent success could match my father's charisma. I almost wished I could think of a way to help Bud out.

Then my quiet, desperate mood was broken by the sound of a truck engine. It was getting closer, even though we were nowhere near the road. As I listened to the gunning engine, the curses of men and the spinning of tires in bog muck, I realized that some asshole was trying to drive a truck right out into the middle of the island. But why?

I pulled the earphone out of Casey's ear and told her to turn off the radio. We both looked as a jacked-up black Ford truck with monster tires came chewing, spewing, spitting and gouging its way across the bog beneath us. It left a trail of deep, ugly ruts that immediately filled in with dark inky water and mud. There were two men in the cab. I had never seen them or the truck before. My instinct was to go running down the embankment, screaming at them to get the hell out of here, but I could see they had a gun rack in the back window with two rifles. Hunters? Nothing much to hunt here but skinny shore rabbits and bushes full of sparrows and starlings.

Maybe they were crazed criminals. What else would explain this illogical terrorizing of the land? If Casey had not been there, I'm sure I would have run down to give them hell, but the way they were tearing up the place was so inexplicable that I didn't trust them at all. So I pulled Casey around to the back of the balanced rock and we lay low to watch.

The truck stopped on a section of level, dry rock — not granite but something that crumbled when you scraped your boots across it. There was a name on the side door of the truck in big bold letters: MANNHEIM/ATLANTA. It meant nothing to me. The two men got out. One was fat at the belt buckle and wore a cowboy hat. The other was tall, bald and impatient. "What kind of god-forsaken place is this?" the fat cowboy shouted in an accent that seemed so out of place here that he might as well have arrived from Mars. I tried to place it. American South. Deep South.

The other man tried to wipe the mud off his shoe onto the fender of the truck. "Goot place, I think. Goot place as any." Another weird accent. Foreign, but not American. "He sounds like Colonel Klinck in *Hogan's Heroes*," Casey whispered to me.

"Let's just get our sample and get out of here before we get our asses sunk up to our eyeballs in this sludge." The American heaved some sort of long pipe-like contraption with a motor on one end out of the back of the truck, pulled on a cord and started up what sounded like a chainsaw motor. He put one end of the shaft to the ground and the engine roared into life.

"What are they doing?" Casey asked.

"They're drilling," I answered.

"Drilling for what? Who are they?"

"I don't know. But I don't like it."

We watched as they made three holes and extracted loose rock which they put into three separate containers. When the drill was back in the truck, they each grabbed a bright red can of Coke, slugged it back and then heaved the cans into the bog.

"Let's get out of this shit hole," the beer-belly with the drawl said.

The German shrugged and got back in the cab. The driver jerked the truck around and headed back out of bog, leaving a new set of knee-deep ruts as they departed.

When they were gone, Casey and I went down to where they had drilled and saw the three perfectly cylindrical holes bored into the crumbling rock. "What are they looking for?" Casey asked again. All I could think of was the gold I had once found near here, the gold my father had asked me to never mention. Around the holes was the dry, whitish-yellow powder of disturbed rock. I put some of the dust in both my pockets and walked Casey home where I told my mother I was skipping dinner.

Hants Buckler was playing checkers with himself when I stepped into his kitchen. "Who's winning?" I asked.

"I am. I always win."

I sat down on an old wooden crate labelled "100% Virgin Olive Oil" with fancy blue-green lettering and a picture of a young Italian woman painted on it.

"Hants, who owns the bog and all the land in the middle of the island?"

Hants kinged his opponent and shifted over to the other side of the board. "Nobody owns it. Guess it's kind of public land. Nobody ever worried about who owned it 'cause nobody ever really wanted it. Not good for much unless you want to harvest sundews and pitcher plants."

I told him what I'd seen today. He said he'd heard all the racket and would have gone to check it out himself only he was in the middle of pickling hard-boiled eggs. "Somewhere on paper, somebody must have legal rights to it," I suggested. "And I'm worried."

"Hell, we're all worried. There'll always be something to worry about. World's probably gonna end next week if they keep building bombs and if that little war in Asia flares up into

Lesley Choyce

something big, it'll probably burn us all to living hell. But you gotta take it like me. Don't pay too much attention to it. Mind your business. Wait and see what washes up. Accept things as they are and make yourself happy."

Hants had turned sixty-nine this year. Maybe I'd see the world the same way when I turned sixty-nine. He got up to pour us both a cup of tea, then sidled over to his cupboard and poured a cap full of black rum into each of our cups. "Here's to 'er," he said. "Barbados tea" he called it.

I sucked on it slowly. It was hot and burned twice on the way down my gullet. "How many acres do you own?"

"Frig knows," he said. "I never had a proper deed. I don't pay taxes, neither. Still doesn't mean I don't own this place. No one really ever owns a place. You borrow a piece of land to live on while you're alive and then you give it to somebody else. Kind of like a contract with the island itself. I figure if I don't take care of the place while I'm living, the island'll get back at me somehow after I'm dead and buried here. Send maggots into me box or something. Who knows?"

"Yeah, but who do you think *the government* would say owns the middle of the island?" I could see it was going to be hard to get an answer here, but Hants was the only real link with the deep past of the island. I was sure he knew what I was getting at despite his attempt to wax philosophical.

He scratched his jaw, producing a sound not unlike a coarse file honing the blade of an axe. "I reckon they'd call it Crown land."

"Which means that it's owned by the government, the province itself, right?"

"Belongs to the people, really. We all know that. Belongs to everyone and no one, just like the entire island, what your father always called the Republic of Nothing."

"But if the government wanted to do something with the land, or if someone wanted to buy it and the government was willing to sell, they could do it, right?"

"Who'd want it, though? Ain't nothing there." Hants was baffled.

I reached in my pocket and poured a small amount of the yellow-white dust on his checker board.

Hants looked puzzled. He slugged back his Barbados tea, wet his finger and lifted some of the dust up to his nose. He sniffed it like a dog would.

"What is it?" I asked

"Whatever it is, it's worthless," he said.

"But you don't know what it's called?"

"Nope."

It was one of the few times that Hants had ever come up empty for an answer. "Thanks, Hants." I had a nice little buzz on from the tea, but I wasn't exactly cheered up. It looked to me like the Province owned the interior of the island. But wasn't my old man helping to run the goddamn Province? I could not imagine that he would have sent the Mannheim/Atlanta truck out here. Something was wrong.

I thought of going the long way home to avoid walking by Gwen's house but, if I did that, I knew it would only be harder to go by there the next time. Tennessee Ernie Philips was out in his front yard making adjustments to his interstellar radio dish. When he saw me coming, he dropped his screwdrivers and came out to see me. "Gwen is not an easy girl to understand, Ian," he said. "We were opposed to her going to Boston, but in the end we let her go. She would have gone one way or the other. I'll tell you the truth. I wish you were down there with her."

"Thanks," I said. I knew her parents trusted me.

"I'm worried about her getting into some sort of trouble. But she's a good kid. I understand why she's doing it. I just hope she doesn't get hurt."

"Me too," I said, not really wanting to continue the conversation. I stuck my hands in my pocket and looked down at the ground. Gwen's father had changed immensely over his years here. He had lost what I remember of the flashy, fast-talking way he had when he arrived. He'd slowed down, become part of the island life. As I started to walk on, I pulled some more of the rock dust out of my pocket and began to sift it out onto the road. I decided to stop worrying about the men in the truck. They were gone. They probably wouldn't come back, there was nothing to it. Then I stopped in my tracks. I went back to Gwen's father and showed him the dust that was left in my hand. "Any idea what kind of rock this comes from?" I asked.

Tennessee adopted the look of scientific curiosity that periodically overcame him when some minor quirk of nature caught his fancy. He held my hand up to the light and looked at it. "Stay here," he said and ran back into his house. A minute later the returned with an instrument I had not seen him toy with for years. It was his old Geiger counter. He flicked it on, set a dial and held the probe out to my hand. The instrument began to make a wild frenetic clicking noise.

"What are you doing with uranium in your pockets?" he asked.

***

38 Tennessee Ernie Phillips set down his Geiger counter. "Would you mind not throwing any more of that stuff around right here," he said. He pointed to his well, only a few yards away. "I've already sucked up enough radiation to shorten my life by ten years and I don't want to lose another day."

I put the handful of dust back into my pocket. I didn't know what else to do with it. What the hell was going on, anyway? Tennessee read the expression on my face. "Look, I didn't mean to scare you. It's not going to kill you. Not right away, anyway. But that seems like some fairly potent stuff for these parts. Of all the rotten luck."

"What do you mean?" I asked.

"I mean, if somebody is going to start ripping it out of the ground here, they'll tear up acres of land, leave piles of residue, contaminate the water, and basically make the island unliveable."

My blood began to boil. "They can't do that!" I insisted.

"I've seen it done. Pick a state: Nevada, Wyoming, Colorado. Very ugly, very deadly and there wasn't a law on the books to stop 'em."

I was glaring at him now. He had to be lying. What was his problem anyway?

"I'll tell you why. Because they take the uranium, refine it, and I mean they process tons of it to make a few ounces of the good stuff, and then they use it to make nuclear bombs."

"But this is Canada, not the U.S. They wouldn't do that here."

"Go ask the people in Saskatchewan," he said.

I didn't now anybody in Saskatchewan, but it suddenly clicked that Gwen's father wasn't bullshitting me.

"Oh, they'll say it's for nuclear power plants and some of it is, but even nuclear power plants aren't ready to be run by human beings for another hundred years because we can't make the bloody things safe. They were just another bad idea that we couldn't resist. In the end, most of it will go to make more weapons. At last count we can blow up the world eight times over. They're working on nine."

But right then, I didn't care a damn about the world. "What about the island? I don't see how any outsiders can come in here and just take over."

"Mineral rights. They buy mineral rights. And if what you said was true about it being Crown land, they can do whatever they want about it. In fact, they can tunnel down under your land and mine if they want. We only own the topsoil and some of those damn rocks sticking up into the air. Government owns the right to sell anything that's under it."

"Yeah," I said. "But my father's in the government, remember. He wouldn't do that."

Tennessee threw his hands up in the air. "Go talk to him. Just don't get me involved. If the Atomic Energy Commission of the U.S. finds out I'm here and decides I'm causing them trouble again, who knows what they'll do. But I'll tell you this, Ian, and I know you love this place, if you let 'em start digging here — even if it's just a pit the size of a backyard swimming pool — you might as well get the hell off the island because it's not going to be fit or safe to live here. No matter what the government or the mining company tell you."

I stumbled off down the road. No way would my father allow something like this to happen. Why would *anybody* do this? For money, of course, but somebody locally must have initiated it. Somebody who knew this place. Who would do that and why?

I explained the situation to my mother and Casey. I took off my pants with the uranium in the pockets and threw them in the wood stove and burned them. My mother told me to go take a shower. When I came out, she and Casey had changed their clothes. "We're going to talk to your father. I already called him to let him know we're coming."

My mother was not the sort of woman who needed long explanations about things like this. Observed fact coupled with intuitive understanding. "I think there is a way out of this," she said to the windshield of my Chevy as we drove west down Highway Seven. "I think this is some sort of test. It's important that we are strong enough to pass it."

"I hate tests," Casey said. "They always make me nervous. Sometimes I forget how to spell properly."

"Don't worry, Casey," Dorothy said, "there will be no spelling involved here."

We were seated in the Bluenose Restaurant. I was beginning to think that my father spent a lot of time in this place. We were all looking pretty uncomfortable except for him. He ignored the food and bit away at his thumbnail until it was down to the quick as I explained to him about the men in the truck and what Ernie had told me.

He snapped a finger and thumb in the air loud enough to stop all the conversation around us. A waiter came. "Could we have a phone over here?" he asked.

Mere seconds passed before the waiter returned with a phone. He plugged it into a jack near the wall by our table. My father dialled, got an answer. "Herb, I need you to check this out for me pronto, if you can, good buddy. Mineral rights for Whalebone Island in my riding — any activity in the last six months. Can you get on it and get right back? I'm at the Bluenose." He hung up. "You know this really worries me. In more ways than you can believe. First, it means that somebody's screwing around my island without me knowing about it. That suggests they're up to something no good. Otherwise, I'd be in on it."

My mother glared at him. "What are you talking about? This is not just your problem. It's not a political thing. It's our problem, our family and everyone else on the island. We're talking about our home here, not your stupid politics." It was the first time my mother had ever exploded that way. Casey looked frightened. I don't think she had ever really heard Dorothy talk to our father this way. They were not fighters and these days they spent so little time together that they could not afford to fight.

The waiter came to take the phone away, but my father waved him off.

"I'm afraid that I've learned there's a political dimension to everything that happens in this province. And right now, it's this way," Everett McQuade, the politician, said. "The party's

Lesley Choyce

in deep shit." My old man would never use the phrase 'deep shit' unless he really meant it.

"How deep?" my mother asked angrily.

"As deep as it can get." He leaned across and whispered. "First off, there's going to be an election later this year as you know. It's already been announced."

I knew about it and was still praying it might be the end to my father's career in the Halifax legislature. I wanted him to lose because I wanted him back home.

"But the real problem is," my father continued, "there's going to be a scandal — an RCMP investigation into Colin's business affairs. It's very messy. Colin's going to step down soon, before the election and, if possible, before the shit hits the fan."

"So what does this have to do with our island?" my mother demanded, much too loudly for my father's liking.

"Just wait." My father looked away from Dorothy and out the window. Then he looked behind him as if he was worried someone was listening. "When Colin steps down, he's making me premier. In a matter of days I'll be premier of Nova Scotia. And I've got to get the house in order and shipshape for election time so *I* can be re-elected."

"Why do you have to do it?" I asked.

"Because I've done a few good things for people since I got here, but now I'll be able to do a whole lot more. The party needs me too. They say the TV camera loves me. They've done secret polls. I'm very popular. The free fish business — it never got stale." My father was beaming. "And I'm going to turn the god damn province around." I'd never seen him so puffed up. I was pissed off. Maybe I wasn't thinking. How could we lose if he was premier? Certainly he'd be able to save the island. The phone rang. Everybody looked at our table. My father picked it up quickly. "Yeah. Herb?"

I guess my father had learned a few tricks during his stint

at the legislature because his face was poker straight. He heard the news, said a simple, "Yep," and hung up.

"Well?" I asked.

"Well, somebody took out the mineral rights and is going to do exploratory drilling for uranium in a big way."

"Mannheim/Atlanta?" I asked. "American, right?"

"Well, you got the name right. They're a mining outfit owned half by the West Germans, half by some American investors."

"You have to stop them."

"So far, what they're doing is legal. Everything is in order. I couldn't possibly interfere. It would look like a conflict of interest and jeopardize my role in the party." My father's eyes shifted uneasily now. He sipped at the cold coffee in front of him. I'd seen that look before. Where was it? Nixon, of course, on TV. My own father had become Richard Nixon.

"They can't buy the land from the government but they have already bought the mineral rights for a hundred years. They now have the legal right to go in and start an open pit mine. Hey, you want somebody to blame, don't blame me. You know who helped them set up the deal?"

"Who?" my mother asked.

"Bud Tillish. Bud wants to get back in his old office so he's starting to make promises. Jobs, new fish plants owned and operated by the Japanese — that son of a bitch is trying to make deals with my contacts. And mining jobs. Guess he did a little leg work of his own and found this turkey from Atlanta who's got a contract to provide as much uranium as he can get his hands on for a new weapons-grade uranium enrichment plant in South Carolina. Son of a bitch."

"You have to stop him," Dorothy said. "It'll ruin the island, ruin our lives, ruin our family. Not just us but Hants, and Bernie and Ben and all of us."

My father looked up at her when she said Ben's name. He was still jealous.

"I don't know if I can," he said. But my father saw the scorn in my mother's eyes, heard his own voice echo like a hollow noise inside her mind. He ran his fingers through his neatly trimmed hair, that rich red hair that was once so wild and unruly. "Look, I'll try, but I've got a lot on my plate right now. A lot at stake here and a lot to worry about — the party, the election. I'll see what I can do, though. I hate that bastard Tillish messing around down there. Just give me a few days."

The phone rang again. My father picked it up. "Oh, hi Herb. What is it?"

This time my old man's poker face didn't work. He didn't say a word but listened and hung up the phone.

"What is it?" mother asked. She could see it was bad news and was reaching her hand out across the table to take her husband's. It had been bad news, very bad. "What is it?" she asked again.

My father let his hand slip into hers, he stared at the dregs in his coffee cup. "The shit just hit the fan," he said. My mother pulled back her hand, her eyes turned to blue ice. My father accidentally knocked the chair over backwards as he went to stand up. "I've got to go now. Not a word to anybody about any of this, okay?" he said. He threw a twenty down on the table. "Enjoy the rest of your meal," he said. "Order some dessert for the kids." But his mind was clearly not on the family, not even on the island.

My father was leaving the restaurant and walking down to the Legislature to take over as premier of the province as Colin bowed out in disgrace. My father would have to overcome the gossip, the slander and the scandal and bring his beloved party back from the grave in a few short months before summer was over. I was thinking about how he had bailed out his son from the Boston jail, how it had all been so easy. He had made a few calls. My old man was now a very powerful politician, and I didn't give a damn. I was wondering just then who I hated more, my father for his new priorities or Bud Tillish for selling out Whalebone Island.

On the drive home, I contemplated burning Bud Tillish's house to the ground. That might get back at both of them at once. Bud would be without a roof over his head and my old man would have an arsonist for a son and have one hell of a time getting re-elected. Casey was asleep in the back seat by the time we passed Chezzetcook. She was dreaming, twisting and turning as the images of God knows what ran through her head. My mother reached back and patted her in a soothing, motherly way as if Casey was still a little baby. Dorothy began to regain some of her calm. She closed her eyes as we drove through the dark countryside around Musquodoboit Harbour and composed herself. Then, without even opening her eyes, she said, "Stop over there," and she pointed to the left. I pulled the car off the road by a pond and turned off the engine. "I want to show you something," she said.

With Casey still asleep in the back seat we got out and walked over to the water. She pointed deep into the night sky and traced something rectangular with her finger. "Orion will always guide you home," she said. "See the stars in his belt."

"Yes," I said. It had been a long time since she had pointed out anything to me in the night sky. We watched as a man-made satellite tracked across the girth of Orion the hunter. "Maybe we can't stop it," I said. "Everything is changing and maybe we will have to accept changes."

"Do you believe that?" she asked.

"I don't *want* to believe it," I admitted.

"What are we going to do?" I had never heard her use this question or this tone before. Her voice was weak and full of despair. "We've lost your father. We are going to lose what's good about our island. Ian, my guides, even Diaz, don't speak to me any more. I'm beginning to have dreams, dreams about my childhood, who I was, what happened to me. I think it's starting to change me. Everything that was good about our lives will soon be gone."

I was thinking of Gwen and of finding her dead grandfather

out on Shag Rock that night. I had sensed that my mother was going through changes, but she was not a talker. How could I fathom the real meaning of her life if she had never even known her origins to share with me?

"I was on a ship," she said. "I was in a dark room on a big ship. I could hear the engines running on and on and on and a man was hitting me in the face. I could taste blood. And it was very sweet and hot. And then someone lit a candle and I saw one face — not a man's but a woman's. And it was full of pain and fear."

I was afraid to speak.

"And the face was the same face I see in the mirror when I get up in the morning. The pain and the terror is there. I have to compose myself. I have to find my other self, the one who is your mother, and bring her back into the mirror before I can face you children in the morning. It's getting harder. There are new dreams every night, and I know they are not merely dreams."

"They're memories, aren't they?" I asked. We were both still looking up into the sky. A meteor shot through the vault of darkness and flared briefly into red before dying.

"Yes, and I always wanted them. I wanted to know the truth. Now I'm going to know the truth and I don't know if I can live with it. The more I remember, the more I lose the skills I've developed with my mind."

There was not much I could say to her. As Orion looked down on me from his lofty perch, I held her to me and realized it was not my mother I was holding in my arms but a frightened little girl. As we looked up at the night sky, I began to tell her a story about a man with bright red hair who rowed at sunrise straight out into the sea and found a young woman adrift in a boat, bathed in beautiful golden light, and how he took her back to an island. I said that they had two kids and lived happily ever after. I promised her that I was not making any of it up.

39 I'm sure that I was not the first son in the human race who became disillusioned and disappointed in his own father. Nonetheless, it put the world on a terrible new tilt. Colin Michael Campbell was at the centre of a doozy of a scandal involving highway construction and dealings in the liquor commission. The party convinced my old man that he was the only one clean enough to hang onto power, so Everett McQuade suddenly found himself the official leader of the government of Nova Scotia. And I could not help but think of him as a traitor to the Republic of Nothing. The summer of 1969 was a summer of madness and revenge. My mother sat awake many nights, wanting to avoid sleep. She took to reading massive paperback novels of pirates and war loaned to her by Jack. She tried to meditate in an effort to relocate her old friend, Diaz, but Diaz had gone mute for her. I heard her sometimes in the early morning hours, alone by the wood stove with a small crackling fire, singing a song in a language I did not understand. It was beautiful and sad and when I went in to ask her where the words came from and what it meant, she told me that she didn't know yet but that she was beginning to understand. It was an old sailor's song and the language was Gaelic. She knew that much.

Casey stayed close to home that summer and practised for sainthood. She did most of the housework during the day and she prepared the meals. What my mother needed was sleep, but she had forgotten how. I wondered how much she could take before she cracked. I drove into the liquor commission in Sheet Harbour and bought her a bottle of rum. At first she protested and said she would not drink. "Then I'll drink it myself," I said. Unlike so many of the guys my age, I had no real taste for the stuff. The world was crazy enough without going around drunk. I threw back a small glassful and it burned like acid on its way down.

My mother looked at me, angry at first, then somewhat ashamed, and ultimately told me she would give it a try. The two of us drank half of a fifth and, while Casey watched us get wobbly and woozy, we invented jokes, games and mind puzzles to fool each other. Mother and son, adrift on a sea of booze until she began to sing again in Gaelic, this time louder, stronger — the melancholy songs, the sea shanties, English and the old language weaving in and out as I fell asleep at the kitchen table. When I awoke in the middle of the night, my mouth dry like a cloud of wool, there was my mother, wide awake.

A few days later, I went over to Hants Buckler's and located some of the young marijuana plants still growing there. Along the lane that wandered up to Hants' shack were dozens of pretty little green plants that would blossom into bushes of cannabis later that summer. I picked a number of them and took them home to dry in the oven. That night, I prompted my mother to smoke some of the weed. She was not afraid of a plant that grew from the ground and, in fact, had read in her various research about how Indians in Mexico had used marijuana as part of a purification ritual.

"What would your father say if he knew we were sitting home smoking dope while he was running the government of Nova Scotia?" she asked me after we had lit up the third joint. With her blessing, I had even allowed Casey a taste of the stuff.

"I think he'd have a hard time explaining it to the other members of his cabinet," I said. The evening ended with us out beneath the stars again, those pinpoints of light that now wanted to climb right down out of the sky and sink into the retina of my eye and crawl into my brian.

"I love those stars," I said, staring at the wide brazen band of the Milky Way.

"The stars had dreams and the dreams were us," my mother

said, which in our condition was a message that took some adjusting to.

"What happens if the stars wake up?" Casey asked.

"Then we might all disappear. The only thing we can do is invent a new planet, fill it with people by dreaming them into existence."

"I think I dreamed this island into existence," I told my mother. "Sometimes I think I made this whole place up. I made it this perfect. I made you both perfect so that I wouldn't have to live here alone." It was the deepest, most honest statement of devotion to my family I had ever expressed. My mother did not look down from the stars and I had this terrible feeling that I was losing her, that if I didn't grab onto her right then, she would drift up into the night sky and be gone. So I grabbed onto her. And Casey, fearing perhaps that we would both drift up to the stars without her, held onto me. We stood frozen like that for long minutes until something reminiscent of a sober sense of reality crept back into us.

Still, my mother could not sleep that night.

I called my father the next day, was put on hold several times; I left messages several times that were never returned. Finally, at 4:45 in the afternoon, I got through to his executive assistant, Herb Legere. "This is an emergency, Herb," I said. "It's Ian, the premier's son. I want to speak to my goddamn father." After a minute of silence, my father came on the line. I explained. "If she doesn't get some sleep, she's going to go crazy. This could make you look bad. They'll say your wife is bonkers."

"I'm sorry, Ian. There's just been so much going on. Take her to a doctor. Not Anderson. He's too close to home. Take her to Whynact in Sheet Harbour. I'll give him a call. I'm sure he can prescribe something. Some nights I can't sleep and I take a few sleeping pills. He can prescribe Valium or something. I'll check back later. Now I've got to go. I'm right in the middle of a cabinet meeting over the Colin mess. If we don't give the press something by five o'clock, they're going to fry us on the news tonight. Bye, son."

"Bye," I said, but he had already hung up.

I didn't say anything to my mother but went over to Bernie's for advice. I didn't like the idea of pills. We weren't a pill-popping family and had generally been able to avoid doctors. My mother, instead, had relied on a cabinet full of homeopathic remedies that had helped us survive childhood. But nothing there, not camomile, not catnip, not any mix of roots or leaves infused or digested could help her sleep. She was possessed by the fear of what she would learn next if she slept, if she dreamed.

"Forget the sleeping pills," Bernie said. "Your mother knows the art of meditation. Tell her to meditate. Your mother is very capable of curing herself. Don't rely on pharmaceuticals!" It was not much help. Dorothy had tried every mental and psychic trick in her possession. She said she could not concentrate, she could not empty her mind. I had a hard time understanding why Bernie was so cold just then, why she had drifted away from us in recent months and why she was not more sensitive to our problem, this woman who had helped deliver Casey into the world on that stormy night.

Like Gwen, I learned later, Bernie had become caught up in the great battles sweeping North America. For Bernie, it was not the war between nations but the war between the sexes. She had read the feminist literature and had grown unhappy with her life with Jack. It wasn't that she wanted more from a man than she could get from one who read books all the time and daydreamed. It wasn't that at all. She just wanted to go off to Montreal or Toronto and fight in the streets, if need be, to liberate her sex from centuries of oppression. Like the Black Panthers in the States, Bernie would confess later that she was contemplating that violence was the only way to bring about change. She could not really say that she was unhappy with her life; after all, *she* had chosen it. She ran the show at her house. It was just that her sisters, her legions of sisters around the world, were still oppressed and it would take decades to throw off the shackles. Sometimes it seemed to her that the only way to get on with it was to get some guns and shoot the balls off a few good men. Such radical feminism, it appeared, had not left much room for compassion towards a daughter who could not sleep and feared her own dreams.

Ben Ackerman was a little more sympathetic. He was working on the roof rafters now. A happier builder could not be found. When I explained the situation and asked his advice, he agreed with my father. "Used properly, the Valium will help your mother sleep. And her sleep will generally be dreamless. I've seen this sort of thing before at the hospital. People do die from lack of sleep. It sounds strange, but it can kill you. On the other hand, what your mother has been dreaming will have to come out of her one way or the other. This is going to be a very critical time if she is beginning to get back her childhood memory." He climbed down from the ladder and now the smile was gone. He was genuinely worried. I understood by that look just how good a doctor he had really been.

"I can't prescribe the drug. You'll have to go to the doctor like your father said. But keep an eye on her. Don't let her take too many. Do you want me to come over and talk to her?"

She and Ben had not been seeing each other lately by a mutual pact. They could no longer create the empathic bond that had linked them. I think they both feared that without that mental transaction, they might tumble into something else. My mother needed him and I almost wished for it to happen. It would serve my father right. But instinctively, these two good, strong people knew it would only complicate things and so they now avoided contact. What kept my mother going were her kids. What kept Ben going were his roof beams and rafters. We were all working very hard at surviving.

Miraculously, the Valium worked. My mother slept the first night for fifteen hours. After that, she began to have an almost

Lesley Choyce

normal ten hours of sleep. "There are no dreams," she said. "I won't be able to dream us out of existence. I think we are safe."

But for me it was a funny feeling to sneak into her room at night after she was conked out, open her bedside table drawer and count the pills to make sure she had taken only one or two.

A larger drill truck came one day and followed the previous ruts of Mannheim/Atlanta, now minor rivers, to the small plateau of crumbling rock. Crouched behind the higher boulders again, like an Indian in an old cowboy film, I watched as three workmen in hard hats went to work drilling into the heart of the island. The four-wheel-drive Mannheim/Atlanta truck arrived with the American and the German, as well as a third man who hopped from the cab looking terribly pleased about something. It was the tall, gangly Bud Tillish and my stomach went into a square knot as I watched him.

I could not remain there to watch. A war had begun; there was no way around this. If Tennessee Ernie Phillips was right, and I believed he was, the uranium mining would destroy us all. We could not let our island be exploited for the sake of a mineral that would make more bombs. We could not let our island be ripped open, even if it was something far less harmful. They would have to be stopped. While young men my own age continued to fight and die for a lost cause in Vietnam, I knew I would have to struggle to my death to save my island. "We're at war," I told my father on the phone. He hadn't returned my call this time until ten o'clock at night. By then, my mother was safely asleep.

"What are you talking about?" my old man asked.

"You didn't stop them, did you? You didn't stop Bud Tillish and his mining company. They're starting to rip the guts out of the island."

"Damn. Look, I've tried to have the mining rights agreement revoked but it's just too hot an issue. If I do that, the

Grits will claim I'm overstepping my bounds. Tillish is already campaigning against me. He's got the people on his side on this one. The people on the Shore want the jobs that will go along with that mine."

"Nobody on the island does."

"Unfortunately, the people on the island don't matter. Tillish got his fish plant off the ground and now he's got this mining thing going. He's winning back his past supporters."

"I don't care about Bud Tillish or his goddamn supporters. I won't let this island be dug up and carted off to make nuclear weapons."

"I'll keep working on it. I'll see what I can do," my father said, if indeed this was my real father, because I felt as if some other life-form had crept into his body and murdered his soul. "Ian, I'm sorry, kid. It's just that there's so much happening now. We're almost clear of this Colin thing. We've got to stay real clean. In two weeks we have the party convention. If I can keep treading water and smiling until then through this mess, I'm a shoo-in. The election will be over in a month after that. It's a lot of damage control between now and then, but everybody thinks I can pull it off. I've got a few enemies, mind you. Remember old John G.D. MacIntyre? Well, I think he's a bit jealous that it's me sitting here instead of him. He's a bit pissed-off. Can't say I blame him. He's put more years in this party than I have. But he's got too much old party baggage. When people look at him they think of Colin. He'll come around. Everyone is very loyal in this party. I'm learning to love these people."

"Dad, I don't give a shit about the party. And I don't give a shit about you!" There, I said it. I slammed down the phone. Then I checked my mother and counted the pills. She was being a good girl.

40 There comes a time in a young man's life when it is absolutely necessary to act, to avoid the great angst of waiting for something to happen and waiting for someone else to save you. The island needed saving and it needed it now. Not tomorrow. Not after some goddamn election or after a dozen cabinet meetings. My father had started out in politics as an anarchist, but now he was something else that I didn't care to think about. I was old enough now to know the true meaning of anarchy. I had been to Boston. I had seen the dark side of the legal and political system. I knew what law and order was doing to that country to the south. They were tearing it apart.

My father had become, in his own way, part of that system, the one that looked out for its own good, its own self-perpetuation. My father was the premier of Nova Scotia and he was no longer an anarchist, no longer an islander. As this fact settled into my brain, I can honestly say that, at that moment, I did not love my father. He might as well have shed his human skin and become a giant reptile — a crocodile or a lizard. I went into the living room, over to that old desk with the rolled wood top that he had once called his office. I tried the bottom right hand drawer. It was locked. I went out to the kitchen for a screwdriver and when I came back I pried open the drawer, found the brown manila envelope and opened it. Inside was the declaration. I wasn't sure it would really be there. I think I was afraid that my old man might have burned it or taken it with him. What would the TV people and the newspapers make of my father's declaration of independence for the Republic of Nothing on Whalebone Island?

Reading the words out loud, I felt filled with self-righteous indignation that the world would dare invade our republic. I folded the letter, put it in my back pocket and went to the tool shed for a small can of black paint and a paint brush. Then I went walking out into the night.

I was alive again. Anger and indignation seemed to emanate from my body and I felt on fire. I almost considered waking Casey to come with me, but I decided this was my work. I was the man of the house. And if someone was going to get into trouble, it was going to be me. My heart was animated with the fire of vandalism. Would I merely paint a message of rebellion, a mere threat, and then go back home to sleep? No, it had to be more. And I craved conspiracy. I believe that conspiracy is another trait of male aggression. If you make a stand, you like to have a comrade. If you are going to die for a cause, you want a buddy there to watch your blood seep into the ground.

The cycle of the uranium was too awful to contemplate. The ore would be ripped from the earth, our earth, leaving us with a big ugly hole and poisoned ground water. It would be shipped off to be used as fuel for the most awful weapon ever created by man. Who else could appreciate the malevolence of this as much as I could? Who would understand? It would be wrong to bring Ben into this. He was too gentle. Hants would not understand. If Burnet had been around, he would come lend a hand for the pure spirit of destruction, but that would feel impure to me. I didn't want an ally who was willing to go off to a foreign jungle and set fire to villages simply because he had been searching all his life for a way to kill with impunity. I wouldn't stoop that low. I touched the sacred document in my back pocket. I was an anarchist, not a terrorist. The liberation of the island was a duty, not a joyride.

But the exact tactic was not clear. Would I just paint a slogan and leave? Would anyone feel the power of the threat? No, there had to be more. And, alas, I did need an ally. Eleven o'clock at night is no time to call on the father of the girl you love. I would walk by the house, anyway, and see if a light was on. The front of the house looked dead and dark, but I could

Lesley Choyce

see a bluish light coming from the back. I walked around to that part of the house where Tennessee Ernie did his scientific research and saw him inside, his face before a small TV monitor, puzzling over something. Sucking in my breath, I knocked on the window. Gwen's father looked up but could not see me in the darkness. He opened the back door and spoke to the night, "Who is it?"

I almost turned chicken and wheeled around to go. There was still time to back out of this.

"Speak up or I'll fry you," the voice said. "I've got cables buried in the ground all around here for intruders. If I go back inside, I throw a switch that will send 10,000 volts straight up your legs and into your balls!"

Perhaps it was the threat, or maybe I was getting my courage back, I'm not sure which. But I was not about to take a chance with a somewhat paranoid ex-nuclear physicist who had once helped to develop the most destructive weapon on the planet.

"I thought you said you were a pacifist, like Gwen," I said. "It's me, Ian."

"Jesus, Ian. Why didn't you say something?"

"Can I move?"

"Yes, you can move. The switch is inside. Besides, it's only 7500 volts at an amperage that would only feel like you stuck your toes in a wall socket. It will hurt but it won't kill. And to set the record straight, I said I approved of pacifism. I didn't necessarily say I was a pacifist. Violence has its place when it comes to self-protection. Get over here and tell me what's going on."

Still a little shaken by the thought of electricity passing up my anatomy to my groin, I gingerly tiptoed to the back door. Ernie seemed genuinely happy to see me. "What are you doing out so late?"

"It's a little complicated," I said, not quite ready yet to explain.

He changed the subject. "I was a young man once, too, you know. Complicated times. Hormones flooding through your system, your whole life ahead of you like an unexplored galaxy. Here, look at this." He led me over to the TV screen he had been monitoring. I wanted to tell him it didn't have anything to do with hormones, but I was still a little reluctant to own up to an adult that my heart was set on vandalism.

"Interesting, isn't it?" he said. I stared at the dots of light on the dark screen. "Right there." He pointed to one that was moving.

I shrugged. I couldn't see what the excitement was about.

"A comet passing close to the earth. I'm picking up its trail with my dish outside. I've been tracking it for days. It's now at its closest point to us."

"That's really something," I said, trying to sound impressed. But from where I stood, the little TV monitor could just have been any portable TV set tuned to a channel where the network had gone off the air.

"The important thing is that this comet has never passed through the solar system before and never will again. It's small and what detectable radio waves it does send off are on such a low band width and frequency that no one but me with this rig would pick it up. You are, my friend, privy at this minute to a phenomena that can be afforded only once in a lifetime — nay, once in the history of the earth." And with that, the tiny dot of moving light moved off the screen and was gone. "Don't tell anyone you saw it. I'm not into sharing my discoveries."

"Okay by me. Does it have a name?"

"Of course not. No one knows about it but us."

"Can we call it Gwendolyn?" I asked.

Tennessee Ernie's face lit up. "You betcha. Comet Gwendolyn it is."

I looked around at all the weird gear — the TV monitors, the electronic equipment, the row of car batteries along the

Lesley Choyce

wall. Tennessee switched off the TV and looked at the can I was holding. "What's the paint for?" he asked.

After sharing the discovery of a previously unknown comet with this man, I felt a little foolish in telling him what the paint was for. "I want to let the uranium creeps know how I feel about them," I said.

Ernie scratched his jaw. "Communication is an excellent idea, Ian. I agree. Just how *strong* a message did you have in mind?"

"I thought I might say that they weren't wanted on the island," I said, still not sure how he would react to the rest. "And then I was going to punctuate the message by pouring sand into the gas tank of the drill truck."

Tennessee raised his eyebrows, shook his head up and down like he understood, then looked around the room. "I'm not quite clear on exactly why you came over here to tell *me* this."

"I guess I was looking for some company. I wanted to see if you wanted to come along."

He looked a little confused. "Son, that is a very interesting proposition for a man like me. A man who has a few gripes, yes, against the nuclear industry but who has declared to his daughter and before her friend that, well, I approve of pacifism. But this, I must say, sounds like an act of vandalism — a destructive act, a hostile one even."

"Yes sir," I said. Maybe I had made a mistake by coming over. "But remember, you just said you *approved* of pacifism, yet you weren't a pacifist yourself."

He turned to me now, a finger shaking at me. "That's right. You have captured the logic of the moment. And, like your father, I can see that you are, in essence, a politician, for this is indeed a political act. And while I cannot fully approve of your act of destruction, perhaps I can do what men of science have always done for politicians down through the ages."

"What's that?"

Tennessee Ernie lit up into a smile. "Improve the weapons

of destruction without feeling any sense of moral responsibility whatsoever."

I didn't understand what he was getting at.

"Sand is not a totally effective revolutionary weapon against diesel equipment. There are gas line and carburettor filters which would catch much of it. I have a better solution." He pointed to the string of car batteries on the floor.

As we walked through the marsh to the drill truck, I held the plastic quart bottle of acid away from my chest, anxious that it would not eat through and burn my hands to bloody stumps.

"You see, Ian, it's very interesting what will happen once the acid is inside the piston chamber and that's why I think this is an excellent revolutionary tool."

"I guess it'll really muck it up pretty bad, huh?"

"I'd say the operative terms are *corrosion* and *seizure*. Those are two very powerful words."

I agreed that they were two powerful words and as we arrived at the truck, each of us carrying one quart of the revolutionary liquid, Tennessee jimmied opened the truck door, popped the latch on the engine bonnet and held a flashlight towards the engine block. "Take off the air cleaner and carefully pour each bottle down the carburettor. Keep your face well away; you'll not like the stench." I emptied both bottles in, replaced the air cleaner beneath the beam of Ernie's flashlight and obvious approval. Then we lowered the hood.

"There's the punctuation," Tennessee said, collecting the two plastic bottles to take home, "Now what's the message?"

I picked up the paint can, pried off the lid and stirred it with the brush. I had thought it over long and hard but wasn't quite sure of how to word it.

"Be direct and to the point," Tennessee suggested.

I dipped the brush into the paint and began to paint the message: "Go Home!" I wrote. "Long Live The Republic of Nothing."

Tennessee shone his bright flashlight on my awkward scrawl.

Lesley Choyce

"I think they'll get the picture. Science and politics sometimes work well together hand-in-hand, don't they?"

Late the next morning, I watched from my vantage point up on the hill as the Mannheim/Atlanta men shouted at the drill operators who screamed back at them. When the shouting subsided, Bud Tillish could be seen walking out through the marsh in his city-slicker clothes and, when he'd had a chance to read my message, he started waving his fists up at the sky and using very foul language. I guess I was fool enough to think right then that it was almost over, that Mannheim/Atlanta would go away and that everyone would leave us alone. I was a fairly inexperienced terrorist and had high hopes for the politics of anarchy.

Instead, two hours later an RCMP car passed over the bridge and began making the rounds, asking everyone if they knew who might have wrecked the diesel engine in the drill rig. The Mountie, a square-headed man who introduced himself as Corporal Bellefontaine, caught up with me as I was walking home from a visit with Hants Buckler. "What's your name, son?" he asked.

"Ian McQuade, sir," I said. I was feeling cocky in the great success of my first truly important act of vandalism. I had already decided I wanted to be an anarchist for life and that my first step beyond mere diesel destruction was to turn myself in and become a full-fledged martyr so as to drum up a groundswell of support for the cause of preserving this beautiful island and liberating the Republic of Nothing from the Mannheim/Atlanta mining people.

"Jesus, are you the premier's son?"

"Yes sir," I said. "Everett McQuade is my old man." This was almost too perfect. I was ready to throw a wrench into the works of my father's political career and get myself busted for a good cause all in the same breath. If only Gwen could be here to see this.

But the cop had lost his cold, businesslike style. "I always kind of appreciated McQuade. He's okay. That free fish thing and then just sweeping into Halifax and showing up those other dickheads. I kinda like the idea of a premier coming from right here on the Shore. I hope he makes prime minister some day. Listen, you don't know anything about somebody vandalizing that drilling truck, do you?"

I swear to God, I was about to tell him the truth. The words were just getting all nervous and jumpy in the back of my throat like a pack of birds ready to get released from a cage. But then I saw something that made me stop. A pink and blue Volkswagen van was just driving over the bridge. As soon as it passed over onto the island, it stopped. Someone looked out the window, someone who clearly didn't like the look of the RCMP car. It was somebody with long hair, but I couldn't make out the face. It could have been a girl or a guy with really long locks. Whoever it was quickly veered left, down the old rutted lane towards Mr. Kirk's old place. The cop had noticed nothing in his rear view mirror. His radio was crackling and he hadn't heard the van as it pulled away.

"Never heard of any vandalism on the island the whole time I lived here and I've lived here my whole life," I heard myself say.

"I must admit that, up until now, you're right. Shit, we never get a call to come out here. Wait till you get a bunch of them miners out here digging that ore they been talking about. Then you'll have a mess of fights and piles of trouble. Wait and see."

"Sorry I can't be of more help," I said.

"Let me know if you see anything odd, okay? And say hi to your dad for me. Tell him he's done real good work."

"Sure thing," I said as the Mountie turned his car around and drove back to the mainland. I couldn't get the image of the VW van out of my head. Whoever was driving seemed to know where to go, and I had the clear impression that the driver didn't want to get seen by the cops.

Lesley Choyce

41 I had never seen a Volkswagen bus come across the bridge onto our island before. It represented an exotic *other* culture — the world of American hippies, protesters, a beautiful bag of mixed craziness and spiritual purpose. But today, to me, it meant only one thing. Gwen was back on the island. I had seen the license plate and had made sure that the Mountie was looking at me so he wouldn't see it head down the lane to the old Kirk house. As soon as the cop was across the bridge and out of view, I ran. I forgot about uranium and remembered my heart, the poor, busted up thing inside me that ached for this girl. I was tired of being half alive; she had come back to me.

Or had she? As I got closer I realized that she was not alone. There was at least one other person in the van. I stopped in my tracks and ran through the scenario — the awful, ugly possibility. *Gwen was back with another guy. She had found herself a new boyfriend, a lover.* I wasn't sure I could confront that. Not here, not now. Not ever. But what could I do? Disappear from the island? Go hide somewhere? I felt completely screwed. Yet I couldn't just stand there forever in the muddy rut and not know. So I walked to my execution.

As I approached the Kirk property, I saw Ben first. He was up on the boards of his roof, talking to someone on the ground. A girl in a long paisley dress. Her long light brown hair spilled out from under a leather hat down to the middle of her back. It was Gwen and, already, I could see that she was different. And yes, there *was* someone else sitting in the van. Definitely male. Something about him seemed dark and sinister. I expected that Gwen had taken up with the devil himself. It could only be appropriate.

Ben saw me and waved, nearly losing his footing. "Look who's back!" he yelled.

Gwen turned around and I could see how different she

really was. The hat. A pair of round, rose-tinted glasses, her long hair dangling down either side of her head. I forgot how to walk. Then I forgot how to breathe. I looked up at Ben who had a shit-eating grin on his face. He didn't understand. I looked at the sinister figure still huddled in the van. He was smoking something. A thin vapour trail rose up out from the window. *The devil smokes*, I thought.

Gwen hoisted her skirt, kicked off her sandals and began to run towards me. "Ian!" she screamed. I could see her teeth sparkling in the sun. I watched her lovely legs bounce from rock to rock along the path — that incredible skill we had learned as children running on the island. But she was not a child; there was no doubt of that. She flowed like a woman as she ran towards me; she floated as if in a dream. *Good news/bad news/good news/bad news? Breathe*, I instructed myself. *Damn it. You remember how to do it.* I let go a lungful of stale air and my throat automatically pulled in one good gulp of oxygen before she pounced on me.

My back, my legs had never been tested by this ma-noeuvre. Gwen took flight from one final stone and leapt upon me, wrapping her legs around my back and grabbing me with two long beautiful arms. I staggered backwards but did not topple. Her mouth was on mine and her tongue shot like a javelin down into my throat. "IanIanIanIanIanIan," she said over and over when she withdrew her tongue. Could I have bargained with the devil in the van or with any god-wielding power, I would have paid handsomely to have us left in that wild, abandoned interlock for then and for forever. Pillar of salt, structure of granite, whatever it would take. This was the moment of my life I had waited for, the reason I had been put on earth, the reason I was alive. *Don't touch anything, please God. Don't even think. Just let me have this forever.*

"I love you," I said to the female creature who had usurped my soul. "I missed you and need you. I can't live without you," I said. These were the words. Others have spoken such syllables, I'm sure, but the text can never do justice to the heart. These were potent messengers, these uttered phrases, and they demanded their audience.

Gwen hopped off me, straightened her dress. "God, it's good to be back. It seems like it's been a long time."

"It has been a *very* long time," I assured her. Time had ceased to be measured by clocks as far as I was concerned. It had gone into exponential overdrive.

"Burnet is in the van," she said.

I looked away from her, saw an arm holding a cigarette and the trail of smoke ascending into the blue sky. "He's here?" An avalanche of confusion swept over me. How could he be here? He was in the military. He had gone to Vietnam. Missing, then dead. Presumed dead, anyway. And now he was back. Gwendolyn had brought him. I was awash in guilt for once wishing him dead, relief in knowing that an old friend had survived the war and then, ultimately, terror at the thought that he and Gwen had come back together, that the bastard had taken her from me once again. I wanted to hug him and kill him in one swift motion.

"Come on," Gwen said, pulling me by the hand. "I think you two need to talk."

Oh shit, I figured. *Here it comes.*

"Be careful what you say," Gwen advised me. "Go easy. He's been through a lot."

The door opened as we approached. He stepped out and stubbed his cigarette out on the ground. "Burnet?" Gwen hung back as I walked up to him. He was almost unrecognizable, thin to the point of emaciation, unshaven with a dark coarse beard and long greasy hair. He was wearing a heavy black leather jacket even though it was a warm summer day. And the face — drawn and pale, eyes full of uncertainty.

I guess I suddenly didn't care quite so much what the news was, good or bad. I could tell by the look in his eyes that this was not the devil unless the devil was a beaten, humiliated creature.

I went to give him a hug, but he pulled back. "It's good to see you again, buddy," I said. "I'm glad you're back." And then what was left of the old bully that was once Burnet collapsed on me and began to sob. He let out a low moan and I knew then that the earth was a place parcelled up between joy and pain and it was very necessary to hang onto the good things because *out there* was a world ready to shred you apart.

All four of us walked into Kirk's old house, into the kitchen where Ben boiled a kettle of water and poured tea. There was so much I wanted to hear from Gwen, but I knew that there was a story waiting inside Burnet, a story ready to burst out like a missile from between his ribs, and that story must come first. Here was a soul in desperate need of repair. He had returned to the safe haven of the republic for mending. Ben gave me a look that said, "another refugee," and I understood. Burnet had been a refugee from the moment he was born. He had weathered his old man's bungled fatherhood and gone off to seek success as a hired killer and now he had found his way back to Whalebone Island. It was ironic that he had begun so close, moved away so far, only to find himself back in Kirk's kitchen.

He lit another cigarette and studied the smoke.

"You can trust us," Gwen said taking his hand and giving it a gentle squeeze. "You can trust all of us. The hard part's over now."

"It's not over until I talk to my old man."

"That's not necessary," Gwen said.

It sounded absurd but I knew it was true. Few people ever even saw his father. Burnet Jr. didn't even look like a shadow of his old self. If I hadn't been told, I would never have recognized him. But what had damaged him so? And why had he arrived like this? "What did they do to you?" I asked. I didn't know exactly who *they* were, but somebody or something more malevolent than his old man had beaten him down.

Burnet took another long drag, looked around him like he

was afraid someone was trying to look through the windows or listen from the next room. "They put me in a uniform. They gave me a gun. They pointed me at the Jesus enemy and they told me to kill anybody who got in my way." He shook his head like it was all a bad dream. "I enjoyed the first three. No shit. I enjoyed it. It felt so goddamn right. Like it was the thing I had wanted to do all my life. I loved pulling that trigger and seeing those little creeps fall down. Once I got started I wanted to keep going. I jumped into a nest of VC and just fired away until I had 'em all hammered good. But then I looked up and there was one more. Up above me. So I let him have it and the sucker didn't have a chance. He just took the lead in his chest and fell down over top of me. It knocked me over and I could taste the man's blood dripping right into my goddamn mouth. And I was laughing. I was really enjoying it until I pushed him off and I saw that it was the captain of my own goddamn platoon. He was dead and up above me now were three of my buddies who had just seen what I did."

The kettle began to whistle and Burnet jerked around until Gwen calmed him with a touch on the shoulder. Ben took the pot off the stove.

"So I just friggin' ran. I got the hell out of there and I've been running and running and running."

"He came into the Quaker counselling centre where I was working in Boston just three days ago," Gwen said, her hand on his shoulder. "He told me who he was. I didn't believe it."

"You change after a couple of weeks in the jungle. I got sick a lot. Puked my guts out. Got captured by some locals who were with the VC. They tied me up in a pig shed and stuck sticks under my toe nails. I got loose and headed south. I slept in a sewer in Saigon for ten days. I'm not even gonna tell you what I had to do to get on a plane and get back to the States. But even then, there was no place for me. I'm a deserter, Ian, can you figure that? I don't think it matters that I was a Canadian who didn't have to go." His face contorted in unimaginable pain. "I didn't have to go over there. Once I realized what I'd done, what I'd become, what I'd been turning myself into all my life, all I wanted was to come back home and make it all different."

"You are back home," I told him.

"They won't come after you here. You're safe. Canada isn't shipping back draft dodgers and deserters," Ben said.

"You know what happened when we were coming across the border?" he asked Ben, like he was about to tell some trivial joke. "Go ahead, Gwen. Tell 'em, what happened."

Gwen just shook her head and sipped on the hot tea that had just been poured.

Burnet stood up and pointed at the yellow stain on his dirty white Levis. "I pissed my pants. I was that scared." He seemed to be enjoying his own humiliation.

Gwen tried to change the subject. "I've been trained by the Quakers in the right things to say at the border. Burnet had fake I.D. He did just fine when they questioned him."

An hour later, Burnet was shown to an upstairs room and he went to sleep.

"Many more like him in Boston?" Ben asked.

"They're not all that bad, but some are worse. Burnet still has two arms and two legs. Some don't. Others just want to avoid the draft. They don't want to go to war and they don't think they should have to go to jail. We help them get over the border. Most are going to Montreal. I thought Burnet would be better off here."

Maybe some of my mother's mind-reading techniques had rubbed off on me. I knew exactly what Ben was thinking as he said, "I've got a roof on my new house — well, almost. I can finish it this summer. I've got a reason to now. I think I can finally put Mr. Kirk's house to the promised use."

I looked at Gwen. "You can stay here on the island then. You can help them adjust — continue being a counsellor. Whalebone Island can be the permanent home of war resisters or a halfway house for those moving up here if they want to go on to Halifax or Montreal."

"It's not a bad idea," Ben said. "I'm willing to have a go at this thing. I've worked in psychiatric units. I can be of some help, I'm sure. Besides, *I* really need something."

Gwen was mulling it over in her mind. I was afraid to speak, afraid to say anything. I could see how everything was fitting perfectly together.

"I've got to go back," she said, finally, shattering my hopes and dreams. "There's not much I could do here. I need to be there. I need to be in the States. You don't understand. I'm good at convincing them it's okay to leave their country when they have doubts. Like Burnet, they come in scared to death. They don't want to fight, but some of them think they can't run away from the war. Some of them are right on the line — they don't know if they have the guts to leave it all behind. Sometimes they decide they'd rather be victims, rather be soldiers in a war they hate than have their family think they're unpatriotic. It's crazy, but you wouldn't understand. You grew up here. They *need* me, Ian. They need me there."

I started to speak; I wanted to plead, to beg. Instead, I told her about the uranium. I told her that we stood a good chance of losing the island, of seeing it drilled and dug and wrecked forever, of having it carved up piece by piece and carted off to be made into fuel for nuclear weapons. "I'm scared, too," I said at last. "I know you think you should be in Boston, but we need you here. You can still help out from this end. And the island needs you. *I* need you." I suddenly felt very small and selfish. But I was trapped. I couldn't leave to go with her, not now. And I couldn't live with her away any more.

Gwen looked straight at me, into me. I saw the confusion in her eyes, the worry in her face. Then she put her hand on my neck and pulled herself close to me. "All right, Ian," she whispered in my ear. "Maybe I should stay. For you. You've done so much for me."

I knew then that I had just won some sort of battle; I had been assured of her loyalty. I guess right then I didn't care if what she meant was love or if it was something else. I didn't care if I was being selfish by keeping Gwen here. All I knew was that I had her back with me here on the island, and I was going to hang onto her. I wasn't going to let her go again.

42 There are times in life when everything falls completely apart and times when all the fragments come back together, coalescing into one magnificent, perfect whole. Order and meaning had fought a war with chaos and destruction; the former alliance had won. Gwen had returned. It became clear as we talked that she cared for Burnet only as a friend, that she would help him in his recovery, but she did not want him as a lover. We achieved a strange and rare conspiracy of compassion. Neither of us felt angry at Burnet for what he had been or what he had done. In fact, there was something very easy and natural about forgiving him now. To forgive was, indeed, among the most divine of human deeds. We would make a pact against the stupidity of grudges and revenge. We were of a new generation that would solve global problems by compassion and forgiveness.

Gwen spoke of the people she met in the States, of the great movement of revolution so powerful that the war would *have* to cease for there would be no more soldiers willing to fight. Burnet himself was a reminder to us of how war destroys even the strong, even those with killer instincts. Reduced to a weak phantom of his former self, Burnet was a victim but also a survivor of his past. We would give him a new name and he would live among us, resurrected. Saul transformed to Paul on the road to Damascus. A living metaphor of the transfiguration of the world that the hippies and their allies would bring about.

After Gwen and I left the old Kirk house at nine o'clock that night, we climbed up onto the almost completed roof of Ben's home-in-progress and sat beneath the Nova Scotia sky as the sun departed and the first stars blossomed in the pink and blue of night. Venus appeared first near the cusp of the horizon, a good omen. I held Gwen in my arms and kissed her with all the strength I had. It was the kiss of our rediscovery. So much time had passed since we had been last together.

Gwen and I discussed the game plan. Ben wanted very much "something to do." The island was a perfect refuge for draft dodgers and for AWOL soldiers. The Canadian government would not object. If questions were raised, I would use my father's influence to protect us. I would put his shameless politics to some good use, although I would not dare mention this until after he was renominated by his party and safely re-elected. The papers made it clear. Despite Colin's boondoggles and sleaze, my father would be a shoo-in. A "man of the people" with a "new vision for the province." If ever I had hated my father, I had forgotten about it. Hate would be dropped altogether from the vocabulary of the new order. Peace, equality, freedom, forgiveness and compassion. We would have a code. It was already being hammered out by the kingpins of the revolution, young American men and women Gwen suggested, so pure in their motives and with such inspiration in their hearts that their followers were now in the millions. We would transform the world without guns or greed.

The sky drew dark and those familiar stars, those friends that my mother and I had dreamed into being, returned. They had been there all along, just hiding behind the light of day. In the dark, though, all things became pure and vivid and the shape of the dream had sharp definition. I told Gwen about how her father and I had wrecked the uranium driller's equipment.

"You and my father?" She could hardly believe it. He was part of the revolution.

"We worked together quite well."

"Beautiful. Wow."

"I'm learning to like the guy. We have a lot in common." Well, maybe not a lot. We both hated uranium and loved Gwen. That was probably the limit of it, but it was enough. "Mannheim/Atlanta will never come back now. They'll realize that they're up against a bunch of crazy anarchists."

But Gwen seemed to have lost interest in my assessment of the battle for Whalebone Island. She stood up on the gently sloping roof, brushed her beautiful long hair out with her hands, undid a couple of buttons and let her long paisley dress slip to the boards beneath her bare feet. She towered over me as I lay on my elbows and I looked up at her long naked, beautiful legs. I slid my hand onto her leg and felt the sheer delight of her warm soft skin. I kissed her delicately upon the foot, then the ankle, then crawled forward on my elbows like a soldier on his belly in the battlefield of love, in a war where no enemy exists.

I heard her let out a wonderful cosmic sigh as she slipped down onto her knees and I made a trail up her thigh until I found her cleft and softly invaded with my tongue. She bent back and as I watched I saw the beautiful arc of her body aglow with the cold, clean light of startime. I dove deep with my tongue and reached up the length of her with my arms until she found my hands and pulled me, a prisoner, now further and further into her. I don't pretend that I have such great skills at such things but a young man invents, improvises, takes tutorial delight from the shuddering of a woman's body. On a divine night like this he takes counsel from the light of distant suns. After the first shock wave of our lovemaking passed, I slid up onto her and we rolled over and over on the roof, our backs occasionally encountering the shock of a renegade roofing nail. If it scratched or drew blood, I'm sure we couldn't have cared less, for we made love until exhausted. Then we fell asleep, right there on the sloping roof beneath the stars.

When I woke, maybe an hour later, chilled now by a light breeze up off of the ocean, I found that we had rolled in unison to the very edge of the roof. Below us was a ten-foot drop to a pile of shingle scraps. As I gently nudged Gwen back from the precipice, she woke up and we laughed, reassembled ourselves, sorted out our intermingled souls and put our clothes back on.

"Beautiful," Gwen said.

"Wow," I added. Those two words had become anthem.

"Beautiful. Wow," we declared together, bumping our heads forehead to forehead.

I walked Gwen home, led her to her door, then evaporated into the night to find my way back to my bed at home, to explain everything right down to our lovemaking to my mother and to prepare myself for the years of euphoria to come.

If any of this sounds naive, I beg you to remember that I had grown up the son of a proud anarchic revolutionary and a beautiful metaphysical sorceress. Dreams changed lives. Wives appeared as gifts from the sea. The distribution of free fish to the masses brought power of political dimension. On an island in the Republic of Nothing, minds were read, dogs brought back from the dead, elephants appeared on the shore, Vikings slept and grandfathers took trains and ferries back to life from purgatory. Certainly in such a republic, mere human happiness was possible. Certainly two people could love each other enough, forge enough forgiveness and compassion in their souls to transform a small planet into a Garden of Eden. All of this was possible.

My mother was asleep when I got home. I counted the pills. She had not taken a single one. I leaned over her, listened to her regular breathing. I decided that I liked the sound of my mother breathing. Something about it reminded me of the sitar music on the Beatles' *Sergeant Pepper's Lonely Hearts Club Band* album. My mother's arm was stretched across the bed where my father had once slept. Her hand clutched his pillow. Every time I saw my mother sleeping alone I was saddened, but tonight was different. I was sure that if things were going so right for me, I could not help but drag the rest of us into good fortune.

I lay down beside of my mother on the place where my father should have been. I lay on top of the covers but put my head on the pillow and lifted my mother's hand, held it in my own. I remained like that, motionless on my back, drifting off into a deep meditative trance, for I was convinced that sleep was no longer necessary for me. I had been revived enough by Gwen's return to remain fully awake for the rest of my days.

I knew that my deep meditative trance might well have something to do with my mother as well. During the heights of her powers, she had some sort of energy field that could stretch out to affect others. Had Tennessee Ernie possessed the right equipment, I'm sure he could have measured this aura, this electromagnetic wavelength that could engulf another mind with her own and bring about a deep, relaxing state. I was like that, lost in the limits of a peaceful, emptied mind when I felt her pull her hand away. I felt the bed shudder and jerk and heard my mother trying to speak. It took me a few seconds to come back into this world.

At first I felt slightly embarrassed that I had lay down on the bed beside my mother and drifted off like this. The old me worried, in my daze, if this was somehow perverse or unnatural, but I quickly erased that from my mind. I sat up. My mother was making noises. Her head was shaking from side to side. Her eyes were still closed but she was trying to talk, trying to let out a sound, but it was as if she could not open her mouth. I knew she was dreaming something terrible and I remembered something about the dangers of awakening someone in the middle of a nightmare. I wanted to hold her to quiet her thrash-

Lesley Choyce

ing, but I was afraid to touch her. She shook her head from side to side rapidly and so hard I feared she'd break her neck.

Still not knowing quite what to do, I got up off the bed and began whispering to her, "It's all right. You're going to be all right, Dorothy." But her movements became more spasmodic. Then her mouth unsealed and she began to say, "No, No, No!" in a hoarse, distressed whisper. Her arms started to strike out into the air at something. "You can't do this," she said in her nightmare and then finally, overwhelmed by whatever had taken possession of her, she let out a long blood-chilling scream and sat bolt upright in bed.

Casey came running into the room and switched on the light. She saw the confusion in my face and the panic in my mother. She took our mother in her arms and began to rock her like a little baby. Dorothy was awake now and crying, a sound of pure agony spilling out into the room like nothing I had ever heard before.

"It's okay, Mom," Casey said. "Ian and I are both here. Everything is all right."

My mother looked straight at me now and I wanted to reach out, to hold her, but I was frightened by the strange and terrible look in her eyes. It was some sort of recognition, but I had no idea what she was seeing. She pulled away from me and wept into Casey's neck. Casey just kept repeating over and over, "It's okay, it's okay, it's okay." I sat on the bed with them, wanting to hold onto them both but unsure of what to do. What had my mother seen in me after her dream, her nightmare? Casey, now grown suddenly older and responsible, rocked my mother until the terror had diminished into soft sobbing.

"It was just a dream," I told my mother, reaching out to her and, holding her tear-ravaged face in my hands. "It was just a dream. Everything is back to normal now."

She shook her head. "No. It wasn't just a dream. And everything is not back to normal."

"What do you mean?" Casey asked.

"I know what happened," my mother said. "I finally know what happened before your father found me."

"Don't talk about it now," I said. "Just try to relax and think about being here with us."

"I want Everett to be here right now. I need him to be here. Why the hell isn't he here?" she whispered.

‹‹‹‹‹‹‹‹‹‹‹‹‹‹‹‹‹‹‹‹‹‹‹‹‹‹‹‹

43 My father would not be coming home that night. The leadership convention was only two days away. He was on a roll. I tried phoning his apartment but there was no answer. So I tried his office. He was there but Herb Legere was the closest I could get to my old man. "Your father is still in a strategy session. It's been going all night," he explained. "It's crucial we iron out one final detail. I'd rather not bother him with a family matter right now."

"Family matter, for Christ's sake!" I shouted over the phone. "My mother is very upset. This isn't like her. I'm not sure what's happening, but I know she's in trouble and my father should be here."

Herb was cool as a cucumber. "I can refer you to a very good psychiatrist. In fact, I think there are a few in the party loyal. Perhaps one would be willing to drive down there tonight. What do you think?"

"We don't want a fucking psychiatrist!" I shouted at him over the phone, then stifled myself, not wanting my mother to hear more of my outburst.

"Please, Ian," Herb cajoled me. "These, as I said, are very sensitive times. I prefer news of your mother's problems doesn't spread. We'll do whatever we can do to help."

"Fuck you, Herb," I said. "Let me speak to my father. And after that, take a pair of vice grips and apply them to your balls."

"I can understand why you feel this way," he said, still cool as a frozen turd. I was amazed at the skills it must take to be a good sycophant. *Never act surprised. Never get emotional and above all, never lose your cool.* "I'll level with you, Ian, because I know you are an intelligent young man. Your father is under a lot of stress right now himself. Another member of the caucus has decided to make a big stink about your father's nomination."

"Well, gosh, who could object to such a sweet guy like my father?" I said sarcastically.

"John G.D. MacIntyre," Herb answered. "You know him."

"I remember him," I said. "He was the bastard who got my father into politics in the first place."

"John G.D. feels your father is too young. John is jealous and thinks he should have inherited the crown from Colin."

"Good. Let him."

"If MacIntyre gets nominated, we won't survive the election. The party goes down the toilet."

"Great news. I'm going to celebrate. Now can I speak to my father?"

"Ian, this is serious. There is a lot at stake here. Can I ask you something? Something personal that won't go any farther than between you and me?"

"Sure, Herb. Let's be bosom buddies. You tell me your secrets and I'll tell you mine."

"Well, I told you about John G. D. Now, would you consider telling me about the Republic of Nothing?"

"What?" It caught me off guard.

"And you wouldn't happen to know anything about somebody pouring sulphuric acid down the carburettor of some equipment on Whalebone Island?"

I felt the blood draining down toward my toes. "What are you talking about?"

"John claims that somebody from the island is trying to discourage one of the best economic opportunities to happen to the Eastern Shore in the history of the province."

"That Jesus uranium pit they want to dig? You've got to be kidding. There will be a few jobs for a few years until they ruin this place. Then the Yanks and their German allies will take the money and run. We'll be left in a pile of radioactive rubble. That isn't what I call a great economic opportunity."

"Thanks for the lesson in ecology, son. But do you know anything about it?"

"Why would you ask me? Think the son of the premier would try to get himself thrown in jail? What are you, crazy?"

"Well, it's just that somebody found something there."

"Yeah, uranium. Just our luck."

"No. A letter. An old typewritten document about something called the Republic of Nothing. It was on the ground. The police don't know about it. There was also something spray painted on the truck, something about this republic. Do you know anything about it?"

"No," I said flatly.

"Your father's name was signed to it. It sounded nuts, the whole thing. But it *was* your father's signature. This is a new one to me. I haven't run across this sort of problem before in our office."

"Who gave it to you?" I asked.

"Well, I don't really *have* it. MacIntyre has it."

"Why? I don't get it. John G.D. hasn't been on the island."

"Yes. But Bud Tillish has."

I guess I was a little slow at putting the pieces together. Slowly, I reached into the back pocket of my pants. I had worn them the other night. They'd not been washed since. It wasn't there. Nothing but sand and lint. I saw the first link in the chain and I realized that my skills as a political vandal were lacking. But I would not confess to Herb.

"Why would Bud Tillish give such a thing to somebody in the opposing party? Why not go straight to the cops?"

Herb let out a small bureaucratic laugh, the most emotion he was capable of. "Because no one would believe it coming from Bud. They'd say he made it up. So he turned it over to John G.D. MacIntyre. John's looking for leverage. Bud wants your old man out of the race so he can get his seat back. Think it through. This is what backroom politics is all about."

"I never heard of anything as ridiculous as the Republic of Nothing," I lied. "It's a hoax, Herb. A laughable joke."

"Well, maybe it is and maybe it isn't. But right now, even as we speak, your father and MacIntyre are hoot to headers ready to fight it out with bare knuckles. I wish you could give me a little insight into this."

"I'm sorry," I said. "I can't."

"If I could get this in focus, make some sense of it, maybe I could put a spin on it, somehow use it to our advantage if John wants to go public. Wouldn't you help us just to save your father's political career?"

"You bet your ass, I won't. I want my father's political career dead and buried."

"I'm sorry you feel that way. But then, we still have the advantage over an old buzzard like MacIntyre. We'll buy him off somehow. Everyone has his price."

"Fuck you, Herb." I had to say it just one more time. "Goodnight."

"Nice talking to you. Let's chat again, after the convention."

I slammed the phone down and ran past my mother's room where I saw Casey still sitting with her, my mother's head bowed down. I knew that I had a sloppy memory. Maybe I had put the document back. I checked the manila envelope in the desk drawer. Nothing. In my room, I pulled out the box from under my bed — the old cigar box with the rubber band around it. This was my box of sacred things and I had this idea — wishful thinking, nothing more — that I had come home from wrecking the machinery and dutifully filed the copy of my father's letter here. Of course the declaration wasn't there either. It wasn't anywhere else in the room.

I went back to the cigar box and looked at the remainder of

the contents. There was a lock of Gwen's hair from when she was twelve years old. Nestled in it was a small chunk of gold my father had found for me. It's funny, but I remembered that it was the island's gold that my father had feared. He used to worry in the old days that someone would discover the fragments of gold imbedded in white quartz all around the island, then come and pit mine the place despite the fact that there would never be enough to make it economically viable. I had a small batch of notes from Gwen, foolish kid things we had passed back and forth in junior high. The picture of Gwen's real grandfather was beneath them, stapled to a picture of old Duke, drowned now and gone for good. And beneath that smiling image of one of the happiest, most peaceful men I had ever met, was a photo of my own mother and father, taken when they were both still very young, soon after my mother had been salvaged from the sea. Two handsome, unbelievable human beings, just kids themselves, smiling into the sun and into the lens of Mr. Kirk's camera, holding each other, frozen forever in this idyllic pose. My hair began to stand on end as I looked at the photo and realized that it was a picture of my own two parents taken before I was born. Why this should send a chill through me, I didn't know. But it made me wonder about a world where, if things had gone otherwise, I would not exist. If my old man had not been fishing at that exact place at sunrise, my mother might have simply drifted away from the coast like old Duke's drowned corpse. She may have ultimately drowned; my father would have returned with a few fish. And where the hell would poor little baby Ian come from?

I stuffed the photos back into the Dutch Masters box and tried to wrestle the rubber band back onto it. Enough reminiscing, enough of futile worries of what might have been. The problems of the present were great enough. Damn. The old rubber band snapped, spilling the contents on the floor. I stared at an item I had not taken out: the finger. The finger of the dead Viking. What would the old boy think if he knew

that some modern pirates with an eye on profiting from thermonuclear weapons were about to disturb his ancient sleep?
Didn't I used to carry the thing around for good luck? Sure.
And sometimes it worked; sometimes it didn't. Then, one day,
I had given up on such childish superstitions and simply
stashed the desiccated finger in the sacred cigar box with other
holy but childish relics. I put the rest of the items back into the
box and slid it under my bed. The finger, however, went into my
pocket. My faith in the charm was not strong, but I figured
that I needed all the luck I could muster. I went back in to my
mother's bedroom. "Dad says he wants you to know he loves
you very much and that he'll always love you. I told him he
should stay there and that I could handle it. I told him everything would be okay for now but that he should get home as
soon as he could." It was a farcical lie. I doubted that Dorothy
had missed the animated phone conversation I had had with
Herb. She smiled and put a hand on the back of my neck.

"Why don't I call Bernie? Maybe she can come over for a
while and you two can talk."

My mother seemed more together now. "No. I think I know
what I have to do. I can't go back to sleep. I can't even start to
tell you about what I know. But you two beautiful kids are
going to get some sleep. I'm going to sit here and write the
story. I've been reading books all my life. I was always waiting
to have a story worth telling. Now I have one that scares the
living daylights out of me, but the only way I'm going to tell it
is on paper."

"Will you let us read it?" Casey asked.

"I think so. But your father should read it first. Now go to
bed."

"Leave the door open, okay?" I asked. I was still afraid for
my mother. Even though she had recovered the composure of
her old self, I knew it would be not easy to reconnect with the
terrified young woman who she had once been. I would check
in on her periodically, make sure she was okay.

"I'll leave it wide open. Now hand me that paper over there and get out. Get some sleep. I guess this is the night I've been waiting for."

I intended not to sleep, but something pushed me over the precipice of awareness into a dark dreamless pit where I lost my ability to conjure the consciousness to check on my mother. My body and mind just gave up trying for the night. In the morning, sunlight lay down a golden ribbon, warm as honey, issuing through the crack between the window shade and the sill. I studied it for a second, almost unaware of the tumultuous events from the previous few days. Maybe I thought I was still a kid. Maybe I'd go out to sea on this warm summer morning with my old man and we'd catch flounder and haddock and come home like heroes to my mother and baby sister. Maybe it was still like that. But all too soon memory reported back like a gunshot and fired all the details of the past few days back into my head. I bounced from bed, threw on my pants and ran out of my room calling for my mother.

"I'm in the kitchen," she said. "Go say hello to your father."

What? My father? Was she out of her mind? Was she dreaming? Had I actually succeeded in transporting myself back into my past? I burst into the living room. There was my old man settled into his favourite chair by the south window — just sitting there in a pool of sunlight, reading.

"Ian," he said, getting up. "Good to see you, son. Thanks for calling. I'm sorry Herb is such a twit. He means well."

"Dad?" I asked, giving him a hug.

"Yeah?"

"How long can you stay?" There was already one miracle under the belt for the day; I was expecting two.

"Not long. I've already been here for a couple of hours. Reading your mother's story. It's your turn next." As he looked down at the handwritten pages, I could tell that he had been deeply shaken by what he had read. "You don't have to read it if you don't want."

Lesley Choyce

"I have to," I said.

Casey and my mom came out of the kitchen and told us breakfast was ready. I looked at the clock. 8:30. I couldn't believe my father had been here since 6:30 and no one had woken me up. Then I realized my lie to my mother from the night before had come true. My old man *had* found his way out of the Tory back room and come home, however briefly. I suddenly felt overwhelmed with love for the old anarchist. I grabbed him and gave him a hug around the neck. He looked immensely pleased and punched me gently in the rib cage like he had in the days when I was a boy. "Ian, you're good kid. But we have to discuss this little rebellious streak you're developing before it gets out of hand."

"What do you mean?"

"The vandalism. Maybe you did what needed to be done. But not so sloppy next time. Besides, learn to work through the system, not against it."

"But what about the uranium? They're going to ruin the island."

He held his finger up to his mouth for me to be quiet. "Not if I'm nominated and re-elected. Nobody will touch this place, I promise you."

I didn't want to ask him about the grief I had brought him by losing the declaration and he didn't seem to want to explore it further. Instead, we all chowed down to scrambled eggs and kippers, bacon, coffee and home-fried blue potatoes. It was a happy family scene. No one spoke a word about my mother's nightmare, about her past, about politics, uranium or elections.

"Gwen's back," I told my father.

"Great," my father said, his mouth full of food. "Marry her before she gets away again."

I was caught off guard. "I'm not sure she's into marriage," I answered.

"Then live with her for a while and see how it works out," he said.

"What?" Casey blurted out, shocked at her father's statement. My mother looked astonished.

"Well, you know. If you love her, let her know it. Make some sort of commitment. Sometimes young people are too afraid to make commitments." This was ironic coming from my old man who had inadvertently sacrificed his family for a life with smelly men who smoked cigarettes in meeting halls plotting the success of the Tory party.

"I'll think about it," I said. There was nothing I'd want more than to live with Gwen, to marry her or settle into any arrangement she liked.

"Maybe the two of you can live in here for a bit if I get re-elected. Casey and your mother can come into Halifax and live the life of Riley with me running the province. He looked at my mother. "They'll treat you like a queen," he said, then turning to Casey, "and you like a princess."

A scowl crept across my mother's face. This was an old battle ground and my father had re-opened wounds.

"Hey, I was only kidding," he said, trying not to shatter the good mood of the morning meal. "I'll call a contractor about building an addition on this old place. Gwen and Ian can live back there."

"Dad, I think I'll move in with Gwen when the time is right."

"Suit yourself." My father checked his watch. "Dorothy, let's go out for a walk. I've got ten minutes before I absolutely have to leave. Even at that, the only way I'm going to get to Halifax in time for the caucus meeting is if I go double the speed limit."

"If the Mounties stop you, I'm sure they won't give you a ticket," I said, thinking about the cop I'd met just yesterday.

"My party is opposed to favouritism of any sort or privileges for government members. Remember that, okay?" he said in a mock official voice, then leaning closer to me, he

Lesley Choyce

joked, "If I get stopped, how much do you think I should offer him? I've only got a twenty on me."

"That's too much," I said. "This is the Eastern Shore. People are poor. Give him the twenty and ask for ten in change. He'll be happy."

My old man winked and gave me a thumbs up. He waltzed my mother out into the sunlight. Casey and I smiled at each other and I watched her eyes light up, sparkling with delight. It was as if last night had never happened.

﹏﹏﹏﹏﹏﹏﹏﹏﹏﹏﹏﹏﹏﹏﹏﹏﹏﹏

44 They walked for exactly sixteen minutes; I timed them. Then my father was in his borrowed government car and gone in a cloud of stone and dust, not even having said goodbye. But I gave him credit for those extra six minutes more than he had committed himself to. I gave him credit for coming home to my mother against the wishes of his advisors. My mother returned inside and picked up the pages she had written the night before from the chair where my father had left them.

She straightened them and handed them to me. With a sad smile, she said, "Your father is a good man. But he's stubborn. He doesn't believe this actually happened to me. He says it was just a bad dream and it was healthy for me to get it out of my system. He said I was a much better storyteller than he realized and that I should start writing fiction."

"How could he say that?"

"I don't know. Your father believes what he wants to believe. I think he feels I went crazy last night so you would call him and he would come running. He says that it was a natural response to him ignoring the family like he does."

"Is that all he said?"

"He apologized for being away so much, tried to get me to move to Halifax again. When I said no, he said that he'd probably be premier for five years, tops. Then he'd get out before he became too much like the rest."

"Bull," I said.

"Your father's a very determined man," she said. She put the record of her dream into my hands. "Now it's your turn, Ian. Read it. Tell me what you think."

Trying to read my mother's handwriting was like gazing at flowers in a garden. Even a story as horrific as this was written in a graceful hand that was hard to resist, the letters were well shaped, attractive and appealing. At first, I could hardly make my eyes focus on the words; I just stumbled around the garden of the flowery script. Maybe I was still afraid of what I would actually read. Nonetheless, I would sit there in my father's chair and read all of it. I would learn the story that had been locked up inside for so many years.

It starts out on a ship travelling along the coast of Nova Scotia. It's dark and I smell oil or kerosene maybe, or diesel fuel. I'm in my bed in a hot cabin beneath deck. I'm afraid of something and I don't know what, but this does not seem unfamiliar to me. I am acquainted with fear. It is an old companion. There are sounds of creaking and moaning. When I am fully awake, I am very confused. It is like waking up from a dream where you are certain you are already awake. Now you're not sure which is real and which is imagined.

I am so used to this confusion that I have a little ritual to calm me down. First I say my name to myself. I am Anna. Then I tell myself where I am. I am on the ship, *Night Sky. Why am I here?* My father is the captain. It is a creaky old steamer that travels to the harbours, the deep ones along the shore of mainland

Nova Scotia, Cape Breton and Newfoundland. *Why, again, am I here?* Because my father loves us very much and wants us near him on his trips. *Us?* My mother and me. She is somewhere in the cabin with my father, somewhere in the darkness. I want to call to my mother but something stops me. It is my father. He scares me.

If it were light, I could see him — he is a handsome man who is always perfectly dressed and well-shaven except for long sideburns. My mother is a delicate, beautiful woman who always speaks in soft whispers. My mother would like to have a permanent house on land, a little cottage with a place for planting flowers and kale. But my father says it would be a waste. So sometimes we live in rented rooms in Halifax or Sydney. Other times we go with him at sea if the season is not too rough.

I want to know why I feel the way I do. I want to know why I am so scared, why I am always scared. I remember that it is because of my father's temper. Among the men, my father is highly respected. He treats his men well and they treat him with great respect. My father's favourite word is "dignity." "The men are creatures," he often says of his crew, "but all it takes is a captain who is well-bred and full of dignity to preserve order." My father tolerates no drinking or fighting. He runs an orderly ship.

Then why am I so afraid? It is because I hear things in the dark. I hear the engines and the moaning ship. That does not bother me. On quiet nights I sometimes hear nothing at all except for the low, almost soothing, rumble of the engine. But then the bad weather comes. It is not the sea, however, that I am afraid of. I love the sea, even though I sometimes get sick to my stomach and throw up in the sink. My mother says this is natural. But when I throw up, it is not because of the sea. It's something else.

At night, during the storms, I hear things in our cabin. I wake up in the morning and I see my mother putting on make-up. She looks different. Sometimes she has fallen out of her bunk at night, or gotten up to go to the bathroom and fallen over, bumped into things as people do on rolling ships sometimes. My mother has bruises on her face and marks on her neck. She is very good at covering them up with heavy powder but then she looks so much like someone who could not be my mother. *What happens on stormy nights when the sea thuds against the hull and the winds whip up nuisances of noise?* I wake this night and wonder. It was stormy the night before and my mother woke up with a swollen face, a cut over her eye. I wonder why I did not hear her wake up or cry out when she accidentally walked into the door.

But tonight it is still. So I should be able to sleep. I lay awake for hours until a new wind comes up and the sea begins to add familiar noises to those of the ship. Always I will fall asleep at this point. I don't know why, but I have learned to fall asleep immediately during a storm. I can never remember being awake during a night of choppy seas. And now I hear it. A dull thud and the sound of pain. My mother has bumped into something in the night. *Why doesn't she turn on the light?* I hear a muffled cry again. I want to call out but my voice does not work. Maybe my father is not there. Perhaps he's gone above to see that everything is tied down on deck. He is a very conscientious captain. Maybe he is not here.

No, I hear the sound of a man in the cabin. I recognize it as my father's voice, but barely discernable. It is hushed and full of anger. *I hear bodies moving,*

Lesley Choyce

wrestling. He is fighting with someone in my cabin. *Who would he be fighting with?* Then I hear the sound of a fist striking flesh, a hard thud followed by the sound of a hand slapping something. *Can it be the sea, the sea stirred to its usual anger by the east winds and a newly arrived storm?* No, it's not outside. It's in here.

"Mother," I cry out. "Mother, are you there?"

But there is no answer. Only my father in that hushed growl of his, a voice I swear I had never heard him use in daylight, cursing at her. "Shut up! Shut up, you bitch." Then another slap and a high pitched wail, cut off unnaturally. Then the sound of someone trying to breathe, the sound of my mother choking for air, unable to get air to her lungs.

I lay still, frozen for several seconds, waiting again to wake up, telling myself this is all a product of my night fears, of too many nights sleeping in hot dark cabins on this ship. Until I am swept into a whirlpool of sounds and images. I realize that what is happening has happened before. *I've woken to scenes like this before. Only on the stormy nights. And I have always gone back to sleep.* But I'm older now. I'm fifteen. Tonight, it is hard to make myself believe that these are merely the fears of my insecure mind. I find that, almost against my will, I am up out of my bed and my hand is on the light switch by the door. I don't want to turn it on but I must. And then suddenly it is on. My hand has moved on its own.

I am looking at my father in his nightshirt sitting up on the bed, his legs straddling my mother who is flat on her back. He has pinned her down and his hands are on her throat. In the cold, terrible light, I see his hands on her throat. I can see that his hands have gone white, he is squeezing so hard. I can see that my mother's face looks swollen. Her mouth is open. His hands are on still on her throat. All at once I remember the other nights. I had never seen anything but I had heard it all before. Despite the light, my father does not turn around. He does not let go. I know that my mother, that fragile, gentle person who brought me into this world, is already dead. My father, only now reacting to my desperate act of turning on the light, turns his head my way and I see the look of anger and hate begin to turn to confusion and disbelief. It is almost as if he had acted in his sleep, that he is now shocked at what he has done and cannot believe any of it. I put one hand on the door handle, turn off the light and run out of the cabin.

Up above, outside in the cold, chill Atlantic air, I stumble around barefoot on the iron plating of the deck. I am alone. Then I hear my father's voice calling to me. "Anna," he is saying. "It's all a mistake. You don't really understand."

But I do understand. I say nothing. I hide from him behind some crates.

"Then to hell with you," he shouts at me. And I know that I cannot live with what I have just seen. I cannot live with all the memories of the other nights along with the true horror of this night. I jump over the rail and into the dark water. The cold water paralyses me and I want to die in it. I want the pain of the cold to punish me for letting this happen. I want to sink beneath the waves but I find I cannot sink. Something is making me swim. It's the pain of the cold water that makes me thrash about and I see that I am swimming away from the ship. I want to die alone at sea like this. I want it very badly.

My arms work to keep me afloat no matter how much I tell them to stop. I try to swallow water to

Lesley Choyce

speed up the process but cannot. I am looking back at the ship. I see a man on deck in the cold white lights. I know it is my father. He is swinging an axe high above his head and bringing it down hard onto one of the fuel drums near the bow. I hear the clang of metal against metal. Then I see him kick the barrel along the deck. He leans over and then there is a surge of fire, a leaping flame that shoots across the deck. I want to turn away but I can't.

Then I see my father himself aflame, outlined against the dark night. He stands with his arms outstretched calling out to me. I watch this human torch burn and think it is not enough. It is too easy. He deserves worse. I watch as he walks to the mounted life boat, unhitches it — this a man whose clothes are on fire and who must be able to smell the stench of his own flesh burning. He succeeds in dropping the lifeboat over the side. Then he falls back against a bulkhead, I see the lick of the flame has nearly encircled the deck now. I hear a horrible deep roar, an explosion surges upward as the ship convulses and erupts into a reddish yellow ball of light. I feel the heat on my face and I like it. With my eyes closed, it feels warm like sunlight on a fine summer day. It is all I have and I decide it is enough to carry me some place else, this warmth.

I clasp my fingers together tightly before me. I feel the heat on my face. With my eyes closed like this, I imagine I can see the sun. I fight the urge to splash and thrash and, at last, bless whatever force allows me to sink.

I expect to lose the light, to lose the sun, the blinding fireball that was once my home but it stays inside my eyelids as I sink. Each time panic and fear burst inside my head, I see the light again, and I hear the song of the sea. I don't know why I begin to struggle again but I do. I am beneath the sea when all goes black and I am afraid. I have lost the light. And now I want it back. I scream and my lungs fill with sea water. Inside my head I go on screaming.

Until I stop. And I am free. Released. Floating. It is less like an ocean and more like a sky but it is because I have been released from my body. My eyes are somehow open, though, and I can see the water all around. I no longer feel any sense of cold. I am released. There is another light now, beneath the water and far off but it is all there is and I must go towards it.

But now a hand has touched mine. A warm, human hand. It is my father. I want to scream again but he smiles — a smile that is at once unbearably sad and full of regret but also it is a fatherly smile.

I begin to try to swim towards the light which now seems farther away, but I must go towards it to get away from him. He does not pull me back. His hand is but a gentle tug and then a request that comes to me in a voice that is truly my father's but also sounds like that of a choir or a chorus speaking to me in many voices, all telling me that I should not swim towards the light. I can barely see the light now. I'm confused. It seems so far away. As I try to focus on my father, his face shifts. I see the torturous expression from the cabin shift to soft sadness, then compassion, then a plea. *Follow me up.*

In the morning I wake up in a small wooden boat drifting at sea. I can remember nothing. The sun is coming up and I feel its warmth. A fiery red-headed young man is rowing towards me. I wonder who I am.

45 "It took me all night to write that," my mother said. "I kept hoping it was someone else's story. I knew it was mine. I was just putting down the pen when your father walked through the door."

"He always did have a sense of timing," I said. I wanted to react to what I had just read, but I couldn't. It seemed inconceivable that the woman who raised me, my mother, had lived this other life and survived this horrible thing.

Casey walked into the room. "I want to read it now. I want to know what happened," she said. I held onto the loose pages as she tugged at them. I looked at my mother.

"Casey should read it, too," she said.

I let go of the nightmare and Casey walked back to her room with it.

"The big question is, can I live with it?" my mother said to me. "Now that I remember, I can never erase it again. I should feel stronger but I feel shattered."

"I can understand that. But you have all those other years of your life on the island. And you have us."

"But there's something else. Remember how I reacted to you when I woke up."

"You were very frightened."

"It's not just that. I looked at you and I saw my father."

"You were just coming out of the dream."

"No. It was more than that. When I looked at you, I saw something — the face of my father as he pulled me to the surface of the sea. Like I wrote in the story, his face was the face of many people — the ones he had been and the ones he would be. And I think one of them was you."

My mother invited everyone on the island, one by one, to come visit her and hear about her missing past. She gave me the written account and told me to keep it in a safe place. I folded it and put it in the cardboard box under my bed where it would haunt me in days to come. Had I been a murderer in my previous life? Had I killed my mother's mother, then pulled Dorothy/Anna back from her own death only to come back as her own child to do what? Good deeds on Whalebone Island? Take care of her? I refused to believe it. I closed my eyes and searched for a murderer within. I searched for something dark and evil inside me. Nothing. Then I remembered two things. I remembered my secret wish that Burnet be killed at war. And I remembered the first time I made love to Gwen; only it wasn't making love.

Still, I refused to believe what my mother suggested. I was neither better nor worse than anyone else alive. I was simply human. Reincarnation, with spirits guiding you from beyond their own demise, was an exotic game my mother had played all my life. I had never challenged her voices, her "spirituality," but it was not a set of beliefs shared by everyone. Part of me always doubted it.

For the next two days, the islanders found their way to our house to hear my mother's story. Bernie came and then Jack. Both were crying as they left. Ben was next. Then Hants Buckler followed by Lambert and Eager, and Gwen's parents, one at a time. I wasn't sure I understood the necessity of this. It somehow reminded me of a funeral. The visitations of friends, the eulogy, but it was something else for it was both a birth and a death. I was hoping that it was my mother's way of getting adjusted to the long-buried facts of her elusive past and of burying them once and for all. My mother had promised not to mention anything to anyone about her bizarre suspicion that I was her father reincarnated. I had convinced her that such a notion was just too crazy and she agreed; at least she said she did not want to shackle me with such a burden. "We can't choose our predecessors any more than we can choose our parents," she suggested. And I realized that there was a curious corollary to that rule because my father had *chosen* Bernie and Jack to be my mother's island parents.

Gwen and I had spent most of those two days in Ben's kitchen, planning for the arrival of draft dodgers and AWOL soldiers. She had talked to the Quakers in Boston and they were ecstatic. There were problems in Montreal, harassment by the city police of the overcrowded halfway houses for Yanks who had come over the wall to Canada. There was a growing need to spread the refugees further afield in Canada. Nova Scotia was wide-open territory. There would still be problems at the border. The politics seemed erratic. Sometimes dodgers seeking asylum were let in straightaway, allowed to immigrate outright. Other times they were harassed, some sent back directly into the hands of U.S. Immigration if they could not prove that they had a guaranteed residence waiting for them in Canada along with financial sponsorship. Some who were sent back ended up in jail for draft evasion. From now on, all would have to come to the country with a guarantee of a place to live and jobs. Eager and Lambert had already declared that they were willing to train and hire "any draft dodger, wimped-out soldier or lady-hair hippie" if they were willing to work hard for low wages.

I kept an eye on the bog and was pleased that no one had returned. There was nothing remaining of the uranium drilling but the ruts and a small muddy pool.

At the end of the second day after my mother's dream, she invited Gwen to come hear her story. I had been hoping Dorothy would not invite her, but there was nothing I could do to stop it. I sat outside the window of my own house and listened to the tale again, deeply disturbed and worried somehow that my mother would break her vow of silence and suggest to Gwen the link between her father and her son. But she did not. Gwen seemed shaken as she left our house. I walked her home and we said very little to each other.

When I sat down Saturday afternoon to watch the Tory leadership convention on TV, my mother immediately switched the set off. "I can't watch it," she said. "If I do I'll be praying for your father to lose. I know it's selfish of me. But I will."

"It's going to be a short convention. He's going to win on the first ballot. All the papers say so," Casey said. "Please. I want to see Daddy give his speech."

"I'm going over to see Ben," Dorothy said and she left the house. "Watch whatever you want. Just don't tell me anything about it when I come back unless your father loses."

"We'll be rooting for him to lose, too." But right then I don't know if I really meant it a hundred percent. Sure, we all wanted my father home, but I was secretly proud of his success, of his ability to become the top dog of all those sophisticated hot shots from all over the province. I figured that Herb Legere must have solved the little problem of the declaration of independence. He must have found the proper sleazy deal to keep Bud Tillish and John G.D. MacIntyre quiet. I was wondering how much it had cost. If MacIntyre had wanted to spill the story, it would have been out by now.

Our TV reception was pretty bad and I kept getting up to move the rabbit ears from one direction to another. The convention looked silly and childish to me. People waving signs up and down, shouting, horns. Somewhere in that mob scene was my father, all prepared, no doubt, to give his acceptance speech when the time came. This was the second day of the convention. All the preliminaries were over. The first ballot had been taken and the CBC reporters were waiting for the results. There were only two other contenders: John G.D. MacIntyre, who was predicted to take only thirteen percent of the vote, and Bill Weaver, a pig farmer from the Annapolis Valley who was running at a mere five percent. But it was hard to pick out their placards among the forest of Everett McQuade supporters.

Commentator upon commentator spoke of how certain it was that my father would win. Dave Jessum suggested that there was a bit of ill-will from some of the older politicians like John G.D. over such a young man stepping into the position of premier so easily, that perhaps he hadn't paid his dues. Casey stuck her tongue out at the screen. As if on cue, Dave said, "The results of the first ballot have apparently been tallied and, in a second, they will be announced from the podium. There's the party chairman, Ike Traeger, now coming up front. We'll let you hear it from him." The camera switched over to a shot of Ike Traeger. He was adjusting the microphone and a loud wail of feedback swept over the hall. "Ladies and gentlemen of the Nova Scotia Conservative Party, the results of the first ballot are as follows: Bill Weaver — 23 votes, John G.D. MacIntyre — 74 votes and Everett McQuade — 245 votes."

A tidal wave of euphoria swept through the hall. Casey jumped off of the sofa and let out a squeal of delight, but when she looked at me she was once again reminded that the province's gain would be our family's loss. She sat down alongside of me and I put my arm around my sister. "Way to go, Dad," I said to the man on the TV screen who was having a hard time getting through the mob of supporters as he made his way to the podium to give his acceptance speech.

With each slow step he took through that mob, I felt that he was moving further and further away from us. I kept waiting for a miracle, kept hoping that something would stop him mid-stride and he would simply turn around, go back up the aisle and out of the building. Maybe he could say it was enough. He had proved his point. The Tories all loved him and he had won. Now he could just forget about it. Let some other bastard run the government. He would come home to us.

But my wishing was futile. Everett McQuade arrived at his destination. He had found his way to the podium and was revelling in the glory of his success. The crowd was going crazy. He was some kind of political hero; he possessed some quality that I think I had always understood but now I could see that it was not just a son's adulation for his father. He had charisma. As the CBC pulled in for a tight shot of his face, Casey and I could not help but feel a welling pride within us. What a handsome man, what cool and calm and grace. He made a damn good winner and he had success seeping out from every pore of his body. "Hi, Daddy," Casey said to the image on TV. "I like your tie." But my father did not hear her.

He pulled out the speech from inside his jacket. He flattened it on the podium before him and held up a hand, like a messiah, to quell the crowds. At first it did no good. Instead, the volume rose loud enough to distort the sound on the CBC audio feed. As I stared at my father, I remembered the younger man who used to wake me before the crack of dawn to go fishing with him. The man I once knew, not this stranger who stood before bright lights and adoring Tories and thousands of TV viewers.

The door to the house opened. My mother walked in. "I couldn't trust myself with Ben," she said. "I kept thinking about a way to get back at your father for not quitting the party and coming home. For not staying here with me. With us."

Casey looked a little puzzled but I knew exactly what she meant. "Sit down, Mom," I said. "Here with us. Dad won the nomination."

"I guess I knew he would. And he'll be re-elected too. They love him." She sat down beside Casey and we watched the two-dimensional grey figure on the screen begin to speak.

"You don't know how much this means to me," he began. "I may have been sitting at the premier's desk for these past few months, but I never felt quite comfortable there all that time. I will be now, though. Because I know I have all of you behind me and when we face the voters of this beautiful province some time in the next few months, I know we're going to win because you are with me." Another eruption of enthusiasm for the man. "And I want to say to you today that I have a vision, I have a dream of where this province is going. We are on the verge of a challenging new era of economic progress and social well-being like nothing anyone has ever seen before. And if we have our way, we will no longer be considered a have-not province. Because, ladies and gentlemen, we are going to have it all, the best of all possible worlds."

As he paused to let the troops go crazy one more time, the TV camera cut to the floor of the convention hall where two men were making their way to the front — the losers: Bill Weaver and John G.D. MacIntyre. "There's the man who got your father into this," my mother said. Both of the defeated Tories would go to the stage and admit defeat, then tell everyone what a wonderful man the winner was and how they would all now work together for the common good of the party. I'd seen this sort of thing before.

Suddenly my mother got up and walked to the window. "I can't watch," she said.

"What is it?" Casey asked.

But I had not turned to look at her. My eyes were still on the screen of the TV as I saw John G.D. step up on the side of the stage and pull something out of his suit coat pocket. It was unmistakeably a gun. The CBC reporter blurted out, "Stop him!" But it was too late. MacIntyre did not take defeat lightly. He had aimed the gun and pulled the trigger twice before Bill Weaver was able to grab his arm and raise the gun straight into the air where he fired four more shots. Then two policemen were grabbing MacIntyre and wrestling him to the floor.

Casey screamed out loud and ran to the TV set, putting her hands right onto the screen as a jerky camera showed my father fallen to the floor of the stage. My mother had never turned around. "Tell me when it's over," she said, for she had seen it all, I am sure, a split second before it happened. Shock, panic and disbelief swept over the convention hall but as I sat there paralysed, I hoped and prayed that the television had lied to us, that we were mistaken. It was not real life, only fiction. Casey was crumpled on the floor. My mother was still looking out the window at the yard. On TV, the reporter was caught off guard with nothing prepared to say but, "Oh my God, Oh my God, Oh my God."

My mother was the first one in the room to gain any control. Not once did she look at the TV screen. Instead, I saw her walk slowly into her bedroom. In a second she returned, walked to the key rack and grabbed the keys to my car. "Let's go. Your father will be needing us. We have to go now."

In a daze I followed my mother. As we were about out of the house I heard Dave Jessum recover his cool and start to say something. "You just saw it for yourselves," he said. "The premier is lying on the floor. That's Doctor Beverly Ware leaning over him. I must say it looks bad. Very bad . . . " and whatever else he was about to say would not be heard in my house. "You're lying, you dirty bastard!" I screamed back and to silence the bastard liar I ran back to the TV, yanked it from the table and heaved it through the front window. I watched the glass of the window shatter and then heard the implosion of the picture tube as the TV smashed hard on a boulder of granite outside.

My mother was taking my hand and leading me away. In a cool, distant voice, she said, "Come on. Ian, I need you to drive. I don't want you to think about anything." It was as if an overpowering grey fog descended on my brain. As I started the car and put it gear, punched the pedal to the floor and spun stone and sand, it was truly as if I had forgotten everything that had just happened. My mother had cast some weird spell over me so I was incapable of doing anything but driving a car.

As we raced across the bridge and onto the mainland, Casey began to sob. My mother reached back, touched her gently on the neck. I reached out and turned on the radio. "A Day in the Life" by the Beatles came up too loud and I had to turn it down. I couldn't believe that they were playing music, that life was going on in Halifax as if everything was normal. My mother would have preferred I left the radio off but she didn't say anything about it. I wanted to hear news of my father, anything at all. I needed to know.

"Ian," my mother said as I pulled out onto the paved highway of Highway Seven, sliding the back end of the car around in a ninety degree turn with the back wheels squealing on the pavement, "Can you keep the car on the road?"

"Yes," I said. "I think I can do that."

46 I drove down the highway to Halifax like a maniac. We were just a little past Spry Bay when the news came on the radio. "As you probably know by now, Everett McQuade has been shot at the leadership convention just this afternoon. The man who shot him is allegedly John G.D. MacIntyre who had just lost in his bid for the Tory leadership. McQuade has been rushed to the Victoria General Hospital where his condition is listed as critical. From reports by eyewitnesses, it appears that he has received two massive wounds to the chest. Right now, things do not look good."

And then, for the rest of the world, life went on as normal. Rock 'n' roll music was back on the air. I went to switch the station to CBC but my mother made me turn the radio off. There was a little store ahead and my mother insisted we pull in.

"No, there's not enough time. Let's just get there."

She shook her head. "This is important. I need to call."

I swerved off the road and stopped in front of a little run-down store with a phone booth out front. My mother got out of the car. I followed but she insisted I stay in the car with Casey who lay curled up in the fetal position in the backseat. I watched as my mother got an operator and eventually began talking to someone. Near the end of the conversation, I saw her take something out of her pocket and put it up to her face. It could have been a handkerchief but I couldn't tell. She jerked her head back as she hung up the phone.

When she got back in the car, her face was pale but she had not been crying. "Everett may not last very long. He's haemorrhaging. One bullet went through his lung, one through an artery near the heart. They say they've done everything possible and we should get there as soon as we can if we want to see him alive."

A shockwave passed through the car.

"But don't worry," my mother said. "I don't want you to worry about it or even think about it. Just get me, get us, there quickly."

We made it to the bridge and over the harbour without getting stopped by police. My mother seemed very odd and had stopped talking. She would not let me turn the radio back on. She leaned her head against the window and said nothing when I asked if she was all right. I ran every red light in my way until we were finally at the hospital entrance. I brought the car to a screeching halt. Casey and I jumped from the car but my mother needed help getting out. She was very shaky on her legs and I had to put my arms around her to help her into the hospital. I realized it was up to me to take charge. My mother was taking things very badly. I tried not to think about my father at all. I tried to act like a man would. I fought back the tears as Herb Legere met us and directed us to the hospital room.

There were two beds in the room, one of them empty. My father was in the other one with tubes in his arms and an oxygen mask over his face. There was a beeping monitor on one side of his bed with a tiny red tracer light tracking his heartbeat. A doctor in his sixties with shaggy eyebrows and a thick Cape Breton accent introduced himself as Dr. MacIsaac. "Right now he is stable. He's lost a lot of blood. We've removed the bullets but they have done considerable damage. I wish I could paint you a rosy picture but I honestly do not think he can survive. I'm sorry."

Casey collapsed on the floor and began to cry. My mother leaned heavily against the wall, her eyes almost glazed over. She said nothing. She looked completely exhausted and somehow removed from us. It wasn't the sort of reaction that made sense. It was like she had given up.

"Is there anything more you can do for him now? Anything?" I asked in desperation because I could see my mother was not going to speak.

"No. It's beyond us at this point. If we do anything, it will only make his condition worse. He could linger like this for a few hours or he could die within minutes. If he survives, it will be a miracle."

"Leave us here then," my mother finally spoke. "Leave us alone. Please."

The doctor did not seemed surprised. "Call if you need us. Otherwise, we will leave you alone."

"Don't let anyone in the room," I said, "Not Herb Legere, not anybody." I couldn't stand to have any of those men from the government here for the death of my father. If he was going to die, he was going to die with his family.

Casey came over and stood beside me. The two of us hovered over our father and Casey began to speak to him. "We want you to live, Dad. We want you to come back to the island with us."

"We want things to be like they used to be. Okay?" I heard myself say.

But my father was silent. He would not open his eyes. His face revealed only absolute resignation. This was not sleep. This was a man whose instincts to live had fled; what was left there of my father was waiting for death. My mother was beside us now. She was groggy. Something was very wrong. Casey and I backed away to let her speak to Dad but she wobbled and I had to grab her to prevent her from falling down. She took a long look at her husband, then reached into her pocket and pulled out a bottle of something. In one quick motion, she put the bottle to her mouth. My mother chewed hard, gagged but swallowed.

I watched as the empty Valium bottle rolled under the bed.

It was the bottle I had emptied and counted all those nights I worried about her. At last count there had been twenty-five pills. I couldn't believe this. Now it was empty. My mother had already taken most of the bottle when we stopped at the phone. Now she had taken the rest. She was trying to kill herself. *How could she be doing this to us?*

I started to say something but she held up her hand, waited to gain some command of her voice. Casey reached out to her but my mother pushed her away. "He's going to die," my mother said at last in a slurred, barely controlled voice. "He's going to die and I'm going after him."

"No! Dammit. You can't just kill yourself. This isn't like you! You're our mother," Casey pleaded with her.

My mother reached out for Casey now and held her sobbing daughter, but it was me she was looking at. "I'm going after him," she repeated. "I'm going to bring him back."

"Mom, you can't do that," Casey said. "We need you here. You can't save him."

She blinked several times, staggered backwards. "Yes," she said. "I think I can. Can't I, Ian?" She was looking at me now in a way I cannot describe. It was like she was looking through me, into me. And as I locked onto her eyes, I heard her question echo inside my head as if her voice was the voice of a crowd, as if I was hearing it with the ears of many, not one. I grew dizzy and closed my eyelids, saw a swarm of faces, some frightening, some familiar, but no one I could recognize by name. They were speaking something and it was all expressed as *we.* I shook my head to rid myself of this confusion and walked over to the window. *What the hell was going on with me? Why was my father dying? Why was my mother trying to kill herself now when we needed her? And why was I losing my mind?*

I looked at my reflection in the window. It was me but it was not me. Someone older, someone who seemed like a shadow of me. I knew it must be my mother's father, that murderous grandfather who I never met. But there was not a trace of evil in him. I tried to focus on that face that merged with mine in the glass. "We think she can do it," said the voice inside my head. "We think she is strong."

I turned back to my mother who was having a hard time standing now. Casey was leading her to sit down on the empty bed.

"Casey, I think she can do it. Can't you, mom?"

She nodded her head yes. "Don't let anyone in, especially the doctors. But you have to keep me awake until your father goes."

"I will, Mom," I said. I was scared beyond all boundaries of fear. Had we all simply gone crazy with grief, tripped over the edge into madness by our impending loss of this man that we loved? I grabbed my mother and put her arm around me and we began to walk around the room. I sang to her an old Gaelic song she had taught me in childhood, a song whose words I did not understand but whose melody spoke of love, of family and of happiness. Ten minutes passed, perhaps twenty. My mother was losing consciousness. I had the hardest decision of my life. Should I call the doctors, get them to pump my mother's stomach and save one life or lose them both? *God*, I begged silently, *give me an answer*. But there was no answer. Inside me, however, I felt the murmur of a committee, as if a debate was going on between my former selves. Finally, a weak chorus was telling me, "It's almost time. Let her go now. Let her go." And so I lay her down on the empty bed and studied her breathing as it grew more and more shallow.

A knock at the door. I pulled the curtain across the bed my mother was in. MacIsaac poked his head through the door but he was looking at my father and at the monitor beside his bed. "Do you need us?" he asked me.

"No," I said, trying to stay calm. "Everything is okay right now. We just want to be alone."

"I understand," he said. He turned and went out. I could hear his footsteps walking away. I pulled the curtain back from my mother's bed. Her breathing was shallow, her face like fresh snow.

At that instant the red tracer line of my father's heartbeat stopped bouncing. The line went flat and the machine gave off a high pitched trill. I looked at Casey. She immediately pulled the cord out of the wall and the machine went silent. I lay on the bed with my mother whose breathing had stopped and held her in my arms. I watched as Casey lay gingerly down beside my father and pushed her face up to his.

And I thought I too would stop breathing. I counselled myself that I was not mad, that we had not just allowed for the death of both our parents. A new fear crept inside me, one too horrible to imagine. *Suppose I was the return of my killer grandfather and that I had just murdered again?* I nearly jumped to my feet to call for the doctor but I was overtaken by a powerful dizziness that left me without balance. I closed my eyes, holding onto my dying mother and drifted back through some grey dominion of voices, faces, confusion. It was not a safe and peaceful place; this was a pathless voyage through my life and the lives of others. There was no map, no guide. Nothing. I wanted to scream but could not. I was simply unable to make sense of anything. Madness prevailed. Later, I would discover that only two minutes had passed, but it might as well have been a lifetime. Then Casey was shaking me on the shoulder. I opened my eyes.

"He's breathing," she said. "He's back."

I shook my head and pulled myself up.

"What do we do now?" Casey asked.

My mother was still lying beside me, her body cooler, her arms feeling stiff. I jumped to my feet and raced out into the hall. I grabbed a nurse. "Come in here, quick!"

Inside the room, she went over to my father but I pulled her towards the other bed. "It's my mother. She tried to kill herself." I picked up the bottle from the floor.

She checked my mother's pulse and ran to the door, told another nurse to get Dr. MacIsaac and an emergency team. I watched with tears streaming down my face as the young nurse began CPR on the chest of my mother, shifting at intervals to breathe air into her mouth. In less than a minute, the emergency team arrived and they applied the electric paddles to her chest. Casey and I both watched in terror as her body jerked from the shock and she seemed to rise up off the bed.

When Dr. MacIsaac arrived, he looked straight at me and demanded, "What the hell is going on here?"

I said nothing. Words had ceased to serve any purpose since none of this could be explained or justified. MacIsaac went over to check my father, saw that someone had unplugged the monitor. "Are you out of your mind?" he yelled at Casey and me. We could say nothing.

I watched my mother's body jump a second time. I prayed. I heard a young man say, "We got a pulse." I watched the young nurse breathe two more times into my mother's mouth.

"Twenty five capsules," I said now to Dr. MacIsaac, handing him the bottle.

"Why, for God's sake?" he demanded but I could not answer.

"Let's stabilize her, then prepare to have her stomach pumped. We're not out of the woods yet."

---

47 It turned out to be a bad year for the Tories all around. Bill Weaver was left to carry the banner for them when election time came around and he was soundly defeated at the polls by Jason Cameron, the Liberal candidate who seemed to have been elected as the only, albeit undesirable, alternative to a party in shambles. John G.D. MacIntyre found himself in Dorchester Penitentiary learning the art of stamping out licence plates. Colin Michael Campbell moved out of the country and took up residence in the Dominican Republic where, he had told the press, he was employed as a consultant to that country's government. The Dominican Republic, conveniently enough, was a nation without any agreement with Canada to expedite criminals back to their home turf for crimes like government bribery and manipulation of public contracts for personal well-being. It was a high old time for the media in Halifax and across Canada as the stories came out. And slowly my father recovered. Of course, it would be many months before he had the strength back in him to chop wood or set nets or do any of the simple tasks he had performed and thoroughly delighted in as a young man. And he could have been a broken man, his political career cut off by a rival with a gripe and a gun.

But it wasn't anything like that. By late fall, he claimed to be somewhere in the top ten of the happiest men in Canada. "And men hate being happy," he would tell me. "By their nature, they like to cause trouble or worry a thing until it breaks their back. I'm the exception to the rule. Men are stubborn too, but look at me. Again the exception. I could take a hint when it was time to leave public life. Some poor assholes stick around until its too late. Like that poor old son of a bitch John G.D. I want you to know I don't hold a grudge against him. John took me off this island and he bloody well helped me to come back home."

My father had one fairly serious setback in his recovery. My mother doesn't like to admit it, but they were making love when it happened. I hadn't heard the bed springs squeak like that in years and, Lord knows, it must have been a bit early in my old man's recovery, what with arteries stitched up and lungs patched up, but they were going at it one Saturday night when something must have gone wrong with the repair work. My mother came into my bedroom and told me we had to drive my father to the hospital again because he was having a hard time breathing.

Poor old Dad was a little embarrassed. "Don't worry, Dorothy," he said to her on the way there, "I'll get my wind back." He did get his wind back, and the squeaking of the bed springs was like music to my ears. But before each session of my parents' lovemaking, my mother asked me to stand by on call just in case there were medical problems. Fortunately I was never again needed to haul my old man to the hospital.

After a while I stopped worrying about my father's health and the dangers of lovemaking on a man who had survived the assassin's bullet. I no longer let myself fret about my mother's mental stability either. Since her own near-death encounter, she had regained a number of contacts in the spirit world. But it was different now for all of us. In her younger days, she had taken to the metaphysical with a serious, sometimes even eerie, tenor. Her guides had been sombre, dark figures, often well-meaning, but not the sort you'd like to have hanging around for a Friday night gathering of friends for beer and chips. Now, my mother's invisible friends seemed to be a friendly, chatty lot who could converse with her about immortality and the ongoing spiritual exchange as readily as they could tell her about a new way to prepare a clam sauce.

My father bought a new boat that spring. We cruised her far out to sea on those warm sunny days, dropped anchor and jigged for squid or simply dropped a hand-line or two for cod and mackerel. And we talked, catching up on years of father and son talk. Casey came along too and got to know her father like she had always wanted to. We had all grown tanned and tempered by that September. Trouble would not return to us until later that fall.

My father was at work writing a book about his philosophy and his days in government and, most of all, about the politics of life and death. "I'm a born again anarchist," he told me. "It wasn't until I was on the other side, sliding down that long, dark, slanty tunnel that I could begin to see how foolish I had been. I was flat on my back and it felt like I was in a flume of dark warm water. The walls were black, but they had a kind of funny glow to them. When I started, there had been this awful pain in my chest. And I was never as scared as that.

I was out of control. I must have gone miles and miles and I kept thinking . . . I'm going down. And if I'm going down, I'm gonna end up in hell. But then I try real hard and I discover I can sit upright and the pain is all gone. I feel like a little kid again on some kind of slide. And up ahead I see a little light that just keeps growing brighter and brighter. I think that when I get to that light, I'll just shoot out onto some goddamn playground somewhere, like that one behind your old elementary school in Sheet Harbour.

"But I see it's not a place — that light up there — it's a person. It's your mother, standing there ready to catch me. I'm so happy I figure I'm gonna pee myself only I don't know if I can pee myself, 'cause I also know that I must be dead. I'm thinking, *so this is dead*. It's funny being dead, a lot funnier than you'd figure. And there's your mom. I think I'm gonna crash right into her, only I don't. I arrive there and the tunnel is gone. I'm standing right up on my feet — no pain, no problems, nothing. And your mother is there. Damn, was I ever happy to see her.

"Then this terrible feeling comes over me. Because *I* was the one who was supposed to be dying. Not her. She holds me in her arms and I want to scream out, 'What are you doing here? You can't be here with me!' But before I can speak she says, 'I had to come here to bring you back.'"

"And, oh boy, I wanted to go back just then. I mean, I think I wanted to stay, if your mother was there with me, but she held up one hand in the air and in the palm of her hand I could see Casey and in the palm of the other hand I could see you, Ian. So I put my hands up to each of hers and I started drifting off backwards until I was back in bed there in the hospital. The pain came back all at once and it felt so bloody awful, I thought I'd made a mistake. And I couldn't find your mother anywhere. Man was I scared."

48 By September the Liberals had been in power for nearly a year. Jason Cameron was an old party chum of Bud Tillish and Bud, his past failures in politics behind him, had been sworn in as minister of Mines and Energy. There was talk of sweeping away all the old Tory misdeeds — the graft, the influence peddling, the patronage and the general squandering of public funds. It was the same self-congratulatory sort of remarks that the public would have heard when Colin came to power and swept away the Liberal's graft, influence peddling, patronage and squandering of public funds. And in that brief hiatus of public cynicism when a people turn the other cheek and are ever hopeful of real improvement from their politicians, a mild euphoria swept through Nova Scotia.

My father sat before the TV and watched Jason Cameron give bold and promising speeches as premier. My father could predict nearly word for word what would issue from the man's mouth. It was an odd form of family entertainment to see my father race ahead with his own version of the speech and then hear the less convincing echo of the man on TV, not nearly as eloquent, forge on with the eminent destiny of this great province.

"I lost one of the best speech writers in Halifax to that bastard," my father said. "We had already been working on this one. After I got shot, Tyrone Glebe went over to the Grits. I liked the man. He had no party loyalty whatsoever. Just wanted to cover his ass and keep his job. He was very up-front about it. He gave me some grand ideas and I fired his imagination with some doozies as well. I'm really quite happy he could put them to use."

But from where I sat, so much of it boiled down to talk about the great two-faced demon goddess of "economic development."

"Ever since I've come back from the hereafter, I'm beginning to think I might have been wrong about this economy stuff," my father admitted. "It was such a beguiling idea. But I think I was taken in." He was still staring at the bland, stone-block face of Jason Cameron. "What we need is spiritual growth. And I don't mean organized religion."

I was really happy to hear my old man talk like that again. There was something about dying that took the Tory right out of him. If he was still a politician, he had reverted to something less organized, more renegade and more homespun. "Look at that dipweed," he said, pointing at the TV screen. "Not an ounce of human emotion in his body. You couldn't get an honest human reaction out of Jason Cameron if you put a cherry bomb up his ass and lit it. The sucker wants to run the province like a goddamn business. Nova Scotia is not a cor-poration. It's a bunch of the most beautiful yahoos with more spunk than people anywhere else on the planet. It's a frigging state of awareness, a realm of possibility, not some goddamn fart factory aiming to provide profit for shareholders."

My mother switched off the set. "We agree," she said. "Now let's go catch some crabs."

Crabbing was my mother's way of bringing the family back together. We would sit on Hants Buckler's dock or hang out down by the bridge and drop lines with hunks of herring into the water, pulling up dozens of rock crabs, blue and orange and black. They would all get tossed into a large bushel basket and we'd take them home where my mother would concoct some exotic new dish of crab meat. My mother said that she had been informed by one of her guides, a young herbalist from the thirteenth century, that crab meat helps to strengthen the heart.

"I'm in favour of anything that strengthens the heart," I said.

It was on a sluggishly delightful afternoon in late Septem-ber when the uranium drilling truck returned. We were on the bridge, leisurely pulling up a crab or three when the truck trundled past us, shaking the whole structure. It was the same truck whose engine I had corroded with the best of acids available on the island. The man driving didn't even look at us.

"This bridge is only rated at two tons. That truck's over the limit," my father said to us. "He's violating provincial law." It was a curious response. I wanted to know what he was really thinking.

A minute later, another truck towing a flatbed with a bull-dozer approached the bridge. The driver cautiously pulled up onto the wooden structure, then gunned the engine and roared across to follow the first truck.

"Son of a bitch," my father said. We had all felt the crack. I lay down on the road and looked at the creosote beams that were the primary supports to the span. "Wilful destruction of provincial property," I said.

A wave of numbness shot through my body. I looked away from my father because I didn't want him to see my face. I looked across towards Burnet Sr.'s dilapidated house where his new brood of dogs, awakened by the trucks, were yelping and tearing themselves against their chains. I could hear Burnet's old man yelling at them from inside the house to "shaddup." Strange to think that he didn't know his son was less than half a mile away on the island and refusing to go see him. I was suddenly thankful that I had a father I could talk to, a father who had returned from politics and the dead to stand by his family come hell or high water.

"War," my father said.

"What?" Casey asked.

"They've declared war on the island," my father said.

An RCMP cruiser now appeared as it came around the turn past Burnet's house and pulled up on the bridge, coming to a stop by my father. The same young Mountie who had questioned me got out and walked over to my father. "Pleased to meet you, sir. My name's Elgin Shaeffer. Sorry to hear about the little accident. My father was a great admirer of you."

"He from the Shore?" my father asked.

"Born and raised here. Voted Tory all his life."

"I'm sure he did," my father said. "What can I do for you?"

"Well, sir, you probably just saw the mining trucks that came by here."

"I did," my father said, "and I'd like to report two significant violations of provincial highway law."

The Mountie shook his head. "Well, I don't know if I can do anything about that if I wasn't here to see it. You could file a complaint, I suppose, but that wasn't why I came out here."

"I'll file a complaint," my father said.

"What I came out to tell you," the young man said, acting a little embarrassed, "is that I've got a court order stating that you not go near the mining site."

My father's eyes flared but he kept his cool, levelled his voice. "Now why is that, son? Why is it that I'm not permitted on Crown land, land owned by the good people of this province for all to use in a proper manner?"

"Well, it has to do with that little incident last year. Somebody ruined the engine of a truck, painted something about a republic of something or other and the Attorney General has informed the RCMP that it was most likely you, sir, behind it."

"Are you suggesting, that the former premier of the province of Nova Scotia drove out here from Province House to wreck the engine of somebody's goddamn truck?"

"That seems to be what the Attorney General is saying."

"My father didn't do anything," I said. And I was ready to blurt out the truth. I wouldn't have mentioned Tennessee Ernie, but I wasn't going to let my father's image be tarnished because of me. But before I could get the words out, my father was pulling me aside.

He spoke loud enough so the Mountie could hear in a cool calm voice, "Ian, would you mind going down to get a look at

Lesley Choyce

the damage to the bridge caused by those mining people? I want to be able to file a complete report here with the Constable before he leaves."

"Yeah, sure, Dad," I said. And I climbed down the side of the bridge structure to get a closer look at the creosote beams that held up the bridge. Sure enough, the one just below us had been splintered in two and another had a serious bow in it, having buckled from the weight of the truck. It didn't look to me like it would take much more abuse. As I climbed back up I told them both what I saw. "If I was you, officer, I'd have this bridge closed immediately to all traffic before the whole thing collapses," I added.

He looked at me befuddled. "I don't think I have the authority. We'll have to have an inspection team come out from Halifax for that," he said.

My father was scratching his jaw and studying Elgin Shaeffer. "Elgin, I want you to know there's a lot at stake here. If they start tearing up this island, there's no telling what might happen. I'm sure that your own father would tell you that, next to loyalty to the party you were born into, there's nothing more important than the land. We start ruining the land and selling it off to the Yanks to make nuclear weapons, we might as well just roll over and die."

"These would be my sentiments exactly, sir, if I had any say in the matter. Liberal scum never did do nothing good for this province."

"Damn straight," my father said, playing up to the Mountie's political prejudice.

"Well, serve me the papers then, Elgin, and you can go on about your work."

"I wish I didn't have to do this."

"It's okay."

Elgin handed over a legal document that my father took and stuffed into his shirt pocket. "You don't have any idea who was behind all this little vendetta to discredit me and put me to shame, do you? Off the record, of course."

Elgin shrugged his shoulders and looked uncomfortable. "I don't really like to say," he began and maybe he was ready to spill the beans, but it wouldn't be necessary. Approaching the bridge was the Mannheim/Atlanta pick-up truck. The guy driving it was the Atlanta half of the operation.

I tried to stop the truck before it got to us. I waved the driver to stop. He rolled down his window and said in the deepest southern drawl I'd ever heard, "You're all in very deep shit, now. Ain't nobody allowed to mess with a man's machinery like that." I just smiled like he had just given me a compliment, looked past him to the man sitting opposite — Bud Tillish.

"Mr. Tillish," I said. "A belated ongratulations on your victory. I haven't had a chance to come by personally to offer my sincere best wishes."

Bud Tillish just looked the other way as if I didn't exist.

"I wouldn't drive on the bridge if I were you," I said to both of them. "Some big flatbed with a bulldozer just drove over, cracked the beam right in half. Nothing holding the thing up but splinters and good will."

"Horse shit," Atlanta said, putting the truck in gear, spinning gravel and pulling up to the ass end of the RCMP cruiser where he lay on the horn.

Elgin looked really annoyed as he saw Bud Tillish sitting in the truck. He gave my father a knowing glance — *Liberal scumbags*. But he sucked in his breath and sat down in his car and drove across the bridge and onto the island where he stopped on the side of the road and studied us in his rear-view mirror.

Atlanta drove up and stopped alongside of my father. Bud Tillish leaned across him and flipped up his sunglasses. "You try to stop this operation, McQuade, and you're in big trouble. I know all about your lunatic schemes and your fantasy republic. If I could only have let the public know what a maniac you were years ago, I'd have had you out of office and into the Loony Bin. Then you could have stopped pretending you were premier or president and been anything you want — Napoleon, Castro, you name it."

"Good to see you too, Bud," my father said. "You working for the Americans now?" he asked, pointing to the Mannheim/Atlanta emblem on the side of the truck. "Or is it the Germans?"

Atlanta stuck his finger in my old man's face. "We're an international corporation, goddamn it. Americans and West Germans — only thanks to you bloody hicks, our investors in Germany are about ready to pull out."

"Uranium sounds like a dangerous business," my father said. "I'd get out if it, too, and into something more . . . what's the right word, more sensible."

"Shee-it," said Atlanta.

"Just remember who's in power now in this province. Just remember who has the real authority," Tillish scolded my old man.

"Bud," my father responded, "Don't forget that it doesn't matter how important you think you are, there are always higher levels of authority."

But Bud didn't seem too impressed. Neither did Atlanta. The truck was stopped dead centre in the bridge.

My mother and Casey had walked to the rear of the truck on the other side. I couldn't figure out what they were up to until, arm in arm, they walked back around the truck to us. "You boys have had enough fun for one day. Time to go home for lunch," Dorothy said to Dad and me.

Atlanta tipped his Braves cap at Mom and Bud settled back into his seat as we sauntered back to the island. We were on solid land when I heard the truck engine rev and saw the truck lurch forward a couple of feet before stalling on the bridge. It seemed to be having a hard time moving. I looked at Casey who held out a little metal spring device up into the sunlight.

She pulled a bobby pin out of her hair to illustrate to me how she had removed the valve core from the tire tube. I looked at Mom and she just shrugged.

Atlanta was still not wise to his problem as he revved the engine and lurched forward again, this time just as the cracked support beam let out a loud status report. One whole side of the bridge gave out. The truck tilted and then slipped sideways off the bridge and down into the channel. The water wasn't deep, just cold, I guess, because I heard cursing as the two men fought to climb out the passenger door and splash their way toward the mainland.

"I'd check into the safety of that bridge just as soon as you can, officer Elgin," my father said to the Mountie as we walked past him. "Somebody could get hurt on a thing like that."

Elgin just shook his head and got on the radio asking for another cruiser to come pick him up at the bridge to Whalebone Island.

---

49 Bud Tillish did prove that he had some muscle in the government because he had a highway crew there by late afternoon towing the pick-up out of the stream and beginning to correct what gravity had done to the old bridge. It was obvious that they were using thicker beams and preparing to make the crossing safe for heavier traffic. We all saw this as an insult to the island. The bridge had been had been out of repair for years. My father had always felt it would have been a sign of favouritism if he had called on the highway crew to repair it. Hants and I had replaced some of the boards on the surface ourselves just to keep it serviceable. But now that we had a burgeoning uranium pit, the highway department was summoned immediately for repairs and we were all certain that everyone would neglect the real cause of the damage.

Bud Tillish and Atlanta had made the mistake of going over to Burnet Sr.'s house to dry off as they waited for the RCMP back-up cruiser to arrive. Burnet's dogs, when they saw a corporate American and a politician coming up the walkway, went completely crazy and pulled their chains loose from the posts in the back yard. Bud and Atlanta were on the front steps of Burnet's house asking for a towel and use of the phone when the dogs tore into them, providing Burnet Sr. with the most fun he'd seen in weeks.

My father, upon settling on the chesterfield back home, stared out the window, waiting for inspiration. "I could have stopped them if I was premier. I should have done something when I was in office. I just didn't want to throw my weight around. I was trying to be fair."

"You were very fair, Daddy," my sister said. "But now it's time to play dirty."

My father looked startled. "What's gotten into you, girl?"

My little sister took a long red handkerchief out of her pocket, twirled it and tied it around her forehead. "I'm volunteering for the Liberation Army of the Republic of Nothing," she said.

"Me too," I added, thrusting my fist up into the air the way I'd seen the America radicals do it.

"Let's not get carried away," my mother said. "Trouble has an easy enough time finding us as it is. We don't have to go looking for it."

My father scratched his stubbled jaw of red and grey hairs. He had become a sporadic, haphazard shaver as in the old days. "Your mother's right. Before we start a revolution, I think you need to give me a chance to go over the head of Bud Tillish."

"That's right," I answered. "Like you said, 'higher authority.'

Why don't you get on the phone to Pierre Trudeau? He's letting draft dodgers into the country. He's not so bad. And if you can get through to him, Tillish would have to listen. They're both in the same party."

My father let out a sigh. "You're probably right, son. Trudeau is a pretty straight shooter. And he's not a big fan of the American nuclear build-up. Only problem is, I met Trudeau. We had lunch when he was in town. I could have liked the guy a lot but I found him awful snotty. A real arrogant man right down to his socks."

"Still, he might listen. I'm sure he would take a phone call from you at least. You, were, after all, premier."

"Yeah. But I made one fatal mistake in establishing a cordial relationship with our prime minister."

"What was that dear?" my mother asked.

"I called him an asshole."

My mother seemed shocked. "In front of others?"

"In front of everybody," my old man asserted. "It was right after lunch and his advisors were there and my advisors were there and all through the meal I got the feeling that Trudeau couldn't wait to get out of Halifax, that he had more important things to do. Just before he left, he said that he found our meeting "fruitful" and me "charming." He said that he was "very fond of men with limited educations who were elected into office by a rural population.""

"And that's when you called the prime minister an asshole?" I asked.

"I think it was a tactical, diplomatic error on my part, looking back on it." My father yawned and I knew we should leave him alone for a while. Never a napper before in his life, he had found it necessary to sleep for an hour in the afternoon ever since recovering from the assassination attempt.

I went to tell Gwen about the impending uranium battle and found her with three new arrivals who had made it across the border late last night. They'd arrived only an hour or so before the bridge went down. She and Ben were cooking up a huge feast for them, and I was introduced as Gwen's boyfriend and self-appointed protector of the island. At least fifty draft dodgers had come to the island so far. Most had stayed for a bit to get acquainted with other dodgers before heading off to Halifax, Cape Breton or points west. Ten had stayed on, including Burnet who had seemingly adjusted to a role as guide-counsellor to any of the hard-core military types recovering from a stint in the jungles of Southeast Asia. Burnet was very proud of his form of treatment which he called "Therapy by Fishing and Clamming." His success rate with truly damaged young men was surprisingly good. Mostly the dodgers kept to themselves, but a couple of the guys had taken to working with Lambert and Eager and three others had made good friends with Hants Buckler, accepting him as a sort of guru who could teach them about the intricacies of inner peace through watching the tides, waiting for free gifts from the sea, chewing tobacco and spitting. Hants Buckler's spitting ability had been finely honed in recent years to the point that even novice spitters like the young American draft dodgers recognized a great talent.

I had been a little jealous at first, what with Gwen hanging around all those American guys, many of them heartsick from leaving behind families and friends and aching for companionship, but Gwen had learned to handle them with the greatest of ease, befriending each but keeping loyal to me. All through the events that year our love had solidified into something new. Dare I say, the great silent adoration I had held so long for her wore off ever so slightly. She had now developed more respect for me. We were equals. It was a great, complex, crazy and unstable world, but we would grow together and create a stable core.

"They're back," I told her. "Mannheim/Atlanta."

"We can't let them dig," she said.

"No, we can't," I answered. "We'll do something. My father's working on a plan." He was at home taking a nap, but that didn't matter.

"There's more of us now. I'm sure the Americans will help."

"I think it might be too dangerous for them. If they were arrested they might be sent back to the States. But don't worry. I'll let you know when it's time to act."

"I'm worrying," Gwen told me. "My father painted the entire picture for me. If they start to strip mine, the island will be ruined."

"They don't stand a chance," I said. "Mannheim/Atlanta and Bud Tillish are up against higher authorities." I kissed Gwen then and had a hard time stopping myself from doing more. I wanted to forget about Mannheim/Atlanta and steal off to the beach at Back Bay with her, swim out to where we could barely touch the sandy bottom with our toes and then make love as we were carried along on the current of the channel. "I have to get home," I said. "I want to be there when my old man wakes up."

As I walked in the front door of my house, my father thrust a letter at me, an old letter postmarked New York City, June of 1951. "Open it. Read what it says."

The letterhead read, "United Nations, Office of the Secretary General" and beneath:

> Dear Sir,
>
> Thank you for submitting a copy of your declaration of independence. While we cannot immediately recognize your republic as a new country, I can inform you that we are willing to consider your case. While it is often a long and complicated process to legitimize "nationhood status" and admission to the United Nations, we do have a committee that is authorized to hear cases submitted by those who claim autonomy on geographical units currently within the boundary of established nations.

To that end, you might consider submitting a brief, outlining your position and we will get back to you as soon as we can.

Sincerely,
Dag Hammerskjold
Undersecretary

I looked at my mother and at Casey. They had already read the letter. We were all thinking the same thing. Maybe I was the first to say it. "It'll never work. They'll just tell you you're crazy. Everyone will think we're all lunatics out here." I handed my father back the letter.

"I don't care if the rest of the world thinks we're crazy." My father picked up another piece of paper and waved it in my face. I could recognize it by the smell — old paper, old ideals. It was a copy of the declaration itself that he was waving in my face, the one that I had lost by the machinery, the one that had found its way full circle back to my father through the back rooms of the Grits and the Tories. "A copy of this has been on file at the UN since 1951. We're a little slow at accepting their invitation to present our case, but we're going to give it a try. If we can even simply get a toe in the door and get something rolling, however crazy it may sound, I think I can at least stop Mannheim/Atlanta from doing any further digging. We've got to try to establish a legitimate claim over that land, over the whole island. We've got to reach over the heads of provincial authority, even Canadian authority, and this is the way to do it. We could, at the very least, create enough public interest and legal confusion that Mannheim/Atlanta won't dare take a rock off this island for years. Then they'll realize it's too much trouble."

I wanted to say that it was wild and foolish, that it would never work. I wanted to suggest we revert to violence and vandalism, but I said nothing. I saw the gleam in my father's eyes, the wonderful, maniacal gleam that had once possessed him as a younger man.

"Don't worry," he assured my mother, "I have a good grip on diplomacy."

I'm sure she was thinking what I was thinking: *Right. Diplomacy. Just like Pierre Elliot Trudeau.*

My father looked at the letter from the U.N. and I saw a momentary flicker of doubt. "Dag Hammarskjold," he said. "Soon after he wrote back to me, he became Secretary-General."

Well, that was different. Maybe a letter from old Dag would mean something, Maybe it wasn't just my old man's fantasy. But something was wrong about the way he said it.

"Only problem is that Hammerskjold got killed in a plane crash over Africa. Sixty-one, I think."

I knew it was up to me to rekindle the flame before my old man's spirits were nothing but a wisp of smoke. "No problem," I said. "I'm sure they still have the declaration and their letter on file. The UN must have world class file clerks. Who's Secretary-General now?"

"U Thant," he said. "He's from Burma. My guess is he's got his hands full with Cyprus, Israel, India and Pakistan. Not to mention Vietnam. I'm not sure he will have been briefed about Whalebone Island and the Republic of Nothing."

"Then we'll brief him," I said, the light of destiny emanating from every pore of the son of the man who had once been premier of the province of Nova Scotia. "When do we leave?" I asked.

My father looked out the window. We all listened to the roar of the machinery shattering the peace of our island home. "Tomorrow, Ian. You and me. We're flying to New York."

My father wakened me at 4 o'clock in the morning. It was pitch black and when he switched on my light I could see that he was dressed in the suit he had worn while in office as premier. My mother had set out my one and only suit as well. I began

to dress. As my old man vanished from the room to finish getting ready he said, "Let's go, kid. Got to move before the tide
slips," and I flashed back to my childhood when he would
wake me up just like this in the dark early morning and we'd
go to sea.

Today it was a different tide. My old man, with me at his
side, was going to barge into the office of the Secretary-
General of the United Nations and remind the world that he
had declared the island an independent nation back there on
March 21, 1951. And today, September 30, 1970, we were about
to reassert our sovereign dominion over the land and drive the
demon land rippers from our borders. And despite the fact
that I was no longer a boy whose feet did not reach the floor
when he sat on the side of the bed, and despite the fact that
neither my old man nor I were dressed in oilskins and rubber
boots, I had the distinct feeling that we were in fact going fishing. Almost unconsciously I reached under my bed, as I had
done so many times before on fishing trips with my father —
I reached for the cigar box from underneath the bed. I flipped
the lid and found the finger of the dead Viking that I would
carry for good luck.

As we walked in the darkness to the car with the giant sack
of food my mother had cooked up for us to eat on the long
dark drive to the airport, I couldn't help but get caught up in
the feeling of euphoria that overtook us. My mother had
packed us a pair of scrambled egg sandwiches to eat on the
road and supplemented it with a monumental lunch to offset
the minimalist Air Canada meal. With so much sustenance, I
was prepared to follow my father on his mission to anywhere
he pleased. Ready to go to whatever higher authority was
needed.

Before we had settled in the car, he stopped dead in his
tracks. "Smell, Ian."

I took a deep, powerful whiff of salt air. It was warm, rich,
luxurious and mixed with the scent of juniper and bayberry

from the interior of the island. I let it sift into my brain like a robust, life-enhancing drug. "Tide's just about to change," he said to me, handing me the keys to drive. "We're going to catch it just right."

My father found a pay phone at LaGuardia, asked for the number and then dialled the office of U Thant. "It's the premier of Nova Scotia," he lied to the woman on the other end of the line. "I need to speak to Mr. U Thant on a matter of grave international consequence."

"No, madam. It's in Canada," he continued to explain.

"Well, can I make an appointment for this afternoon?"

Disappointment. I toyed with the Viking finger in my pocket.

"Perhaps there is someone still with you who was close to Dag Hammarskjold. My business concerns a petition for United Nations membership that was delivered to Mr. Hammarskjold in 1951. He was a great man and a very close friend. Is there anyone still there who was an associate of Mr. Hammarskjold's?"

My father held his hand over the receiver. "All we need is a foot in the door," he assured me. As he waited for the woman to come back on the line, I looked at the frenzied crowd of people moving to and fro in the crowded airport. I wondered what it was about this city that had drawn me back here for a second time in my life.

"Yes," my father said. "My name is Everett McQuade. 2:30? Fine. Thank you." He placed the phone back in its cradle. "Per Lindquist will see us at 2:30," he said. "U Thant is apparently busy today."

At precisely 2:30 in the afternoon the heavy mahogany door to Per Lindquist's office opened and an aging, silver-haired gentlemen extended his hand. My father greeted him like a long lost friend.

"Please come in," he said. And we followed him into his office. "Sit down."

"I am Everett McQuade, and this is my associate, Ian

McQuade. I understand you worked closely with Dag Ham-marskjold," my father began.

"I came over with him from Sweden when he first worked here at the U.N. He is gone, as you know, but I have stayed on." His voice was cold and clinical. My father's charm had not sliced through the formalities yet.

"A great man," my dad said. "A tragedy he was lost."

An uneasy silence fell over the room. I looked around. The room was full of old artifacts — a stone axe head, small soap-stone statues of unidentifiable figures — warriors perhaps, a tattered piece of clothing was encased in glass on the wall. I nervously toyed with the Viking finger in my pocket.

"Mr. McQuade, I have only the vaguest notion as to why you are here, but I must say I do not appreciate the false pretence. A: I suggest that you were not a friend of Dag Hammarskjold and B: I gather that you are no longer premier of Nova Scotia."

My father, rather than looking defeated, seemed duly im-pressed. "Then you *do* know why I'm here," he ventured.

"Yes. We do keep files. No matter how silly, we keep all such declarations as yours on file. My secretary found it with little trouble after your phone call. You'd be surprised how many individuals like you there are out there, how many minority groups wanting their own countries, how many megalomaniacs hoping to establish their own kingdoms. At least you had the respect for us to tell us your truthful name. At least I hope that is the case. You are Everett McQuade from Whalebone Island?"

"Of the Republic of Nothing," my father concluded the statement. "And you must forgive my blundering. It is a mat-ter of utmost importance necessary to save our island, to save our home." He proceeded to explain about the uranium min-ing, about the island, about us. My father stood up and walked around the room as he talked. He wove a tapestry with words about our home that made it sound like the most beautiful and majestic of places on earth. His voice was the sea itself, cares-sing the shores of the island, recounting its history, our lives, the unique character of the people who lived there and ultimately asserting our right to be free and independent of all other governments.

Per Lindquist listened patiently. The muscles in his cheek had loosened ever so slightly as he absorbed the resonant oration of my father, the master speech-giver. And when my father had finished, having recounted the story all the way up to the very minute we had walked into the office, he stopped, sat down and waited. Per Lindquist folded his long slender hands together in front of him creating something akin to a cathedral spire. "I am moved," he said. "I too am a man who feels certain passions for a place. Your home does not sound unlike the island I grew up on along the Baltic Sea. I am deeply touched."

He paused. The world stopped. I knew that the next word would be *however*. Nothing good in my life ever followed that disaster of all words. All praise, all kind remarks, all good whispers that trailed with *however* ended in bad news. I scanned the room again, taking note of the artifacts. The crude stone implements on the table by the window. The drawing on the wall.

"You have come here, Mr. McQuade, asking for the absurd but believing yourself to have a legitimate case. If the United Nations were to give you even the benefit of a hearing we would open the floodgates to the mobs, the madmen and the revolutionaries from around the globe who would wish also to create their own countries. I cannot help you. Alas ... " Lindquist now appeared to be little more than a tired old man, a bureaucrat who had sat too many days behind the same desk. The air filled with a heavy sodden quality that made me feel tired, defeated. I could not even look at my father.

Then there was a voice in the back of my head — a memory, a thought, a fading echo of sound in a language that I was not familiar with. Almost without thinking, I reached into my jacket pocket and pulled out the desiccated finger. And then I

Lesley Choyce

was on my feet, leaning across Per Lindquist's desk. On the immaculate, green ink blotter before the man whose hands were folded like a church spire, I dropped the curious object. I hovered above him as his face contorted into a frown and he stared at the bizarre gift before him. "What is it?" he asked.

"A finger," I said, another promise broken in my life for I had vowed to my father I would never speak of the ancient dead man who slept on our island. But now I had a reason. Maybe it was the Viking himself who had spoken to me, maybe he wanted to be permitted the luxury of his repose in the bog of Whalebone Island without being dug up by uranium miners. "It's the finger of a dead Viking."

A look of astonishment and curiosity replaced the frown on Per Lindquist's face as he picked up the finger, curled as it was like a question mark, and held it up to the light of the window. "And what about the rest of the poor man's anatomy?" he asked.

"Buried on Whalebone Island. He was the first citizen of the Republic of Nothing," I asserted.

I felt a momentous panic of possibility rise in my chest as if something was emanating from the finger that Per Lindquist held. My father was staring at it, too, but he knew that his turn to speak was over, that this son had ventured into the slippery world of international diplomacy and the negotiations of sovereignty.

"You're suggesting you have evidence of the visitation of Vikings on your island. Has this information ever been revealed before?"

"No," I said, looking at my father. "We kept it a secret."

"Why?"

"We didn't want people coming to dig up our island for relics."

"And now you are considering the lesser of two evils."

"I'll take ten archaeologists to one American entrepreneur any day."

"Why is it that I want to believe you?"

"Because it's important," I said. "Because you believe in our case."

Per Lindquist did not admit I was right. "If you have the entire body of a Viking explorer on your island, then it would be a travesty for a strip mine to be developed. We have very little concrete evidence of the Vikings along the coast. They were restless, brave adventurers. The world was a less interesting place when they settled down and faded into European civilization." Lindquist cupped his hand around the dried finger and held it to his chest.

"I'm going to have to verify this," he said. "I can run a cursory dating check on this today. If what you say is true, then I can help you after all."

"Really?" my father asked, amazed and baffled.

"If there is sufficient evidence of Viking presence on your island, we can attempt to establish protection for the entire island under the Charter. Canada has always been most cooperative in setting aside any Viking settlements and ancient arctic digs. When will the mining exploration begin?"

"It's already started," I said.

"Then, if the test proves you are being truthful, I'll establish protocol proceedings with your government."

"I think that's a fine idea," my father said.

"You're going to have to put up with a few archaeologists, I'm afraid. But they tend to be very careful these days with how they dig and what they dig up."

"I'm sure they'll respect our island," my father responded.

"I'm looking forward to being there to make sure they do, Mr. McQuade."

50 Bud Tillish had not figured on being defeated by a dead Viking. Mannheim/Atlanta's security guards had settled in for a few slack days of listening to the drills pound away at the rock. A small pit had barely been started in the centre of the island before the bulldozer had found itself up to the driver's seat in a thick dark ooze, a seemingly bottomless pit adjacent to the uranium ore. There were some fears that the dozer would, in fact, sink out of sight so they had to attach several chains to it and anchor them around the rock outcroppings. But the bog was only the beginning of the end for the mining operation.

Bud Tillish was gravely disappointed to learn that it would forever be impossible to mine uranium in a World Preservation Site, and many people along the Eastern Shore of Nova Scotia will never forgive my father for the potential job loss and blow to the economy left in the wake of the pull-out of Mannheim/Atlanta.

Soon the archaeologists arrived, as did a few historically curious tourists. My friend, the dead Viking, with a borrowed finger stitched back on by the most diligent of cadaver surgeons, became something of a celebrity and I hope that he will forgive me for disturbing his rest. I felt a bit like a traitor to an old friend, but Per Lindquist convinced us all that the soul of a Viking was very resilient and would not object to disinterment of the body if it meant saving Whalebone Island. He was hauled off to The Museum of Civilization in Ottawa and I felt bad he would have to exist there so far inland.

There was digging in the bog on the island even after the uranium hounds had departed. For the most part, they were meticulous scientists and their helpers who sifted through dirt and dried peat like they were sifting flour for a cake. A small party of them hung around for nearly two years, making an exodus for indoor work as the winter months approached. Hants Buckler made many new friends from the parks people and the visitors who found him more interesting than the Viking site. Gwen's father found himself drawn into the work concerning the island's past and even landed a job doing research into the history beneath his feet instead of the stars above his head. Per Lindquist became a regular visitor and a great friend of the island.

Then, after two years of spade work, of bagging samples and sifting, there was a freeze on spending at both the U.N. and in Ottawa for archaeological digs, and the work was put on hold. Bureaucrats decided that, despite the authenticity of the dead Viking, there was nothing more of any great value to be found on the island.

I honestly think they were correct. Yet, my friend the Viking had done his job. He had been waiting around all those years to save us all; after being so rudely interrupted, Mannheim/Atlanta would never come back now. The island had given them enough grief and there was easier uranium to be had out West or in South America. Somebody somewhere else would always be willing to give up the land to fuel weapons of mass destruction if the price was right or if the will of the people was soft. And so, I wanted to believe that the Viking had come here for a larger purpose so many years ago and he was part of the grander scheme of things. He had come here to safeguard our island.

Maybe he had been murdered; maybe there was greed and bloodshed, but it was the dried blood of history sifting down to the present in the form of good will. His tragic death miraculously meant that no hydrogen bombs would be made from the rock of Whalebone Island, this Republic of Nothing. Small victories like this quixotic twist of human fate are to be counted as the greatest of blessings. Among those blessings was a university student by the name of Barry Weeks who came to scratch through the peat for pots and bones, only to find love. Barry, the son of a Cree woman and a hardware store owner from Parry Sound, was immediately attracted to my

Lesley Choyce

sister, Casey. There was an age difference to be sure, but they became close friends and fell in love and we all knew that it was more of the work of the Viking. Barry was as thin as a rail and had a dreamy look about him. When he smiled he lit up from within in a way that could break the code of parental disapproval of an older boy in love with a younger girl. The Cree and the merchant had conspired a great soft soul in the form of Barry Weeks and for once in her life, my sister had found a companion other than me. Barry went back to school the first winter, returned the next summer and stayed on in Halifax after that, transferring to Dalhousie University to finish a degree in geology. Since archaeology was not available as a major at Dal, Barry would always say that Casey was responsibile for his commitment to rocks and sand instead of pots and bones.

The Vietnam War would eventually come to an end and most of the draft evaders would go home, forgiven by their countrymen for refusing to kill. Some would stay on in Nova Scotia, however, and lead vital, happy lives. Burnet had chosen to remain anonymous on our island even after the war was over, working on the boat with Lambert and Eager, pretending he was another displaced American. He did, however, get into the curious habit of sneaking into his father's back yard late at night to feed the dogs and become friends with that new generation of slobbering, raging canines, turning them into gentler, friendly creatures. Despite his nightly visits, he avoided contact with his brutal old man until the time his father had a stroke and was rendered partially paralysed and almost speechless. When news reached Burnet, he discarded his American identity and went immediately to the hospital. When it was time for Burnet Sr. to go home, his son was there to take him. Burnet guided his father back to mobility and speech and they became tolerable friends, bridging the gulf of a lifetime of family cruelty.

With the draft dodgers all settled on the mainland or returned to the States, Gwen and I began to plan a life together.

We moved into Mr. Kirk's old house and stoked the wood stove and the fires of our love that winter. We were not married, but no one disapproved. On Sundays we attended giant family meals with my folks and Gwen's parents, Ben and Bernie and Jack and Hants. It was potluck fare and everyone ate like a horse and there was always plenty of home-made English bitter to go around.

I began to write. I kept a journal and tallied the times that Gwen and I made love and the precise circumstance and location. Why I would choose to document those immaculate moments is no surprise to me, and I could only wish that it was the story of all my days henceforward. In the depths of winter, when the snow was deep and the gales would wail, the house grew small and we would hike off in opposite directions around the island's perimeter until we met. Wherever that spot was, we would find a refuge — under a rocky ledge of slate with nothing more than a blanket for a bed, or beneath an impromptu shelter of spruce bows or driftwood. We would lie in the snow on a sunny February day, the sun not ashamed to oversee our lovemaking. And I assure you that I always thought that this was enough. I had no further ambition. My life with Gwen was why I had grown to manhood. Someday soon she would stop taking the pill and we would have children — one or five or twelve, whatever she liked. Our love was deep and pure and for me, enough, and always would be. By spring, however, I knew something was wrong.

"I love you, Ian," she told me. "I love you, I always will. I love our life. I love everything about this place. I love this crazy, perfect set-up we have. I just wish it wasn't so good. That would make all of this easier."

But it could never be easy. We had succeeded in making the world go away for one winter and a month. I would do anything I could to stretch out the tenure of heaven. So, like a dreaming fool, I pushed away the world beyond the threshold of the island for another summer. But when the arguments started, I knew there was no holding on. I wanted us, but Gwen wanted more. She wanted the twentieth century. I wanted no century at all.

"I want to leave while I still love you," she said finally on a dark August night when mosquitoes pinged against the screens of our windows and fireflies lit up the night like miniature flash bulbs.

"I want you to leave while you still love me, too," I said. "I want my love to embrace you no matter where you go or what you do."

And in the morning, Gwen was gone.

She wrote to me often. She enroled at Boston University in International Peace Studies. She would train to be a diplomat and a negotiator. She would live what she believed, just like me, the only tragedy being we could not live our beliefs together. But she never married. She returned to the island at intervals. I always knew when she was about to arrive although there was no calendar to her return. I stayed in the big Kirk house by myself despite the fact that I felt guilty about the empty rooms, so I moved my sleeping quarters from one to the next each month, always remembering my time with Gwen in that particular sacred room (for we had made love in every room of that place). And only when feeling heartsick beyond recovery would I take out my journals and read my meticulous record-keeping of our love.

Each time Gwen returned, she would move back in with me, sometimes for a weekend, sometimes for a month — she would move back in as if nothing had changed. I grew adept at accepting this and believed that, if this was the way I could have Gwen for a lifetime, I would accept it; I would crush my ego and my pride in favour of our love and I would not feel jealousy or anger. Like any man, I sheltered within me a volcano of commingled frustration and anger that might well have erupted and ruined our sporadic life together. But I was not any man, for I held within me the cautioned voice of my mother's father whose lessons of unhappiness and pain I had inherited. His presence allowed me a singular destiny of loving Gwendolyn whose mind embraced larger empires and greater politics beyond the limited rocky shores of this place.

The bottom fell out of the Spickerton blue-eye clam after a Japanese gourmet magazine published a poorly researched article about the potential for the blue-eye to actually cause impotence in men. It meant little when the research was shown to be faulty, for the importer would not touch another blue-eye. Rumour can be as good as truth when it comes to the seafood industry. So we were all left searching for cod and mackerel and chasing a flounder or two or jigging for squid. If the money had once been there in doryloads for Lambert and Eager, it had drifted away somewhere by the time the clam boom ended, slopped off into who knows where like so much fish guts splashed off the dock with a pail of sea water. Yet somehow, no one felt the worse. "I think of economics as the tides," my father would say, himself a poorer man now that the exotic species of sea life no longer appealed to the foreigners. "There's a tide to everything."

After the Vietnam War had ended and after Gwen left me for her university and diplomatic career, a third American phenomenon seemed inextricably entwined with the history of my family. It was evening of August 8, 1974. How strange to think that the life of the president of the Republic of Nothing was so closely allied forever in my mind with the political career of Richard Nixon. For years ever after, although I can hardly try to express a logic to this, I would voraciously read about the sallow American president. I would read all his books, his letters, his biographies, the tomes of his admirers and his detractors. For it was on that night of August 8 when I switched on the CBC ten o'clock news and saw a battered Richard Nixon tell a startled American public that he was resigning from office.

Because of the war and the death of students at Kent State

and so many other reasons, I had learned to hate Nixon with passion. Nixon represented everything I despised about the United States and, even though Gwen had shared my disdain for so many things American, it was that terrible country to the south that had lured her away from me. So I should have cheered like thousands, if not millions of others, when Nixon read his resignation speech and walked off stage into ignominious history. But I did not. Instead, I felt a great wave of empathy for this man. Perhaps I always cheered for the underdog, always identified with the defeated. Was it because I too felt like a failure? Had I resigned from living, allowed Gwen to leave and live out her own mandate with me left behind to be there for her only when she wanted me? Was that it? I begged of Nixon as I watched him nearly stumbling away from the podium and the presidential seal.

I decided it was not that at all. I decided it was something else. My mother and father had given me the great human gift of compassion for the injured and a biblical ability to love my enemies. Beyond their instilling these qualities, I have no idea how I had survived a prolonged male adolescence, how these two temperaments had wrestled their way through a male ego into adulthood. But there I sat, nearly in tears because the president of the United States looked to be in such bad shape. The phone rang. It was my mother. I almost thought she was going to tell me the news, what I already knew about Nixon. But I was wrong.

"It's your father," she said, choking back tears. "Something happened. He's dying."

"I'll get Ben and Bernie," I said, stunned. "Be right there."

All three of us were there within minutes. Casey was beside the bed, holding my father's hand. My mother had her cheek up against my father's face as she lay beside him. What I noticed first was that she had on her sexiest of nightgowns, the one my father had given her for a birthday present last year. I knew at once that they had been making love. My mother looked up and I saw that she was not crying. There was sadness in her face but also something else — resignation.

Bernie bent over my father and listened to his ragged breath. Ben reached for my father's neck and checked his pulse, counted it against his watch. Everett McQuade looked pale, but peaceful. Here was my father, dying, and I wanted to know what to do for him.

Ben was reaching in his bag for something. I found myself at my father's feet and I took one in each hand, began to massage them. I had probably never even looked at my father's feet since I was a child but as I held them — bony and pale, the feet of a fishermen with calluses in all the necessary places, I thought they were the most beautiful feet in the world. I believed I could massage vitality back into this man who was my father by delivering my energy to him from my hands into his feet and up into his heart and his mind. My strength could be his.

Ben had taken a stethoscope out now and had placed it on my father's chest. Ben's eyes were closed as he listened. He moved the silver medallion from one spot to another, listening to lungs, heart, arteries. He looked up at Bernie. "I think there's new damage to the repairs. I'm not sure. I'm fairly sure there's blood spilling out of his arteries, into his chest cavity, into his lungs."

My mother did not look up. She cradled my father's head in her hands and whispered something in his ear. Casey was holding onto his hand and sobbing.

"We have to get him to a hospital," Ben said.

"Too far," Bernie said. She took the stethoscope from Ben and listened for herself, shaking her head sideways. "He'll never make it. We need to do something else." Bernie was a good nurse. She didn't like to lose a patient.

"All we can do is cut him open, insert some sort of tube into the lung. Suck out the blood. Otherwise, he'll drown in it."

"Can you do that?" I asked Ben. "Have you ever done it before?"

He looked at me, understood my doubts.

Lesley Choyce

"Yes," he said. "I've done it in the emergency room before. In New York."

I looked at Bernie and could see she had doubts. I could see in her eyes that it was a procedure fraught with danger, the last desperate attempt to save my father. "Do it," I said. "What do you need?"

Ben looked in his bag and put up his hands. "I need a very sharp knife and some tubing. Fuel line. Anything. Clean it in boiling water."

As I ran out of the room, I saw Ben undo my father's pyjama shirt and begin pressing down on his ribs, studying my father's chest, trying to decide where to cut.

I found a good sharp gutting knife and a couple of feet of clear plastic gas line from one of the boat motors. When I came in through the kitchen, Bernie was boiling some water. We waited until the kettle whistled, then Bernie poured the scalding liquid over the knife and tube. When we returned to the bedroom, I first saw the lipstick mark on my father's chest where Ben had decided to operate. "If I can't get a good cut, I might have to break a rib as well. It's all been done before in cases like this," he said, trying to sound calm and matter-of-fact.

My father's breathing was shallow, his face looked drained. My mother sat upright and looked at each of us. "No," she said. "It won't be necessary."

"What are you saying?" Casey asked, trying to stem the tears that were flowing down her cheeks.

"I'm afraid it's not like before," my mother said. "I think it's too dangerous. It's wrong."

At first I thought she was considering the alternative. Like before, she was preparing to "go after him" and bring him back. But then it quickly became clear that this time it was different. Ben was poised with the knife in the air. The reflecting light shot like cold arrows around the room as he lowered it and held it before him. "No," my mother said. "There would be great pain either way. Great pain and great loss. Everett and I have known a time like this would come. This is the time."

I looked at Bernie who nodded her head. And at Ben who suddenly seemed so greatly relieved that he would not have to attempt such a difficult task. I guess I knew that if Ben had been right, the bleeding would continue anyway. Once the lung was drained, the heart could just go on beating blood out through the torn artery. John G.D. MacIntyre's assassination would finally be complete.

"Your father's been there," my mother said. "This is going to be an easy trip for him."

Ben and Bernie left the room. Casey and I joined my mother on the bed, all three of us lying there, our arms wrapped around each other. We waited for my father to die and as I closed my eyes I realized how lucky we had been. He had found his way back to us and we had been granted those five extra years together. As his breathing grew fainter and fainter, I could feel his life slipping out of him, but at the same time a wave of peacefulness came over me, the fear replaced by the certainty of things to come. We lay together on the bed as the night began to swallow us. His pulse, his heartbeat, diminished to a rumour and then a memory. I think all three of us shared what my father was feeling as he left us — my mother, Casey and me, all drifting off into the warm tide of death and aware of the dim light shining from the farther shore. And there, in that other place of darkness and distant light, I knew that my mother was no tourist. She guided us to the point of my father's departure and then turned us back towards the other light of our own lives on the island of nothing and everything.

And in the morning, the sun returned and the island remained itself and I knew once again that all things were possible, that even the pain of this final loss would pass and I would go on living.

Three days later, we scattered my father's ashes on the sea at sunrise, at the precise location my mother believed that she had first met the young man with the fiery red hair. I looked down into the deep waters and found myself remembering my mother's awful story of the sinking of her father's ship. I wondered again what had become of that tyrant who had murdered my grandmother and then saved my mother. I continued to fear that maybe I had inherited something of that killer who had driven my mother into the arms of my father.

My curiosity was maddening and I wanted to scream, but as I watched the ashes float upon the water, I discovered that I loved my father more than I had known, that I was more like him than I believed myself to be. I knew that I needed celebration for the life of my father and his spirit that was still in me. I would not grovel in the twisted wreckage of a forgotten life.

So when our boat had returned to shore and we had gathered for a meal among great friends of the island, it was Hants Buckler who had presented me with the gift that came as no surprise. Three sticks of dynamite tied together with a red ribbon.

"They washed in?" I asked.

"I liberated them from the uranium miners. Was saving them for a birthday or something, but this is close enough."

Later that day we all walked to the renovated bridge that tethered the island to the mainland and as we stood on the new government issue structure, I read aloud my father's declaration one more time, reminding all of us that we of Whalebone Island were apart from the world, that we were unique, that we had personal dominion over our lives and wanted renewal of our freedoms. With ceremony and great caution, I lashed the three sticks to the cradlework of the bridge and walked the wire back the length of the road.

Looking landward, I saw Burnet Jr. come to the door of his house. He waved, went back in and came out with his father in a wheel chair to watch. I expect it was the sort of spectacle that Burnet Sr. might appreciate.

And when the bridge blew sky high, raining down the

shattered handiwork of the province of Nova Scotia and putting to waste a princely sum of the taxpayer's money, I felt like
the Republic of Nothing had survived its first twenty-three
years in reasonably good shape, that we had adhered to the
principles my father believed in. We were still an unruly, anarchic sort who would be troubled by too much intrusion
from the outside world and give that trouble right back when
necessary, for it was not a very broad channel that separated us
from the mainland.

But for now, with this act, the spirit of my father remained
alive in his son. And it was good to be alive, good to be free
and crazy and unencumbered by the politics of success and
failure, dream and reality, war and peace and all the other foolish dualities the civilized world live by.

And now, sometimes on a still night when all the Vikings are
sleeping quietly again, I walk the island where I had been born,
alone or with my mother or Casey or with my gypsy lover,
Gwen. On these nights I prepare to undertake the next phase
of the subtle research into the nature of the power of nothing
— the sweet centre of all the chaos that is our lives, the cher-
ished republic my father had declared so long ago on the day I
was born.

Lesley Choyce